Julene Wood is a South African author. Her work, *Immortal Fire*, is her first book series. She is currently also working on an exciting second adult series – *House of Wings and Shadow*.

Julene grew up traveling across South Africa and abroad to countries such as Italy and Malaysia for motorsport racing, in which she competed from a young age in karting. While traveling, Julene could always be found with a book and art supplies, as her passion has always belonged to literature and art. Now that Julene is older, she has decided to finally devote her time to her true passion – writing.

To find out more about Julene, visit linktr.ee/julenewood or follow @julenewoodwrites on Instagram.

To those who see beauty in the dark and only need a moment in time to reveal their extraordinary potential.

Julene Wood

House of Wings and Shadow

Chained

Austin Macauley Publishers
LONDON * CAMBRIDGE * NEW YORK * SHARJAH

Copyright © Julene Wood 2024

The right of Julene Wood to be identified as author of this work has been asserted by the author in accordance with sections 77 and 78 of the Copyright, Designs and Patents Act 1988.

All rights reserved. No part of this publication may be reproduced, stored in a retrieval system, or transmitted in any form or by any means, electronic, mechanical, photocopying, recording, or otherwise, without the prior permission of the publishers.

Any person who commits any unauthorised act in relation to this publication may be liable to criminal prosecution and civil claims for damages.

This is a work of fiction. Names, characters, businesses, places, events, locales, and incidents are either the products of the author's imagination or used in a fictitious manner. Any resemblance to actual persons, living or dead, or actual events is purely coincidental.

A CIP catalogue record for this title is available from the British Library.

ISBN 9781035831739 (Paperback)
ISBN 9781035831746 (ePub e-book)

www.austinmacauley.com

First Published 2024
Austin Macauley Publishers Ltd®
1 Canada Square
Canary Wharf
London
E14 5AA

As soon as wolves roar and ravens flee,
A betrayal brings to life a new life
There comes a day when what is green turns to moonlight
A creeper of shadows Manipulator
A man clads in crimson, born of emerald sight
Shall bring forth the overthrowing of royalty
As soon as the blind man sees once more,
Siblings bring forth the clash of Titans
It shall be on the day that the true one reveals herself,
The two-faced one brings forth an almighty darkness
Upon the day the water rises to the sky, the guilty shall reap
Once stars fall from the sky,
A surrender awakens the downfall of an empire
When the moment comes that the wolves howl together,
The young one shall cause the rise of what was forgotten
The black rose and thorn shall conquer.

Prologue

"You ruined it," I moaned, squinting my eyes and pursing my lips as I looked back and forth between the boy grinning at me and the rose I had engraved on the tree trunk.

"I don't think so. It's much better now." He continued grinning at his handiwork as if he was as grand as Picasso himself, his pocketknife twirling expertly between his fingers.

"Gods, you did not need to add so many thorns and make it seem like it's been hacked away at. It took me ages to get it just right!" Simmering, I continued to look over the disgusting spot on the tree that held my perfect rose a few moments ago. Now, gouges had been added along the stem, etched deep and rough into the bark, making it appear like more thorns than an actual rose.

Looking away from the tree trunk, I looked him over. Hair as dark and silky as midnight, taller than me by an inch or two, and aqua eyes that matched the cerulean sea my parents had taken me to visit a year ago. A ring of amber on the outer edge of his irises and pupil. *Exceedingly rare…*

He caught me looking at him in disgust, my arms taut at my sides from my ire. A hearty laugh escaped him as he stepped away and back to the spot where our card game sat unattended on the forest floor.

"Come on, let's finish the game. My parents said I need to be home before sunset." He huffed out as he picked up his cards, peeping at me to ensure I did not look at them before he pulled them against his chest, scowling at me as I drifted past, closer than needed, just to try and get a glimpse.

Sitting on the moss-covered ground across from him, I picked up my cards, eyeing him just as suspiciously before I eyed what I had been dealt.

"Gods! You must have cheated!" I squinted at him as I looked over my cards once more, knowing I had already lost this game against my nameless companion.

We had been meeting here every day at precisely four pm since we first encountered each other a month ago. It was quite a surprise as the Whispering Woods were off-limits, save for every two years when the sacrifice would take place in honour of our gods. I had been too young to go before, however, that had recently changed, and I would be expected at the next sacrifice when all the great houses would commune in the sacred temple of the woods.

I had snuck out of my family's estate that bordered the woods as usual when I had met him. Seeking refuge amongst the ancient land, quieting my mind, and controlling myself.

I had no idea what his name was and had yet to tell him mine. It didn't seem important at the time as we first eyed each other suspiciously that day, before becoming fast friends. It seemed ridiculous to ask his name now after a month of spending time together every day in these woods.

We had discovered that our birthdays were only a day apart, both of us having turned thirteen a week ago. It was a horrible age. I knew that my parents and our heritage enforced much once I turned thirteen. I hoped that the boy did not have to endure the same…

"I did no such thing," he mumbled, shuffling his cards into the correct order he deemed necessary, eyeing me from lowered lashes.

"You must have. If not, how did I end up with the worst cards in the deck?" I retorted back at him before shoving some crisps into my mouth that he had brought with him.

"I did not!" he snapped right back at me before he eyed his cards and then placed them down on the ground between us with a heavy sigh.

"Give me your cards," he mumbled, shaking his midnight hair away from his eyes.

I did as he asked and watched him, chewing away at more crisps as he reshuffled the deck and began dealing them out once more.

Reaching for my cards after rubbing off the crisp crumbs on my dress, I glanced at them and couldn't stop the smile that widened on my face as I now had the perfect stack. I looked over to the boy and giggled as I got comfier on the ground, crossing my legs beneath me.

"Oh, I know that look, that's not fair," he mumbled again, scratching his head grumpily as he looked over his cards, seeming to find some semblance of a plan of how to play the cards he had been dealt.

We continued playing. Myself being victorious for two of the three rounds, and the boy grew more agitated before he finally won the final round.

Looking overhead at the sky between the tall ancient trees, it was clear that sunset was mere minutes away. The boy began gathering his cards and the packet of crisps, but not before offering me a final handful which I greedily took and was still chewing away merrily when he stood, his backpack now being slug across his shoulders.

I stood, swallowing as I once again rubbed my greasy crisp covered hands along the skirt of my dress. Gods, I hated dresses. Hated them, but my mother was insistent on my wearing them. I somewhat hoped the greasy stains from my hands would cause her to get rid of this particular white, frilly monstrosity.

"I'll see you tomorrow." The boy smiled at me before looking at my stained dress and laughing. "You try everything to get rid of those dresses your mother loves so much, don't you?"

"Yes well, *try* is the operative word," I mumbled with a faint smile as I looked down at my ruined skirts. Crisp crumbs, grease smears, and mud as well as moss clung to it.

I watched as he walked away, in the same direction he always did, his pocketknife twirling between his fingers expertly. I wondered where it was he went and came from. Perhaps tomorrow I would ask him, and possibly even ask his name…

I turned on the spot and began my walk home, passing the weeping willow with my rose and the boy's thorns etched into its ancient bark. I crossed the stream, the sounds and whispers of the woods speaking to me, granting me solace as they always had.

In our society of great houses, demigods of the gods, we each served the god of our direct ancestry. We were a dark world, hidden in plain sight of the humans. Cartels and businesses were run by the houses in service of the gods. I did not know everything, but I had been told enough to know what a dark world it was and that each house served its purpose.

The Whispering Woods were taught to us as almost being an entity of its own, something to be avoided at all costs except when it would welcome the houses for the great sacrifice every two years.

I did not know why it had been feared so as the woods had become my form of solace since the first time I had entered it. It had beckoned me, with whispers along the wind, almost breathing a sigh of relief as I had finally arrived beneath its veil.

Seeing the straight path towards my family's estate, I looked around, ensuring that the boy had indeed gone on his way before the soft caress of a whispering breeze of the woods flittered around me, tickling my skin, and winding away amongst the trees once more.

Shadows crept from my feet, twirling around me before I vanished in the blink of an eye, shadow-stalking, traveling from one shadow to the other, undetectable to anyone and everything except for that of the Whispering Wood, which seemed to breathe out heavily as I expelled my pent-up power.

Arriving at the border of our estate, I emerged from a shadow, caught off guard as my mother was standing there with one of the goddesses waiting. The goddess constantly whispered secrets in her ear. My mother had a vicious look upon her as I began to feel the panic rise within me.

"Mother?" I stammered, running my hands down my filthy dress as she scowled at me. "You disobeyed again. You know you are not allowed in the Whispering Woods. Development has taken place, and house Katopodis has been issued a warrant of the hunt. You foolish girl!" My mother snapped at me, the venom in her voice causing my eyes to well with unshed tears. "It appears that you have not headed your mother's warnings of the importance of your existence being kept secret. I will be ensuring you are thoroughly punished as this cannot happen again." Hecate spat from beside my mother, coils of dark, purple magic flitting around her form.

"Mother?" I managed out softly as I looked at her. My mother ignored me, clasping her hands together before her as she turned and walked toward the manor across the perfectly manicured grass.

Leaving me alone with the goddess Hecate who smirked wickedly at me.

"This way, child." Hecate snapped, heading toward the back end of the manor. She did not wait to see if I followed.

Stalling, as I swallowed back my tears, I turned shakily and followed Hecate. I managed one last pleading look toward my mother as she climbed the marble steps leading to the gigantic wooden and gold overlay front doors of the white marble manor, her expensive heels audible to my supreme hearing across the great distance. The large golden lion's head eternally roared above the doors – the symbol of our house. House Sarris, the keepers of the law and justice in our hidden world, serving under our goddess Themis.

She did not look back at me once.

Wiping at my tear-filled eyes, I bumped into Hecate as she suddenly stopped in her tracks. A loud curse escaped her lips before she yanked me forward harshly by the hair on my head. Her small delicate hands were stronger than I ever could have imagined. A scream escaped me as she shoved me against the cold stone of the well-house.

The cold was biting into my shoulder and cheek as I tried uselessly to pull myself away from her crushing hold. It was futile.

The heavy doors opened with a loud moan, the darkness, and dampness of the air hitting me full force as she shoved me forward once again and dragged me up the winding stone steps of the well.

It was not a standard well. No, the well upon my family's estate rose high as the ancient and cold stone circled and high like that of a silo. The god's well was kept in place by powers ancient and unknown. Its knowledge lost over the millennia. Up and around we went, my skin scraping over each stone step and the wall of the well the higher we went as I struggled against Hecate's hold. Finally reaching the top, Hecate still held to my hair painfully and waved a hand across the top of the well.

The stone covering the top shuddered much like myself before it slowly slid to the side with a loud groan, scraping along the granite stone top before finally stopping, leaving the top open to the endless waters below. Only darkness lay within.

Dropping to my knees, I pulled uselessly against Hecate's hold on my hair as I felt my heart would rip from my chest and wails filled the air. A blind panic filled me as I realised what my punishment would be.

"Please! I… I won't go into the woods again!" I screamed, struggling to breathe as she pulled me forward toward the gaping hole of the well. "No! Please, no!"

Hecate loosened her hold on my hair, only to instead grab a hold of my dress front as she held me dangling over the well. I struggled to keep my feet planted on the cold stone edge as she held me over, my back stretching over the darkness below.

"You foolish child. This has nothing to do with the woods. It has to do with the prophecy. You are risking everything by being discovered before it is time! Some time alone to think of your priorities should do you well, my little soldier.

Tell me, how did they gain knowledge of you? Whom have you spoken to?" She sneered at me, her eyes glowing with ominous power.

"N-no one," I stammered, not willing to let any harm fall back on the boy. I could not think of anyone else it may have been, but I could not believe my friend would have betrayed me. He had not even bore witness to my powers. And I did not know if he was even aware of our world…

"Very well, perhaps the waters shall loosen your memory and tongue of who it is you protect." Hecate snapped before shoving me forward and letting go.

A scream escaped me, so loud it felt as if the air vibrated around the well-house. An uncontrollable power emitted from within me, causing the air to shudder and the water within the well to slosh against its sides. I fell, my dress billowing up around me as I tried uselessly to grab at anything. It felt like an eternity of falling, my heart beating a war drum against my chest as I descended through the damp air, no hope of escaping…

I finally hit the dark water below, crashing through its surface like ice embracing my being. My scream cut off as the stagnant water filled my mouth and nose, cutting off all supply of air. Down and down I sank, my body went limp from the shock and chill.

Finally, my descent slowed beneath the water, my eyes still somewhat aware of the opening high up above. I watched from beneath the water, ripples up ahead obscuring much of my vision, as Hecate peered in from her perch above a great distance away. She stood from view before the stone covering began to slide back into place.

I began to swim, my lungs burning and protesting for air as I tried to reach the surface and uselessly tried to get out. Breaking the surface with a mighty splash, I screamed as the top of the stone structure slid closed above me, out of reach, and effectively cut off all forms of light.

Darkness filled the space, the kind where you cannot see your hand before your face, and I began weeping. My treading of water, splashes and wails were the only sounds that carried in the well.

After what must have been an hour, my muscles burned with exhaustion as I attempted to stay afloat in the darkness. My thirteen-year-old body screamed in protest at the exertion. My mind had been playing tricks on me, having me imagining creatures beneath the dark water, and the silence deafening.

My tears had since stilled, officially drying out. I struggled to stay afloat as my mind drifted to my mother and Hecate's words. Had it been the boy who betrayed me? That would mean he was a part of our world. I had thought of him as my friend. If I was honest, he had been my only friend, besides my older brother, Dorian… but it wasn't the same.

I lost track of the time I was within the well, minutes could have been hours, days, or weeks. I was exhausted. Having sunk below the surface every time my mind drifted off to sleep had me choking on the water before I returned to the dark surface, struggling for air.

Over, and over again. It never ended.

I had attempted to shadow-stalk around the dark open space above the water's surface, however, I soon found myself utterly exhausted and pummelling straight through the ice-cold water once more.

Vibrations of my power were sporadic within the water around me, barely keeping me afloat for a few minutes of rest before I woke to sink and choking, only to force my aching muscles to swim back to the surface.

Finally, a noise had me looking up at the top of the well overhead. The sound of stone sliding across stone groaned out before light spilled down to me. My eyes detested it after being isolated in utter darkness for so long. I could not bear to open my eyes and did not even have the strength to scream out as I felt my body held firmly by magical bonds and lifted out of the water. Water dripped from me, splashing back to the well below.

I was shivering when I felt a cold stone beneath me as I was placed harshly on the steps beside the opening, once again scraping my skin open. I was numbly aware of the strips of skin that had peeled away from my body in various spots after being submerged for so long. My skin against the stone simply smeared away leaving a bloody mess trailing down the ancient steps that wound their way down and around the silo.

Forcing my eyes open, I squinted at who was before me, struggling to focus.

My mother and Hecate stood before me, scowling at my pathetic form drenched at their feet. The sounds of the estate and smells from the open well-house door assaulted my senses, making me cringe.

"Have you learned your lesson, child?"

It was Hecate who spoke, not my mother. I could not find my voice as I squinted between the two of them. My eyes finally landed on my mother where I watched her.

There was no remorse on her face whatsoever. Only that scowl she wore constantly as of late. It was at that moment I realised what it was to hate someone.

Hate her with my entire being for allowing this to be done to me without so much as a second glance whatsoever.

"I spoke to you, child. Answer me!" Hecate snapped, her magic hauling my chin up and toward her harshly, causing my teeth to knock against each other as the force of her magic gripped my jaw painfully. The skin of my face was just as sensitive as the rest of my body.

"Yes," I answered pathetically, my will a flurry of whimpers and snarls, each contradicting the other as I struggled with my anger and fear.

Hecate nodded and led my mother away who had still not said a word or shown any sign of remorse. I watched them go as they left me on the cold stone to find my way back by myself...

Pushing myself to my feet and standing on shaky legs, I heaved heavy breaths as my trembling became uncontrollable, my knees buckling more than I cared to count.

The water-clogged wrinkly skin of my feet peeled away with no restraint against the stone. I managed after a few hours to make it down the icy stone steps and out of the well-house, the estate before me and the sun setting in the distance.

I almost gave up, wanting the pain and suffering to end. It would be so easy to do, but something deep within me refused. Refused to give them satisfaction. I may be a mere age of thirteen years old, but something changed inside me during that time in the well.

Something ancient and powerful had awoken as if from slumber, rearing its head to me and smirking in awareness...

Hecate had asked me who it was that I was protecting, and in all that time I had been in the dark confines of the well, I had plenty of time to think it over.

I knew my answer upon being let out of the well, its embrace having scarred any trace of who I had once been before going in.

Walking slowly, struggling across the manicured lawns, I made my way to the manor, shivering as I went.

The staff passed by, avoiding my gaze, acting as if I was a ghost in my own home. Or possibly fearful of showing any kindness towards me for fear of retribution from my mother and Hecate. As I passed the edge of the estate, near the Whispering Woods border, I felt a caress of its awareness, almost in sympathy before a sense of rage retreated with it, leaving me alone once more.

Entering the manor, I stopped as I saw Hecate on the grand staircase, chatting with my mother. No, not my mother… just a monster.

I never saw the boy again.

Not until the great sacrifice, and every great house gathering after.

Braelyn

Running through the Whispering Woods, I could feel my legs burning as I pushed myself harder, further than I had before. Jumping over the stream that ran through the woods from the temple a mile away, I rolled as I landed and kept going. Fallen leaves crunched beneath my feet as I was as swift as the wind itself.

Twelve years had passed since the day of Hecate and my mother's punishment. Twelve years of training to become their weapon. A soldier as Hecate always referred to me as.

I had finally worked up the courage to return to the woods in secret after two years. Its whispers calling to me incessantly since that day. I had struggled to ignore its calls, fearing the punishment I would receive if I was caught.

I had never seen the boy in the woods since that day. The boy was now a man. Theo Katopodis. I had discovered his identity a year after our final meeting in the woods when I had been brought along to the great sacrifice. I had been in disguise, by instruction of my parents and Hecate's insistence.

I was never seen by anyone off this estate unless necessary. When I was, I adorn a blonde wig, covering my jet-black hair. My family was known for only having blonde locks. To have my raven hair on display would cause an uproar. It was the reason no one knew of me until I had turned thirteen and attended the sacrifice a year after.

I had been my family's dirty little secret. The staff on the manor had to sign a blood oath, binding them to secrecy for fear of a painful death if they ever let slip about what I was.

As for my eyes, I would be forced to always wear a blind mask, its intricate, beautiful, and haunting design covering my eyes entirely. No one may know of my bottle-green eyes. People of my world, the great houses, all had particular shaded blue eyes, no one had yet to be born without blue eyes until me that is. Luckily for me, I did not need to see with my eyes and was content with everyone thinking that I was indeed blind. A peculiar thing to happen to a demi-god, but still believable and less terrifying than the truth.

My powers had increased over the years. I would be able to see within my mind by using my shadow-stalking abilities, my vision a kaleidoscope of all around me without the use of my eyes. My hearing was far superior to what was normal, even for the demigods of our world. My appearance alone, as well as my powers, would cause the downfall of my family's house, everyone wiped off the map out of fear of a prophecy I had been drilled about since I was able to speak and comprehend the world around me.

I had been startled when I noticed the boy across from me in the temple. The grand floor swept out between where my family stood across from his. He had grown taller in the year since I had seen him, muscles already filling out his hard body and it was then I knew he was indeed a part of this dark world I lived in.

His family had been speaking to each other softly, however, I had heard his name for the first time when his mother had called him.

Theo.

His demeanour seemed different from the boy I had played cards with. Darkness and coldness surrounded him. He no longer wore anything besides the training leathers of his house. The thick material, almost like leather but stronger and more flexible, covered his body. He also wore gloves, no matter how hot it was…

I felt my heart split in half at the realisation that it must have been him who had indeed sold me out, and whom his family was still hunting for.

I realised it, and yet could still not bring myself to hand over the information to Hecate who in all these years still hounded me over whom I was protecting. I don't know why I protected him when he had deceived me most horrendously. I continued watching him from the shadows over the years, catching him looking at me strangely when I would be forced to be at events. A scowl was permanently on his face as he watched me. I had panicked, thinking he knew who I was but found myself relieved yet incredulous as I caught him and his companion making rude remarks about the 'blind princess' and had never ventured close again.

Jumping from rock to rock, I spun in the air and threw my throwing knives at the target I had on a tree in the distance. Twisting, I landed on my feet and continued running, finally coming to a stop before the weeping willow. Its wisping branches swayed in the summer breeze drifting through the woods.

I plucked my knives from the target, all of them hitting true. I eyed the target, trying to forget that day. The rose and thorns etching across the bark had been split and sliced at, but the image remained.

Wiping at my brow, I was sweating as the heat of summer, accompanied by my attire, had me wishing for a much-needed shower. I had my training leathers on, the jacket with a hood that covered most of my face, and a slip of silk that covered me from the nose down. All that could be seen were my eyes.

I would need to head back soon as tonight was the grand Servile. The pairing of a couple from two different houses in the form of marriage. Marriage isn't exactly how it was though. The Servile would select usually the oldest from one house and the same from another. The oldest chosen woman would enter the man's house and continue the bloodline of his house.

It was archaic, but I was expected to be there with my family as a show of support. My brother may be chosen this year and I knew he detested the idea just as much as I did. The servile would be held on our estate this year, and an entire weekend event would be made of it.

The other houses started arriving just before I had come out to the woods and I needed the escape as the idea of being so close to all these strangers and enemies for an entire weekend had my skin crawling.

A crunching of leaves to the left of me had me whipping around, searching the surrounding area. A tremor worked its way up my spine as the footsteps grew nearer and the scent hit me. Thankfully, my scent was covered by a spell Hecate had cast as an extra precaution.

Theo Katopodis stepped from behind a tree, seemingly lost in thought as he froze, having sensed me now as I stood only a few feet before him. His keen senses would have noticed me sooner had I still been running and if my scent was not being covered.

It was the first time in twelve years we had looked eye to eye. The first time in twelve years I had seen him in the woods which everyone else avoided like death itself.

His eyes widened in disbelief before he looked to the tree, our etching still visible, although now mangled by my many throwing knives. I swallowed the lump in my throat as fear overtook me. He would hand me over. He had been searching for me. Hunting with his family over the years to find me. And here I was. My green eyes were clear as day to see. It was clear he remembered me.

"Fuck, it is you," he finally managed to say as he took a step forward. His voice was a deep baritone that held a threat. A threat of what I wasn't sure about and did not plan on finding out.

I took a step back, eyeing him in shock as I tried to think of what to do. I needed to get back to the estate. I should have covered my eyes. I should have stayed in my room. *Shit!*

He stopped as he noticed my retreat and placed his tattooed hands up in a placating manner.

Theo had racked up a great number of tattoos since he stopped wearing those leathers. His arms and hands were covered in them, and one could be seen on his neck. The crisp suit did not hide the fact that he was lethal in every sense of the word.

I dared not to say a word back as he would no doubt recognise my voice instantly after having heard me speak as the blind princess over the years. Theo always seemed to be watching, calculating. I did not doubt that his mind was a brilliant and terrifying place.

Theo and I watched each other, neither of us saying a word. He began slowly stepping toward me while holding my gaze with his. Fear pounded through me as he neared.

He almost reached me when my mind shot an image of that forsaken well through my vision and I was gone in an instant, submerging myself within the shadows, effectively invisible to him. The air shuddered where I had been a moment ago.

Theo whirled around, trying to locate me, however, he was unsuccessful.

His jaw grew tight, and a tick worked its way there. I almost breathed a sigh of relief when he turned around as if to leave. I froze as he cocked his head as if listening and a raven landed on his shoulder.

Gods, I had forgotten he had inherited the rare Chaos Handler gene of his ancestors – Ravens being his arsenal.

Theo whirled around and looked straight at me, or rather where I was standing hidden in the shadows. He smirked before taking a step toward me. I did not wait to see if he would find me. I hurtled my being from one shadow to the next, racing back to the estate with him close behind. I then realised that he would figure it out, all of it, if I went straight home.

I then used my training and circled back to the willow tree, Theo arriving shortly after. We once again eyed each other as I stepped from the shadow's embrace.

"Why are you running from me? Why won't you speak to me?" he gritted out angrily after coming to a stop six feet from me. Theo scrunched his brows in confusion and ire as he watched me keenly.

I ignored him, refusing to speak. This seemed to irritate him further as he took large steps toward me again. Using my power, which I had yet to perfect, I could hear the growling of the sacred wolves of the Whispering Woods as they stalked closer, circling us, or rather Theo.

I did not know how I could control the wolves or communicate with them, yet I had always found them loyal and bending to my will. Theo rotated where he stood, spotting the wolves as they neared. He didn't seem afraid in the slightest, only confused and somewhat in awe.

Not waiting for him to land that keen attention back on me, I shadow-stalked back in the direction of the estate, as fast as I could go. It appeared my distraction worked as I found myself hanging in the shadows below the window ledge of the third-story window.

I listened keenly, hearing no one else inside, and willed myself to the shadows of my brother's bedroom, finding him struggling with a tie around his neck.

I stepped from the shadows, startling him. "Gods, Braelyn! Don't do that!" he scolded, before taking in my appearance.

"You went to the woods? Are you out of your damn mind!" he whispered toward me before checking his bedroom door was locked and the windows were thoroughly closed, to avoid any unwanted listeners.

Pulling the silk wrap from my sweating face and pulling the hood down, I stalked past him to his bathroom, leaning over the marble vanity and splashing water over my now grimy face before I looked at him.

"Yeah, I did," I answered, my heart still racing after the encounter with Theo.

Not even Dorian knew about Theo and my past, and I intended to keep it that way.

Therefore, any chance of me telling him of our little encounter just moments ago would be nil to none.

"Are you trying to get killed? Get all of us killed? You know what happened last time you were caught and the risk with every other house here..." He snapped at me; the tie was long forgotten as it dangled in a mess from around his neck.

"Relax, Dorian. It's fine." I lied, knowing damn well what he said made sense.

"Don't do that. Don't act coy! Not around me... I can't have them do to you what they did last time." Dorian snapped at me before spinning away to avoid looking at me. His neatly cut, blonde hair reflected the setting sun from his window.

Dorian and I had inadvertently grown much closer since my punishment twelve years ago.

Upon returning to the estate after dragging myself from the well-house, I had found him in my bedroom, his blue eyes bloodshot with tears and pale. He rushed to me and embraced me as gently as he could considering how deteriorated my body had become. It was only then that I took his appearance a bit closer. His wrists had been chaffed raw from what appeared to have been handcuffed.

Hecate had ordered him locked in the dungeon of the estate as she had caught him trying to get me out of the well. He had been locked up and caged like an animal for two weeks, while I had been in darkness and drowning in water. He had only been released after they had left me alone and shivering on top of the stone silo. It had never been the darkness that had bent my mind in wicked ways. It had been the silence and the water that broke me.

Sighing, I walked up to him and spun him around before grabbing his tie and undoing the mess of a knot he had attempted to make. "You know I will not let anything happen again. I just... I needed a breather. I'm not used to so many people around me like you are, Dor." Dorian said nothing as he eyed me while I fastened his tie for him, a perfect knot once again. I always had to help him with his ties. He could never get it right. We had laughed about it many times, and it had somehow become our thing, along with being extremely protective of each other. We were all we had in this dark world.

Stepping back, I looked up at him. He had grown to be as tall as our father, standing at six-foot-two. However, I had inherited the monster's genes... I was only five foot three, much like our mother. Dorian tended to refer to me as a short stack.

"Father hasn't returned yet, has he?" I asked him as I stepped back, inspecting my handiwork. "No, he should arrive soon though. Hopefully, he can keep mother under control, at least until the end of the weekend..."

Dorian entered his walk-in closet for a moment and returned with a suit jacket slung over the bend of his elbow whilst he placed his cufflinks in position. The gleaming golden lion of our family's crest.

"Father should be returning with Themis, which means Hecate will be absent. It's not much but perhaps maybe, try to relax a bit in the knowledge that the witch herself won't be around to torment you," he mumbled as he stood looking at me where I now sat on the edge of his king-sized bed.

I rose a speculative brow and was about to reply when someone pounded against Dorian's bedroom door. Jumping to my feet, I readied myself for an attack, still jittery from my encounter with Theo not so long ago. Dorian eyed me in curiosity before he called out, "Yes?"

"Dorian Sarris, where in the nine hells is your sister? She is meant to bathe as well as get ready for the welcoming of the guests!" our mother roared from the other side of the door.

We both cringed, knowing the tone of that shrill voice far too well. She was on a war path yet again it seemed. Dorian watched me as he called out to our mother, nodding at me to get going before the monster would storm in here.

"I saw her in her bedroom not even a few moments ago. Surely your age has not affected your sight so much?"

I had to hold back my laughter as we heard the shriek of fury from the other side of the door before the door handle was yanked at harshly. "Dorian! You open this door right now! I know she is in there!"

"Go," Dorian whispered to me whilst smirking before pulling me into a side hug and heading for the door.

I did not stick around after that and caught the sound of the door being opened to allow my mother in just as I slipped into a shadow, then shadow-stalked right out of the bedroom, barrelling to my own on the other side of the manor's third floor. I stepped from the shadows within my bathroom and quickly shut the door, locking it.

No doubt my mother would be here any moment, and any evidence of my leathers and trip outside needed to be eradicated immediately. Stripping in a rush, I threw the dirty clothes into the hamper and stepped under the shower head, having it automatically switch on.

I forced myself to calm my racing heart as I washed, taking special care with my hair that would constantly tangle due to the wig and blind mask. It had become especially tangled and dirty after my time in the Whispering Wood this afternoon.

My mind kept going back to the encounter with Theo, my body trembling at the thought of it. He had recognised me so quickly, clearly not having forgotten about me after twelve long years… although for someone like him, a reaper for the gods, a Katopodis, I was merely a long overdue hunt within his grasp.

Being reminded of the reality was a slap in my face. I had trusted him, and he had betrayed me. It seemed that is what he was lately… news had travelled fast amongst our world of his part in removing Hades from the plane of existence. It had been ordained by Zeus himself, but still had many demigods and gods and goddesses alike murmuring about the infamous '*God Killer*' in hushed tones when he passed them.

Hades had been neglecting his duties as the king of the underworld, leaving it in disarray for years. His obsession with a girl near New York was the final straw for Zeus, after many years of distress amongst the gods at the disappearance of Persephone. Hades had initiated the killing of many innocents and sired a demigod in secret – which had been outlawed for longer than I cared to remember.

The outlawing of new demigods was the reasoning for the Servile. The servile would ensure the continuation of our services to gods, the cartels, and the whims of the gods by ensuring the bloodline remained true.

It was surprising Theo had even come to the servile as the encounter and elimination of Hades happened only a few weeks ago. It was customary for all family members to attend, however, a bit of reprieve for such an action would have been justified in my eyes.

What am I even doing? Theo does not need my support. The bastard betrayed me.

I had deliberately kept him from my thoughts for years, merely watching as instructed from a distance. Always having to be aware of everyone's movements and thoughts.

I would be lying if I said that I hadn't slipped and paid too much attention to the man on more than one occasion.

"There you are!" my mother shrieked from the other side of the bathroom door, causing me to jump, almost slipping on the wet marble of the shower.

"I will be out in a minute, mother," I called back, blowing a breath through pursed lips at having to act submissive and respectful to the woman I loathed so much.

Shutting off the shower, I wrung out my wet hair before reaching for a towel. I stepped out of the shower and observed myself in the mirror. My green eyes stared back at me. Eyes Theo had recognised…

Shit! He would no doubt have informed his family of the encounter! What the hell was I going to do? I had to attend the ridiculous welcoming ceremony in an hour, and I would be walking right into the viper's den…

Trembling, I turned from my reflection and counted to ten before unlocking the bathroom door and smiling serenely at my mother who scowled at me from the side of my bed, her arms crossed in rage.

"Where have you been?"

Lovely as ever then… "What do you mean, mother, I have been in the bathroom showering as per your instruction to get ready for the ceremony…" I replied, ever playing submissive.

My mother eyed me, knowing I was lying yet could not outright accuse me as she had no proof to state otherwise. Smiling sweetly at her, I turned and headed to my vanity, sitting on the antique seat whilst reaching for my face cream. I had just scooped some of the jasmine-scented concoction when she stepped up behind me, scowling at me in the mirror.

"You shall behave as instructed, gathering information on our targets as usual. You shall refrain from getting into intimate conversations with anyone and will remain by my side until the ceremony is over, after which you shall return to your room and remain here until summoned. Do you understand, Braelyn?" she sneered the same instruction that it always was…

I almost rolled my eyes at her, instead smiling sweetly at her.

"Yes mother, crystal clear."

She turned from the mirror, heading toward my closet and I had to school my feature as I watched her go from my mirror with a look of absolute disgust. Returning to the task at hand, I applied my face cream and other essentials before drying my hair. I glanced at the wig on my dresser, detesting the foul thing.

My mother returned with a garment bag that I had seen delivered this morning and had chosen to ignore. Unzipping it, my mother pulled out a mint green dress that reached the floor. I could not see its full grandeur from my position but decided to ignore it as it was most likely just as horrendous as the rest of them.

"Perfect," I heard my mother mumble, knowing far too well that when she did that, she was up to something, and it meant trouble.

Scrunching my brows in curiosity, I placed my brush down on the dresser and stood, going over to look at the dress. My heart sank at the sight of it. She couldn't be serious. Was I to be her whore now too?

"Mother?" I asked, not able to form the correct word to enquire why she had chosen such a dress for me to wear tonight.

"Perfect," was all she mumbled yet again and placed it across my bed before venturing to my jewellery stacks in the closet, as well as the masks. After a few moments, she returned, gold glinting in each hand.

"Mother," I called out to her, my agitation slipping through now. I immediately regretted it as her icy blue gaze shot to my emerald one.

"You will wear it, and I do not want to hear a word from you. You will wear this jewellery and mask. Have your hair up tonight." She snapped, now venturing to the farthermost part of my large closet and opening the cupboard that held my wigs. I always had my hair down. By my mother and Hecate's instruction of giving the impression of innocence.

I had a wig right at the back that already had been styled in a soft updo, soft wisping tendrils of golden locks cascading romantically around the face.

My mother grabbed it and then proceeded to stalk over to my dresser, yanking my usual wig from the mannequin head and throwing it carelessly to the floor. I eyed her with a rage building within me as I clenched my fists. The air around my hands visibly and audibly shuddered before I reeled it back in. She had noticed though and snapped her eyes to me as she placed the new wig upon the mannequin. "You will reign it all in, or would you like to be reminded of the well?" she said softly, sleazily like that of a snake.

My throat constricted at the thought of the well. I never wanted to be submitted to such a fate again... I was still in prison twelve years later, yet here I was not drowning.

"I understand, mother," I managed out defeated in her presence.

"Good, now get finished. Your father will be arriving soon and then the ceremony will begin. I expect you to be there when he does. Dorian will escort you," she said, almost switching personalities as the preppy tone and confidence exuded from her before she exited my bedroom, readying herself to play the perfect hostess and lady of House Sarris…… Our house of law and justice as dictated by the God Themis whom we descended from.

Law and justice – a disgrace for us all after all the secrets and torments of the years.

Staring at the bedroom door for a moment, I sighed and ran my hands through my jet-black hair as I tied it up and out of the way. Picking up the dress, well an excuse for a dress, I cringed.

To call it anything other than a sleazy scrap of fabric gave me the shivers.

She could not be serious in wanting me to wear this, especially in front of all the houses attending this evening. The more I thought about all those eyes that would be on me, the more I felt disgusted, however, I knew she would have no qualm shoving me in that well yet again…

Groaning, I got dressed in the mint green monstrosity and tried to avoid my body's reflection in the mirror as I sat to do my makeup and wig. The stocking and glue irritated my sensitive skin from the wig and mask constantly being adorned. My makeup irritated my skin too and I already could not wait until I could return to my room to remove all this mess…

The wig finally being tightly in place, as well as my makeup done, I grabbed the jewellery my mother had instructed me to wear. The gold was cool to the touch as I inspected the pieces. Two armbands twirled around each bicep, imitating laurel wreaths. I placed them first, hating the feeling of the constriction.

Grabbing the chain she had chosen, I scoffed at the piece. It was a body chain… wrapping around my neck, only to drop between my breasts and encircle my waist. It reminded me of a leash… it was most likely why she had chosen it.

As I stood, I looked myself over in my entirety finally. I did not recognise myself. The mint green dress reminded me of a hooker's toga if there was such a thing. I had heard of the sex houses owned and frequented by the gods and goddesses and could assume they wore such things.

The mint-green layered chiffon gown dropped from each shoulder to a wide V-line between my breasts and ended just above my navel, where a band around my waist then fell in a soft layer before splitting at each hip, leaving a strip of fabric barely covering the middle of my legs and crotch area, the same pattern of dress lay at the back, barely covering my ass. It was impossible to even wear any form of underwear, top or bottom.

Of all the areas to cover, they decide the outer thighs would be good… I felt uncomfortable and was about to protest when a knock sounded at my door.

"Are you ready, short stack?" Dorian called from the other side.

"Um, I… Uh…" I stumbled over my words, causing Dorian to open the door timidly before peering in, his jaw fell slack before he rushed in, slamming and locking the door quickly before he turned back to me, clenching his jaw.

"What the fuck is that witch up to?!" he seethed as he took in my appearance from top to bottom and back up.

It took a lot for Dorian to swear in front of me. He may be two years older, being twenty-seven but he still did not cuss around me as if I was still just his baby sister.

"You can't go down there dressed like that." He snapped, heading to my closet in search of another dress. He knew far too well that every dress I wore to events was meticulously chosen by our mother. My heart hammered as I looked on, and flashes of the well flew through my mind. Snapping my head up and pushing my shoulder back, I expelled the pent-up tension and called out to Dorian. He returned with a mass of dresses in his arms that he threw upon my bed.

"I will do it, now let's go," I muttered, not wanting to meet his face as he saw my resolve and no doubt knew why I had decided to comply instead of enduring the wrath of our mother.

"But Brae," he said softly, urging me to reconsider the spectacle I was about to make of myself.

Stepping to the dresser, I grabbed the golden mask, encrusted with jewels and moulds of stars, and placed it over my eyes, my senses and shadow-stalking giving me a sense and view of my surroundings immediately.

"Brae," Dorian sighed one last time as I waited for him by the bedroom door as he rubbed at his eyes in frustration. Finally, he walked over to me, opening the door and letting me exit first.

Upon shutting the door, he turned back to me as he held his arm out for me to take.

Taking his arm as he escorted me down the corridors of the manor, I could feel the tremble from his arm as he held back his rage. "Dor, there will come a day when I get us out of this mess but today is not that day," I whispered to him, feeling him stiffen beneath my hold.

"You are my little sister. I am supposed to protect *you*," he mumbled as we neared the grand staircase to the foyer below, already filling with the other houses. We both peered down for a moment, nervous for our reasons.

"Yes well, your little sister is not so little anymore and besides, at least I don't have to look them in the eye as they judge me." I smiled a small smile at him and flicked the golden mask that covered the top half of my face.

Dorian sighed heavily and chuckled softly before looking back down at the foyer in silent contemplation. "You ready, princess?"

Braelyn

Stepping down the grand staircase beside Dorian with me on his arm, everyone who was entering stopped and watched us. The faces showed a clear shock at my appearance.

"You okay?" Dorian leaned over and whispered in my ear whilst still looking ahead.

"As okay as I can be," I whispered back, smiling softly to the crowd as I did so.

I felt sick, their gazes drinking up every inch of me. The men especially. I caught sight of one of the women smacking her husband's arm angrily before walking back outside.

Finally, we reached the bottom, my heels clicking loudly against the white marble floors as everyone was silent. I felt my brother stiffen as he took in all the gawking. I needed to do something before he did something stupid. "Welcome to our home," I spoke softly, serenely in the manner I had been trained to do. "I hope your stay will be a blessed one," I finished before subtly pulling on Dorian's arm as I began towards the ballroom, knowing that is where my mother would be expecting us.

Dorian sighed and led me away, my keen hearing still focused on the crowd that had been silent near the entrance. Many began muttering about me. Some were shocked, others lustful. It made me queasy. I had picked up on the family I dreaded the most as they entered the manor, myself and Dorian still heading away to the ballroom.

Gods, was that Braelyn? Where the hell is Theo? He needs to see this! Kason Katopodis, the youngest sibling said.

Shut up, the eldest brother, Trey, responded sounding bored.

She's smoking! Kason continued

Kason has a point, where is Theo? Layna, the eldest Katopodis spoke – the only female out of the four siblings of House Katopodis.

I felt tense at the mention of Theo. The fact he had not returned had my stomach rolling with anxiousness. What would he say when he returned? Surely this evening would turn into a blood bath as they hunted me down on the news I had been spotted in the woods.

"There you are," my mother's pathetic preppy voice pulled me from my thoughts as she strolled over and embraced me at the ballroom entrance. It was all a farce. All of it. Playing alongside her, I smiled sweetly and returned the hug, imagining the day I would end this woman finally…

"Mother," Dorian greeted tensely from my side. "Dorian dear, why don't you show our guests to their correct seats? Your sister will be by my side."

Dorian raised a brow, side-eyeing me in quiet speculation at our mother's words.

"That's what worries me," he muttered under his breath. Mother heard and snapped an icy glare at him before schooling her features once more and smiling.

"Welcome, welcome! Dorian shall be escorting you to your seats, right this way," she said to one of the houses who entered the ballroom and ushered them along with Dorian leading the way. I could not focus on whom it was who had entered, my panic over Theo and the repercussions eating me alive. Having to be around so many people did not help either.

I smiled sweetly and nodded in greeting to everyone who began entering the ballroom, a blur of faces passing by. The sickening looks of lust crept over my body as I stood to attention like the good little soldier I was.

House Katopodis entered, at last, the nearby houses shying away from the sheer power of their presence. The house of Hades' descendants, trained by Ares himself. They were reapers of the gods, and mercenaries when needed. Ensuring the cartels ran as smoothly as expected by the gods and overseeing shipments of souls as well as the usual drugs and weapons through the human realm.

Enforcers. God killers.

All of them, although it had been Theo himself who had dealt the deathly punishment upon Hades, ushering in a new ruler of the underworld.

Dante, Theo's father led the group with his wife Alaia by his side. Dante had the same overwhelming presence as Theo and all the sons had inherited his midnight hair, aqua eyes, and olive skin. Theo took after him the most, their height was the same at six-foot-six of raw, lethal power.

Alaia was shorter, at an average height of five-foot-seven, and had milky pale skin and vibrant red hair. Their daughter and eldest child, Layna, took after Alaia inheriting the same gentle look and vibrant hair, however, I know they were just as lethal as the men in the family by the conversations I had overhead over the years. "Good evening, Kaisley," Dante spoke to my mother directly, before turning his attention to me at her side, "Braelyn," he nodded to me, all the while Alaia smiled softly at me before looking to my mother and a look of dislike swept over her face too quickly before she schooled it and smiled at her. I noticed it due to my keen senses, yet my mother had been oblivious. *Strange...*

"Welcome to our home. Dorian shall show you to your table," my mother crooned beside me, sweeping an arm out indicating toward Dorian who was on his way back to us through the crowd, a tick of irritation in his jaw I knew too well.

"That won't be necessary," Alaia spoke up firmly, before smiling at me again and stepping away from us, Dante placing a soft hand on her lower back as they wove their way through the crowd.

I had been too panicked by their presence that I had remained silent during the entire exchange. My heartbeat was thunderous in my chest as the siblings walked past us, all nodding in greeting. Thankfully Theo was nowhere to be seen... Although, *Shit, had the wolves torn into him?*

A new kind of panic washed over me, and I stumbled where I stood. My mother gave me a harsh look before returning to her pointless conversation with another house member.

Looking around the ballroom, I did not spot him anywhere. He had not spoken to his family since the incident in the woods and I worried about what that could mean...

Dorian returned to my side. His irritation was clear. "I need a break from those old pervs mother invited. I feel like I need a shower. Mrs Adamos cannot keep her old wrinkly hands to herself. I have never had my butt cheeks pinched so many times in my life. I need to shower I feel so disgusted." He rattled off beside me for only me to hear.

I was still searching for Theo when Dorian nudged me softly with his elbow, squinting at me.

"What is it?" he whispered, noticing my lack of interest in his story. Usually, I would have laughed at him, but not today. My head turned ever so slightly as I surveyed the ballroom, searching with my senses, still standing beside my mother with my shoulders back proudly and hands clasped together in front of me.

"Brae," Dorian asked yet again, gaining my full attention at last.

"Nothing is wrong," I answered, disgusted with how easily I could lie to him of all people. Hecate and mother had trained me well, far too well it seemed.

I snapped my head in the direction of the foyer just beyond the ballroom, my powers sensing and snagging on something just beyond. I knew it was not the man I sought but my worst nightmare all the same.

Stepping into view, my father walked in proudly alongside, yet slightly behind, as protocol dictated, Themis herself. Behind them, Apollo.

Themis was tall, standing at almost seven feet, with cascading blonde hair and blue eyes that twirled like that of a whirlpool. The goddess of justice. Her lithe form was covered in a floor-sweeping golden dress that accentuated each curve perfectly, and no makeup adorned her face, save for the ruby red lipstick. The colour of blood.

"Themis," my mother spoke in greeting as we all bowed, not yet allowed to stand until she allowed us to. Every cell in my body fought against my will to stand. That dark ancient power slammed against my hold stating that I should never bow. I ignored it, feeling sweat gather on my brow from the exertion, within the confines of my golden mask.

"Rise," Themis purred, finally allowing us to stand. My fingers trembled as the power within me recoiled at the disgrace I had just made of myself by bowing. I clasped my hands together tightly to hide the tremble, my knuckles going white. I could never understand it. It was a part of me, yet somehow wholly separate. No words had ever been passed from the power to me, or vice versa, yet it would communicate on a different frequency I could not explain, like that of a different entity altogether.

A ringing began in my ears that drowned out all other sounds and I stumbled slightly as the power within me tried to show itself, show all these monsters what

I truly could be. Who I was. My brother noticed my misstep, and stepped closer, leaning into my side to keep me up without anyone noticing. He knew this happened whenever one of the gods or goddesses had me bow to them. Being in their presence was torture, yet being forced to bow… My weathered and stubborn determination was the only thing keeping me undetected until now.

My father noticed as Themis spoke with my mother, and a look of fear crossed his face before he spoke to Themis, gaining her attention. "Themis, allow me to show you to your table, I am sure you will find it to your liking. Kaisley has ensured it is only the best for you," he spoke, sweeping an arm out, ushering the goddess in the direction of the dais that had been erected for her in honour of being the goddess of the house tonight.

Themis nodded and allowed my father to show her the way, my mother following closely behind. *Thank the gods…*

"I need to get out of here for a minute. Cover for me," I whispered to Dorian who nodded, knowing the routine. He squeezed my hand softly before stepping in front of me, covering me from view as I turned and left. I had just made it out when I heard Mrs Adamos call out to him yet again and a very audible groan escaped him.

My heels clicked and clacked along the white marble floors that shone brightly, reflecting the crystal chandeliers that hung from the high ceilings. The manor was massive, erected with only the finest materials. The rarest of antiquities filled its spaces. Rooms larger than necessary took up the space. I continued, finally turned a bend, and looked around that no one was looking.

The air shuddered around me as I stepped within a shadow, moving from one to the next as fast as a blink of an eye. I found myself in the woods faster than I thought possible and let it all go.

I released the power in all its rage, holding on to the leash that bound us together.

A sense of the entity within me roared and chuckled, dancing with the Whispering Wood that answered its ancient call.

The leaves rushed around in a frenzy, the branches swaying and rustling in the light of what it was and could be.

I extinguished what I could, yet it would never be enough to keep the danger away…

Never enough.

Theo

I found myself wandering through the Whispering Woods that lay in the centre of all the houses of the gods. I had not stepped foot in here in the last twelve years.

I tried not to think about that time of my life or the mysterious girl with emerald eyes. For the past few weeks, she had been running through my mind uncontrollably. It grated me, the entire fucking situation of now and then…

I had just returned from a mission of sorting out an issue with one of the cartels in South America and needed some space. The fucking assholes thought it would be a good idea to go against orders and start moving merchandise without consent.

My father had insisted my brothers and sister accompany me; however, I did not take too kindly to that and went by myself and sorted the issue in record time. I seemed to be filled with this nagging feeling as of late and it was driving me nuts. No amount of fucking, killing and training seemed to shake it from my system.

Shake her…

So, when the mission came up, I jumped on it and heads rolled faster than what was probably necessary.

My family had wanted to wait for me to attend tonight's Servile, however, I sent them ahead and told them I had shit to do and I would meet them there.

Which is how I somehow decided it would be a good idea to wander through the place I had avoided for twelve years.

I could not believe my goddamn eyes when I came upon the spot of that fucking willow tree and there she stood.

I saw the etching still there and those big green eyes staring at me in fear. *Fucking fear?!* I knew the hair hidden beneath that hood would be midnight black.

I was shocked when she refused to speak and even more annoyed when she slipped away. Shadow-stalking. I should have guessed she would have had some form of power. Especially one that had only been recorded once over the millennia, so rare that its origin could not be told, lost to history. She had never shown any indication of it in all the time we had spent together in the woods so long ago.

She was smart, very smart.

I had been chasing her when she doubled back. Not to let me know her destination. I noticed that her scent was missing, which was strange, as I remembered her always smelling of jasmine and some earthy scent I could never quite name. I finally felt like I had her where I could get to her when the wolves of the Whispering Woods began circling me.

I looked back and she was gone. I cursed so loudly I swore the woods itself recoiled at my blasphemy of losing her yet again.

I saw three wolves, larger than normal, circling, snapping, and growling at me, keeping me in place.

"Well, come on then," I growled at them.

One jumped at me, which had been a bad move on its part, and I grappled with it, slamming it into the harsh ground. It rose and snarled before all of them stopped, their heads lifting, and ears raised as if listening. A breeze flew through the winding trees before disappearing. All three wolves turned and ran, away from me as if being called.

I watched in disbelief as I surveyed the area, my blood still pumped with adrenaline, ready for a fight. *Had she done that?* Looking down at myself, I saw my suit and shirt had been ruined by the chase and now the wolf.

"Fuck," I mumbled, dusting mud and blood from my ripped shirt, seeing a scrape across my ribs from the wolf who had lunged at me. Just another scar, I guessed.

I would need to head home and change before I went to the Servile. My mother would have my balls if I arrived looking like this. My family had already taken my bag with clothes for this fucking ridiculous weekend escapade, but I couldn't just wander through the estate looking like… yeah, I would need to go home.

So that's exactly what I did, thinking over a million possibilities of how it was that the girl from twelve years ago had been there. Every soldier had been sent out to comb these woods that day and months after that and had found nothing. Not even tracks leading anywhere.

I figured the reason was there had been no tracks was because she had been shadow-stalking… Smart indeed.

A wicked smirk pulled at my lips before a scowl took its place as the memories slammed into me, making my skin crawl beneath my tattoos.

I scrubbed harder than necessary in the shower, trying to rid my skin of that feeling, and rushed to dress and entered my family's manor garage, all our vehicles and motorbikes lined up and looking spectacular, every single one shining black as night. Lights on the ceiling lit up as I went, deciding that I would be taking my favourite baby tonight.

My customised, black Ducati Panigale V4. Swinging a leg over the Ducati, I sat and pulled my helmet over my head and started it, revving it loudly before tearing out of the garage, it automatically closed behind me. I raced down my family estate's long winding driveway and out of the tall gates.

The sun had just disappeared over the horizon as I raced down the road toward House Sarris. I knew my absence would be noted by now, which I honestly couldn't give a shit about.

It was the ire that was simmering in my blood as the events of this afternoon raced through me.

I was racing down the highway alongside a section of the Whispering Woods and cut through the traffic with ease. I was turning off the highway when in the distance, within the woods, I caught glimpse of a section above the canopy where the air seemed to shudder and shake before leaves rushed in a cacophony of chaos and dropped down as the shuddering stopped.

I pulled over to the side of the road and peered out toward the woods, having a nagging feeling that it had to do with her. If it was indeed her, to hold so much power was impressive, yet even more terrifying. I wondered if anyone attending the Servile had noticed it. If they did, I had no idea how to navigate the situation.

My mind raced with the possibilities and how to handle the situation. There was still a hunt order issued for her…

I continued to watch before my cell buzzed, and it was a text from Kason.

You need to see Braelyn. My god's, bro, I didn't realise she was so fucking hot. You need to see this! Where are you, dick?

I rolled my eyes at my younger brother's text. He was two years younger than me, at twenty-three years old, and knew I had always found Braelyn to be obnoxious.

Blind or not, I couldn't stand the way she always paraded around as if superior to everyone, and that mother of hers, gods it's no wonder Braelyn was so fucking stuffy. Braelyn also seemed too important to be involved with anyone or anything and only showed face when she had to. Too good to even have a conversation with anyone besides that brother of hers, Dorian. I tried to avoid even looking in her direction.

Pocketing my phone, I revved the Ducati once more and raced toward the estate I would be forced to stay for the weekend. Thank fuck I was not the oldest and would not be involved in the Servile.

I arrived at House Sarris' estate and was let through without questions, the guards knowing me and my reputation. I continued up their bricked and perfectly manicured driveway, stopping and shutting off my bike next to the large marble fountain that sat in the circular drive.

I'm here, see you soon. You better have a drink waiting for me, I texted Kason back, knowing he wouldn't take the chance of not having my drink waiting for me. He knew the repercussions of his older brother.

Climbing off my bike, I removed the helmet and shook my hand through my black hair, and placed it on the handlebars. I looked around the estate, everything far too preppy and perfect for my taste and internally cringed as I thought of having to stay here all weekend. Maybe I could show face and ditch. *Sounds like a fucking plan.*

Straightening my suit jacket, I walked up the steps and looked around, the back of the estate catching my eye. I halted on the steps as I noticed none other than Braelyn speed-walking through a different entrance into the manor. It was so fast, but the glittering mask had given her away as it reflected from the garden torches that were lit around the garden paths.

I didn't think too much about it and continued my way, servers ushering me toward the ballroom, glowing chandeliers hanging from the ceiling every several feet. It was too much. Too much opulence, and too much starkness with the golds and whites.

I noticed just above the arched entryway of the ballroom, a large golden lion head, its features eternally roaring, and rolled my eyes at the madness of it all.

Entering the ballroom, I noted it was packed full, Themis sat on a dais at the head of the room and tables ran the surround of the grand room, one for each house. People noticed me and spoke in hushed tones, some turning away and some staring blatantly as I passed them, heading to my family's table.

God killer.

Yeah, I guess that was my name to all of them now. I smirked casually as I neared my family, my seat vacant. Mom and Dad were speaking to each other softly and smiling, Layna was sipping at a glass of wine and scrolling through her phone, Trey was looking bored as fuck and Kason was lining up shot glasses in front of everyone, laughing at something he found hilarious as usual.

"When I said a drink, I didn't mean a shot, asshole," I said as I reached the table and took my seat next to Kason, nearest to the opening of the room. We each had our usual seating as accustomed to strategic purposes. I always sat with the fastest way to intercept any form of threat as well as a clear line of vision of everything.

I had inherited the Chaos Handler gene in our bloodline. The first in a very, very long time. What some would say was chaos, I called calculation.

I know my staring and calculating looks unnerved most, but that was exactly what it was… I took in every facet, every detail, calculating, chaos rippling from a chain reaction I could control. The ravens were my inherited weapon. I could control, whisper to them, or split my consciousness between a swarm of them, the calculation too much for most to even comprehend.

"The shot is a warm-up, bro, your whiskey is coming." Kason laughed as he handed me a shot and the others lifted theirs in cheers before we all downed our own. The sickly-sweet godawful tartness had us pulling faces and I almost pummelled Kason as I reached for water to rinse my mouth.

"What the fuck was that shit?" I growled at him as I drank more water. Layna and Trey both had the same idea. Kason looked at all of us like we were out of our damn minds.

"Cherry something. I don't recall," he replied, with an incredulous look. I was about to rip into him when Trey said something.

"You are officially banned from shot duty. That was revolting."

"I second that," Layna said around a cough. Kason looked to me for help, which he was not going to get.

"I agree, that was the worst one yet, dick," I called him out and he slumped in his chair with a huff as a server placed my whiskey down in front of me before swiftly departing. My rings that covered every finger clanged as they contacted the crystal tumbler. Taking a sip, I felt myself relax a little bit. That was until Layna had to ask the one question I hoped to avoid.

"What took you so long?" Her blue eyes bore into me, waiting for an answer.

I felt nervous for the first time in twelve years as they all waited for my answer, even my parents were now waiting for an answer. So I went with the best excuse that I knew they wouldn't want details of…

"I had needs that needed to be satisfied," I mumbled, taking another sip hoping that they would buy it. Why I was lying to them, I had no fucking idea. I had never lied to them, and it was this fact that had me pulling on my shirt collar and loosening the tie and top button.

"Oh gross." My sister fake gagged, before continuing, "You and Calista need to stop what you are doing. She has a job to do and so do you. Don't think I haven't noticed how long a mission takes when you two work together."

I eyed her, not caring she had figured out who my fuck buddy had been for the past year.

Kason and Trey however stared at me wide-eyed, and Kason choked on his drink before catching his breath enough to speak.

"You are telling me you and Calista have been fucking?" Kason almost shrieked. Trey got to him before I did and smacked the idiot on the back of the head for being so loud.

"Yes," was all I said as I looked around the ballroom casually.

"Shit, well, congrats to you man," Kason saluted me and downed the rest of his drink before standing. I finished mine and stood too, knowing he was headed to the open bar at the back of the room.

Following him through the crowded ballroom, a strange scent hit me. Stopping me in my tracks as I swivelled on the spot, trying to locate it amongst the crowd.

Too many people… too many scents. Shit!

"You good dude?" Kason asked from the bar a few feet ahead of the spot I had stopped. Ignoring him, I looked around once more, trying to locate the scent. It was familiar and had traces of the Whispering Woods. Which meant…

"Yoh, Theo, you good?" Kason called me again with a frown.

"Yeah," I mumbled and headed to the bar and ordered more whiskey as Kason watched me speculatively.

"You better stop looking at me like that, bro," I mumbled in his direction as I surveyed the room, waiting for my drink.

"Shit, there she is," Kason spoke up excitedly. My stomach dropped before I caught on to whom he was referring. "Look!" Kason nudged me and tilted his head in the direction of the head house table next to the dais – Sarris.

"I told you," Kason was chuckling beside me as my eyes went wide at the sight before me before I quickly schooled my features.

Braelyn-fucking-Sarris was hot. Gods, I'll never admit it but…

That dress showcased everything, from her voluptuous curves, and defined muscles, which I knew you did not attain without rigorous training, to shimmering olive skin, her hips, and the swell of her breasts were exquisite and not hidden beneath the dresses she usually wore. I could tell from here there was not a strip of underclothing on that body.

Her hair was done up for the first time and her slender neck was on full display, leading down to those perfectly carved collar bones and those breasts… The body chain though… *gods*…

"I don't see it," I mumbled in nonchalance to Kason who stood stupefied at my side by my lack of interest. Taking a sip of my whiskey that had been laid on the bar top, I looked around the room once more.

"You have got to be kidding me," Kason deadpanned.

"Nope, still can't stand the bitch," I replied and downed my drink in one go and ordered another.

"Fuck that bro, you must be the blind one then," Kason grumbled grumpily beside me with a shake of his head.

I ignored him, giving him a clap on the back before strolling through the crowded room in search of that scent that had taunted me minutes ago.

I couldn't find it anywhere on the current side of the ballroom and decided to casually venture closer to the dais side. I caught a whiff of it and knew I had finally found her and would be able to track her down. Had she been hiding in plain sight all these years? Had she been shadow-stalking the events of the great house such as these? Who the fuck was she? Where was she? I was a man on a mission and was nearing the tables closest to the dais when Themis stood and the ballroom shushed, Apollo, striding casually toward her.

Apollo's golden blonde hair was slicked back, his neon green eyes blazing. He walked casually with his hands in his suit pockets as usual and smiled at everyone as he passed. Out of all the gods, I got along with him. Zeus had left him in charge of the earthly plane, so he was the head honcho so to speak.

Apollo stopped beside Themis who was taller than him by a few inches. He spotted me across the room and nodded in greeting, which I returned, although feeling agitated that my hunt for the scent had been put on hold by whatever was about to be announced.

"Welcome, children of the gods," Themis spoke sickly sweet, her whirlpool eyes unnerving as she looked out toward the crowd.

"Tonight, we celebrate our long-standing survival by the rite of the Servile. Please may I ask that you return to your seats as we will be commencing the ceremony on the hour?" Themis finished, sitting back down.

The room erupted in noise and movement as everyone began moving about, tangling every possible scent, and dragging away any chance I had of finding her.

Fuck!

I headed back to my family's table, still hopelessly scanning the room for any trace of that scent. I grew immensely agitated that I was unable to keep track of it as I had never had an issue tracking anything before, even in crowded spaces. I was the best at what I did for a fucking reason.

Slamming my drink down on the table, I sat and ripped my tie completely off and removed my suit jacket, rolling up my sleeves, and leaving my tattoos that covered every inch of my olive skin from my hand and up the length of my arms, on full display. I sat back with a huff and grabbed my drink, taking a large sip, and feeling the whiskey burn its way down my throat. "What's the matter?" Layna asked with a frown having noticed my mood.

"Just drop it, not now Layna," I muttered, knowing my sister wouldn't push me.

"Well. good luck to you two, it could be either of you chosen," my mother spoke up to my sister and Trey who were the eldest. Layna being the firstborn, yet female, meant that it could be Trey that was selected for marriage. There weren't many houses that could be chosen tonight. I think it was about seven different houses that had children of the correct age. I didn't pay any mind to it though because it wasn't going to be my fucking issue anyway.

Trey said nothing yet stared ahead of him tensely and Layna offered my mom a soft smile before gulping down her entire glass of wine that had just been placed before her a moment ago. My father began laughing.

"Don't you mean to say good luck to whoever else it will possibly be stuck with them?" He cracked up even more as my sister winked in agreement and my mom slapped his chest.

"Dante!"

I felt a rare smile tug at my lips as I watched them and felt it disappear. I heard the room quieten down as Themis stood once more. "We shall begin."

The ballroom grew still as a large golden disk was brought forward by the priestesses of the temple in the woods. Never to be seen except for during the Great Sacrifice and the Servile. Their robes were an ivory colour, golden disks covering their faces as hoods concealed their hair.

They placed the golden disk before Themis and then poured water from the ancient well, that was on this estate, onto its circular concaved surface. The water rippled and shimmered as the lights caught the golden disk.

The priestesses bowed and left the ballroom, no doubt heading back to the woods and the temple where they dwelled. Apollo stepped up beside the disk and blessed it with an ounce of his power, all of us having to bow our heads and close our eyes as golden light erupted in the ballroom before dying down.

Themis stood before the disk and twirled a slender, perfectly manicured finger through its water, a whirlpool much like her eyes began to spin as she whispered the ancient rite that would show who it is to be wed for the best possible bloodline.

I began feeling hot and uncomfortable.

Shit, maybe I had too much whiskey too fast?

I began fidgeting in my seat and my father noticed as he scrunched his eyes watching me and cocked his head. I grabbed my drink and gulped it down. The uncomfortable heat tingled through my body.

What the fuck?

I reached for my glass again and dropped it as searing heat flashed across my hand and wrist. I jumped back, out of my chair and I watched in horror as black, midnight swirls appeared twisting around my thumb, swirling like vines with small thorns around and down toward my wrist, over my tattoos, and finally ended at my elbow.

The ballroom gasped at noticing what had happened at our table, their glances shooting back and forth between my shocked expression and the mark.

Fuck.

I looked at my father who was wide-eyed like the rest of my family as I heard a clash of glass and a small whimper near the dais. Braelyn shot to her feet as the same brand appeared across her skin. She was trembling as she raised her head and found me immediately even with that blind mask covering her eyes.

I eyed her in absolute confusion at how this could have happened and then the rage began to build within me like a god-dammed inferno. "Theo," I heard my family members calling to me, yet ignored them as I looked from Braelyn to Themis and back to house Sarris. My anger grew and grew, my pulse thundering at the madness of it all.

"No," was all I managed to grit out before leaving the ballroom, slamming my chair back with a loud bang against the wall.

Just fucking... No!

Braelyn

I had just exited the woods and made my way back to the side entrance toward the back of the manor when I heard the roar of a motorcycle pulling up to the front. The sun had set, casting the estate in shadows when I stopped in my track, curious of who it may be.

Stepping from the path, my heels dug into the lawn slightly as I peered around the corner and saw that it was Theo. He had a different suit on, black as usual, even the button-down collared shirt he wore. His tie of black satin added a slight contrast yet looked very dapper as he always did.

Sin incarnates.

I shook my head of the thought immediately, not sure where it had come from, and turned, heading back toward the entrance that would sneak me back inside, undetected.

The lit torches along the garden path illuminate the garden in a golden glow as I went and I pushed against the French door, entering one of the many lounge areas of the first floor, my father's study being always the room to the right and off limits.

Opening the door to the corridor, I peeked out, looking both ways to ensure no one was around before venturing out and closing the door silently. I eyed the staircase near the entrance, knowing that I should shower to rid myself of the scent of the woods, but my mother spotted me as I took a step toward them.

"Braelyn, where the hell have you been?" she snarled at me from the arched entrance of the ballroom, her voice just loud enough for me to hear with my sensitive hearing. I froze, eyeing the stairs before I slowly turned and smiled at her serenely, acting as innocent as could be.

Submissive to her.

"I just needed some air, I was on my way to you right now, mother," stepping toward her and halting before her, the family sigil of the golden lion roaring above our heads.

My mother eyed me, looking for any evidence of me being untruthful. I hadn't exactly lied, I just left out the part of me expelling an insurmountable amount of my power in the woods, more than I had done ever, yet not as much as I needed to if I was being honest. The power still hissed and writhed through my blood, wanting to be let out and angry at me for holding its leash.

I found myself twirling the golden signet ring that I always wore upon my forefinger, around and around I would spin it using the thumb next to it. I found the effect of it calming, and grounding when needed.

"Very well. Come, Themis is going to announce soon that the ceremony will take place at the hour. I would like us to all be seated before then," she quipped before turning on her heel and heading back to the ballroom, expecting me to follow, which I did.

I eyed my mother from the back, her ice-blonde hair perfectly combed and twisted into the perfect chignon, her slim frame straight and adorned in an expensive pantsuit, the colour a deep navy, almost black.

Much like her soul… dark and uninteresting, I guessed and shook my thoughts away as we wandered through the ballroom. I noticed immediately that Kason and Theo were headed our way, toward the open bar. I turned my head back toward the table we would be sitting at up ahead and pushed faster to reach it before Theo would be anywhere near me. My mother eyed me suspiciously as I passed her and finally got to our table. I grabbed a seat next to Dorian, who had a glass of whiskey before him. Sitting, I grabbed it and downed it before placing it back before him, hissing as the liquor burned my throat and heated me from within.

"Shit Brae, what the hell?" he asked, eyeing his now empty tumbler and my tense disposition beside him.

"Did you not manage to, um," he trailed off quietly, leaning toward me so no snooping ears may hear.

"I'm fine. I did. Thank you for covering for me," I whispered back, still feeling the burn of the whiskey.

"Braelyn, it is so lovely to see you again," Apollo said, heading my way smiling. I immediately stood, hating the exposure this dress enforced upon me. Ignoring it, I smiled sweetly as he stopped in front of the table.

"It is good to see you too, Apollo. I hope you enjoy your time here," I replied, sweet and submissive. Apollo smiled wider at my words, his hands still in his pockets.

"I am sure I will. Please, have a seat, I did not mean to interrupt," he said before smiling at Dorian and casting a brief look over my mother and father before heading off toward Themis.

I had always gotten along with Apollo. He had never given me any indication of dark intent, like much of the gods and goddesses. I liked him even more because he seemed to have a special dislike for my mother and father, however, it seemed to run deeper for my mother. I never knew of the cause yet found it amusing all the same.

I could feel eyes on me and tension. I cast a side glance and found it to be Theo and Kason at the bar who were staring at me. Kason's was an obvious look of awe, but Theo. I gulped back the strange emotion as a look of pure disgust shone on his face before he clapped Kason on the back and headed into the crowded room.

I found my seat once more and twirled the ring around and around. I then spotted the wine before me that Dorian had ordered and took a large sip.

"Holy shit, Brae, what is going on? You have never downed a drink like this? Did mother do something?" Dorian scrunched his brows together as he asked me, placing his elbows on the table and eyeing me intensely.

"I said I'm fine, Dor. Too many people…" I mumbled, knowing it was partially true. I saw his eyes soften and he released a sigh and sat back in his chair, turning slightly toward me as if to speak, but Themis stood, cutting him off from whatever it was he wanted to say.

I did not pay attention as I knew that Themis was about to get everyone seated and perform the ceremony just as my mother had mentioned. I twirled the golden ring around and around beneath the table. My mind kept going back to that disgusted look I had witnessed on Theo's face moments ago.

Did I disgust him? I had never even spoken to him directly in all these years as he seemed to have always avoided me, and if I was honest, I had avoided him too. I could not risk the chance of discovery.

My mind then ran over our encounter in the woods earlier. Why had he even been there? No one ever dared enter the woods and he had not been there for twelve years. Looking over in his family's direction, I saw how relaxed his family was. Dante was laughing and Layna winked at him before Alaia smacked her husband in playful scolding. I was always envious of the familiar bond they seemed to share compared to most houses. It struck me then that Theo must have remained silent, not mentioning our encounter.

If he had said something, they would not be sitting there casually. House Katopodis would be on the hunt. The hunt order still lay upon my head, and I found myself frowning in confusion as to why Theo would remain silent. He was the most lethal of them all and knew of the order. Peculiar did not begin to describe the situation.

As I continued to watch, lost in my thoughts and deaf to my surroundings, I began to feel uncomfortable. My body heat rose, and my pulse thundered in my head.

Had I not extinguished enough of the ancient power? I twirled the ring around my finger furiously as my body thrummed with an odd sensation of heat and vibrations. A burning began near my thumb, causing me to look down at my lap, the skin on my hand darkening in a swirl near the apex of said thumb. A glass being dropped at the back end of the ballroom caught my attention. Whipping my head up, I saw Theo standing, the Servile brand coiling its black vines and thorns across his skin from his thumb, down and around it went, only ending near his elbow. It was stark against his tattoos that already covered his skin, impossible to miss.

A gasp rang out from the guests that filled the ballroom.

A whimper escaped me as I pushed away from my chair uncontrollably, trying to grab at the table or anything as pain seared through my skin. I inadvertently knocked my wine glass clean off the table, its shattering like a bomb going off in the ballroom. Pulling myself straight, I saw the same brand across my skin and couldn't stop myself from looking at Theo across the room immediately. Confusion was clear on both of our faces.

How?!

We were not the firstborn from our respective families and out of everyone, it had to be *us* joined.

My mind raced in shock as we stared at each other. My mind slowed, as a look of unfiltered rage crept its way over Theo's face. Dark and menacing. His family looked back and forth between me, him, and each other. They each tried calling out to him, yet Theo heard nothing as he glared at me, as if I was the foulest, most enraging thing in this world.

"No," he finally gritted out before shoving his chair back into the wall violently and leaving the ballroom in a rage that had me trembling.

I remained standing, the guests silent as they all turned their gazes to me. I was meant to be blind, as far as their knowledge went, however, I felt a part of me shatter under their gazes, Theo's reaction.

All of it.

Inhaling a shaky breath, I raised my chin and pushed my shoulders back. My hands trembling but clasping them tightly to hide them from view and turned toward my family who watched silently.

Dorian's face was the only one I faced, and his expression had shock and worry written all over it. I then looked toward where Themis stood eyeing me. Apollo standing a few feet back from her, his arms crossed, and brows drawn together in thought as he too watched me.

I nodded to them slightly before turning and walking toward the ballroom exit.

My heels were the only sound as I weaved my way through the guests that remained seated in silence. I kept my chin raised, not allowing anyone to see my weakness. See how deeply affected I was by the spectacle that had been made.

Even House Katopodis remained silent as they watched me pass by them. All of them watched me go as I left through the arched entrance and down the corridor.

White marble clicked beneath my heels and the further I got from the ballroom, knowing fully well that they all watched my back, I let out a shaky breath as the emotions threatened to overwhelm me as I shoved it deep down.

I had no idea where I was headed, only that I needed to be alone. I passed by the staff of the household and ignored their efforts of trying to open the door for me as I neared the large double doors that led outside.

They must have known to not push me as I raised a hand signalling them to stop.

The man nodded respectively and stood back to attention against the wall near the door.

Grabbing the large golden handle, I pulled the enormous and ridiculously heavy door open and stepped out, pulling it closed behind me.

I stood upon the threshold, still holding the handle behind my back as I leaned against the doors, releasing a large pent-up breath as my head tilted back against the cool surface, my golden mask facing skyward. I counted to ten before releasing my hold on the handle and stepped forward, retreating down the steps, into the cool night of the estate.

The gurgling of the fountain in the circular drive bubbled as I passed, and the crickets called out from the foliage around the gardens that stretched to either side of the manor. A soft breeze carried past me, carrying the scent of roses and wildflowers as well as the hint of a summer storm on the way.

I followed the torch-lit path around the manor, not sure where I was headed, only that I needed to think.

As I strolled, my thoughts ran over the humiliation of what just occurred within the ballroom. There was also the issue that I was now chained to the one person who had betrayed me in the past and would hand me over to be annihilated. His entire family would surround me for execution as well as be the ones to carry it out. My identity…

Gods.

How did this even happen?

The sound of the heavy double doors of the manor's entrance caught my attention and I did not care to linger and find out who it may be. I was surprised my mother had even allowed me to leave in the manner which I did.

I would surely be receiving punishment for such a show of disrespect.

I finally stopped and found myself in a part of the gardens that were solely used for the plantation of black roses. They bloomed at night and were extremely rare as they shimmered under the moon and starlight. A gift from the gods and only for the demigods as a show of faith between the houses. I always found them utterly beautiful and spotted the bench within the blooms that I had sat upon many times over the years of my isolation.

Their sweet, spicy aroma filled the air around me. I plucked one, staring at the thorny stem and shimmering black petals.

They shimmered in shades of gold and silver, completely charming. My gaze finally acknowledged the brand upon my skin, much like the rose. The similarities are palpable. No brand had ever been the same as the previous one. Mine and Theo's was wholly unique.

I knew what would be expected of us for the rest of the weekend. Two days of being forced to spend time together as more celebrations took place and after that, come to the end of the weekend, I would be leaving to start my life within the Katopodis household.

My head turned in the direction of the manor's guest houses that sat further back upon the small hill of my family's estate. Apartments used to house the other houses during occasions such as this weekend. House Katopodis would be staying in one of the houses on that hill this weekend…

Sighing, I leaned back and closed my eyes in contemplation. I knew that I was my mother's and Hecate's soldier, and I had my orders, the circumstances were nothing as I imagined they would be. I felt as if I had it all wrong and I was running out of time…What I wanted did not matter.

Looking back toward the well-house, I knew I would not fail my orders.

I couldn't.

Theo

I was sitting on my Ducati, the cool night air helping slightly with my simmering rage after having left the ballroom. I was smoking a cigarette when I heard the doors opening. I watched in silence as I noticed Braelyn exit the manor with that holier-than-thou attitude. I watched on in confusion as she shut the heavy door and leaned back against it, exhaling loudly. All traces of the snarky princess were gone.

She had not noticed me and thank the gods for that. I wanted absolutely nothing to do with her. She descended the steps, each heel clicking against the marble, only irritating me further.

She ventured down the path towards the gardens and a breeze floated by her.

I froze as the scent of the girl from the woods floated by. I sat up straighter, squinting around the area and seeing nothing besides Braelyn and the Whispering Woods further ahead in the direction she headed. The scent must have come from the woods, but…

No, it couldn't be… I thought deeply as I watched her go when the doors opened once more and it was my mother who exited the manor, her red hair loose and fluttering about as the breeze picked up once more. She spotted me upon the Ducati and frowned at me as she began heading my way.

I placed the cigarette between my lips and had a drag, the smoke easing some of the tension in my chest before I exhaled. The white cloud of smoke filled the air before me, before being dragged away by the night breeze.

My mother stood before me now, scowling at me before she grabbed the cigarette from my fingers and stomped on it. I was about to protest when those blue eyes held my tongue. "What was that, Theo?" she spat at me.

"What was what?" I asked, feigning nonchalance.

My ears rang as my mother slapped me. Hard. I blinked and eyed her, incredulous about what the fuck was happening. I had never seen her so angry in the past twelve years. The speed and strength with which she had slapped me had caught me off guard and that was saying something. I'm pretty sure as sweet as she was, there was a reason she was chosen at the Servile to be the lady of House Katopodis all those years ago when she had been joined by my father. "What. Was. That." She enunciated each word, her anger clear through her words.

I did not have an answer for her. How the fuck was I supposed to answer a question where I couldn't even explain it to myself.

"I can't stand her. I wasn't even supposed to be eligible to be fucking chosen." I snapped, knowing I was pushing my luck by being disrespectful right now.

My mother eyed me, raking that gaze up and down me in a way that had me readjusting my seating on the motorcycle. I leaned forward, crossing my arms over the handlebars, and stared ahead. I could still feel the sting of her slap against my cheek and found myself grinding my teeth, jaw clenched tight as I stared ahead, noticing that I could see Braelyn sitting amongst a grove of black roses.

"You have no idea how disappointed I am in you. You weren't supposed to be eligible tonight, but guess what, neither was that girl. No sorry, she is not a girl, but a woman. And how do you think she must be feeling knowing that she is bound to someone who just humiliated her like a child? In front of their house goddess, Themis, Apollo, and every single house that is here tonight?" My mother ripped into me.

I clenched my jaw tighter as I stared ahead, trying to avoid my mother's judgment and ignore the site of Braelyn in the garden yards away.

"For someone so attuned to every detail and chain reaction, you sure are fucking stupid sometimes," my mother snapped further.

"Excuse me?" I recoiled at her words, my brows raising at what she had said and the fact she had cursed. She never used foul language.

"You heard me. Do you honestly think Braelyn wants to be stuck at her mother's side non-stop? If you didn't avoid her over the years, you would have seen that as soon as she steps away, she is hauled back. Dorian acts as the buffer between them, stop looking everywhere else besides at her. I raised you better than what you showcased tonight and expect you to make this right, Theo," she finished, the silent threat clear in the air between us.

Was she right? To be honest I didn't know and still didn't give a shit.

"I am fucking daring you to try anything like that again," she snapped, having seen my thoughts cross my face as well as read my emotions. My mother was a powerful empath… I blanched yet again.

"You do know I am twenty-five years old. Not a fucking child to be scolded," I huffed out, sitting up and running a hand through my hair.

"Then don't fucking act like one."

I looked at my mother, never having seen her so passionate about anything like this, that wasn't a part of the family.

"She is now," she snapped one more time and then turned and headed back inside, leaving me reeling at what the fuck just happened.

"Fuck," I groaned as I clenched my jaw again and tilted my head as I watched Braelyn amongst the black roses. I could see them shimmering under the star and moonlight from here.

Digging in my pocket, I dug out my pack of cigarettes and lighter, immediately lighting one up and gods help me, I couldn't even stomach smoking now. Flicking it away in disgust I started the Ducati, its engine roaring only to settle down to a rumbling purr as I placed my helmet on my head. I looked toward the garden once more and Braelyn was gone.

I tore down the driveway, the guards barely opening the gates in time for me as I raced into the night.

Braelyn

Sitting in my bed the following morning, my black hair was a curtain hanging past my shoulders. I had shadow-stalked back to my bedroom after having overheard Theo's mother laying in to him about his behaviour. I was surprised that I had walked right past the area he had been sitting in and did not even notice him sitting on his Ducati.

I had been shocked at how she knew so much about me and my mother as well as the dynamic of our relationship and Dorian's input. It was startling, to say the least, and I feared the day she ever found out the intricacies. It appeared Alaia was an empath and something I would need to be mindful of going forward.

My mother had found me in my bedroom late last night and was furious over my exit during the ceremony, however, her features cooled when she informed me of Hecate's return to the estate sometime this weekend. She would not yield any further details of the reason behind the visit, other than I had better pay attention as it had to do with what I was trained for…

Staring out of the third-storey window, I could see the sun had risen slightly higher in the sky as I had been morbidly sitting in my bed the past few hours, my mind reeling over every detail. I could hear the commotion outside as the caterers set up for this evening's activities which would be held until the late hours of the night.

A knock at my door startled me from my thoughts and panic set in as I sat in bed, my wig and mask long forgotten in the bathroom upon the vanity.

"Who is it?" I called out wide-eyed as I began hurrying to the bathroom.

"It's just me," Dorian's gravelly voice ran out from the other side of the door.

I felt myself relax and headed to the door, unlocking it, and stepping away so that no one may see me whilst he entered. Dorian was dressed in casual clothes today. A dark pair of jeans and a simple white t-shirt brought out the blue in his eyes and the golden tones of his hair. "Hey short stack," he smiled softly at me as he shut the door and locked it behind him.

"Hey," I mumbled, placing my waist-length hair over my shoulder.

"How are you holding up?"

I don't think he realised what a loaded question that had been. I contemplated how to answer and simply shrugged as I answered. "As good as any other day I guess."

"Brae."

"What? This is what has happened and there is nothing to do about it. I just will have to endure as always until the time is right. Somehow, I expect mother and Hecate's hands are in this."

"Did you hear she is returning sometime this weekend for instructions?" I said in a rush as I flung myself backward across my bed, the mattress bouncing beneath me. I lay staring at the ceiling, my thumb twirling my signet ring.

"Yeah, mother told me last night after you left," he added, before sitting on the edge of my bed, the satin comforter matching his shirt. "I wanted to say, the way you handled that was beyond impressive."

"Yeah right, I can only guess what those vultures have to say about the snooty, blind princess now." A huff escaped me.

"No one said anything after Layna Katopodis snarled at everyone to get back to minding their own business and the show is over. You should have been there to see all those houses buckling under her gaze." He laughed as he shoved playfully at my knee.

It was a conundrum of why the Katopodis' ladies seemed to be so highly protective in the situation. I also noted the spark in my brother's eyes at the mention of Layna and eyed him keenly while he stood and walked over to the window. His gaze now cast out toward the gardens and no doubt the caterers.

"I never thought this weekend's festivities would be celebrating your Servile bond, and even less so that you would be joined with Theo Katopodis of all people," he trailed off, the protectiveness clear in his stance and tone.

I didn't respond, instead casting a look at my arm, the vine-like brand across my skin, and my hand. I ran my fingers over the mark, tracing the twirling lines in an absent-minded caress. A shiver worked its way down my spine, and I dropped my hand, frowning at the odd sensation.

"I don't know how to help you in this situation, short stack," Dorian said frowning as he crossed his muscular arms and leaned against the bay window.

"I don't need you to help me in this," I mumbled in reply whilst standing and heading over to my closet, rummaging through the hanging dresses, trying to find one that was slightly less appalling than the last. Gods, if I never wore a goddamned dress again, I could die happy…

"How are you so calm?" Dorian called out to me, still in his spot near the window. I spotted a simple, strappy emerald, green satin wrap dress and grabbed it, not bothering with jewellery. After last night's spectacle, I would prefer to not have any further glittering adornments covering my body.

Walking out of my closet, I threw the dress carelessly across my bed and stalked to the dresser, placing what I would need for the wig and mask out in a neat line, ready for me once I exited the shower.

"I am not calm, I am contemplative. I am aware of the situation and contemplating how to go about it. So, no, I'm not calm, just biding my time, Dor," I mused, placing the final item in place before turning to my brother.

Dorian eyed me in return, his gaze softening as a thousand thoughts and emotions flittered across his face before he sighed, dropping his folded arms, and pushing from the wall.

"Sometimes, I worry that they have trained you too well over the years, short stack," mumbling the words, he passed me, ruffling my midnight hair as he passed on his way to the door. "Don't be late for breakfast," he added before unlocking the door, casting a soft smile my way, and then he was gone, the silence of my bedroom embracing me once more.

I immediately locked the door, never being comfortable with the vulnerability of it being unlocked. I quickly showered and dressed, ensuring my blond wig sat just right and was immovable before placing my makeup. I did not bother with eyeshadow or mascara as the mask would be covering it, however, I had been drilled by my mother of the importance of appearance and that I should always have perfect rosy skin and plump, pink lips. I could gag at the thought. I did not mind makeup but placing so much importance upon it and the rigorous routine of every day added by the motives of my mother and Hecate had me loathing the feel of it against my sensitive skin. The mask I would wear today was a simple gold one, all my masks being gold as it was stapled metallurgy and colour for all houses. It had a simple design moulded into its surface. The lace-like pattern was subtle and not garnering attention like the ones my mother preferred.

I stared at myself in the mirror, not looking like anything as I was underneath the disguise. The blond hair of the wig fell in soft waves down my back, the mask only allowing my face to show from my nose down. I twisted my signet ring on my forefinger with my thumb, the only piece of jewellery on me except for the mask that may be considered as such. Exhaling, I counted to ten and schooled my features, pulled my shoulders back, and raised my chin.

***

Walking into the dining room on the ground floor of the manor, the smell of breakfast hit me, making my stomach growl. I had skipped the meals that had been served last night after everything that had happened. I stopped only for a second as the chatter in the room died down. Walking over to the empty seat beside Dorian, I sat down and was grateful to Dorian when he cleared his throat, and everyone got the hint and continued chatting.

The members in the dining room were me, Dorian, and our parents, the others were House Katopodis. I did not see Theo anywhere and gritted my teeth in annoyance that he was continuing this debacle. It was customary for the families of the two houses to share breakfast the following morning, which should most definitely include Theo himself.

I noted how House Katopodis had still somewhat kept their distance from my family, deciding to sit two seats down from the first available chair of the long table. Dante sat closest to my parents, the two seats separating them, followed by Alaia who smiled at me as I sat, and then the rest of their children.

I smiled softly in greeting them and felt nauseous as my plate was served before me. Gods I did not know whether to be relieved or furious at the blatant disrespect Theo was showing. I was somewhat grateful I did not have to see him, yet I was infuriated at his actions.

Taking a sip of my orange juice, the man himself entered and the chatter died down once more.

Theo strode in, his anger rippling off him in waves as he harshly withdrew his chair and sat, not even glancing in my direction or any of my family which irked me further. He too was dressed casually in dark jeans and a black T-shirt that left his tattoos on full display down his strong arms. His usual adornment of a ring on each finger shone against the morning rays hitting them from the bay windows. I found myself inspecting the tattoos of ravens that crept down below the side of his neck and disappeared underneath his shirt for too long. A tattoo of a rose covered the skin between his collarbone and throat on the other side…

"Good morning, Theo," I shocked myself when the words left my lips, the venom of my tone palpable. Everyone froze as they looked between us. Theo finally looked at me and the hatred on his face was clear as we glared at each other.

"It is a terrible morning," he mumbled just as his father kicked him beneath the table, his disapproval clear as he frowned at his son who was now clenching his jaw.

"Mmm, I would think so too if I was a miserable goat like yourself. I would presume wallowing and brooding are what I should expect in the future. What a miserable habit to have, not only for those around you but for yourself," I finished in a bored tone as I took a sip of my orange juice casually.

Kason burst with a laugh, only to shove his hands over his mouth wide-eyed as Theo turned his death glare to his younger brother before he looked back at me, fire in his eyes.

"And what would you know of it, princess," that deep baritone of his voice rumbled as he spat the word princess as if it were poison upon his tongue.

Dorian was about to jump in. Placing a hand on his arm, he settled beside me, his jaw clenched and muscles tense as we eyed Theo. I cocked my head as I watched him in silence. I could just imagine how unnerving I must have seemed as the blind mask was all that stared ahead from his perspective, and directly lined with his sight.

Theo began frowning in frustration as he eyed me back and the rest of the members at the table began fidgeting, not sure what to expect until I finally answered him. My voice was cold and deadly as I did so, a tinge of boredom covering it. "I know more than you know and know that there is much to fear in this world, Theo Katopodis, but to me, even as you sit there, a god killer, a reaper, a thorn upon a rose, or simply a miserable goat." I paused, shuffling in my seat to lean over the table slightly as everyone eyed me keenly and leaned forward, tilting my head again as I watched him, my hair tumbling over my shoulder. "You do not frighten me and you will not disrespect me in my own house, as *I* am sovereign here," I finished with as much authority and venom that I could manage, not recognising my voice.

I sat back in my seat, casually brushing my hair back over my shoulder as everyone's mouths fell open before they quickly covered it by taking a sip of their beverages or a bite from their breakfast. Theo's jaw had a noticeable tick in it as he barely contained his rage. Kason was grinning like a Cheshire cat, and I could feel the pride rolling off Dorian who relaxed in his seat beside me.

"The breakfast is wonderful mother, thank you," I said cheerily before continuing to eat not once bothering to look back at Theo. My mother and Hecate had bred a warrior within me, their motives, and practices malevolent, yet I did take pride in myself despite it.

"Yes, thank you Kaisley, it is lovely," Alaia, Theo's mother piped in with a smile and everyone returned to their chatting and eating around me, all the while Theo remained silent. A thunderous storm was brewing within the six-foot-six dark lord who sat down at the table from me.

I suddenly realised that this morning had been the first time in twelve years I had spoken directly to him, and it had been in the form of a battle. I also realised that my comment of a thorn upon a rose was a referral to much, yet also the etching upon the willow tree within the Whispering Woods. *Shit.* Why did I mention such a specific detail?

I cast a glance in his direction, and I found him leaning back in his chair, his heavily tattooed arm slung over the back as he eyed me suspiciously, no longer filled with rage. The contemplative and calculating look on his face was clear. He did not shy away from being caught staring at me, so I stared right back, not willing to give him the satisfaction of evening the score between us.

Theo's brow rose in surprise at my brazenness and a hint of a smirk formed on the side of his mouth before he quickly covered it with a sip of black coffee and turned to Layna and Trey. I did not listen to what they were saying as I finished my breakfast. My father's voice had me whipping my head up, as well as everyone else at the table.

"I would like to take a moment to say that although we were all surprised by the joining of our children by the Servile last night, I hope that the two of you will take this weekend to get to know one another before you are to return to your House come Monday."

My father looked between me and Theo, his sandy hair being lit up by the morning sun filtering through the window behind him. My mother had remained oddly silent during the exchanges this morning and I did not know what to make of it as she sat silently beside him. "We agree then, Mathias," Dante spoke from his spot, before he turned to me, offering a slight smile before he looked to his son, and no words passed between them as Theo stared blanky back.

"I would also like to have a meeting regarding the latest developments after breakfast," my father added, having the entire Katopodis household looking at him. My father, as leader of House Sarris, had authority over House Katopodis, as it was over all the houses. Ours was the house of law and justice and Katopodis our enforcers.

I had noted my father being called away for longer and more frequent business trips and had been stewing over what it may be about. By the looks upon the family seated down the table from me, I could tell they were involved in whatever business it had been. A silent nod was all Dante gave to my father before he glanced at his family and returned to his meal.

We ate in silence after that. My father excused himself as well as my mother before Dorian left. I was heading for the door wanting to head to the gardens and follow the Katopodis household out when Dante halted and spoke to Theo who had ignored me after the escapade within the dining room.

"You will sit this one out. You are to spend time with Braelyn," Dante issued his order, and I halted a few feet behind, with no way past and listening to the exchange.

"What the fuck? You're cutting me out of a meeting?" Theo seethed silently beside his father.

"You heard me, I'll fill you in later," Dante answered sternly before heading down the corridor and entering my father's office, effectively leaving me alone in the hallway with an infuriated Theo who had his back to me, his muscles tense.

I cast one last look at him and walked past, continuing my way, not bothering to see what he would do. I would be quite content not having to see him, I had avoided him for twelve long years for a god-damned reason. I exited the manor, using a side entrance as I pushed the French doors wide, the warm morning sun hitting my skin and the smell of wildflowers filling my lungs.

I hated being inside for extended periods. The feeling of being contained was like an oil slick over my skin that would drive me mad. I stepped across the flagstone path before turning and heading across the green grass. I halted and bent down to remove my sandals, immediately wiggling my toes against the tickling grass. It was still damp from the morning sprinklers and cooled me down immediately.

"You have got to be shitting me," Theo scoffed from behind me. Whirling around, I found him standing there, cocky as ever eyeing my bare feet with a look of disgust before his eyes rose to my face.

"What do you want?" I snapped, my sandals still dangling in my grasp.

"What I want is to not be forced out of an important meeting, not forced to spend time with a barefoot gypsy princess and not to have this shit dictating the rest of my life," he growled out as he rose his arm, the Servile brand as clear as day.

"Too bad we both don't have what we want then," I snapped back, my grip on the sandals tightening. Theo noticed as he dropped his arm and smirked as he eyed me up and down. A smirk that held so much danger in its silent promise.

I froze as Theo stepped closer, his height and muscular form dwarfing me and quite literally blocking the sun from view as I tilted my head up, the mask suddenly feeling heavy across the top of my face and head.

"How is it that you always know exactly where to look?" he purred seductively as he traced a tattooed finger over the mask, making my breath catch – in fear as well as a foreign feeling. I was broken out of his spell as the cocky bastard then flicked his finger harshly against the part that covered my forehead, the clang of his ring against the metal making my jaw clench.

"It's impossible to miss your disgusting aura," I snapped, taking a step back and turning. I began walking away when he called out.

"Likewise princess. Your presence disgusts me just as much," I froze. Those words... *Your presence disgusts me...* I felt the ancient power thrashing against my will, wanting to be let out at the reminder and tear him apart, tear everything apart. My grip tightened on the sandals in my hand as I closed my eyes and willed the power to submission.

Whirling around, I threw the sandals straight at Theo, who dodged them with ease as he casually sidestepped them. He stood with his arms crossed and head cocked as he eyed me without so much as a word.

I turned and continued across the lawn, counting to ten over and over to calm myself. I had not expected to be transported right back to the moment my mother and Hecate had stood over my bleeding body after a rather gruelling training session as my mother glowered at me, the words, *"You disgust me,"* spat down upon me. It had been a year after the well-house… fourteen years old.

Gods.

"Where are you going?" Theo called out as I heard him now following closely behind.

"Away from you," I mumbled, any fight I had in me a moment ago now replaced by a slow-burning loathing.

"Okay well, that isn't going to work for shit. You know how this weekend is supposed to go and that we have no choice but to spend time together unless you want to explain to Themis and Apollo that you know better. It won't go down well, I already tried," he gritted out in irritation.

The words caused me to stop yet again, turning and facing him as he looked at me bored.

"You did what?" I seethed.

The god-damned gall of him! Theo raised a brow as his aqua, amber-rimmed eyes took in the entirety of my face and mask.

"I tried to get out of it, even tried to have the fucking brand removed. It won't work. So, I guess we just must get through this shit storm, and I am already in a fucking foul mood, so I would prefer it if we just got this fucking weekend over, and once, I get home, you can do your own thing and we don't even have to see or speak to each other. This weekend, however, eyes are watching everywhere," he said, his voice rumbling with distaste.

I felt that power thrashing within me yet again, hissing and thrashing at the disrespect for me, the Servile, all of it.

"Go fuck yourself, Katopodis," I snapped after a silent minute of watching him.

I never cursed so plainly. It wasn't usually in me, and this was new for me. Theo's eyes widened in shock as I turned and headed toward the shade of a large oak tree, my satchel with my books still laying there where I had left them yesterday just before having headed to the woods…

A laugh erupted from Theo, loud and rapturous before he followed me to the shade of the tree and sat down on the grass, his large frame looking odd in such a casual setting.

"You seem to be surprising me today, princess." He chuckled before turning toward my books and picking one up, turning it over as he inspected it. He rose a brow as he side-eyed me, placing the book down and inspecting the second.

"Very surprising indeed," he muttered eyeing me keenly. "What is a princess, who is blind, doing with a book of ancient artefacts and then, a naughty little novel?" he said plainly, trying to lure me into a trap.

I felt my cheeks flush at the mention of my novel but quickly recovered myself.

"I can read," I answered sarcastically, avoiding the topic of the subject matter.

"How?" he straight-out asked, his voice now serious.

"Hephaestus makes them," I muttered, indicating to the mask. "I can feel the words upon the paper, much like an aura," I lied straight through my teeth, hoping my training would help in making it believable.

Theo eyed me for a silent minute before turning his gaze away with a barely audible, "Mmm." *Gods, was he going to sit here and irritate me all day?* I decided to ignore him and read. It was unnerving sitting in silence under the tree and I eventually gave up on reading after twenty minutes, throwing the book back into my satchel with a huff. Theo looked at me, a smirk on his lips.

"Great, I was wondering how long it would take you to give it up. Let's go, I'm bored out of my fucking mind," he said, standing and beginning to walk away, hands in pockets. I found myself staring at the muscles that rippled along his back with each step, straining against that black T-shirt.

"Come on," he called back, sounding irritated once more.

"I am not at your beck and call, Katopodis," I snapped at him as I stood and grabbed my satchel, dusted off my dress skirt, and slowly followed him, hating that I was even doing so with every step.

Theo stopped up ahead of me, my sandals laying on the grass where I had left them after throwing them at him.

He bent down to retrieve them, and his head whipped in my direction, a stern look on his face before he looked away from me. I frowned at the action and came to a stop beside him, hands outreached for my sandals that he held in an iron grip.

"Can't go walking around barefoot, princess," he snapped, shoving them at me before continuing his way.

"What is your problem?" I snapped back at him from where I stood incredulous.

Theo stopped in his tracks, a heavy sigh leaving him as he rolled his neck and shoulders before turning back to me.

"I need a drink, and you are going to show me where the good stuff is." He smirked at me.

"And why would I do that?" I asked grumpily as I began to walk toward him.

"Because, you know what happens tonight, and I would prefer to have a relaxing day before then, so drinking all of Mathias' most expensive whiskey seems like a good way to start it," he chirped, extending a tattooed arm, indicating for me to show him the way.

I eyed him suspiciously and felt my gut tighten at the mention of tonight's ceremony and celebrations. I had tried to ignore that part, hoping to shy away from the reminder, if possible, but clearly, he had no intention of shying away from it.

"Okay then," I finally stated, having no other choice than to spend time with him, and maybe if I got him drunk, I would be able to sneak away for a few hours.

Sneak away to the Whispering Woods to unleash…

"Follow me," I stated as I walked on ahead, Theo ensuing.

Theo

I do not know who will cave first.

We had been in one of the many rooms of the manor's ground floor for two hours. The stocked liquor cabinet now missing a few prestigious bottles that would surely grate Mathias. I felt myself smirk at the thought of getting on that prick's nerves.

After I had left last night, I travelled to the underground market – The Agora. A market that held the undesirables of our world, the dark and twisted side, which was saying much. I knew of a few witches that traded there and the fear the patrons of the said market had for my family's reputation, my reputation, had them answering immediately upon my arrival. To my absolute frustration, no one could help me in removing the Servile brand, which led to me returning and cornering Apollo and Themis. Apollo had remained eerily silent, which was unusual for him during my ranting plea of putting an end to this madness. Themis had seen it as a direct insult and refused to remain any longer after many curse words flying between us.

So here I was, the following day, first shocked by the mere essence of Braelyn at breakfast, not hesitating in putting me in my place like a viper. It had been the first moment words had ever been exchanged between us and it was a glorious, heated battle. I had to give her credit, not many people had the guts to speak to me like she did, and it had caught my attention.

Even more so in the gardens earlier when she had thrown her fucking tiny sandals at me and cussed me out like a heathen.

I had noted the way my words had affected her before she covered it up and realised my mother had been correct in that I needed to pay attention.

I still couldn't care less, but I was intrigued.

I thrived on minuscule details, and I noted the challenge in Braelyn. This was going to be fun… or so I had thought until I had picked up her sandals, the scent of the girl from the Whispering Woods sticking to them.

How? How was it that her shoes alone held the scent? We were standing along the edge of the woods, so perhaps it had drifted by while I held them?

I then decided to get her drunk. Not my classiest move, but it was an attempt to get her to speak, nothing more. However, what I had not anticipated was the woman's ability to outdrink maybe even myself. I also suspected that she had the same idea of getting me drunk… for what reason, I did not know.

I suspected we were both drunk at this stage, yet neither of us was willing to admit it, even after five bottles lay empty on the coffee table between us.

"Your turn," I said, leaning back against the sofa with my hands behind my head while I eyed her.

She looked in my direction, that mask covering where her eyes should be.

"Why do you have all the tattoos?" I felt myself stiffen and dropped my arms. A tick worked its way into my jaw.

"Because I like them; my turn," I answered in a gruff voice not wanting to go down that road at all.

"What do your eyes look like beneath that mask," I asked casually as I took another sip of Mathias' whiskey.

I acted disinterested; however, I noticed the way she began spinning that ring on her forefinger using the adjacent thumb.

"I do not have eyes, hence the mask," she answered icily.

I could see how that may have been uncomfortable to answer, but something still felt off.

"What happened to them?" I squinted through the drunken haze as I pressed her further.

"Why all the interest in the blind girls' eyes, Katopodis?" she snapped, standing, and going over to the cabinet, grabbing another bottle of whiskey.

Bingo.

"It's just a question, why are you avoiding it?"

"Why are you interested?" she snapped right back at me, leaving us both eyeing each other with suspicion.

Braelyn then turned, pouring us each a new glass before she placed mine before me and sat across the table on her sofa, sipping at hers, still that mask facing me point blank.

"Why do you think we were chosen? We can't stand each other… with all due *disrespect*," she asked slightly humorous, smirking as she said the last part.

I felt myself relaxing further into the sofa as I laughed and took another sip.

"Fuck if I know, we will end up killing each other before the weekend is up. I would rather give up a limb than remain stuck in this nightmare…" I said the last part more to myself but caught sight of how she tensed, taking another sip, and setting the tumbler down harshly before stepping around the coffee table and standing before me.

She bent down, placing her face right before mine and I felt my body go lame.

Shit. She drugged the whiskey. This woman! How could I have made such an amateur mistake? I clenched my jaw as she smirked and stood again, sighing.

"Remember, Katopodis, that could always be arranged," she said and was walking away as my world went dark.

***

I awoke, my body stiff and the sun setting by the look of the light filtering through the bay windows. I groaned, pushing up and scrubbing my hands down my face and then through my hair.

I sighed, looked around, and froze when I spotted my siblings sitting on the sofa across from me, all three of them holding back smiles as they eyed me.

"What?" I mumbled, my mouth feeling as if it was full of cotton.

Layna, Kason, and Trey all erupted in raucous laughter, and it only irritated me further.

"What the fuck is so funny?" I snapped, running my hands over my face again, willing the fog away and in desperate need of water.

"Why don't you have a look in the mirror, T," Layna spoke through her fit of laughter as she flung an arm over the back of her sofa.

I scrunched my eyes in confusion and stood up on stiff legs as I walked over to the large mirror on the wall.

Gods…

"I. Am. Going. To. Kill. Her." I gritted out each word as I saw what she had done to me.

Upon my forehead in permanent marker, she had drawn a crude rendering of a cock severed from its ball sack, little squiggles around the jagged edges as if to be blood spraying. On my cheeks, she had written, *"Would this limb do?"* I scrubbed furiously at my face, the marker remaining intact, and my pulse pounded in my ears.

"Where is she?" I snapped at my siblings who still sat back laughing at me and ignoring my question completely.

"This is going to be so much fun to watch every day once we get home," Layna quipped, followed by Trey, "I want to know what conversation they were having before he passed out. What did you do this time?" and finally Kason, "I love her already."

I glared at them each, none of them letting up.

"Where is she?" I asked quieter this time, my rage simmering.

"I don't know, I saw her leaving here about an hour ago and haven't seen her since. We just found you ten minutes before you woke up."

"How did you manage to pass out though? I've seen you drink more than this," Layna spoke as she picked up an empty whiskey bottle, inspecting the year and brand with a low whistle.

"Mathias is going to be pissed. I love it!" she burst out laughing, only encouraging the other two to laugh at my expense yet again. I remained silent about the fact that Braelyn had managed to drug me. I could only imagine how they'd be making fun of me then… pricks.

Ignoring them, I exited the room and looked down the hallway, not spotting her anywhere. I turned right, heading to the main entrance with my brothers and sister now following closely behind. My feet thundered against the marble floors as I passed the shocked staff of the house and out into the circular drive, taking the steps down two at a time, all the while, scanning the area for the little shit.

I ground my teeth as I turned, stopping as I noticed the commotion that would be tonight's festivities and the arrival of the other houses further in the distance. Marquees had been set up as well as garden torches and potted plants and sculptures of the gods and goddesses.

"Where the fuck has she gone?" I snapped at my siblings who now stood around me.

"Shit T, calm down man, it was just a prank," Kason said from my left and I spun around on him faster than he could blink, shoving at him before turning once again and heading to the housing we had been staying in.

I thundered up the grassy hill, the white apartments up ahead.

I was halfway up the hill when I noticed dampness in my socks that had not been there before.

I felt sick as realisation began setting in. Stopping, I looked down, removed my Adidas sneakers, and felt the blood drain from my face further before it returned in one almighty rush of rage.

"Fuck! I'm going to fucking wring her neck!" I roared, inspecting my shoes over and over. My favourite pair of sneakers had been sliced through the bottom of the soles, allowing the water from the recently watered lawn to creep inside.

"Oh shit," Kason murmured in fear as they saw my shoes, knowing that I collected them.

These specific ones were rare and my favourite. I had paid a fortune for them!

Braelyn had no idea what kind of shit she just landed herself into. Stubbornly not wanting to admit that maybe I had met my match in being an asshole, I angrily shoved my now wet feet back into my sneakers and stood, exhaling loudly, and rolling my neck and shoulders before I started forward again.

"I'm going to kill her," I murmured happily and quietly, sloshing over the wet lawn, and headed straight to the apartment.

"Shit, he's gone psycho mode," Kason murmured to our brother and sister.

I ignored them and entered the apartment's French doors that led to the living room from the veranda.

"What…" My parents both stared at me wide-eyed and stupefied as I walked past them, the severed cock across my forehead and my shoes sloshing and squeaking across the marble floors.

Ignoring them except for a silent enraged glare, I head straight to my designated suite and shut the door with a loud bang, the windows rattling as I then ripped my ruined shoes and shirt off, flinging them across the room. I heard Trey retelling my parents what had happened before the two of them also joined in on the laughter.

"Pricks," I fumed.

Heading to the bathroom, I stopped before the mirror, staring at the graffiti Braelyn had left on my face. Sighing, I began scrubbing at it, but whatever marker she had used was stubborn. It took me a good thirty minutes of scrubbing my skin raw before any trace of it was removed.

By the time I had finished showering and got dressed for the ceremony, I had calmed down to a simmering rage, and I planned on finding Braelyn and confronting her. I had admitted to myself that perhaps what I had said was shitty, however, I was not known for being friendly and she had just declared all-out war when she decided to fuck with me.

Tonight was going to be fun.

I was now down near the marquees, silently taking in my surroundings and watching for any sign of her, my siblings standing nearby, chatting about gods knew what. I was leaning against a beam of the massive marquee, ignoring the blatant stares of all the other house members that passed by when I spotted Calista headed this way.

"You do know that needs to come to an end, right?" Trey said beside me, Kason and Layna now looking in Calista's direction too.

I was an asshole, but not the kind to fuck around. I had my morals... although ninety percent of the time they were grey... I guessed I would have to speak to Braelyn about all this. A conversation I loathed the thought of. Detested that I had already somewhat accepted my fate. What the hell was going on with me? I ignored him, as movement caught my attention, far in the distance near the side of the manor.

Got you.

Pushing off the beam, I headed through the crowd, torches casting an orange glow around the area.

I avoided heading in the direction of Calista and saw her pace falter as I kept heading in the direction of the manor. Mathias and Kaisley were chatting near the fountain and did not notice me as I swiftly headed around the side, searching for her. I halted near the black roses and scanned the area.

Shit, how did she disappear so soon? I had seen her near this area not even a moment ago.

Frowning, I called upon my Chaos Handler gene, my eyes now glowing amber in the dark as I tilted my head, scanning every detail. A raven landed on a nearby tree that sat on the edge of the Whispering Woods.

"What the fuck are you up to?" I mumbled to myself as the raven indicated that she had been within the woods yet was no longer there.

The longer I thought about every detail, the colder my blood ran. *It couldn't be. Could it?* No, my mind was playing fucking tricks on me as there was no chance in nine hells…

My mind fumed at its ridiculousness as a movement caught my eye through the French doors of the manor to my right. I watched in silence as I witnessed Braelyn busy in her father's study, rummaging through his desk. I knew that his office was strictly off-limits unless you were called in for a meeting and even his own family had never been allowed within the space.

Taking a step, then another, I leaned casually against the French doors of the office. Crossing my arms, I watched her in silence, wondering what it was she was up to. I watched as she was dressed in a midnight black dress, much the same as the one from last night, leaving very little to the imagination.

I would be lying if I said my eyes could not stop drinking at the sight of her. She was gorgeous, I don't know why I had never noticed it before. Probably because I avoided her like a plague over the years and that she rarely was seen at any events or meetings of the houses…

Her mask tonight was of a dark pewter colour, stars and black roses embellished the mask and small dark diamonds glittered against the light creeping in from the moonlight streaming through the glass panes of the doors.

She reminded me of the black roses of the garden just to my left and I mentally shook myself, focusing once again on what she was doing.

She slid the desk drawer closed before standing and spinning that gold signet ring whilst she scanned the office as if looking for something specific, an anxious tick I had noted in less than twenty-four hours, she did quite often. She then exited from view as she entered the domain of the manor, closing the office door silently on her way out.

Stepping away from the doors, I returned to my siblings, trying to figure out what it was she sought. It was a slow trek back to the marquee. I had hesitated near the steps of the manor, hidden from view. I grew more agitated as the minutes ticked by and she never appeared. I had been surveying the sides of the manor and the only way down to the spot where everyone was congregating.

Fuming in irritation, I eventually gave up on catching her on her way there. I was halfway to the marquee when I spotted her standing alongside her brother, just within the tent. I halted immediately, confused as to how she had slipped past me. I had every way covered, it was impossible to miss her.

Kason came up beside me, noticing my line of sight and a deep frown.

"What?" he asked, knowing my facial expressions far too well.

"Find out everything you can on Braelyn. Now."

"But T, isn't that taking it too far? It was just a prank," he started to say but cut off when I turned my gaze to his.

"Now," was all I responded before I looked back to her and grabbed a drink from a passing server.

"But," he began but gave up when I headed over to where she was standing.

She seemed to notice my approach from too far away for anyone to be able to, particularly someone who was blind. I arched a brow as I took another sip of my drink and eyed her from across the crowd, never wavering as I eventually came to a stop before her.

"Hello, little rose."

Braelyn

I was searching through my father's office looking for something, anything…

I had overheard him and my mother arguing earlier whilst they thought no one had been listening. It had been over whatever the meeting had been regarding earlier and a hunt to do with the prophecy and missing shipments. I had never read the prophecy yet had been warned about it my entire life, hence my life was shrouded in secrecy.

My mother had been livid that he would not tell her the details of a hunt that was underway currently by House Katopodis. I had to know if it was me they were hunting, and that Theo had told them about our encounter in the woods yesterday… *If he had, oh gods*… but I would cross that bridge when I came to it. Theo Katopodis did not intimidate me. Going up against his entire family of reapers, the Bloodhound Brothers as they were known to some, did make me uneasy.

At the thought of him, I fought the laugh that wanted to work its way up my throat at the memory of the sight of him lying passed out on the sofa, my fantastic rendering sketched across his forehead. I had just planned on getting him drunk enough to pass out so that I could return to the woods to expel the power that had been banging against my chest and ribcage to be released the entire day. However, the fool drank like a fish with little to no effect of the liquor. I had eventually resorted to drugging him with a powder I kept hidden in my ring for emergencies from Hecate herself. I loathed the goddess but found her wickedness handy.

After Theo had said those godawful words in arrogance, I couldn't help myself. I could not find it in me to harm him, but to make a fool of him… Yes. With no shame, I may add… I had taken it a step further by destroying his irreplaceable sneakers. I had taken note over the years that he tended to always wear the rarest, most expensive sneakers, ones that were difficult to come by, when he wasn't dressed in his combat gear or formal wear. It was easy to presume they were important to him. It would no doubt annoy him to nine hells and back, which was perfect.

In frustration, I could not find anything in my father's office regarding the hunt order and knew that if I was spotted there, I would be punished severely. I was busy scrummaging through his desk drawer when I sensed Theo nearby, his presence crawling across my skin stronger than ever before. It was as if the longer we spent time together, the ancient power within me grew curious. I did not turn toward the French doors where I simply knew he stood watching. Glancing at the reflection of my father's antique vase on the desk, I spotted him leaning casually outside, watching me. *Shit.*

I closed the drawer silently and surveyed the room once more, all the while knowing Theo stood just outside. I did not let slip that I was aware of his presence and headed for the door leading to the corridor within the manor.

Shutting the door quietly behind me, I was relieved to find the hallway empty. I had just turned toward the main entrance when my mother and father were deep in conversation and headed that way. I checked over my shoulder, ensuring once again no one was watching when the air silently vibrated around me, and I disappeared into the shadows.

Thankfully my parents had not seen me, and I continued through the manor, shadow-stalking from one shadow to the next, all the way outside and down toward the marquee. It was risky, however, I sensed Theo waiting for me near the main steps and wanted to avoid him for as long as possible. I eventually stepped out from the shadows behind the massive tent, with no one spotting me. Straightening my pathetic excuse of a dress and stepping around the construction's ivory side, my heels threatened to get stuck in the lush lawn as I spotted the Katopodis siblings off to the side, their parents nowhere to be seen. Thankfully no one had spotted me yet.

"Brae," Dorian called to me, having spotted me sooner than I would have liked, however, I was thankful it had been him and not a certain brooding warrior.

"Hey," I responded, making my way over to him just within the tent.

The surrounding estate had been decorated with statues of our gods and goddesses, flaming torches illuminating the area in a golden glow. "Where have you been?" Dorian asked quietly beside me as we smiled politely at the guests that greeted us in passing.

"Do you know anything of a hunt order father has the Katopodis household working on?" I asked, hoping he had an idea and completely ignoring his inquiry.

"No, why?"

"I heard mother arguing with father about it, but he refuses to divulge any details."

Dorian looked to me then, his face deep in thought before he schooled it, his air of politeness returning as someone passed by where we stood.

"I don't know but I'll try to find out what I can." I was about to ask him yet another question when my skin prickled in recognition.

Turning my head in that direction, sure enough, there he was. Dressed in a black Armani suit, black dress shirt, and no tie tonight as the top buttons were undone, his tattoos showing. I could not take my eyes off him. He was gorgeous, I would give him that. The cocky bastard knew it though... He stood eyeing me before Kason walked away from his side, Theo ignoring him and grabbing a drink from a passing server.

Dorian had been calling for my attention yet noticed my gaze which had been stuck on Theo as he now approached. I sensed him tense beside me before standing protectively at my side, exuding the House Sarris manner we had been bred into us to exude in all situations. Theo came to a stop before me, completely ignoring Dorian as his eyes, aqua ringed in amber, held me in place.

"Hello, little rose," he purred at me, causing me to pause in whatever retort I had prepared. "Let's take a walk, shall we?" I had no response as I felt the power within me grow curious, wanting to reach out to him.

I held it at bay, yet his words, what he had called me repeated over and over in my mind. Little rose. Had he figured out my secret, or was it just to annoy me by giving me a nickname that could hold so many different meanings?

"Lord of death," I finally responded as he and Dorian stood watching, waiting for my response.

A small smirk worked its way to the side of his mouth before he finally looked to Dorian, placing his free hand in his pant pocket and then back to me.

"Lord of death does hold a certain ring to it, doesn't it?" I did not respond to him, instead wondering what he was up to. Dorian, bless him, held an arm out to me, offering an escape.

"We are needed inside before the ceremony starts," he said, and I took his arm as he led me further inside, leaving Theo standing in the spot, watching me.

As I looked back, I saw the smirk had grown on his stupidly beautiful face, as he knew I was avoiding him.

"Nice shoes by the way," I called back, smiling serenely. Theo's smirk fell, only to be replaced by a clenched jaw. Smirking at him, his eyes grew wider before I turned my attention from him and back to ahead of me, where Dorian led us further into the tent.

"Do I even want to know what that was about?" Dorian asked in a hushed, amused tone.

"Probably not," I laughed, only for it to fade as soon as my eyes settled on a certain guest that stood chatting with Dante and Alaia Katopodis near the main table.

I halted in my steps, causing Dorian to come to a halt.

"Let's go somewhere else," I spoke timidly, in a manner that made me sick to my stomach. It went against all fibre of my being feeling and acting this way yet the man that stood beside Theo's parents… *Gods…*

Dorian eyed Ezio Katopodis up ahead, frowning at him and then at me.

"What?"

"Nothing, I just want to go somewhere else," I stammered. God-damned stammered! Dorian dropped my arm and stood before me, his eyes blazing as he watched my features and then back to Ezio.

"What in nine hells, Brae? You better tell me right now," he hissed in anger under his breath so no one would hear.

"I said nothing, now let's go," I snapped back, turning on my heel, but freezing as my name was called.

"Braelyn!" *Shit, shit, shit.*

"Dante, Alaia," I smiled at them before turning to the bastard who was beaming at me. My face cooled into a look of boredom, of superiority.

"Ezio." I deadpanned, envisioning doing terrible things to him.

"My, you look exquisite. How long has it been? Seven years?" he crooned, watching me with a hateful smile.

"Too short I am afraid," I deadpanned once again, now standing as tall as my small stature would allow as I held my hands together before me, eyeing him down from behind my pewter mask. Dorian cleared his throat, knowing something wasn't right, yet also a subtle reminder that people were watching. Our house reputation was on the line, as well as mother's wrath…

"Oh, I didn't know that you knew each other. I don't think I had ever seen you together before," Dante spoke up, eyeing us both suspiciously while Ezio raked his gaze up and down my body like a gods damned pig.

"Yes, we have met in passing," Ezio replied to Dante. "But I am surprised that my cousin is now joined to you, Braelyn. What an interesting turn of events. Perhaps I'll be seeing you more often now, all the family get-togethers and such…" He smiled slyly at me, causing Dante and Alaia to look to each other in silent conversation before Dante frowned, but quickly smoothed his features.

"Perhaps," was all I gritted out, my ring now being twirled around my forefinger in rapid succession. "Excuse me," I forced a smile at Dante and Alaia before turning and heading to the tent exit, my heart hammering, and the power hissing within me. I was barely keeping it under control when Dorian caught me gently on the arm, pulling me to a stop.

"Brae, what happened?" he asked yet again, the anger still simmering beneath the surface, but his approach on the matter was much gentler this time.

"Nothing, I need air, Dor. Cover for me, please. I won't be long, I promise," I held conviction in my words, giving his hold on my arm a pat in a comforting manner.

Dorian eyed me before sighing and nodding before he looked away. I did not wait for any further interaction as I exited the tent, the cool air outside a much-needed therapy for my burning lungs as the ancient force twirled, crashed, and hammered me from within.

I worked my way quickly across the lawn, well as quickly as I could without being suspicious. I had made it past most of the guests and was near passing the garden benches set up sporadically under a set of their awning. Areas of seating, lit by torchlight filled the open lawn for many yards, with only a few guests making use of them. Some chatted quietly, others laughed some used the distance from the marquee to smoke. As I passed a set of benches, the Katopodis siblings were sitting in discussion and turned to watch me pass by without interruption. It was only two of the siblings, however. Theo and Kason. A cloud of smoke was expelled by Theo as he blatantly watched me go before, he stood casually and headed after me in a lazy gait.

I cursed under my breath as I continued, knowing he followed and made the mistake of looking back. Theo saw and smirked as he placed his tattooed hands in his pockets and continued to trail behind.

Shit! Looking around, I knew I could barely handle the power within me much longer and would need to lose Theo soon. I reached the manor, the ground beneath my heels crunching as I passed by the fountain out front, and the Whispering Woods up ahead, to the side of the manor's enormous ivory structure. Turning a corner, to the path that led around the side, I glanced to be sure he wasn't close enough and shadow-stalked along the edge, hurrying for the woods. I entered, stalking along the usual path and into the small area by the large willow tree before I exited the shadows. The woods whispered as if in welcome to my presence. I turned at the sound of a crunch behind me and froze as Theo stood there, arms crossed and a frown on his face, his eyes burning amber in the dark.

The ancient power that had been hissing beneath my skin and bones quieted down to a lazy purr immediately, confusing me on top of my near hysteria about him having found me.

"Hello again, little rose. What are you doing here?" he grumbled, the deep baritone of his voice causing my breath to hitch.

Ignoring him, I turned slowly to face him entirely. He watched me in silence, before his gaze drifted to the etching on the willow tree behind me and then back to me.

"It was clever of you, the shadow-stalking, as there was no way to track you," he finally said and I was sure that all blood drained from my face.

He took a step closer, dropping his arms to his sides. It was then that I noticed the hundreds of ravens that sat perched in the canopy around us, each of their beady eyes trained on me. I took a step back myself, refusing to speak. I wanted to know how much he had figured out. Yet, there was only the shadow-stalking, which he could not prove to anyone.

"If I were to remove that mask, I think I know what I would find. So why don't we look?" he said, taking yet another step closer, causing me to step back again. Theo grinned at the movement, halting, and eyeing me with a cocked head.

I readied myself to flee, but Theo's phone began buzzing in his pocket. Never taking his eyes off me, he reached into his jacket and frowned at the screen before answering. His eyes held me where I stood frozen in place.

"Ezio, what the fuck do you want?" he growled at his cousin through the phone.

At the sound of his cousin's name, I felt my spine stiffen and struggled to inhale a breath. A small tremor began in my hand, which I quickly covered by twirling my ring, around and around. Theo noticed my changed demeanour immediately and frowned deeper, his eyes trailing from my face, down my arms, to my fingers, and back across the entirety of my face. I could have listened in on the phone call, knowing what was being said, yet my anxiousness at the mention of Ezio made it impossible.

"We are on our way," Theo snapped and hung up, pocketing his phone yet again. "We need to head back. Now," he said, eyeing me suspiciously while I calmed my beating heart.

I finally managed a sharp inhale of breath, easing it out sharply, and pulled my shoulders back and straightened my spine. I began trudging back down the path and passed Theo, still ignoring him.

"This discussion isn't over," he said from behind me, where he now trailed closely. Far too close for my comfort.

"There is nothing to discuss, lord of death," I snapped, never turning to him as we neared the edge of the woods.

Exiting the woods, and walking along the side of the manor, I froze and stumbled, having Theo catch me before he looked at what had caught me off guard.

"Ezio," he grumbled, stepping away from me as he looked to his cousin who stood near the fountain.

Ezio stood tall and cocky as he beamed at us sickly. He was shorter than Theo, standing at six feet, and had the Katopodis staple black hair and aqua eyes. He was on the skinnier side of the spectrum yet still muscles formed neatly across his body. He had a runner's build, nothing like Theo's warrior one.

"What are you doing here?" Theo growled at his cousin who did not waver his gaze from me. "I asked you a question, asshole," Theo finally snapped, stepping around me and heading toward his cousin who finally acknowledged him.

"I'm waiting for you. I do hope you had fun. I'm kind of jealous." Ezio smirked at Theo, which had his jaw ticking in anger. Ignoring them, I continued my way, highly uncomfortable by Ezio's innuendo and wanting to get away from both Katopodis men.

I left them by the fountain, not listening to what was being said between the two cousins, and reached the lawn, my heels threatening once again to sink into the damp grass. Dorian spotted me from further down and he hurried over, matching my quick pace back toward the tent.

"Mother is looking for you. I told her you went to the restroom. She seems on a war path tonight," he spoke, glancing over his shoulders from where I had come. "You were with them?" Dorian asked confused as he looked back at me. I ignored him, my thoughts racing as I sensed Theo trailing behind, his eyes on me to the entry of the tent.

"Ah, there she is." I froze, not believing my ears, and bile rose in my throat.

"Hecate," Dorian and I answered, staring at her.

Theo

Kason and I had been sitting in the gardens, the furthest away from any possible listening ears. He had his phone out, reading to me what he was able to find, which wasn't much.

"I don't know what to tell you, man, there is hardly anything I could find on her. It's weird, even for our world," he mumbled grumpily, annoyed his elite hacker skills could not get me the information I needed.

"All I was able to find was the first public sighting of her at the Great Sacrifice eleven years ago, she is barely seen at other events, except the big ones where attendance is mandatory. She is two years younger than Dorian, whom I can find plenty of information on… She doesn't even have credit, which is weird." He finished, frowning at his phone with a sigh.

"Did you tell Layna and Trey about what I asked you to do?" I queried casually as I took a deep inhale of my cigarette.

"No, I didn't think it necessary." Kason eyed me suspiciously.

"Good, keep it between us," I spoke, mulling it over until something snagged at my memories. If she had first attended the Great Sacrifice a year after the incident… Well, if she attended it for the first time, just like I did eleven years ago…

"When is her birthday?" I asked, snapping my head in his direction. Kason looked back at his phone, doing whatever weird tech shit he did, and his eyebrows rose before he chuckled.

"A day after yours. July thirteenth."

I froze mid-inhale of my cigarette as the words left his mouth and the devil herself walked past, heading to the manor. I exhaled the small cloud of smoke as she noticed us and her steps quickened, amusing me even though I was incredulous at the revelation. A revelation that my brother had no idea about.

Casually I began following her, leaving Kason to his musings of gathering more information. I now knew it would be futile.

She glanced back at me as she went, her lips downturned in what I could easily assume was displeasure and grinned. She hurried then, trying to get away. My eyes snapped amber as I called my ravens to track her through the darkness of the night and wasn't surprised when I turned a corner to the side of the manor, and she was gone. I almost chuckled at the lunacy of it all. *Was it her all this time?*

Something rotten and dark began swarming me as the amusement faded. Memories I would rather forget filled my mind as I followed my raven's silent call. *Fuck...*

I followed to that fucking willow tree; the etching still carved there after all these years yet beaten by what I could easily tell were knives.

There she stood, snapping in my direction as I arrived. I had not bothered being stealth, she and I needed to talk, one I knew would be monumental, yet atrocious.

"Hello again, little rose. What are you doing here?" I grumbled, the deep baritone of my voice letting slip of my rising anger as the memories flooded my mind.

I noticed her breath hitch, my eyes snapping to the base of her smooth throat for a second, too fast for her to notice.

She ignored my question, only turning to face me fully now. I watched on in silence, before my gaze drifted to that twelve-year-old etching on the willow's bark and then back to her.

"It was clever of you, the shadow-stalking, as there was no way to track you," I finally said casually, noticing as she paled before me in an instant, only confirming my suspicions more than ever.

I still needed proof, however. It could all be a coincidence…

Taking a step closer, I dropped my arms to my sides. I watched on as she then tilted her head up and scanned the canopy of the forest, my ravens filling the branches in the hundreds, all eyes trained on her for the instance she decided to disappear again.

She took a step back yet again, like a caged animal, and remained silent. It was beginning to enrage me. I needed to know for certain. So far, I had only figured out the birthday, the timeline matching up with her appearance at the Great Sacrifice, and the shadow-stalking, which I had no proof of, only the musings of my ravens.

"If I were to remove that mask, I think I know what I would find. So why don't we look?" I finally said, taking yet another step closer, causing her to step back yet again.

I grinned at the act, noting how we appeared to be stuck in a game of cat and mouse since Friday evening, perhaps spanning over a decade already. I cocked my head then, eyeing her as I noticed her anxious demeanour. Was it me she feared?

I noticed her muscles tensing as if readying herself to run away when my fucking phone began buzzing in my suit pocket. Never taking my eyes off her, I reached into my jacket and frowned at the screen before answering. I watched her intensely, noting all the slight tremors and barely noticeable shakes in her breath.

"Ezio, what the fuck do you want?" I growled at my cousin through the phone. I didn't like many people, yet my cousin had been on the top of my hit list for quite some time.

If he wasn't family, I would have killed the sleazy motherfucker years ago. At the sound of my cousin's name, I noticed immediately how Braelyn froze in fear. A small tremor began in her hand, which she quickly covered by twirling that golden ring.

Around and around, it went. I frowned at her reaction to his name, suspicious as to what may have caused it and not liking any possible scenarios that popped up. My anger at the thoughts had me clenching my jaw tight. I could not stop my eyes from trailing her face, down her tense arms, to her fidgeting fingers, and back across the entirety of her face. What could be seen of it that is…

"Where are you? The ceremony is about to begin. Let me guess, taking your new bride for a spin? Cheeky, I like it!" the fucker spoke across the phone, only increasing my anger.

Not bothering to answer him or correct him as I snapped at him, some of my anger sounding through the line

"We are on our way," I hung up, pocketing my phone yet again. "We need to head back. Now," I said, eyeing Braelyn suspiciously while I tried to figure out what to do about my suspicions and my cousin.

It was clear something had happened… I watched her in silence as she managed a sharp inhale of breath, easing it out sharply, and pulled her shoulders back and straightened her spine. Exuding to the princess attitude I had witnessed far too many times over the years. It was impressive now to catch a rare glimpse at what I was beginning to think no one ever saw from her.

She began trudging back down the path and passed by me, chin raised, and ignored me blatantly. I spun on my heel and followed her, watching the regal way she meandered through the dark woods.

"This discussion isn't over," I called out from behind her, trailing closer this time. So close that I could note that she had no scent.

Interesting…

"There is nothing to discuss, Lord of death," she snapped, never turning to me as we neared the edge of the woods. A smirk broke its way through to my face at her attitude and new little nickname. It was meant to be insulting, I knew as much by which she flung it at me venomously, but I would be lying if I said I didn't kind of like it in a sick way…

Exiting the woods, and walking along the side of the manor, Braelyn froze in front of me, stumbling as she did so. I caught her before she fell completely and frowned as tiny vibrations in the air around her bare skin fluttered against mine where I touched her for the first time.

Looking up after standing, that simmering rage began to erupt like a blazing inferno.

"Ezio," I grumbled, stepping away from her, dropping my hold as I looked to my bastard cousin who stood near the fountain.

"What are you doing here?" I growled as I noticed how his fucking gaze lingered over Braelyn, only taunting my anger further, a reaction that surprised me. "I asked you a question, asshole," I finally snapped loudly, my muscles tensing as I stepped around her, effectively becoming a barrier between the two of them, heading toward my cousin who finally acknowledged my presence.

"I'm waiting for you. I do hope you had fun. I'm kind of jealous." Ezio smirked at me, which had my jaw ticking in anger.

This motherfucker…

I noticed Braelyn make her retreat while Ezio was distracted by me and felt some of the tension in my body dissipate the further she got from him.

"She is quite the woman, isn't she?" Ezio turned his gaze back to her retreating figure, before running his thumb over his mouth, covering the obvious smirk.

"Watch your fucking mouth," I hissed, taking a step back and turning to head back to the marquee, Braelyn's brother reached her in the distance as Ezio came to stride beside me. "Quite possessive already, cousin, remarkably interesting. So, I can only assume that means…"

"It means fuck all and if you wish to keep that sleazy tongue of yours, family or not, I suggest you keep quiet," I snapped at him, clenching my fists as we headed to the marquee.

Dorian had glanced back toward us numerous times, Braelyn refusing to. I could only imagine what was being said.

"Too bad, I think she was rather fond of my tongue, so I'll prefer to keep it for her future pleasure," he chuckled, before disappearing beside me, into The Shiver.

A realm between realms, that only some may enter for use of transport from one spot to another, yet never linger. He was lucky he did so, as when the words left his mouth I had reached for my blade, hidden within my suit jacket, and whirled on him. I groaned in frustration, my eyes blazing amber for a second before dying down. I ran my hand through my black hair as I pocketed the blade, my gaze returning to Braelyn who now stood frozen just within the marquee.

Frowning, I pushed aside my absolute fucking rage and headed over, noticing Hecate the closer I got, who was in a deep, tense conversation with Braelyn who had her back to me, her long blonde waves reaching the base of her spine. Dorian was visibly tense at her side. He noticed me as his head turned to the tent opening, silk drapes billowing in the night breeze, and I recognised that look on his face. One I knew too well from past experiences.

A plea…

Not giving it a second thought, I strode over, grabbing a whiskey from a passing server yet again, and came to a stop beside Braelyn, her short stature almost comical beside me. I noticed the stiff posture she had to stiffen further as I approached, her having sensed me somehow, and then somewhat relaxed as I stopped at her side.

Peculiar…

"Hecate, I did not know you were going to be here," I spoke disinterestedly and rudely to the goddess who I knew hated my family, and grinned around the rim of the crystal tumbler as her eyes blazed in all too familiar wrath.

"This is a private conversation, Katopodis, and such disrespect, as usual, I see." The goddess snapped at me, her long raven hair hanging loose to her waist with beads adorning the lofts of hair.

Her green, cat-like eyes reflected and tendrils of purple magic wafting around her frame. I looked her up and down, disinterested.

"And barefoot as usual I see." Cringing as I eyed her bare feet and took another swig of my whiskey before turning to Braelyn who stiffened at my side as I insulted the goddess.

Dorian was staring dead ahead, yet I saw the twinkle of amusement in both their eyes that others would have missed.

"Come on," I said, placing my hand on Braelyn's lower back, sucking in a stealthy breath at the odd sensation of vibrations that circled the air around her.

She didn't argue, much to my surprise, and allowed me to lead her away from a seething Hecate, who I knew was glaring daggers into my skull with every step I took.

"What, no thank you?" I mused to Braelyn as I led her to the head table, where she and I were to sit alone until the ceremony had been concluded.

"I did not need your help, Katopodis, so no, there will be no thanks given," she snapped, hellfire in her words.

"Didn't look like it to me, Sarris," I quipped, putting special emphasis on her surname with as much disgust as she did with mine.

"We need to finish our conversation, little rose."

"We will do no such thing. There is nothing to discuss," she deadpanned as she took the seat at the table before I could pull it out for her.

She grabbed the nearest glass of champagne and downed it, placing the now empty flute harshly back on the table. Rolling my eyes at her, I grabbed the seat beside her and leaned back casually as I eyed her, the crystal tumbler spinning in my hold, and I ran my thumb back and forth over my mouth. I felt my brows scrunching the longer I stared at her, trying to figure her out and doubting one suspicion after the next…

Gods damn me to nine hells, but this woman was infuriating me to no bounds, yet something was captivating me. What the fuck was it about her?

"Unless you want a repeat of your shoes, I suggest you quit staring at me like a lab rat immediately," she hissed under her breath, not bothering to look in my direction.

My anger flared again at the reminder of this afternoon.

"About that, you owe me a couple thousand."

"Add it to my tab then Katopodis." She sighed, leaning over the table to grab my champagne flute, which I allowed her to do, watching her intensely.

"I will, but seen as though you are twenty-five with no credit whatsoever, which tab would you like me to add it to? Should I enquire with Ezio?" I gritted between clenched teeth, deliberately letting slip I was on to her and wanting to know what the hell that shit around Ezio had been about.

Braelyn dropped her glass, the flute luckily falling over on the table and not shattering, but the champagne had run off the edge, splashing all over her barely-there dress. "Excuse me?"

"You heard me," I retorted when she snapped her head toward me, her mouth in a thin line and pale as she ignored the champagne now dripping to the floor.

She was trembling as she eventually grabbed the nearest napkin and began dabbing at her dress. I watched her in silence, not bothering to help her. I frowned as I noticed the tremor in her hands growing more prominent and realised I had it all wrong with Ezio, my own body beginning to tremble in rage.

"What the fuck did he do to you?" I said quietly, deadly as I leaned forward, trying to get closer to her, so no one would overhear.

She froze, her hand clenching the napkin tightly, her breathing deep as if trying to calm herself.

She did not respond to my question, leading me to ask again.

"What did he do to you, Braelyn?" It was then she looked at me, slowly and somewhat collected, not saying a word as we eyed each other.

"Fuck you, Katopodis," she sneered under her breath, slamming the napkin on the table, making the glass wear and silver wear rattle.

A few of the surrounding tables turned and looked in our direction quizzically before returning to their conversations. I noticed my own family across the marquee eyeing us suspiciously and knew I had to get this situation under control. How I was going to do that, I had no fucking idea. The woman beside me seemed to be the most stubborn as they came.

"Relax, you are causing a scene," I whispered as I placed my glass down casually and eyed the crowd, noticing some still watching and Hecate in deep conversation with Kaisley up ahead, both staring at us in unison.

"Fuck you," she whispered under her breath, the venom clear in her tone.

"That's for another time, right now you need to calm the fuck down as there are too many eyes on you, little rose," I whispered, smiling at her, trying to deflect the onlookers from what was going on.

I noticed the air vibrating around her, little visible pulses being seen. Thankfully, I doubted anyone but me had noticed it. I did not know what the fuck I was doing, what the hell she was doing, but an instinct came over me to protect her.

Grabbing her clenched hand under the table with my large one, I held her softly yet firmly. She tensed, the vibrations flaring under my palm, but I watched in awe as the rest of the pulses dissipated, nothing to be seen, only the flickering of energy and power between our touching skin.

"That's it, calm…" I whispered, grabbing my whiskey with my free hand above the table and downing it, incredulous as to what the fuck was even happening and why I was doing this and what… just… *Gods*…

The minutes ticked by as I felt her relax under my grip when suddenly she twisted her hand within my grasp and she clutched at mine, surprising me.

Did it feel… good? I was surprised and mentally recoiled from the idea as the memories resurfaced. It took all my willpower to leave my hand there, upon her thigh, one hand holding the other for a few silent minutes.

The vibrations finally ceased, only a sense of static energy floating between our skin. "Thank you," she whispered, with no sign of anger, venom, or disgust.

Only pure gratitude. I looked at her then, finding her head turned to me before she looked away.

"All right," I responded casually and removed my hand, noting the icy chill upon my skin as I did so.

Braelyn looked at me, her shoulders sagging slightly before she cleared her throat and sat up straighter in her chair, running her hands over her bare thighs that showed fully through the slits in her dress. I had to stop myself from staring as I noticed my gaze lingering over her smooth skin and the fold of her leg near her hip that was exposed.

Thankfully she didn't seem to notice, and I ushered a passing server to get us more drinks. I had a feeling she needed one just as much as I did. After getting us drinks, I eyed Hecate and Kaisley still in hushed conversation.

"I did not realise that your family was close to Hecate," I casually mentioned, noting her posture stiffen once more.

"We aren't, my mother is…" she mumbled, taking a sip from her champagne to avoid my gaze that lay on her now. *Odd…*

I wanted to know more but noticed the priestesses from The Servile entering and the rest of the guests gathering at their allocated spots. Looking at my family, they seemed tense, yet excited. I looked over to Braelyn's family, and they seemed tense, expectant of something, yet Kaisley, she seemed eager…

"It is time," the priestess said as she stopped before our table.

Braelyn froze mid-sip and lowered her glass, pushed from her chair, and stood regal, just like the princess she was. All fear had vanished from her as she stepped from the table, not looking back at me as I finally, and reluctantly followed her to the ceremonial table set up in the centre of the tent. I caught my family's sight yet again and wished I had not.

This was all fucking bullshit.

Braelyn stood before the priestess, me standing to her side now. The priestess said a prayer of gods knew what, blessing our union or some shit and all I could think of was how the fuck to get out of this.

I barely registered as the priestess took my hand and cut a small line along my thumb pad, my blood pooling on the tip. The sting did not register, only my mind internally freaking the fuck out as I grew more and more infuriated about this even happening and what would happen next. The priestess then did the same to Braelyn's finger, and yet again no scent erupted along with her pooling blood.

I tilted my head toward her, frowning, yet she stared ahead, as if I was not even here beside her, being dragged into this mess.

"You may complete your union," the priestess' breathy voice announces, causing both Braelyn and I to turn toward each other. I was sure she could read the displeasure across my face as she sighed quietly.

"Let's just get this over with, Theo," she whispered, snapping me from the cage of my mind. She had said my name, not *Lord of Death* of *God Killer* or even *Katopodis*.

I don't know why but it meant something to me… Sighing, I stepped closer, running my bloodied thumb across her lips, leaving them plump and crimson. A small shiver worked its way through her before she reached up and did the same to me, a shiver working its way down my spine as she smeared her bloodied thumb across my lips. Clearing my throat, I looked to the priestess who nodded.

"Fuck," I moaned to myself in annoyance, expelling a deep breath and just wanting this shit over.

I looked back to Braelyn, sensing how she was exuding nonchalance, yet she did not want this either. We both knew the repercussions though if the Servile was not upheld.

Death to both of us and a member of our household.

"You ready, little rose," I whispered so no one besides the priestess could hear us.

A nod was my only response, and I took it as my sign to just get it over with. Grabbing her, I pulled her close in a rush and touched my bloodied lips to hers.

That was a big mistake.

I was royally fucked from this moment on. Oh, I just knew it. Royally fucked…

We only needed to touch lips, however, as soon as we did, those vibrations around her swarmed me and her scent hit me in full force.

I broke away breathing heavily as I held her shoulders, staring at her wild-eyed. She was breathing heavily too, her mouth slightly open. "It is you," I said so softly that not even the priestess heard me but the way she stiffened under my hold confirmed it.

I couldn't stop myself as I crashed my lips to hers, having her grant me access to her mouth when I pulled her flush against me.

A loud commotion erupted through the marquee at the sight of me kissing her, and she froze.

Braelyn

Shit, I'm screwed…

The thought raced through me as he touched his lips to mine.

That ancient power within me clawed at him, reaching out, caressing him. It was then I knew there would be no escaping Theo Katopodis.

Ever.

A shiver worked its way through my spine in delicious waves of ecstasy before it all turned to dust as he pulled away, wide-eyed, and whispered so softly, only my proximity and sensitive hearing heard him.

"It is you."

Gods… I didn't know what to do, the revelation clear across his face had me freeze up.

There was no denying it now. It was when his mouth crashed to mine unexpectedly in a heated kiss that had my toes curling, that my mind went blank for a brief second.

Holy gods and goddesses!

An eruption of cheers from the surrounding houses had me ripping away from him, brought back to the painful harsh reality that was my life. He still held his large, tattooed hands around my neck, his lips flushed and the scent of him swarming when I took a hasty step back.

I avoided his gaze as he noticed the shift in me, dropping his arms to his side and I looked at the priestess.

"Welcome to House Katopodis," she said in that eerie, breathy, teeth-chattering voice.

Nodding to her, I inhaled a shaky breath, my lips still tingling in the aftershock of Theo's brief kiss.

"Excuse me," I muttered to them both before turning and walking through the still-cheering crowd as quickly as possible.

Some tried to stop me, to congratulate me, but I continued my way, knowing all while that Theo was coming after me. I could sense exactly where he was now, like a beacon on the darkest night.

The Servile bond had magnified that strange sense of him tenfold, perhaps even more. As I turned the corner, exiting the tent, I caught sight as he watched me go, his face tense, just as his family swarmed him, all congratulating him. I did not want to be around when he told them.

When he sold me out a second time.

As soon as I was clear of the tent, with no one around, I shadow-stalked right to my bedroom on the third floor of the manor, packing hastily in my effort to leave. I had been warded from leaving the estate unless permitted to do so, but now that I was bound to Theo, I felt its sickly tendrils vanish along with its hold on me.

The only loophole I had managed to find in the ward upon me had been the confines of the Whispering Woods all those years ago. It had somewhat seemed as if the power of the woods outmatched even the wards themselves.

Removing the ghastly wig and mask, I loosened my hair, feeling the sting of it being tied and confined for too long. I rang shaky fingers through it as I exited my closet, bag in tow, and froze.

Hecate stood casually beside my dresser, toying with my jewellery before chucking it aside carelessly.

"Planning on going somewhere so soon?" she called from across the room as her eyes snapped to mine and then the bag.

"I was just getting a head start for when I leave for House Katopodis." I cooled my features, using her training to hide from her.

"Is that so? I'm happy to hear that you are so eager to get our plan underway. You do recall the instructions you were given earlier this evening before that excuse of a man interrupted us?"

"Yes, Hecate," I answered firmly, not allowing her a glimpse of the unease and poison running through my veins at the mere thought of it.

At her referral to him... I could tell her that my cover was already blown, that Theo knows... but I just couldn't. There were too many factors and my mind raced over them all.

"Repeat the mission goal," she said, stepping before me and gripping my face painfully.

"Seduce and destroy," I gritted out.

She smiled sinisterly before dropping her grip and stepping back.

"Good, very good," she purred with a twirl, purple magic drifting from her skirts as she headed to the door. "I look forward to your feedback," she added, eyeing me suspiciously and then the bag.

It was only after she had left my bedroom and shut the door that I slumped on my bed, a loud sigh escaping me. I looked around my bedroom, the colours of ivories and gold scattered around. I hated it. All of it.

But I was a soldier in a war, and I would endure. Standing from my bed, I looked to the mirror, my bright emerald eyes staring back and my black hair falling in a heavy, silky mass to my hips.

I then heard music playing in the distance, the party now well underway at the marquee. I eyed the open window, the breeze from outside carrying the smell of an oncoming storm through the night.

So many shadows to stalk, only one place I needed to be right now.

Not even two minutes later, I found myself in the Whispering Woods, its calls answered across the breeze as I arrived through the shadows.

I had not bothered with a wig and mask this time, knowing the only person that may find me already knew my secret.

Well, one of them.

I was standing under the willow tree when he arrived. I had been sensing his encroachment since he left the party. I had my back to him, my midnight hair cascading down in waves, with nowhere to hide. He said nothing, only coming closer to stand behind me, his fingers running through the ends of my hair.

I had to bite back the urge to moan at the feel of it, and the sudden urge to lean back into him. I had my arms crossed to stop myself from grabbing him, to either attack or finish what he started, I did not know or care to indulge the thought further.

What the hell was happening to me? I hated him, I reminded myself...

"Have you come to collect me for the hunt order? Hand me over to your family?" I said tensely, still not facing him.

I felt his hand still in my hair before he dropped it altogether.

"Why would you ask me that?"

"It's what you are here for, isn't it? To sell me out again…?" I snapped, turning around, and having him visibly freeze as he saw my eyes for the first time since we were thirteen years old.

I felt my temper flare as the words left me, the reminder of his betrayal and the punishment I had to endure for so long.

"Well? Isn't it?" I snapped at him, shoving at his chest, causing him to step back by sheer force.

A frown grew on his face, either by my words or sheer strength, I did not know, nor care.

"I don't know what game you are playing at, Theo Katopodis, but I will not let you destroy my life for a second time!" I snapped, the air around me vibrating as the power hissed protectively around me, yet hesitant to harm Theo. It caused me to frown inwardly.

"What the fuck are you talking about?! Gods, it is you…" he snapped back at me enraged, before his gaze took in my features, no longer disguised and calmness settled over him.

"Yes, it is me, dickwad!" I retaliated, spinning on the spot to leave, feeling my anger grow.

A peal of raucous laughter had me stilling. As I turned, I spotted Theo hunched over laughing, a laugh I had not seen from him nor heard since we were children in this very spot of the Whispering Woods.

"What the bloody hell is so funny!" I fumed, only to have him eye me for a moment before he laughed again.

"Prick," I muttered and headed deeper into the woods, only for him to stop and my training set in.

He came up behind me, ready for a sneak attack when I ducked, spinning behind him, grabbed his elbow, twisted, and knocked his feet out from under him. He spun and landed with a heavy thud on the forest floor, myself straddling him and my arm pressing against his windpipe. "Well, that was surprising," he spoke hoarsely with raised eyebrows.

Releasing him, I sat up, eyeing him suspiciously as he remained beneath me on the ground.

"Are you going to tell them about me again?" I gritted out, needing to know the answer, and looked away.

His strong hands, covered in tattoos and rings, gripped my face, turning me to face him.

"I don't know," he muttered, his eyes dancing between mine.

Something in me died when he said that. I had not realised what little hope I had been holding onto for so long, but it crumbled away, decaying as he held my face.

"I don't know what to do, but I did not hand you over all those years ago. Gods, do you think I did that?" he asked me, now sitting up with me still on his lap, the atrocious dress showing off almost every inch of me.

His frown turned to an amused smirk. "Gods, you have turned into a fine woman," he mumbled, his tone and train of thought completely doing a one-eighty.

He was now eyeing my figure before his eyes landed on my lips. "I always had hoped they never found you, that you got away..." he murmured, still focused on my lips, growing closer.

I felt him stiffen beneath me, my lack of underwear making it even more prominent as his arousal grew.

I felt my arousal grow as his scent filled the air in my lungs. I could not stop the draw I felt toward him. I was about to succumb to it, let him kiss me when reality set in yet again. "What the fuck?" he mumbled against my fingers as they pinched his lips together painfully. I had done it to block his lips from mine and stood up and away from him, wanting to laugh at his shocked and irked expression. "Sorry Katopodis, but one terrible kiss is enough for me," I deadpanned as I turned away being sure he didn't see.

Hearing him get up from the ground, cursing under his breath, I felt my amusement grow, yet showed nothing of it.

"Terrible kiss? Gods, fucking nine-hells, woman! That was barely a kiss, and it was far from terrible! You know it too!" he called out to me grumpily.

"It was terrible, Katopodis," I called back over a shoulder, seeing him following a way behind.

"*It was terrible, Katopodis.* Bullshit. Get back here so that I can prove it," he mimicked me in a high-pitched voice before calling me back aggravated and with a huff of indignation. "And just so we are clear, you are a Katopodis now too, sweetheart, so I would cut the bullshit toward *our* name," he continued grumbling in irritation.

I stopped in my tracks, only to look over my shoulder at him with a brow raised.

"*Our* name?"

"Yeah, *our* name, *wifey*. Do you have a problem with it?" he said, crossing his ink-covered, muscular arms cockily as he stood before me, towering over me like a giant.

Wife... oh shit. The Servile was not marriage by any means, but in simple human terms, I guess it could be considered that, as there was no closer description.

Rustling near the edge of the woods, on the side of the estate, caught both of our attention. Our heads whipped in the direction of the noise. I didn't have my wig or mask on, *shit!* "Theo? I know you are in there, you bastard! Come on out!" Ezio called drunkenly from the perimeter, not daring to step within the woods for fear of its secrets and power.

I began trembling, my eyes wide before I shook myself, forcing a state of feigned calm to come over me. Theo eyed me before he looked back in the direction of his cousin.

"Fuck, I thought he would still be in the fountain," he whispered with a frown.

"In the fountain?" I whispered back, now being the one to frown confused.

"Asshole was following me. I may or may not have helped him in." He shrugged casually.

"Theo!" Ezio shouted into the woods again.

"Go." Theo crossed his arms, watching the direction of Ezio the entire time.

I stood, unsure of what to do. Would he use this as his chance to rat on me? More rustling sounded before Theo looked at me.

"Fuck's sake, Braelyn, go!" He snapped, his voice barely a whisper as he frowned at me in frustration.

"Don't use that tone with me." I snapped out at him in ire before stepping into a shadow, disappearing from his view.

I was going to head away but instead lingered nearby in the shadow, watching, and listening to the two of them. Theo eyed the spot I had been with both eyebrows raised in surprise, before running a hand through his dark hair and smirking.

"Nine hells, Theo!" Ezio called out again, sounding frustrated and a crash near the perimeter had Theo dropping his arms and throwing his head back in frustration as he groaned loudly exasperated.

"What!" he shouted, a tick in his jaw as he started forward toward Ezio, who now lay sprawled amongst the bushes near the end of the woods, drunk as I had suspected.

"What the hell do you want?" Theo asked sounding as bored as nine hells.

He kicked at his cousin's shoes with his hands now on his hips as he looked down at the fool. "You slimy shit, you just left me in the fountain!" Ezio slurred from the ground as he looked up at Theo.

"Your point?" he asked, now crossing his arms yet again, head cocked, and I noticed the tick in his jaw.

"That woman of yours, oh man, you have no idea…" Ezio began but did not get to finish as Theo's hold on his irritation snapped in an instant.

He was faster than a blink of an eye, his knee pressing against Ezio's throat, cutting off all air. Ezio struggled beneath him, his face turning shades of red and purple.

"Let's get one thing straight, cousin, it is only the fact that you are family that has kept you alive so long. I could kill you now and be on my way," he gritted out in a casual tone, taking a blade from his suit jacket and swinging it up and down, all the while, Ezio struggled on.

"And if you think you can go anywhere near Braelyn, mention her name, or refer to her in any way, I will not hesitate to follow through. So yes, I left your pathetic ass in the fountain, just be grateful I didn't leave you scattered around the estate. I'm fucking on to you, cousin, your dirty little secrets won't be so secret for long." He sneered venomously at him, getting close to his face.

"Do we have an understanding?" he asked, feigning friendliness with a twisted smile as he lifted his knee, allowing Ezio to suck in ragged lungsful of air before he slammed it back down, a gun now pressed to his head faster than I had to realise what was going on.

"I said, do we have an understanding, cousin?" Theo gritted out yet again, the barrel of the gun pressing firmly against Ezio's temple.

Ezio's eyes widened, and he tried to speak but could not form words.

"What's that?" Theo mocked, pressing down harder before lifting his knee yet again.

He cocked his head as if listening intently to hear the words that could not escape Ezio's mouth.

"What was that?" he deadpanned, all playing aside as he waited for an answer.

"Y… yes," Ezio croaked.

"Good." Theo smiled sinisterly and slapped at his cheek twice, harshly, and stood, his knife and gun already hidden from view as he straightened his suit and stepped over his cousin who still lay sprawled amongst the bushes, gasping for air, some colour returning to his face.

I was frozen in the spot of the shadow within I hid, not sure what to make of what I had just witnessed. I knew Theo was lethal, I knew I hated Ezio's every breath… God's what was that? And about me?

I looked back at Ezio one final time as he lay rocking in the bushes, hands cradling his already bruising throat.

Shadow-stalking, I followed Theo as he headed toward the apartments set up for the other houses' stay. The party was still in full swing down at the marquee.

Braelyn

I followed Theo to the apartment, over the veranda and within the confines of the lush space. He headed over to the suite on the left, before disappearing. The tension rippling across his body was clear to see and I was thankful none of his family was around now to see what was going on.

It would surely raise some questions.

"I know you are here, Braelyn," he called out from the suite in an irritated huff.

I exited the shadows, stepping into view at the threshold of the entrance to his domain for the weekend. I looked at him silently before my eyes scanned the contents of the room. Weapons of every make and size littered the space, although neatly.

"Planning on going to war?" I deadpanned as I looked back at him, a brow raised. "Or a hunt order?" I added, not being subtle at all.

Theo rolled his eyes at me as he sat on the edge of the bed, removing his gun and knife, and setting them down beside him before he removed the suit jacket and began unbuttoning his shirt. He noticed me watching and stopped as he reached the button just below his chest. He then leaned forward, placing his elbows on his thighs, and the rings adorning his hands caught the lamp's light from across the room.

"You think I'm following through on that order?" he deadpanned, the tick in his jaw now more than prominent.

If it were possible, I was sure smoke would be exiting his ears. He shook his head and stood, heading to the bathroom. I watched him go, not sure what I was even doing there. I heard the shower turn on as I walked further into the room, and removed my heels, placing them beside the dresser that stood covered in guns and knives. I knew each of them, calibre, make… but continued my stroll over to the window, pushing the blinds aside to ensure no one was headed this way. I should not risk being here.

What the hell am I doing?

Closing the blinds, I looked around once more, the shoes I had destroyed lay haphazardly in the corner of the room, appearing to have been thrown. It would not surprise me if that were the case. I almost felt guilty about it but shrugged it off.

The asshole had deserved it.

The bathroom door opening and the scent of Theo flooding the room had my mind going hazy for a moment. He stepped out, dressed in black sweats that hung lowly on his body. I could not help but stare and did not even manage to get a good look as he immediately pulled a grey T-shirt over his head, covering his rippled abs, covered in tattoos, and the deep V-line that led to below his pants. Theo froze, cocked his head, and smirked at me.

"That smell… it's sinful," he said, now smirking even more when he noticed me turn away embarrassed.

I was exuding indifference when he came to stand behind me, towering over my small frame while I picked up a nearby gun.

"Be careful, that's a…" he began, but I interrupted him as I cocked it, aimed, and then disarmed it.

"Glock twenty, twice the ammunition capacity of the nineteen-eleven. Hits twice as hard too. The recoil sits well… an old one but one of the best," I finished, stepping away to inspect the assault rifles.

Theo froze, then chuckled as he followed me, his mood seeming better than earlier.

"How do you know this stuff, princess?" he mocked me, using that horrid nickname once again as he emphasised it.

"I told you; I know more than you could ever imagine."

I mused as I placed the throwing knives back on the coffee table and turned to him, crossing my arms.

"Care to explain what that was about with Ezio?" All the air left the room at the mention of his cousin's name.

Theo crossed his inked arms as he eyed me tensely.

"What did he do?" he asked me right back. I found myself freezing as we stared at each other, none of us willing to cave to the other.

Theo noticed my unrelenting stance on not answering and stepped to the front of me, merely a hair's width between us as his body heat swarmed me, and I was forced to tilt my head up to look into his eyes. He then gingerly grabbed my wrist, the one with the Servile brand, the brand much like a tattoo indicating our joining like vines with intricate thorns wrapping along my skin up until my elbow. "You see this? This means you are mine to protect now. I might not have wanted it, but that's how it is. It makes no difference to me who you were, are, and I may be many things, dark twisted things, and certainly no fucking hero… but this means you are mine and I protect what is mine." He dropped his hold on me, my skin scorched by his touch and goosebumps erupted across my body.

"Maybe it's everyone else who needs protecting, Katopodis," I whispered and stepped away from him, needing the space to think.

I could not deny his claim over me mended some piece within me, but I had a mission I needed to see through.

"What happened to you?" he asked, unusually quiet as he remained where he stood beside the coffee table.

"What do you mean?" I asked, now sitting on the edge of the bed.

"I mean what happened to you twelve years ago," he spoke up with more conviction as he poured himself a whiskey at the small bar across from me.

"It does not matter," I sighed, images of the well-house snapping like an elastic band across my mind, causing me to flinch.

He noticed and slammed the glass tumbler down harshly as he turned to me.

"It fucking matters to me!" he snapped, breathing heavily, a strange look on his face.

"Why the hell does it matter to you what happened to me? You sold me out!" I snapped right back, getting to my feet in a rush and heading to the door, ready to leave.

"Don't you walk away from me! Not after everything!" he yelled, now heading toward me.

"Screw you, asshole!" I sneered over my shoulder.

I exited the suite, marched down the small hallway, and was yanked back, firmly yet gently as he pushed me to the wall, a hand over my mouth. I screamed into his hand, my eyes glaring daggers into his head as he looked away from me and to the rest of the apartment. He began moving his hand, only for me to snap my teeth around it and bite down hard, his blood entering my mouth.

"What the fuck is wrong with you?! Are you god-damned feral?!" he hissed in a whisper, yanking his hand away as he ushered me back to his suite, and closing the door quietly just as the sound of his family entering could be heard.

"Fuck!" he hissed into a fist as his hand dripped blood across the marble floor of the suite.

"You," he snapped his fiery gaze toward me, and raised a finger, pointing it at me as he began chuckling menacingly and headed to the bathroom, shaking his head incredulously as his temper rose to dangerous heights.

"Never in my fucking life…" I heard him grumbling to himself as the faucet turned on, the steady stream of water was audible from his bedroom. I wiped at my mouth, seeing my hand come away crimson. I then headed straight in beside him, noticing the glare he gave me as he washed his hand.

I stepped around him, cocking an eyebrow, and then bent over to rinse my mouth and chin of his blood. He stepped back, grabbed the navy hand towel, and wrapped his hand in it. He was watching me in the mirror as I turned off the faucet, water dripping from my chin, down my breasts. I noticed his lingering stare and cleared my throat annoyed.

"Not even a sorry? Your manners for a princess surely are lacking, little rose," he tsked and smirked as my frown deepened.

"Stop calling me that," I hissed in annoyance as I followed him out of the bathroom and back towards the bed.

"Calling you what?" I could hear the eye roll in his voice which enraged me further.

"Little rose! Stop calling me that!" I sneered at him, trying to be as quiet as possible.

Theo turned his head to me as he grabbed his drink and downed it, the towel still wrapped around his other hand, and he began cleaning the bloody mess on the floor.

"And why would I do that?" he deadpanned, sounding disinterested as hell.

"Because I don't like it, and it doesn't make any sense!" I blabbered in a rage, knowing *I* was making no sense and sounding like a child.

Gods he was infuriating.

"Well, I like it, *little rose*, and as for making sense, it does to me and maybe one day I will let you in on the secret." He smiled and winked at me as he came around the bed and fell on it, laying his head across the pillows and sighing.

"What in nine hells do you think you are doing?" I quipped, noticing him getting far too comfortable and closing his eyes.

"What does it look like I am doing?" he asked sarcastically, peeking an aqua, amber-rimmed eye at me, his black hair still damp and falling across his forehead.

"I need to get out of here! Get up," I snapped at him, pulling at his leg. It was as useful as trying to move a mountain.

"No can do, little rose. There is no way out, even by shadow-stalking your way out of here. I chose this suite for a reason. The windows are sealed and the door. My family has gone to bed and has set tripwires within the apartment. You don't think we of all people would go somewhere and sleep there without preparing for every possible scenario, every possible creature, did you?" he finished, shuffling further down the mattress as he adjusted his position, getting comfy.

I felt pale at the realisation.

"You mean to tell me I am stuck here all night?" I said, not believing my ears.

"Yep," he sounded out, the amusement clear in his voice.

"What am I going to do all night?" I asked, more to myself, but Theo sat up on the bed, his brows scrunched together as he eyed me.

"What? What the hell do you think?" he was being sarcastic again as he rolled his eyes and fell back against the mattress, throwing a tattooed arm across his face groaning before dropping it and eyeing me through lowered lashes.

"Just go to sleep, Braelyn. I promise I won't do anything." He grumbled, tapping the far side of the enormous bed that could fit six people.

I hesitated, eyeing him and the room, then the weapons...

"Don't even fucking try it," he mumbled, not even looking at me.

I scowled at him, deciding to flip him off before glaring between the door and window.

"I saw that," he grumbled sitting up yet again, frowning at me.

"What is the problem?" he gritted out, eyeing me.

"I cannot stay here. I need to get back to my room. My absence will be noted."

"Your point is?"

"My point is that I cannot stay here and need to get back. It isn't difficult to understand, Katopodis," I snapped, crossing my arms as I glared at him.

Theo eyed me, a frown growing deeper across his forehead.

"You are making it fucking difficult to like you, you know that?" he finally said, shaking his head as he got off the bed and began putting his socks and shoes on.

"I don't like you, so perhaps the feeling will be mutual," I seethed, the prompt of the punishments I had to endure over the years due to his betrayal crossing my mind.

Did he honestly think I would welcome him with open arms? Gods he was an infuriating, cocky imbecile!

Theo stood, his shoes now on and it was odd seeing him dressed so casually. I frowned and stepped back as he neared me like a predator, caging me between the wall and the solid form of his body. I continued to glare at him as he placed his forearms flush against the wall, his body now pressing against mine and the sheer, flimsy fabric of my dress made it feel like he was caressing every part of me. He looked down at me, his hair hanging low over his forehead.

"What…" I started in a petulant huff but was cut off as he lowered his head, his cheek, then open mouth ran softly over the skin of my neck, from my earlobe to my shoulder.

A shiver worked its way down my spine straight to my core, and I clenched my thighs shut at the sensation, his silky raven hair caressed my skin as he worked his way back up and hesitated at the shell of my ear.

"Your lies smell sweet, little rose," the deep baritone of his voice and his hot breath as he whispered caused goosebumps to erupt across my skin.

I could not help myself as I closed my eyes for a moment, the feel of him made my heart run rampant.

Theo then moved his mouth to my jaw, grabbing the side of my neck with his hand and trailing it across the planes of my skin, stepping even closer to me, his body flushed and pressing hard against mine. It was then he ran his lips lightly across mine, back and forth at a torturous pace.

A barely audible moan left me and he froze, his lips still covering mine. When he did not move, I opened my eyes, finding his aqua ones already staring at me, the amber rings swirling around the irises.

Amusement lit in his eyes, and I narrowed mine in defiance. His mouth still covered mine, and we were waiting to see who would cave first, by the large bulge pressed against my stomach, it was clear how much he was affected too.

Raising an eyebrow, I reached around him, my hand slipping beneath his shirt, caressing softly over his skin. The way he had me pinned, it was difficult to reach any higher and I dragged my nails down his skin before I grabbed his ass and squeezed.

A shiver worked its way through him, and he still made no move. Our mouths remained pressed against each other, and our eyes never wavered.

Gods, he had no idea how dirty I would play to beat him at his own game... fool!

Cocking an eyebrow at him, only had him frowning in confusion before I once again ran my hands under his shirt, feeling goosebumps across his skin as I wrapped one leg around him, then the other. His eyes went wide at my actions, and I pressed my upper back into the wall as I moved my hips higher, shuffling myself to the spot I needed to be in comparison to his height in one swift movement. I was now pinned to the wall, my legs firmly wrapped around his waist and my hands running over the planes of his bare skin beneath his shirt. He made no move as we eyed each other, our breaths mingling.

I began moving my hips, rubbing his hardened, concealed cock against my core in slow movements, his eyes shut tightly, and his breathing turned ragged, I noted how his arms tensed, the hand on my neck holding firmer and the one against the wall now in a fist.

I felt myself grow more aroused and I knew he could smell it in the air, but I did not stop. His eyes flashed open, the amber completely having taken over the aqua, my own eyes narrowed once again and then grew wide in shock as he moved his hips against mine, the force almost sending me over the edge completely.

We eyed each other for what felt like an eternity when he grabbed both sides of my face and kissed me.

And gods, did he kiss me well!

Theo's lips, full and plump were soft yet harsh as he consumed me, I did not stop him as his tongue invaded my mouth caressing me further.

I kissed him back feverishly, the friction between our grinding hips and kiss sent me over the edge, moaning against his mouth, which earned me a moan from him as I ride it out against him, my body locking his to mine as wave after wave of ecstasy rippled through me.

It was a clash of mouths as I rode it out, not able to have him close enough. I knew he was close too, and that's when I bit down harshly on his lip, having him recoil from me in blinding pain. "What the fuck?" he snapped at me wide-eyed, in shock.

"I don't like you, Katopodis," I said sounding bored as I pushed him away and dropped to my feet, straightening my dress and hair, before wiping my lip with a thumb.

"Now get me the hell out of here."

Play dirty indeed…

Theo

Blue balls…

Never in my fucking life had the shit that went down last night happened to me… now I was suffering with god-damned blue balls!

After Braelyn had ordered I get her back to the manor last night, I wanted to wring her little neck. I had gotten her out of the apartment and flipped her off as I remained within the threshold.

She had been about to retort when I had shut the glass French doors, effectively cutting her off.

She could find her way back…

I could see the amusement across her face which only irked me further.

Matters only grew worse when I returned to my suite and the smell of her arousal filled the space, drowning me in it. I had to have four cold showers just to be able to sleep!

"What's got into you?" Layna asked as she came up beside me outside the manner, having noticed my brooding mood as I stared down the large front doors while I leaned against my bike smoking a cigarette.

Flicking it away, I crossed my arms, frowning at the double massive doors, willing the fucking monster to make her appearance.

I had a suspicion she had been avoiding me all day and we were due to leave in the next few minutes. The sun was already setting, and the estate was quiet as the other houses had returned to their estates earlier in the day.

Mathias had my father in meetings all day, presumably regarding shipments and managing the cartels.

Gods, how I wasn't supposed to kill her within five minutes of her moving in was beyond me, the thought crossed my mind for the hundredth time today...

"Nothing," I mumbled to my sister, who only eyed me and the manor, back and forth, before chuckling.

Trey and Kason headed over from their car, having loaded up everything we needed. "She is already under your skin," she crooned, nudging her shoulder into mine.

"No, she isn't," I snapped under my breath, not taking my eyes from the doors.

Where the hell was she? I was about to tear down the front doors when they opened and Mathias and Kaisley stepped out, followed by Dorian and the devil in a red dress...

"About fucking time," I mumbled, pushing away from my bike at the same time Layna did.

"I trust all is in order?" Mathias spoke to my dad who had come up with my mother beside him.

"Yes," my dad responded.

The way they eyed each other, subtle yet intricate details I lived for, had me questioning what it was they were referring to. I also noted how Kaisley was glaring daggers at my mother, before looking away bored with the whole interaction. Dorian and Braelyn stepped around our parents who were in discussions and stopped before us.

My sister smiled widely at Dorian who smiled back at her. *Hold the fuck up, what is this?!* I was frowning between the two of them before I decided I really did not care and finally looked at *her*...

Braelyn stood beside her brother, the blonde hair, which I now knew was a wig, and the golden mask covering her green eyes. I eyed her up and down, taking in the details I had been blind to over the years, and it was clear she was tense, standing stiffly in a red summer dress that ended over her knees...

I did not greet her, still seething from last night, and took her bags over to the car, placing them in the trunk, cursing under my breath the entire time. How many fucking bags did one woman need? I felt her, the Servile bond enabling me to track her anywhere without a second thought. She came up behind me, still silent as I placed the final bag and slammed the door closed. "Good evening,

Katopodis, it appears you have forgotten how to greet me yet again," she said with a sigh as she eyed me from behind that mask.

"How is your lip? It appears a bit swollen…" she chuckled softly yet mockingly.

Gods, the shit I would do to that pretty little mouth of hers if she wasn't such a pain in my ass.

I crossed my arms, leaning against the car.

"It is perfectly fine thanks, I had Calista kiss it better for me," I deadpanned, an outright lie, but I noticed her stiffen at the words.

I smirked sinisterly, only to have it fall away as she spoke.

"Poor girl. Sometimes charity can expect too much of someone," she said in false endearment. I did not have a comeback fast enough as I gritted my teeth, eyeing the little monster before me.

She began grinning, knowing she had gotten under my skin.

"You fucking enjoyed last night!" I hissed under my breath, pushing away from the car.

"I did," she deadpanned under her breath, so no one else heard us. "I got off, and I went to bed. A simple evening," she added.

"What the fuck does that mean?!" I was whispering but my anger simmered as I drew closer to her, before stepping back to act casual before the others noticed.

"It means, asshole, I got off, I left, and went to bed. I told you I don't like you so what more is there to it? Nine hells and you are the ones who killed Hades? Thick is what you are…"

"Yeah, thick is what I am. I could prove to you just how *thick* I am if you didn't fucking bite me twice in one night like a fucking animal," I hissed, my fingers already digging for a cigarette and coming up empty.

So much for quitting if I had to endure her for the rest of my life.

Gods dammit to hell. She was infuriating!

"I felt enough last night, there wasn't much to brag about or even mention, so if you'll excuse me," she said, that bored as fuck tone back.

Oh no, she did not just insult my cock!

My eyes widened in disbelief at her statement, and the woman had enough nerve to smirk at me before turning and heading away, back to her brother who was in deep conversation with Layna.

Fuck it all to nine hells!

"You okay, dude? That vein in your neck is doing that popping shit again," Kason said to me as he came and stood beside me, his headphones slung around his neck.

He did not go pretty much anywhere without them.

"Do you have a cigarette?" I hissed, eyeing Braelyn across the driveway, my eyes narrowing on the little shit.

"You're joking, right? I don't smoke." Kason laughed at me but kept quiet when I turned my head, glaring at him.

"Um, I think I saw a pack in the console of the car," he mumbled, knowing I was in no mood for shits and giggles today. Pushing away from the car, I went to the driver's door and got in, finding my cigarettes.

Lighting one, I ignored everyone outside and watched Braelyn from the rear-view mirror of my Mustang GT. I had allowed my siblings to drive over here with it while my parents came over in the Land Rover. Trey was going to ride my Ducati back to our estate so that I could be in the car with Braelyn, but I was considering telling him to drive with her…

"Finally," I mumbled to myself as I saw everyone dispersing. The Sarris family, returning to their manor, and my mom, dad, Layna, and Kason getting in the Land Rover. Trey climbed atop my Ducati, placing my helmet on, and revving it as he started it up. Braelyn eyed me sitting in the Mustang and headed over. She could open her door for all I cared, and I started the car, the deep rumble and purr relaxing me to some degree.

Braelyn opened the passenger door and got in, her red dress stark against the black interior as she closed the door. I waited for her to buckle her seat before I put the car in gear and headed down the driveway, the Ducati, and Land Rover just up ahead. She was silent, her body tense as we neared the gates of the estate.

The guards already had them open and I watched her in the reflection of the console as she held her breath, tensing as we crossed the boundary before she exhaled and turned to look back at the now-closing gates.

"What was that about?" I asked, not being able to damper my curiosity.

She turned to face me in her seat, chewing the side of her cheek as if contemplating telling me. "It's the first time I am out of there without my family," she said softly before clearing her throat and straightening her dress skirt.

"What? You never went out by yourself?" I asked, my brows scrunched in confusion.

"No, I couldn't before…" she mumbled, sounding uncomfortable.

I turned my head then to look at her briefly before looking back at the road as we neared the highway.

"What do you mean you couldn't? You're twenty-five years old…"

"I couldn't because I was warded. The only time I have stepped foot off that estate was when it was mandatory, and my mother was with me." She snapped, ire in her voice, not at me, but at her circumstances…

I felt my anger rise at the thought of how they had kept her locked up like some zoo animal.

"What would happen if you tried to leave? Surely you tried to even if it was just once…" She kept looking ahead and then at me as if debating telling me.

My hands gripped the steering wheel tighter as I waited, a million scenarios playing out in my head.

"I would be… punished. After the wards would alert that I was too close to the boundary, I would be punished after the ward would incapacitate me, leaving me lying on whichever spot I fell…" she said eventually.

I pulled over hastily to the side of the road, my family still ahead on their way back to the estate.

"What are you doing?" Braelyn said, yanking her mask from her face, leaving her staring at me wide-eyed.

"You are going to tell me everything right now, or I swear to the gods, we will go back there right now, and I will make them tell me," I gritted out, my anger threatening to implode any second.

"You can't do that!" she yelled, her anger rising as we faced each other within the confines of the car.

"I fucking can and I will!" I yelled back, beyond infuriated that she wouldn't just tell me! "You know I will," I gritted out quieter this time, breathing heavily.

"Gods, I don't understand why you need to know! Why are you so god-damned adamant about knowing every single detail?" she hissed, turning to face the road ahead, the cars on the highway buzzing past in the distance.

Braelyn's face was scrunched in frustration, the mask having left imprints along her cheekbones that were now flushed red in anger.

"Because I have spent twelve long years not knowing and it twisted me up!" I snapped, falling back in my seat with a loud groan and smacking the steering wheel before I was pinching the bridge of my nose, eyes closed while I tried to reign in my emotions and temper. My breathing was heavy, the sound of it filling the car. I dropped my hand, looking out ahead at the road when I finally calmed enough to continue.

"I never told anyone about you. That last day I left, the day you did that ridiculously over-pretty rose etching… I returned home to a meeting my father was having. I was still eating those fucking horrendous crisps that you loved so much when I heard them mention a hunt order for a girl with green eyes… Only then did I pay attention, but I had missed enough of the conversation that I didn't have much to go on. I couldn't exactly make it obvious why I was so interested or that I even knew what they were talking about. Something in me just knew I needed to warn you. After the meeting, I snuck back to our spot by the Willow tree, and you weren't there. Instead, I was caught and brought in for questioning by Hades himself…"

I found myself reliving those memories, my skin crawling with the thought of what happened after that.

"I never heard from you, saw you, or even heard my family speaking of you again. I never found out what happened…" I mumbled and then sighed loudly as I rubbed at my face and then turned to her.

"So, can you please just tell me everything? No more of this back-and-forth bullshit," I said, eyeing her.

She sucked in a breath, her face pale as she turned her golden mask repeatedly in her hands. She turned to me, about to respond when my phone went off across the speakers of the car.

"Yeah?" I answered it, not taking my gaze from hers.

"Where are you guys?" Trey's voice sounded over the speakers.

"Just taking a slow drive home. What's up?"

"We have orders for a new mission. You need to get your ass back here," Trey said. I eyed Braelyn, hating the timing of this.

"I'll be there in five," I gritted out annoyed, and ended the call.

"This conversation isn't over," I said, turning in my seat and pulling back onto the road.

Braelyn

The drive to the Katopodis Estate took us three minutes to get there…

Theo had been driving at ridiculous speeds through the traffic, albeit as smoothly as any professional.

We did not speak any further after Trey's phone call and I watched him in silence. I noticed the tick in Theo's jaw, how his tattooed arms and hands were covered in those rings and clutched at the steering wheel.

There was so much tension in him and something was not adding up. If he truly did not rat me out, whom the hell had? I also sensed there was more to his story that he had not shared. I had no idea what I would tell him once he returned from whatever orders they had received…

The driveway leading to their estate was winding, and seemingly never-ending. The road took us through the hillside, large trees shadowing the road. The sun was barely lighting up the sky when we arrived at the colossal gates, larger than the ones for our estate. It was shocking, to say the least. The gates opened faster than I had ever seen before Theo thundered on through, then closed just as fast.

I had whipped my head around to have a look when he spoke up for the first time since the phone call.

"They need to be fast with the type of work we do…"

That made sense, and I found myself looking forward yet again marvelling at the estate, everything making mine feel like a cottage in comparison, yet still understated in the sense they did not need to showcase their wealth or power by displaying everything for the world to see. I was silently counting in my head, watching the speed we travelled when he spoke again.

"You will need to put your mask back on now," he said softly, looking at me briefly.

I did as he said and just as I finished, we came around a bend and the large manor of House Katopodis loomed before us.

"Gods! That's your house?!" I exclaimed in disbelief.

I felt like a pauper in comparison the longer I marvelled at the sight before me.

The Katopodis manor was styled like a fortress, an ancient temple from our ancestry, reminding me of the Parthenon if you will, with the surrounding hills covered in the same archaic trees as the Whispering Woods. The ancient stonework tones of greys and white with lattice work forged from Adamantine – the impenetrable, unwavering metal of the gods.

The abode reached high into the sky; five stories high.

"Yeah, not the dungeon or torture chamber you were expecting then?" He smirked at me. "Sorry to disappoint you, little rose." He chuckled as the garage doors at the very bottom of the colossal structure opened and he pulled in, cutting off the Mustang's roaring motor. "Come on, princess, I've got shit I need to do," he chirped before climbing out and shutting the door.

Climbing out myself, Theo was already unloading the trunk, my bags now beginning to surround the car. Looking around, I found more bikes and cars, the marble floors gleaming and a workstation skilfully placed on the other side. Everything was high-tech within the garage, which had me curious as to what the inside of the actual residence would be like.

Holy shit… Katopodis was fancy. Who knew?

"Do you honestly need all this? What the hell is in here?" he protested grumpily as he removed the final bag.

"Yes, I do, and you should never ask a woman what she has packed in her bag," I replied sweetly.

"Knowing you, probably a mace to smash my head in with while I sleep," he murmured, now beginning to haul as many as he could in one trip while I trailed behind.

"Probably," I smirked back, chin held high.

"You could help, you know," he called over his shoulder as we neared a door.

"And why would I do that when you can do it yourself?" I asked in mocked shock.

Theo halted just before the door, dropping my bags with a loud thud against the marble floors. He spun around frowning as he crossed his arms.

"Do it yourself then," he sneered at me, trying to get under my skin.

I smiled at him and began gathering the bags, piling one atop the other, almost taller than me, and heaved the load up, peeking around the side at him.

"Lead the way then," I smirked, his eyes scrunched in disbelief at my short stature carrying such a heavy load.

He had forgotten about my highly unnatural strength then…

He turned to the door, before turning back to me, then the door again, and then finally back to me, his hands now on his hips.

It was comical to watch as he battled with himself internally, his stubbornness or his chivalry…

"Put it down," he said annoyed.

Cocking an eyebrow at him, albeit behind my golden mask, he huffed in annoyance, pinching the bridge of his nose yet again in frustration.

"Hells, Braelyn, just… put the bags down…" he gritted out, forcing himself to try and sound polite, well as polite as he could be.

"Okay," I said cheerily and dropped them. Theo's face scrunched up in pain and he yanked back, the tower of bags wobbling as he blew a heavy breath through his mouth and shut his eyes.

"Is there a problem?" I asked, cocking my head, acting innocent.

"No, not at all," he said through clenched teeth and eyed me while I smiled at him.

Mumbling under his breath about being the death of him and some nonsense about killing me before the week is through, I stood proudly as he limped over, he gave me one last glare before picking up the bags yet again and turning to the door. I had to bite back the laugh that threatened to escape me as I watched him stepping gingerly with his right foot.

"Yoh! Hurry up man, we have a hunt order to get done. I want to try to get back in time to go to Holy Roller!" Kason yelled from somewhere up ahead.

It was difficult to see anything past Theo and the mountain of bags as I trailed behind.

"I'm coming, you dick," Theo mumbled under his breath, readjusting the bags as we passed by an expansive formal dining room and then the most enormous, incredible kitchen I had ever witnessed in my life. The countertops gleamed with white marble, grey cabinets, and top-notch stainless-steel appliances. The fridge seemed to be as big as my closet. It was strange seeing such an open-plan space as in my own home, the kitchen was hidden away, nothing luxurious about it, and servers worked in it tirelessly throughout the day and night. Something about this appeared like a true home, one I had read about or seen on television.

"This way," Theo called out to me up ahead as I found myself standing in the hallway, admiring everything. I reminded myself why I was here which brought me back to reality. I followed along silently, my eyes taking in every detail as well as counting my steps in my head. I noted all the immediate entrances and exits, no doubt which would be rigged. Theo had let slip more than he would ever realise over the weekend, particularly their family's use of security. The ancient power within me reared its head as I passed by a closed door, its attention peeked as it vibrated against my bones.

"What's in here?" I asked casually, noting that it was the only door that appeared locked so far. Theo halted, turning, the bags still in his grip, to see what I was referring to.

"My sex room," he deadpanned before continuing. "Now come on, I need to go," he said casually before heading down another hallway and up a set of stairs, then another, and another, and *another*. Nine hells…

"You do know there is this thing called an elevator, right?" I whined as I saw him heading down a hallway again with, gods kill me now, *another* set of stairs.

He did not bother to wait for me anymore. "Yeah, which is an easy way to get trapped, ambushed, or killed, among other things," he called back from up ahead.

"Planning on having a killer in your home anytime soon, Katopodis?" I snickered, his words amusing some dark twisted part of me more than it should have.

"We are all killers in this home, little rose."

"Duly noted," I deadpanned, the reminder making my skin crawl and Hecate's instructions repeating in my head.

Seduce and destroy…

Shaking the thought, I looked around yet again. Antiques lined the hallways, yet not overbearing. I noticed each one as we had gone through the manor and found it impressive that they owned such a collection and managed to keep the house from feeling imperious. A feat my mother had failed at dismally. The manor at home had always felt too stuffy, too much like a show of power than a home...

"T, we are leaving in five," Layna called from a room down a different hallway leading to the right.

"Yeah, I'll be there," he called back to her just as she stepped into view, shutting what I assumed to be her bedroom door.

Her red hair was braided, and she wore all-black, combat boots, leather pants, and a jacket to match, like the leathers I had seen Theo wearing nonstop as we grew up. Her hands had fingerless gloves and she held a Barrett M eighty-two sniper rifle over her shoulder as she headed our way.

"Hey," she smiled at me before continuing her way, walking backward as she spoke to me. Theo was now heading up the stairs.

"Welcome to the family! Oh, and give him hell." She winked before turning and disappearing down the flight of stairs, taking them two at a time.

"Princess, you better get your little ass up here, so that I can go!" Theo's deep voice yelled out from somewhere up the stairs.

I rolled my eyes at his annoyance. I chanced a glance down the hallways one more time before heading up what would hopefully be the final set of stairs. They twisted around the last few feet, and I entered what could only be called a complete bachelor pad. God's...

"I am not staying in here; this is your room..." I said indignantly.

Theo was rummaging through his walk-in closet across the expansive space, the room large enough to take over the entire side of the manor, and windows covered both sides. A wall of glass allowed in the sight of the surrounding hills and the courtyard between the two halves of the manor. The vaulted ceiling gave it an airy feel and no walls divided the space whatsoever.

"It's an attic," mumbling, I looked around.

"Best damn attic I've ever seen," he shot back as he stuck his head out from the closet, no shirt covering him.

"That's beside the point," I gritted out annoyed and trying uselessly to remove my eyes from his tattooed body in the closet. It would remain an attic, and I would never admit that it reminded me of a skyrise penthouse. The bastard was cocky enough as it was...

"Where is my room, Katopodis?" I huffed out, crossing my arms as I looked around, my curiosity getting the better of me.

"In here," he deadpanned, sounding bored again as he exited the closet in what I could not decide was tech-wear or combat.

All black.

It seemed to be a mash of the two and a hood hung from his back, a mask in his hands as he headed over to a table on the far side of the room, closest to the right, overlooking the woods.

"Why in nine hells would you assume I am going to share a room with you?" My anger snapping as I headed over to him as he began buckling weapons of every shape and size to his person.

"Because, *wifey*, it's the only place no one can get to you, now if you will excuse me, I have someone to hunt down." He smirked, flicking his black hair away from his face as he smacked my ass, hard I might add, in passing, heading to the door.

Jumping from the sting of his hand, he began chuckling at my expense, loading a rifle as he walked away, not a care in the world.

"Prick!" I seethed, glaring daggers into the back of his head.

"Might as well get unpacking little rose. You are stuck with *me*, just as much as I am stuck with *you*," he sang back descending the stairs and the door shutting of its own accord.

Screaming in frustration, I threw myself across his colossal bed, staring at the vaulted ceiling. I could hear their voices in the distance, then the rumbling purr of the mustang and three bikes before it faded away into the expanse. Rising on my elbows, his disclosure abruptly registered, and my mind did not know what to do with the information.

Because, wifey, it's the only place no one can get to you…

Theo

"*T, where are you?! They are getting away!*" Trey's frustrated voice drummed through my earpiece.

"*Two at twelve,*" Kason's voice followed over the coms, Layna's sniper rifle blasting off. Ignoring them, I was battling my opponent.

Dodging his onslaught, ducking low, I twisted around his legs, knocking them out from under him, immediately reaching for the gun he had been firing in my direction.

Snapping his wrist, a gargled cry escaped before the gun was pointed, now held within my grip and I fired off two shots right between the asshole's eyes.

I watched as he dropped like a rag doll and emptied the gun, bullets rained around my bloodied boots.

More of Layna's sniper shots rang through the air in the warehouse district we were in. It was the dead of night, and the ground was slick from the storm that had passed through a few minutes ago, rivulets of blood still running down the street, disappearing into the storm drains. My eyes glowed amber as I lifted my head in the direction of the scuffle further up. Kason and Trey were still fighting against two of our attackers.

Shaking the rainwater from my hair in a swift flick, I disappeared into a mass of chaos.

Ravens erupted in a great swarm, like that of a tidal wave, flowing through the area, taking down any hidden rivals in my wake.

"He's on his way. You, babies, know he doesn't speak when he's on a killing spree," Layna chuckled through the coms, seeing my swarm on its way toward our brothers from her perch upon one of the warehouse rooftops.

I reached them just as Trey took down the one guy, Kason still playing with his opponent.

Kason wore his signature headphones, dancing around the poor bastard who decided to go against him. He may be a goofball, but the guy was second to my deadliness.

"Took you fucking long enough," Trey rolled his eyes at me as I arrived, my ravens disappearing leaving me standing in their stead.

I crossed my arms, looking at him bored as fuck while Kason continued his taunting of the guy. "Just finish it," I grumbled to our youngest sibling.

Kason sighed dramatically, killing the guy in one swift move. "It is too easy," Kason was moaning, running a hand through his hair, which was also slick with rainwater and presumably blood.

I looked my brothers over, our signature death masks stared back at me. We each had a distinctive mask, each equally terrifying. It covered our full faces, only allowing holes in our eyes. Technologically a masterpiece, they allowed us coms amongst other neat tricks, including safety from any poisonous gases, which these assholes had thrown at us upon our arrival.

"They are getting away if you wanna take this, otherwise I will," Layna's voice spoke sternly over the comms, yet again.

A wicked smirk worked its way across my face. Disappearing in a swarm of ravens, blocking out the light or the surrounding streetlights, I rose high into the night sky before dropping at incredible speed, already having spotted the five men making a getaway in their van. Twisting through the buildings, my ravens swarmed in a colossal tornado around the van, banging against its side and blocking their view of the outside world.

I found it amusing to see the terror on their faces as the van rocked, banged, and groaned against the metal…

"Boo," I chuckled, as the five grown men shrieked within the van as I formed right beside the driver's window, my ravens disappeared in the blink of an eye.

The van still rocking before it came to a stop. They recovered from their startle, immediately pointing each of their guns at me. Leaning my shoulder against the van's driver door, I crossed my ankles as I peered in at all of them, not saying a word, being sure to stare each of them down, my glowing amber eyes unnerving them through my death mask.

I was aware of my brothers who were now getting into position around the van as I noted their movements in the van's reflection. The men inside were arguing with each other about who should kill me, speaking in Greek. I arched a brow, it was strange having Greeks in this part of town, and there was no known affiliation to the cartel this current issue revolved around.

Sighing, I stood, readjusting my leather jacket which hugged my body.

Grabbing the door of the van, I yanked it open harshly, only to open it wider in a slow, taunting manner, the hinges moaning as the metal bent from the force exerted when I forced it open, against the locking mechanisms.

"Out," I spoke back to them in Greek, their faces paling further.

The pricks remained seated, earning a jerk of my head annoyed, indicating to the outside of the van. The distinctive click of a gun to the back of the van, of prick number four, whom I had been eyeing through everything had me whipping my gun up in a millisecond, firing at him swiftly, his body slumping back against the van's interior. It happened so incredibly quickly that the others in the van weren't sure what happened before they eyed me in speculation. Shuffling my weight from one foot to the other, I crossed my arms, having already holstered my gun, repeating, "Out."

This time, they did as they were instructed, never taking their pale faces from me. "*Stop playing, T.*" Layna's amused voice echoed through the coms, earning a small devilish smirk from me as I flipped her off, my arms still crossed as they piled out of the van before me. "*Asshole,*" she laughed through the open coms.

Trey and Kason crept closer, now a few feet from the backs of the four remaining men.

"Who do you work for?" I deadpanned in Greek as I eyed them bored, my arms still crossed, Adamantine covering my arms and hands.

They continued to ignore my question, pushing my patience. Unholstering my gun and throwing knife in one swift move, I shot one in the knee, having him collapse wailing into the night, before finishing him off with a second shot and flung the blade, it lodged itself deeply in the throat of the other. He collapsed too, gurgling, and choking on his blood. I holstered my gun, stepped forward, and yanked the knife from the throat of the other, a slick pop noise sounding out at its removal. I wiped the blade against his shirt before he fell to the wet ground. The remaining two were shaking in terror as I stepped back sighing.

"Who do you work for?" I gritted out, hating to repeat myself.

Usually, Trey would do all the speaking, however, after the weekend I had, I somehow ended up taking the lead on this hunt. Trey's methods may be cleaner, but mine were more effective in the line of work we were in… The two of them eyed each other for a moment. I watched as the look turned to one of finality. I noted how the one clenched his hand, his arm muscles tensing uncontrollably in spasms. The sweat that dripped down the other's neck and the dilation of their eyes.

Both men swallowing at the same time… *Fuck.*

As soon as the realisation of what was happening dawned on me, there was nothing for me to do, nor my brothers who stepped forward while I remained standing, not having moved and my arms still crossed, a gloved finger now tapping against my elbow in thought.

The two men dropped lifeless to the floor, foam emitting from their mouths.

"Poison?" Trey spoke up as he knelt inspecting them, holstering his weapons that had been at the ready.

I eyed the bodies of the two men with a cocked head, deep in thought. Kason checked the pulse of both men before standing.

"That's a new one for the cartels."

"It's not cartel business," I mumbled my thought out loud.

"What do you mean?" Trey asked brows scrunched in confusion.

All the minuscule details of the evening, calculating the possibilities…

"They knew we were coming. It's not cartel business. They were scared shitless, yes, but they knew my abilities. The poison is not the cartel's way of offing rivals, and they did it willingly instead of naming whom they worked for. They were also speaking Greek." I frowned, trying to figure it out more when Layna arrived, her sniper rifle slung over a shoulder, backpack on, and a flight case in hand.

"I'll take a sample. Maybe we can trace it," she said, grabbing a vial from her backpack and getting down beside the bodies.

"Who issued the hunt order? What details did they give?" I turned to Trey, as he was the one the orders would be issued to.

"Dad got the order from Mathias. I'll try to get more details when we get back," he spoke, deadly serious as what was usual for him.

Layna gathered what she needed, before stepping back, and Kason released one of Hephaestus's many marvels.

The metallic creatures, the size of mites flew from the containment they were housed within and filled the air, their metallic bodies buzzing as they destroyed and consumed all evidence of our being here. The bodies vanished, the blood strewn over most surfaces and the van itself.

Kason pressed the button along the side of the adamantine container, a high-pitched whistle sounding out before they returned, and the box sealed. Trey headed over to his flight case Layna had brought over and dropped the shield. The waxy sheened globe that had encased the surrounding area as it concealed what occurred within and subconsciously deterred any innocents from the area, collapsed in on itself, leaving the area appearing as if nothing had happened.

In silence, we headed over to our bikes a block away in an underground parking space and the mustang beside them. Trey helped Layna load the equipment into the mustang before he and her left. Kason and I had come on the Ducatis, both our family's signature black. Black to cover up any evidence of the gore and violence or to match my soul, I didn't know nor care, as both were well suited to the colour.

"We are heading out to Holy Roller after a shower, are you coming?" Kason called out as I mounted my bike, my helmet already on.

"I need to check the brat hasn't blown the house up," *or found my shoes.*

I had already hidden them in the closet, hoping to all the gods and goddesses the sassy wench would not discover them, I mumbled.

Kason's laugh filled the air as he got on his bike. "I love her already." He chuckled, the engine roaring to life beneath him.

"Then you take her," I gritted out, immediately having to cover the rage at my own words as some primal part of me felt incredibly territorial even against my brother. *What the fuck is this?!*

"If you aren't careful, I just might." The asshole chuckled and sped away, leaving me stewing in rage alone in the dark abandoned parking.

Gods damned, woman!

***

Entering the estate, I groaned silently within my helmet as my bike went over the gate rail.

The manor further up ahead the twisting road glowed in the dark, its warm lights the only ones around for miles. Our estate bordered the Whispering

Woods, however, more on the hillside of the land, a fortress from the eons and placed here for its strategic position. It bordered the woods just like House Sarris, as well as the rest of the houses. A few of the lower-class houses were scattered amongst the world, each serving its god and purpose.

This, *home*, was what could be considered the main hub of our secret society. Mortals had no idea of the shit that went on around them and just how much of their world was ours; they were merely playthings of the gods and goddesses used for their entertainment and enrichment. Passing the final bend, the manor and the garage nestled beneath the hillside, adjoined to the temple-looking structure I called home, came into view.

Parking my bike, I removed my helmet, leaving it to hang from the handlebar as I took in the sight of the mostly empty garage.

My Mustang and Kason's Ducati were gone, they had already left for Holy Roller.

I had taken a slow ride home, somehow making my way to the spot on the side of the highway I had stopped and witnessed that show of power on Friday from the woods. I was uncertain as to what it could be, yet I had my suspicions. The brat upstairs was too much of a coincidence to not be liable suspect. I wouldn't force her to reveal more than she wanted to though as I still had that hunt order to consider, and I did not want to deal with that shit anytime soon.

So, to make life a bit easier for myself, I'll pretend to know nothing if possible. I did not even know why there had been a hunt order against Braelyn. The realisation had my mind spinning as I dismounted the bike and made my way inside, finding the house silent in the early morning hours.

I did not need to go looking for Braelyn, as the Servile brand and bond had me instinctively knowing she was upstairs where I had left her.

Holding my side, I entered my room, halting immediately. My black hair was dishevelled, and my body was still covered in the evidence of tonight's battle, I froze as I looked around my room wide-eyed.

"What the fuck have you done?!"

Braelyn, the nerve of this woman, sat up from my bed and eyed me with indifference. "Excuse me?"

"What in nine hells is this?" I snapped, my irritation knowing no bounds.

The brat had dumped all the items from my closet across the floor and I could see she had used the space to fill with her clothes and garments, masks, and jewellery.

"My shoes…" I said barely audibly as I rushed forward, finding them all dumped from their spot and strewn across the bathroom floor, spots of water marring them. "My fucking shoes!" I bellowed, turning back to her on the bed and yanking on her ankle as I dragged her forward, as I now towered over her, my chest heaving, and jaw clenched.

"You said this is where I am to stay, so where did you expect me to place all of my things?" she answered tartly, crossing her arms defiantly as we eyed each other.

"I said you are to stay in this room, not butcher my belongings!" I yelled, pinning her down on the bed. Her eyes went wide at my actions before a sinful smirk played on her lips.

"Oops."

"*Oops*? Oops!" I tossed back at her, pressing myself closer.

I knew my eyes were shining amber in the dimly lit room as I stared into those emerald orbs, almost forgetting what I was so mad about. That was until her scent hit me. Pushing away in a rush, I forgot about my side and flinched.

"What is it?" she asked concerned, sitting up immediately.

That gods damned scent of her arousal was filling the space and making it difficult to think. She was just as fucked up as me … Ignoring her, I walked into the bathroom and slammed the door shut, immediately thumping my head against the back of the door.

"Fuck!" I yelled angered before pushing away and turning on the shower.

The shower was a long and cold one. My body healed quickly, a lucky perk of our family, yet one of the pricks from tonight had gotten a lucky shot on my side while I had been occupied, my thoughts distracted by none other than the devil outside this bathroom.

She had been doing something across the brand which sent tingling erotic shivers through me in the middle of a fight. My side was bruised and bleeding, the adamant armour not protecting against the weapons of the gods. Another reason I knew this Hunt was not normal cartel business. But I was not going to get the family in on panic over a stupid wound that would be gone in the morning.

I'll tell them then…

Exiting the bathroom in a pair of sweats, I shook my hand through my wet hair, tiny droplets spraying everywhere. I halted, noting how the room had been tidied up, my belongings hanging neatly in the closet beside Braelyn's and the culprit herself fast asleep in my bed, the black silken sheets a pool of darkness around her as the light from outside filtered through the glass walls that ran the expanse.

Sighing I sat harshly on the mattress to stir her. There was no response.

Bouncing, there was no response yet again. "That is my side, and this is my bed. Move," I muttered grumpily as I pushed a tattooed finger against her shoulder, causing her to roll and then fall back, a soft snore escaping her.

"Fuck it all to nine hells," I was muttering under my breath as I slipped in on the side next to her, hating that my bed was reeking of her tantalising scent.

Running my hands over my face as I stared at the ceiling, my body felt like a live wire. Her presence and scent were driving me crazy, and it was making me mad.

So, gods damned mad I found myself glaring at her beside me while she slept. A small snore escaped her once again and I envisioned smothering her with a pillow, immediately finding myself smiling at the thought of it. "Don't even think of it," she muttered sleepily before turning around, her naked back to me. I froze as I looked up close and the strangest patches of scarring marred her back. Silky smooth, with slightly raised bumps. It was like a patchwork of skin, so faint that only being this close allowed me to witness it.

"What. Is. That?!" I found myself snarling out loud.

Braelyn shot up in bed, her midnight hair a curtain around her face as her nightgown hung loosely, its halter neck strung around the nape. "What?" she asked wide-eyed as I too sat up facing her.

"What the fuck happened to your back?" I snarled, reaching around to see it again but she stopped me with a slap at my hand.

"It's nothing," she hissed at me, her anger storming in her eyes.

"Bullshit," I gritted out, once again reaching for her back, only to have her smack me away glaring daggers into my skull.

Losing patience, I grabbed her, my training taking over as I spun her around and pinned her beneath me, face down and arms pressed against her sides by my thighs.

"Get. Off." She huffed, blowing her hair from her face while I felt pale at the sight the longer I looked at it.

I knew from personal experience that the type of scarring was caused by skin peeling away like melted butter. I ran my calloused fingers across the planes of her back, struck speechless for once in my life.

A first…

"Who did this?" I felt myself shaking with rage and clenching my jaw in fury. My eyes glowed amber in the dark and every single detail of her skin was burned into my mind.

"You did," she hissed before kicking her heels up, straight into the base of my spine harshly and twisting, my side protesting in pain. Before I knew it, she had me pinned beneath her, her arm pressed against my throat and her right hand digging painfully enough to the wound. "You did, Theo Katopodis, or someone in this house did," she sneered, wrath coating every word she spat at me.

Braelyn

Shoving away from Theo, I disappeared within the shadows, my chest pounding in anger and humiliation.

I had let my guard down and he had discovered my scars. Scars littered much of my body from the time in the well when my skin had peeled away on contact with anything after being submerged for so long. My back had it the worst, having the most damage inflicted when I had been hauled and dropped so casually out of that prison cell upon the cold stone steps.

Luckily over the years, they had faded to such an extent that only once someone truly inspected my damaged body would they discover it…

Of course, Theo Katopodis would be so inclined as to see them and demand answers… the prick. "You can't hide from me, little rose," he grumbled sitting up in bed and scowling around the room as I shadow stalked from one part of the room to the next, his eyes darting in every direction I travelled.

The ancient power within me stirred, reacting to my erratic heartbeat as I tried to control my anger. Hecate's instructions repeat within my mind.

I had been doing a lousy job of seducing, a part of me was reluctant to do it, but my anger that was becoming a simmering brew of malice beneath my skin had my mind made up for me. "Come and find me," I whispered from a shadow around Theo's ear.

His body went taut, muscles tensing at the sound of my disembodied wispy voice. I watched as he stood, eyeing the shadows as he did.

His full body was on display save for the sweatpants he wore. Tattoos of our gods, creatures, and symbols lined his skin; ravens sporadically covered a large majority of his bronzed body. Most of them covered his one pectoral, traveling in differing sizes up to his neck and down his shoulder and bicep. The other side of his neck was covered in a black rose, its petals and shape reminding me of the etching on the willow tree.

"What happens when I find you, little rose?" he grumbled, the deep baritone of his voice like a lick of flames across my skin.

Theo ran a hand through his ink-black hair, leaving it in disarray, a flick of it covering his brow.

Traveling around the shadows where he stood, I knew he felt my presence as I shifted from one to the next. Eyeing him, I reminded myself why I was there…

Hecate's reasons, as well as my own. I appeared from the shadows on the bed behind where he stood, my feet rolling to find balance on the mattress.

At this moment, I was tall enough to stand behind him and whisper in his ear as my fingers travelled down his spine, causing his abs to pull tight and his breath to hitch as I whispered in his ear, "You get what you want." Theo whirled around, but I had disappeared yet again, traveling from one shadow to the next around the great expanse of his room.

Theo smirked wickedly into the darkness, a thumb wiping at his bottom lip, back and forth in slow succession before he chuckled.

"I don't think you can handle what I want." My heart jittered at the sound of his voice, the multiple meanings behind his words.

I eyed the open window within the wall of glass that travelled the expanse of the floor on the side of the inner courtyard and took the opportunity to escape through it without a second thought. I shadow-stalked from one shadow to the next, the darkness of the early morning hours making it simple to do so at a speed that would have Theo chasing me with little luck of success.

I entered the courtyard of the manor; birch trees and an array of plants covered the space between the paved walkways. The manor rose around me, caging in the courtyard as colossal columns rose high into the sky, supporting the five stories of the building. I took a moment to appreciate the grandeur and history of the space before I noted the carved sigil of House Katopodis in the centre of a large pond filled with brightly coloured fish.

The metallic serpent coiled around a skull that glimmered against the light of the moon, ready to strike. It was bigger than I expected, sitting atop an obsidian platform, gold streaks covered the serpent and jaw of the skull. It was a reminder of their heritage, legion to the underworld, and reapers of the gods, yet it was beautiful.

Its darkness telling tales of romanticised horrors…

Ravens erupting from the window five stories up had me whipping my head in their direction, the flapping of their wings stirring dust and fallen leaves around the area. Slipping within the shadows once more, I hurried along, travelling faster than ever before, Theo's ravens a swarm of darkness behind me.

I found my way to the Whispering Woods that resided beside the manor, the hilly decline a stark contrast to my family's estate which was mostly flat. I shot from one shadow to the next between the trees, moss and fallen foliage erupted with the scent of earth and nature as I passed, quickly followed by the ravens. I erupted from the tree line upon the shore of a lake, no shadows for me to hide within as the moon cast a silver glow upon everything it touched, the water reflecting quicksilver as it lapped at the pebbled shore in lazy strokes. "Shit," I expelled under my breath as the fluttering of wings ceased behind me.

"I told you, little rose, that you cannot hide from me," Theo's deep, gravelly voice spoke from behind me.

As I turned, my bare feet felt the cool crunch of the slick pebbles beneath my toes. Theo stood a few feet up ahead of the tree line, his eyes glowing amber in the dark before the slowly returned to his normal aqua with amber only showing along the rings of his irises. His eyes travelled the length of my body which was covered only in a white halter neck nightgown, the silky fabric ending mid-thigh.

"So, what do I want, little rose?" he spoke, taking slow predatory steps toward me. The look in his eyes said it all, making my cheeks flush. It was one thing being trained in this regard, but executing it…

"Answers," I replied with a lift of my chin, proud of my quick thinking.

Theo halted before me, his eyes scanning my face in silent wonder. He began clenching his jaw, his body tense with anger yet again as his eyes landed on my thighs, the scarring more visible there like my back.

"Who did this to you?" he gritted out before looking into my eyes yet again.

"I already answered that," I said, my spine stiffening as the water swept over my bare feet, the notice of its great body of endless depths causing the fear to grab a hold of me.

Sidestepping him, I walked further away, trying to avoid looking at it at all costs and pushing my terror aside.

Theo noticed, that calculating gaze of his taking me in, then the water…

"You are afraid?" he asked, not sounding like a question, so I avoided it completely, pushing my dark hair behind an ear.

"What do you want to know?" I asked, raising my chin defiantly, bringing forth my princess of House Sarris etiquette yet again.

My shield.

"What happened after I left you that day in the woods, twelve years ago?" he asked, crossing his arms, the action bringing attention to his godly build and tattoos.

"I returned home, only to be punished for venturing into the woods. My mother was waiting for me when I emerged. I was told about the hunt order and punished, never allowed to venture out again and wards placed on me. You can guess the rest as I'm sure you already know I was only out in the public when necessary," I pushed out between clenched teeth, the reminder of being imprisoned my entire life and having the power within me grow agitated as it squirmed and hissed against my bones.

"What punishment did you receive?" he asked, his fingers flexing and clenching into fists beneath his folded arms.

He appeared to be struggling to maintain his temper. I cast a glance at the lake, my vision clouding over with memories of the well-house, being cast in and locked away within the icy waters of the silo-like structure.

"Braelyn?" Theo called to me, gaining my attention yet again, and I noticed he stood directly before me now, his arms hanging at his sides.

Still clenching and releasing fists, his jaw tight and eyes calculating my every action, every hitch in breath…

"The gods' well…" I started in a mumble, my gaze back toward the lake and then to him with a shiver, "I was placed within the gods' well for two weeks. Locked away…" I whispered, the air around my body vibrating in sporadic shudders as the power grew agitated by my anxiousness, readying to protect and maim anyone who dared anything…

Theo's eyes went wide before he squeezed them shut tight, his jaw clenching and releasing, his chest rising rapidly as he struggled for control of his anger. When he looked at me again, the amber in his eyes was glowing hot. "They put you inside that fucking well for two weeks, and locked you up? In that water and darkness for two-fucking-weeks?" he sneered; his anger not directed at me but at what had been done.

"Yes," I mumbled, stepping away to further increase my distance from him and the lake, its body of water giving me the chills. I avoided his gaze altogether. I willed the ancient power within me to recede, which it reluctantly did, its displeasure known only to me.

"You were just a child, only thirteen years old!" he snapped, turning to me.

"I know!" I snapped back, my temper snapping with the hellfire of the gods, and the air around me pulsed, the pebbles at my feet vibrating in rhythm with my racing heart.

"I know, Theo Katopodis! You did this to me! You were the only person outside of my house that knew of me. Your family is the one with the hunt order against me! I know I was a child, the memories of drowning over and *over* again in the ice-cold water of that god-damned well for two weeks and my skin peeling away as if it were nothing will live with me forever! So yes, I know!" I snapped, my chest heaving as I struggled for control of the power that wished to raze the Katopodis household to the ground.

Why in nine hells had I spoken of the truth of my past to him?! I shouldn't have…

"And all because of some imprudent fact that I decided to trust a boy in the woods!" I finally finished, squeezing my eyes shut tightly as I breathed through my nose, counting to ten and forcing the ancient power to recede a second time.

He was standing before me yet again; his eyes had softened slightly at my outburst if such a thing were possible for him…

"I did not betray you, little rose. I did not tell anyone about you, ever. I thought you were dead all these years… that they got to you," he forced out, the baritone of his voice deeper than usual as he eyed me, his attention going to my clenched hands and then my face again as he stepped closer.

"I will find out who betrayed you, but it was not me, and never will be me," he spoke with determination pouring over each word.

We stood facing each other, both breathing heavily and not willing to look away.

Theo raised a large hand, cupping my face as he drew nearer, his body flush against mine. He held me in place as I had to tilt my head up to see him. We were both glaring at each other, our anger melting together into something else; something equally heated. My blood was thrumming through my veins. The power within me curled around its eagerness at having Theo so close, tantalising its senses. "What are you?" he asked, barely audible as the power reached out a tendril, caressing him seductively.

He closed his eyes briefly and when he opened them again, I felt myself go weak, all anger leaving me. His eyes had softened yet again, want and curiosity clear in his gaze.

"What are you, little rose?" he murmured as he ran his mouth over the shell of my ear.

My breath hitched at the sensation, causing my eyes to close and my mouth to part. Theo then pressed me closer to him with his hand, the other stroking gently at the juncture of my neck and jaw.

"I..." I started to say but didn't finish as his tongue swept over my bottom lip, causing me to tense up as a shiver of pleasure erupted through me.

"You what?" he asked, the sound of a smile in his gravelly voice.

Not bothering to think any further, I crashed my lips to his, catching him off guard. He froze for a second before running his hand through my hair and pressing me close as he began kissing me with hunger, his craving matching mine. Theo tilted my head back, his hand a fist on my hair as he kissed me deeper, his tongue invading my mouth, warring with mine sending shivers down my spine.

"You are mine," he growled out before picking me up and holding me against him while he stood along the shore. My own hands gripped his face while my legs wrapped around him. He had laid his claim on me, and I did not refute it. *Seduce and destroy. Seduce and destroy. Seduce and destroy...* Hecate's mantra kept repeating in my mind before vanishing as Theo pressed my body impossibly closer to his and nipped at my lip before running his tongue over it, the heat easing the sting.

The kiss then turned brutal, a war of mouths and tongues and will. Each of us fought for dominance over the other, his hands gripping tightly at the back of my neck as he devoured me, and me him.

"I need more, gods, I need more of you," he mumbled against my throat.

A moan was my only response as he nipped at my skin, a mixture of pain and pleasure. Rolling my hips back against his groin as I pulled his mouth to mine, a shudder went through me at the feel of him and the sound of his moan of pleasure and pain as he strained to withhold himself.

Gripping his silky black hair in a fist, I yanked his head back harshly. His eyes went wide in shock as I glared down at him, my fist still brutally tugging on his hair whilst he held me. My aching breast's pressed firmly against his bare chest.

"You will not have me until you beg me, Theo Katopodis, and certainly not beside a lake in the woods like some animal," I spoke sinisterly, licking my way up the base of his throat in one swift move.

A shiver worked its way through him at my actions, causing his eyes to shut briefly before they opened, glowing amber as they drank me in heatedly.

A sting against my scalp was the only warning I had before Theo yanked me back as I did him, his fist woven into my midnight hair. Both of us were breathing heavily as we glared at one another, neither of us willing to submit. "Don't try this game with me, little rose, I'm not the good guy. You won't win," he said, his eyes trained on my rapidly rising and falling chest. The heated need dripped with every syllable that left his swollen lips.

"Good thing I don't plan on winning," I started before running my tongue sensually across the planes of my lips, and Theo's eyes focused on them just as expected, a smirk playing on the corner of his mouth.

"I plan to dominate," I finished with a harsh tug on his hair still firmly in my grip, and rolling my hips against his hardened length.

His eyes flashed in a sense I had yet to see from him, and his mouth pulled into a straight line before parting ever so slightly, causing me to smirk triumphantly when his widened eyes met mine.

Running my free hand along his muscled forearm leading to the back of my head, I began dragging nails down the inked skin, causing goosebumps to rise across the bronzed surface. Trailing it back up, I wrapped my hand around his, my hair a knotted mess behind my head, and began rolling my hips once more.

His grip loosened just enough for me to vanish into the shadows and away from him, smiling at his profanities that filled the air as I returned to the manor.

A ghost amongst the shadows.

Braelyn

Waking amongst the sea of black silk sheets, I found myself staring out of the glass panels that ran from floor to ceiling across the floor.

The day was sunny, the golden globe rising in the distance, not yet near its peak; mist drifting near the lake in the distance, held within the grasp of the Whispering Woods.

Sitting, I glanced around the room, no sign of Theo's return after our tense encounter last night. Had he returned at all? Pushing the sheets aside, my bare feet touch down on the smooth ground, chilly in comparison to the warmth of the massive bed.

Standing and reaching for my robe, I strode around the room inspecting every detail. There was no sign of his return at all...

Had I pushed him too far last night?

After leaving him alone on the pebbled shore of the lake, I had returned to the manor, hearing him cursing loudly most of the way. It had been amusing teasing him in such a way. My body was burning with molten need upon my return, causing me to shower before getting into bed, falling asleep against my will as I waited for him to storm into his room... but he never did.

Scrunching my brows in confusion, I hurried as I got dressed, adorning the wig and mask yet again. I had opted for pants instead of the dresses mother had insisted I pack. Dorian had managed to purchase a few items for me at my request and had managed to sneak them into my luggage.

Glancing at myself in the mirror of the closet, I felt slightly more myself as I stood in a simple pair of black skinny jeans and a crimson chiffon blouse. I could do without the dainty blouse, yet I still needed to keep up the pretences to some extent.

Exiting the room, I began the blasted descent of the stairs to the main living area, step after step after step. If it were not for my extensive training, I figured I would have collapsed out of breath after the first two flights. Finally reaching the last landing, the smell of bacon filled the air along with the sweet aromatics of maple and strawberries.

My stomach growled in hunger, reminding me that I had not eaten since my arrival here yesterday. Alaia had knocked at Theo's door last night extending an invitation to eat; however, I declined to feign exhaustion. I had been inspecting every inch of his room instead, gaining as much information as possible before his return.

"Good morning!" Alaia called from the kitchen, working away as she smiled near the stovetop. Immediately, I placed a shield around my being, the ancient power cocooning me in its embrace before she could decipher any more details about me. Theo's mother who I now knew to be a powerful empath needed not to learn of my plans…

"Good morning," I answered softly, hovering near the threshold.

"Are you hungry?" she smiled, flipping the sizzling bacon in the pan.

"A little," I answered, twirling the ring on my finger as I eyed everything.

"Hey," Kason greeted casually, smiling as he entered past me and grabbed a seat at the island, his headphones slung around his neck. A normal thing for him.

"Don't you dare," Alaia called, her back turned to us as Kason had been leaning forward, ready to swipe a handful of bacon and waffles.

"Your hangover can wait for everyone else to get here," she continued, having Kason slump back with a sigh before smiling at me defeatedly.

"You going to stand there all day or are you going to grab a seat and help me?" he chuckled, earning a smack across the hand with the spatula from his mother as he attempted to steal food yet again.

"Ouch, dammit," he hissed, shaking his hand. I couldn't help the chuckle that escaped me as I neared, grabbing a seat beside him.

"Where is everyone?" I asked casually as Kason began pouring the two of us glasses of orange juice.

"No idea, Layna is probably in the dance studio, Trey in meetings, and Theo… whom the hell knows. I thought you would know?" he finished casually eyeing me.

It was the first time we had spoken, and I found him easy enough to speak to, but I knew he was getting a feel of me, just as I was with all of them. I had used the bond to locate Theo earlier when it had been clear he had not returned, however, he was in an area I was not familiar with…

"Speak of the devil himself," Kason said with a chuckle, as he looked behind me.

I felt his presence wrap around me, sending a shiver down my back. Theo entered the kitchen, slightly sweaty and dressed in training gear, his tattoos on full display down his arms. He grabbed a seat beside me harshly, and sat down, not greeting me as he placed his elbows on the large kitchen island, staring at me, those eyes calculating as they always were.

"Good morning," I spoke up serenely, taking a sip of my orange juice.

Theo's eyes narrowed on my mouth, then the length of my throat as I swallowed.

"Morning," he grumbled before reaching for his glass and pouring it for himself.

"Where did you go?" Kason enquired from my other side, leaning forward to get a better look at his brooding brother beside me.

"I had shit to do," Theo grumbled yet again, now fully facing me, his wide legs caging me in as I sat on the stool beside him.

He was staring at me blatantly, not even looking at Kason as he responded to him. He was leaning an elbow on the countertop, his thumb swiping at his bottom lip as he eyed me. I knew what he was doing. He was attempting to get me to squirm under his gaze and proximity. It would not work. Quirking an eye at him, I finished off my juice as the rest of the family entered, taking up seats opposite us, and Dante went straight over to Alaia, kissing her forehead tenderly before his eyes found mine.

"Good morning, Braelyn," he spoke, nodding to me before he began helping with dishing up alongside his wife.

Theo was most like his father, with the same tall build, muscular definition, and that icy stare that no doubt had their foes trembling in fear. Layna was the perfect likeness to Alaia, their fiery locks identical and the soft features of their faces unmistakable. Trey and Kason were a good mixture of the two heads of

House Katopodis, their features a mix of both parents, but Dante's dark hair shone through brilliantly. Each of them had a tattoo of their house sigil inked across their skin. The men near the apex of their elbow on their right arm, along their forearm. Alaia and Layna were nowhere to be seen, but I knew that it must appear somewhere upon their bodies.

Layna had a tattoo of an extended laurel wreath on the side of her neck, intricately and beautifully woven around her skin.

"Apollo has called us in for a meeting, after which we need to discuss shipments with Hayden," Dante spoke up, taking a bite of his waffle as the rest of us began digging into our food.

Hayden was the new ruler of the underworld, Hades' replacement after he had been executed. He was chosen for the role by the Moirai, or The Fates as some would refer to them. He had been killed over two years ago in an attack orchestrated by Hades, resulting in many lives having been lost. Hayden was also the mate of the Angelis Mortis – Angel of Death, which resulted in a loophole in his taking up the role of King of the Damned.

Apollo had orchestrated the execution and new line of regency under Zeus' command as well as the Moirai and House Katopodis. Theo had been in the centre of it all, having dealt the final death blow using Ares' sword. Theo had been known as God Killer since that fateful day. Some whispered it in awe, others in fear… I had not been privy to all the details that led up to the actions being taken and was in the dark as many others. It seemed to become something most feared to discuss amongst our worlds.

"What does Apollo want to discuss?" Layna asked, her hair tied back in a neat braid and sitting across from Theo and me in what appeared to be dance tights.

Kason had mentioned a dance studio and it piqued my interest.

"He didn't say but I have a feeling it has something to do with last night's hunt order," Dante spoke, before casting a weary look over to where I sat, my blonde wig and golden mask meeting his gaze.

Theo shuffled in his seat, having said nothing, and began eating, his right arm slipping beneath the countertop and landing upon my thigh. I ignored his touch, knowing he did it as payback for my actions last night. The others began chatting amongst themselves whilst they ate, and all the while I attempted to do the same. It became increasingly difficult as Theo's large hand began running up and down my jean-clad leg, squeezing intermittently.

I turned my head to cast a glance at him and found the bastard chewing on a mouthful of waffle, as he stared at me and then away, the wicked amusement shining in his eyes as he slid his hand lower, near the apex of my thigh, torturously too close to a spot that had begun to burn in need once more. His thumb drew lazy circles, inching ever closer. I could not focus on what was being said around me and had to fight back a groan as he cupped my sex under the counter, no one was privy to what he was doing.

I felt my spine stiffen as I coughed around a mouthful of food to cover the moan that threatened to escape. Theo rubbed up and down, his large hand holding me in place firmly, pressed against the tight jeans. He was chatting with his father of gods know what, not a hint of what he was currently doing slipping through his bored as fuck expression and tone to match. I felt the wave of ecstasy threatening to wash over me, my heart hammering against my chest as I struggled but was successful in remaining casual. No sign of the storm brewing within me. The ancient power grew excited, twirling along my bones as the precipice to which Theo urged me grew nearby.

Shit...

As close as what was possible, he drew pleasure from me, and just as the wave threatened to crash over me and consume me, had my spine pulling tight, he withdrew his hand altogether.

"I'll go get ready, meet me in five," Theo grumbled to Trey, seeming bored as he pushed away from the kitchen island and left.

My body sagged slightly, but the thrumming of my blood still echoed in my veins. The power within me hissed at Theo's retreated figure, never allowing the rush of ecstasy to race through me. My jaw pulled tight and I counted to ten, spinning my golden ring in a flurry as I tried to calm myself. Smiling at the rest of the family, I excused myself from breakfast and exited the kitchen.

Theo was nowhere in sight as I walked the halls, the twenty-foot ceiling glinting in gold and depictions of the wars over the years. Titans and the gods, the underworld, and creatures of myth and legends to the rest of the unknowing world covered their expanses.

"Looking for me, little rose?" Theo murmured near the shell of my ear as he slammed me against the wall, the kitchen filled with his family just down the hall.

The smell of his scent washed over me; my breathing rushed as I blew a stray strand of hair from my face.

"Absolutely not. Why would I be looking for you, Katopodis?" I asked defiantly as his face hovered ever so close to mine.

A chuckle escaped him as he pushed away from the wall and me in turn. He began walking down the hall, heading to the staircase.

"Your lies smell so sweet," he called back, not bothering to look at me.

Bastard!

The scent of my arousal hung over my skin like a siren call. Making quick steps, I passed him on the staircase, wanting, or rather needing a shower immediately. Theo smirked as I passed him, traipsing up the endless stairs behind me.

Finally reaching the room, I was reminded of last night, and the question left my mouth sooner than I had a chance to stop myself. "Where were you last night?"

Theo halted as he changed within the closet, dressing in his usual reaper attire.

"As I said, I had shit to do."

"That is not an answer," I retorted, far too quickly.

I had no idea why it bothered me so. Why I allowed him to bother me… Theo exited the closet, the sight of him terrifying to most, but to me he was exhilarating. He stepped before me, still buckling weapons to his person as his eyes held me.

"Why did you come after me?" he asked, avoiding my question altogether and seeing right through me just moments ago.

"I did not," I replied, lifting my chin as I glared at him.

"I wonder… do your lies taste as sweet as they smell, little rose?" he said, stepping closer to me, his voice gone husky.

I did not respond, my mind going blank at his forwardness and the weakness it brought upon my knees.

"Perhaps you could find out," I snapped out of the daze, smirking at him as my eyes landed upon the servile brand on his skin, matching mine. I needed to follow through with the plan… or at least part of it… Removing my shirt, leaving me in nothing but my bra, I threw it aside. Theo's eyes turned dark as he unashamedly drank me in. Placing my hands on his chest, I ran them down and over his armour, my hands hitching over the multiple weapons during my descent before they landed on his belt buckle, tugging him closer to me. A tick worked its way into his jaw as he tried to restrain himself, the smell of his arousal filling the air around us.

"But it won't be today, Theo Katopodis," I whispered in his ear as I went on to my tippy toes and then nipped his earlobe.

Theo pulled stiff at my actions and only turned his head as he stood and watched me head toward the bathroom, shutting the door.

I was only in the shower for a minute, reeling over having seduced him, teasing him of what he could not have when the door to the bathroom banged open, startling me as I stood naked beneath the spray. I quickly recovered, standing proudly and an air of defiance hovered over me as the water pummelled me, causing my long dark locks to stick to my body and the bathroom to fill with steam.

"What the fuck are you doing?" I growled at him.

Theo appeared lethal as if he would shred the world apart with his bare hands and laugh about it afterward. He did not respond, only standing outside the glass shower door glaring at me as his chest heaved in anger.

"What..." I started, my anger ripping through, but was interrupted by a deadly flat voice as he swung the shower door open in one swift move and had me pinned beneath the spray, his own body now sopping wet.

"Shut up," he growled out before slamming his mouth to mine, the coolness of the shower wall against my back and the heat of him pressed against my naked front sent a shiver from my head to my toes. "Just shut the fuck up," he whispered against my mouth as the kiss turned even more feral, each of us pushing and then pulling on each other.

Both of us fought to have more and then shoved it away in wrath. It was a wicked dance of our wills, only the yearning and lust simmering through our veins. Theo's hands gripped my hip, squeezing harshly, enough to leave a bruise before he slid it between my legs, the water of the shower only heating us more. A moan escaped me, which he quickly covered with his mouth as he began stroking me, no barrier between the skin of his fingers and my core. I felt my body tighten, my back arching as I pushed against his hand.

"I don't like you," I mumbled dumbly between kisses, panting and moaning, opening my mouth in a silent gasp as Theo slid two large fingers within my clenching core.

"I. Don't. Fucking. Like. You. Either," he gritted out in between the panting of his desire escaping each hot breath against my face, being sure to plunge his fingers in deeper as if proving a point at the sound of each word leaving his lips.

Dropping to his knees in the shower, Theo lifted me, laying my molten core right against his mouth. A squeak escaped me, and my slick back slipped against the shower wall. The shower rained down on him, his midnight hair an untamed wet mess between my legs.

"Fuck," I hissed in a breathy moan as he began devouring me, causing me to bite down on my fist, head tilted back and my other gripping his hair.

Theo's tongue travelled the length of me, savouring every drop of my arousal, and began paying particular attention to the bundle of nerves threatening to send me over the edge. As he placed two fingers in me once more, I felt my world shatter as wave after wave of pleasure rolled through me. I found myself moaning loudly as I gripped his hair tight enough that it surely stung and rocked my hips against his mouth. Theo made sure to see me through each convulsion of pleasure, his free hand holding the back of my buttocks tightly as he drank me up.

Every. Single. Last. Drop.

We were both breathing heavily as the high of my orgasm began dissipating and he looked up at me from between my legs, the shower still raining down upon us.

"Your lies taste even sweeter than I imagined, little rose," he smirked at me, making a show of sliding his tongue over the two fingers that had been inside me only a moment ago and licking his swollen lips.

Unwrapping my legs from around his shoulders, I stood on shaky legs as Theo once again towered over me, pressing me against the wall of the shower. The bulge pressing to my naked stomach was a clear enough indication of his desire.

Reaching out, I grabbed a hold of it firmly, Theo jerking slightly as he closed his eyes tight before opening them and looking down at me, his lips parted, and eyes hooded with lust as the stream of the showers water ran in rivulets down his face, dripping upon my breasts. I began stroking him, gripping him through the pants he wore, and almost let my fear stop me by the sheer size of the man within my grasp. Theo gripped the sides of my face, moulding his mouth to mine once more, the taste of myself still lingering on his lips.

"T! Hurry up man, you said five minutes, asshole!" Trey's voice called from the bedroom, causing us both to freeze in our actions.

Theo removed his mouth from mine with an almost feral growl as his anger at Trey peeked through. Leaning his forehead against mine, still gripping my face, Theo's eyes shone a brilliant amber as we eyed one another in silence. The sound of the spray and our haggard breathing filled the confined space.

"Theo!" Trey called annoyed from the bedroom threshold once again as he could not enter the room, never mind the bathroom on the other end.

"I've got to go, but this isn't finished, little rose," Theo murmured against my temple as his hot breath fanned my face which he had not yet relinquished his hold of. I stood in shock in the shower as he dropped his hold and stepped back, a heavy sigh escaping me.

I watched in silence, my heart jackhammering within my chest, the ancient power purring within me as he eyed me, taking a step back, the water of the shower now a wall between us.

"Later," he reminded me yet again, his eyes traveling up the length of me, a dangerous smirk playing at his mouth as he shoved his wet hair back from his face. Theo then exited the shower, grabbing a towel from the vanity before exiting the bathroom, the door clicking shut as he went.

"Holy nine hells," I whispered to myself as I ran my hand across my mouth and down my stomach in disbelief. The ghost of his lips still playing against my own.

"*Braelyn, my sweet soldier,*" Hecate's wispy voice echoed in my mind, having me freeze, all joy or excitement I had experienced turning to shards of ice within the pit of my stomach.

The ancient power within me reared its head, hissing and snarling at the sound of Hecate and the audacity of showing up within our mind, interrupting our moment of… pleasure.

"*Braelyn,*" her voice called to me again this time in anger, the burning sting of her magic blazing at the base of my skull beneath my ink-black hair.

"Yes, Hecate," I whispered back, hoping to gods that Theo would not be lingering nearby.

A quick assessment through the bond had me relax somewhat.

I slid to the floor as she began her instructions on war.

Theo

My mind kept spinning around and around over the memory of Braelyn's moans, her hand in my hair, the stinging pleasure of it. The way she had come undone upon my tongue…

Shuffling on the spot, I remained stoic, no one having the faintest idea how my body blazed like a live wire beneath my armour. It had taken all my self-control not to rip Trey to shreds for interrupting us, the level of possession I had felt in that moment over Braelyn was a new one for me.

I had no intention of it reaching the point that it did this morning. I had simply wanted to get under her skin, the way she had done to me last night… but that damned scent of hers had my body and mind in a frenzy.

The need to claim her had been almost animalistic. When she had taunted me by removing that blouse of hers, I snapped. Some part of me could not just walk away, the draw to her was beyond comprehension, and when she threw words at me like daggers, using that brilliant mind of hers, my blood boiled in every sense of the word…

"Are you even listening to me? I swear this smartass just keeps fucking ignoring me on purpose," Kason moaned amused besides me as we waited in the lobby of one of Apollo's many establishments alongside our father, Layna, and Trey.

"Pretty much," I responded with a scowl, shuffling on the spot yet again, growing agitated for having to wait.

I had no fucking idea what Kason had been saying and had to admit, being distracted was rare for me. Finally, the door to Apollo's lavish office was opened by his secretary, Ms Rose, the woman who had worked for him for the past multiple decades.

"He is ready for you," she said, gesturing to the now-open oak doorway.

"About fucking time," I mumbled, not bothering to wait for the rest of my family as I entered, finding Apollo pouring a round of whiskey near his bar.

Apollo looked up at me as I entered, followed by my family, his neon green eyes and golden hair shining against the morning's sunlight through the windows.

"Always so impetuous, Theo Katopodis," he said with a sigh, rolling his eyes – a habit he seemed to pick up after spending so much time with Aria Silverton, the Angelis Mortis the past couple of years.

"Yeah well, shit to do, people to hunt… You know the drill," I said, taking the whiskey he offered and throwing myself down on one of the many costly leather seats that filled the space.

"Dante," Apollo greeted my father next, shaking his hand in welcome.

Apollo was a decent guy, a guy in the sense he was a god. Most of the gods and goddesses still treated many of us as their pets. Apollo provided everyone the respect they deserved. I imagined it was why Zeus had left the earthly plane to his son to manage.

Apollo sat down, twirling his whiskey in a hand after greeting my siblings, who had decided to remain standing, our training never slipping in the least.

"How is it going with the Sarris girl?" Apollo grinned at me as he took a sip.

The asshole probably knew this was going to happen. He was the god of many things, prophecy being one of them. My family's attention had now turned to me entirely, their inquisitiveness taking root as I had been avoiding broaching the subject with any of them. "Fucking fantastic," I grumbled. "But you already know that, don't you?" I asked, a brow lifting incredulously.

The asshole had mentioned during the assassination of Hades that I would be in this situation, using a play of words… however I had refuted it all together, knowing that I should not have been selected during the Servile. Apollo chuckled, crossing his suit-clad leg over a knee as he leaned back eyeing me. His neon eyes knew far too much.

"I will admit, I had seen visions of you with someone with a fire to match your own, however, I was surprised when it was you who had been selected at the Servile. The woman I had seen was meant to be your equal, with no need for a ceremony. It appears I have misunderstood the meanings of my visions. It is… odd, but…" he trailed off, his brow scrunched in thought before it cleared and he continued, "We have urgent matters to discuss. What happened last night?"

"We intercepted the shipment as planned, but they were gone, only a few rogue soldiers occupying the area. The shipment containers had been breached, not a soul to be found and no tracks whatsoever," Trey began explaining, his hand held behind his back and chest out in a military manner.

"What do you mean no tracks? Surely the Hounds of Hephaestus could track where the souls had gone? No mortal, demigod or not, could leave no trace," Apollo enquired further, sitting straighter now as he spoke with Trey.

"The hounds found nothing. It is as if they vanished, we did however find traces of adamantine shards near the container," Trey finished as Apollo eyed him intensely before setting his gaze on Layna, who straightened immediately, respect shining through her eyes.

"Your father tells me you retrieved samples of poison?" Apollo asked, setting his now empty tumbler down upon a coaster.

"Yes, after eliminating the enemy, we had two left for questioning. They had ingested poison, effectively taking their own lives as opposed to answering whom they worked for," she spoke before retrieving her phone and handing it to Apollo to read the results himself.

"I ran it multiple times to be sure," she added, stepping back in line with Trey and Kason.

"We shall keep this to ourselves for the time being. Ichor has only one source, and that is the blood of the gods. It appears we have someone working against the operation from within," he spoke, his neon eyes flashing quickly as the only indication of his anger over the situation.

He held out the phone and Layna stepped forward retrieving it quickly with a small nod of affirmation.

"What of the target, the one who has been hitting all the most recent shipments? Was there any sign of them after you arrived at intercept?" he asked, his fingers thrumming against the leather armrest of the couch.

"No, there was none. As Trey mentioned, not even the Hounds of Hephaestus could find them, along with the stolen shipment," I answered, finally cutting in on the debrief. "They knew we were coming. They knew of our strengths and abilities and made damn sure that we could not trace anything back to anyone," I gritted out, annoyed over the conversation.

There was something I was missing here.

All the details, a million scenarios, and calculations ran through my mind as I thought it over, my eyes glowing amber as I downed my drink, the burn of the whiskey having nothing to do with my frown as I finally felt the details click into place. One after one, it made sense; not the entire situation but a massive part we had been missing.

"The Shiver," I murmured, sitting back as I stroked my chin, all eyes on me. "The pricks are using The Shiver," I spoke with determination as I eye Apollo who sat back at my declaration, his mind seeming to mull it over.

"It makes sense why they cannot be traced," Apollo spoke. "But it is such an extremely rare ability to wield that the numbers needed for hijacking that the number of souls do not correspond. Not with the exceptionally fast way they do it. There would need to be at least fifty of them capable of traveling through The Shiver at once."

"I am telling you; it is the only way it makes sense. The Ichor also proves that there is a god or goddess involved, perhaps they are aiding in the hijacking?" I continued.

Apollo mulled it over, his jaw tense.

"The Ichor does indeed prove that one of the gods is involved, but even a god or goddess has no sway over The Shiver."

I huffed in annoyance, knowing I was right as I rose from my seat, grabbing the whiskey and pouring another. It was during moments like this that I somehow hoped that alcohol would have any effect on me. The amounts I would need to consume to even feel the slightest bit tipsy would have a mortal man dead and buried. "I know I am fucking right," I mumbled, taking a sip, then another as everyone eyed me in thought.

"Let me think it over. It is a valid explanation; I just need to figure out the details of how such a feat would be possible. For now, the details of this conversation do not leave this room under any circumstances, save for informing our new Hades," Apollo spoke as he stood, readjusting the lapels and sleeves of his expensive suit.

"Where is Hayden?" my father asked, standing too. "We are to meet with him after this."

"He should arrive any minute," Apollo spoke as he looked at his Rolex.

Just then, a black swirling mass appeared within the corner of the room, the shadows and mist of the Underworld twirling and expanding before a portal opened and Hayden stepped through. He appeared different since the last I had seen him as he had been resurrected and swept away to his new kingdom that day so long ago now at Apollo's temple in Delphi.

My family pressed a fist to their heart and bowed slightly before righting themselves as the new head of our Household stood before them. I did no such thing. My time of bowing before gods had ended just over twelve years ago. I would rather fucking die than bow to a god ever again. They knew my reasons and said nothing as Hayden's gaze found mine, alternating eye colours staring back at me. One eye sapphire with a crimson ring, the other crimson with a sapphire ring. Two sides of the same coin on one face.

"Sorry, I am late, I had matters to finish up," he spoke, eyeing the rest of the room.

He had died a mortal. An elf. Elves being the descendants of the gods as we were, however, they had branched out, their bloodlines being diluted over the millennia, whereas the demigods such as my family and the other Houses had remained pure, the Servile serving to maintain those bloodlines. His once shaggy blonde locks now cut close to his head, an undercut beneath the longer strands on top. He had also gained quite a bit more muscle since his resurrection, the tattoo of our house now branded on his arm.

"They can fill you in, I have shit to do," I spoke, placing my tumbler down and smirking at Hayden as I headed for the door. Luckily the bastard, all of them, knew it was nothing personal. I was just an asshole to everyone.

"I will be expecting you in a day, Theo."

Hayden called out as I reached the door. Looking back at him, I eyed him calculative. "And why the fuck is that?" I responded sounding bored.

Hayden stepped forward, his six-foot-five height an inch shorter than me as he stood near the bar and poured himself a drink before looking at me yet again.

"It is custom that the next head of House Katopodis receives their Servile cache from the Underworld within days of the ceremony. I will be expecting your arrival," he spoke before he took a sip and turned back to the others, a smirk on his lips as he knew I loathed being at someone's disposal.

It was a situation consisting of respect and hate between the two of us.

"Oh, and don't keep Charon waiting. He can get quite dramatic when he must wait to ferry someone."

Staring at him, I looked him up and down before nodding and exiting the office, my jaw clenching at the thought of once again the situation of the Servile. I was never meant to be the head of the house, that was meant to be passed down to Trey. I stopped in my tracks as I spotted the last person I expected to see waiting down the hall, no doubt to see Apollo.

"Dorian," I greeted blandly and had his head whipping in my direction.

Braelyn's brother neared and looked past me to Apollo's office.

"She isn't here," I spoke, crossing my arms as I looked him up and down.

Had the asshole done nothing to help her when she had been stuck in the fucking well? The thought alone had me grinding my teeth.

"Is she okay?" he asked, being sure to keep his voice down.

"She is safe, which is something I can't attest to while she had been living on your estate," I gritted out, my eyes flashing amber in a warning.

Dorian's face paled and he looked around before eyeing me in what appeared to be concern and doubt.

"She told you?" he spoke barely above a whisper.

"Yes," I mumbled, my muscles tensing at the thought of her suffering.

The door opening and my sister stepping out had us both looking over at her. The smile that spread across her face had me frowning in confusion as I looked between the two of them. Back and forth I watched as the sight of the two of these morons was brazenly obvious. The fucking asshole was smiling at her as if he worshipped the ground she walked on, however, the anxiousness of our passing words still lingered upon him…

"You have got to be shitting me," I deadpanned, the timber of my voice almost a growl in annoyance.

Dorian's face fell, his worried expression returning.

"Shut up," Layna hissed at me under her breath with a scowl. "Mind your own damn business, little brother. Didn't you have shit to do?" she moaned at me; her eyes threatening violence I know for a fact she could deliver on.

"Whatever," I mumbled, heading toward the main entrance once more, and not sparing them a glance. "Not my fucking issue," I scowled at the thought of my sister with Dorian fucking Sarris of all people.

Gods, I would need methanol to burn the image from my mind.

How the fuck they had managed to even manage it was beyond me. It was no fucking secret that yes, we worked as enforcers for House Sarris, but the tensions between our two families were tense. False politeness was always adrift in the air at gatherings between us.

Exiting onto the street, I climbed into my Mustang GT, the engine roaring to life as pedestrians and cars made their way by the building, no idea of what the fuck resided within. Pulling out my phone, I hit the speed dial for one of my contacts, the same one I had visited last night.

"Hey, have you got what I asked for yet?" The sound of a voice on the other side of the line croaked before coughing, giving me the news I needed to hear. "I'll see you in twenty minutes," I deadpanned over the line before ending the call.

Glancing at my arm which held the intricate vine and thorn tattoo of the Servile brand, I put the car in gear before pulling away from the curb.

There was still much that did not make sense surrounding the Servile and Braelyn herself.

The hunt order…

Finally, I would be getting some answers.

Braelyn

Hecate's impromptu discussion had me simmering with rage yet again, tainting any form of unrealistic peace I had slipped into.

The sting at the base of my skull, hidden beneath my hair, still stung painfully. It was a solid reminder of my mission, one I would not fail in.

The manor was quiet after everyone had left for the meeting they had with Apollo, leaving only one Katopodis upon the estate.

Alaia, I had found was in the gardens, her hands covered in dark soil as she appeared to be gardening herbs of every kind, hunched over a spot in the garden, her knees flat upon the grass. I watched her from a window inside, finding it odd, to say the least. It was highly uncommon for any member of the great houses to not have staff attending to such business. Cooking, gardening… it was exceedingly unusual and had my mind reeling over what else this family may perhaps do themselves. I had yet to witness any staff upon the great estate and found it hard to believe that the family maintained the grand space…

Pushing the curtain back into place after giving her one last glance, I turned, examining the space.

Hecate had a grudge against this family that had lasted for millennia, although in recent times the disappearance of Persephone from the underworld had the goddess on a literal path of war. Her instructions were clear, seduce the family, especially Theo as he posed the greatest threat to her plans.

Seduce and then destroy them using assassination from within.

I would need to keep my distance and remind myself of their place as mere targets. I had been slipping and the reminder from her this morning had been the much-needed kick up the ass I was due.

The terrifying reminder of the well-house as well as many other punishments had me swallowing back bile. She too had me in search of an ancient artefact that was said to be held in the Katopodis armoury. I would need to retrieve it, and once it was in my possession, I was to eliminate any threats that may disrupt her plans – House Katopodis.

My gut clenched painfully in disgust at myself as I thought of her instructions.

Shaking the thought from my mind, I ventured down the great halls, drawn near the door I had seen the day prior and Theo had avoided answering my questions about.

The ancient power within me felt the charge of what lay within the closer I drew to it. Standing before the door, I glanced around ensuring I would not be spotted, and pulled on the handle, jiggling it as it remained locked. The power within me vibrated in anticipation, in turn causing the air around me to shudder. I cursed under my breath as I tried once more.

Voices near the front of the manor had me whipping my head around, my hand immediately dropping from the handle. I moved to the corner, disappearing within the shadows as Layna and Trey came into view, both discussing a shipment that had been hijacked, before disappearing upstairs. The sound of Kason speaking with Dante in the kitchen had me eyeing the door once more. A quick check through the bond had confirmed Theo was nowhere near the estate. He seemed to be miles away. It was impossible to even guess where he was exactly as my knowledge of the outside world was limited due to my being warded; locked away in my family estate over the years.

The hissing of the power within me grew enraged the longer I stood in hiding, not entering through the locked door. Ensuring no one was around, I exited the shadows once more and felt the power take over me, which it had never done before.

My eyes grew wide as my hand of its own accord hovered over the handle, the air vibrating in violent shudders visible to the naked eye around the handle.

A barely audible click sounded, and my hand dropped, my will my own once more. Shaking, I lifted my hand eyeing it as I turned it over, fearsome of what had happened.

The ancient power prowled against my bones, slithering as it hissed, wanting me to enter immediately.

Looking around, I opened the door in a swift move, slipped through, and silently closed it behind me praying no one had seen me.

I found myself in a stone chamber, with no light in sight as the damp smell coated the air. My eyes flashed as they adjusted to the shadows, allowing me to see perfectly.

It appeared to be an ancient chamber, nothing within the fortress of House Katopodis being changed over the millennia within the space, unlike the rest of the manor. Steps descended before me; the dark stone was worn smooth over the years.

Listening for any sign of the family outside the door, I started forward. The power within me had the air vibrating around me in pulses, the rhythm like a heartbeat.

Each pulse had the dust at my feet roll away as if the earth itself recoiled from my very existence. The stairs spiralled down into what I could only assume to be the hillside that the manor stood upon.

There could be no other explanation.

Down and around I ventured, still with no light within the space. The only redeeming quality for myself was my affiliation with the shadows as they greeted my sight with a world no others would be capable of witnessing.

The darkness and enclosed space reminded me briefly of the well I had been sentenced to twelve years ago and had me pausing as I counted to ten, reminding myself it was not the well as I twirled my ring. My thumb spun the gold around my forefinger incessantly. The power hissed once more, urging me to continue forward as it caressed my being in a form of agitated comfort, aiding me, yet wanting to find what it was I sought to push through.

Forcing myself forward, I finally descended the endless stone steps and came upon another door in the dark, the antechamber in which I stood was covered in murals of the underworld.

The chill in the air had me shivering as I surveyed the ancient murals. Touching my hand to the stone, I felt a wave of ice sliver its way from my palm and through my veins, immediately having me recoil, gripping my palm as the iciness of the strange force lingered. Frowning, I examined the mural once more, not daring to touch the cold stone again. It appeared to be of the war of the Titans, Zeus and his siblings locking them away in Tartarus for eternity. The fearsome sight was that of nightmares. I found a mural depicting the worst of them all, Typhon, the Titan known as the father of all monsters.

We were told stories of him as children, a way to keep us in line, or have the wrath of Typhon befall us…

The ancient power within me turned its attention to the depiction, silencing itself as it watched on. Looking away, a shiver from the chill working its way through me, I found the locked door, the call of what I sought like a beacon from the other side.

"Shit," I moaned in agitation as I could not open the door, the ancient power within me now hissing in rage as it hammered against my ribs, wanting to open the door, but failing to.

Slamming my body against the large door, I bounced from it painfully, the locking mechanism twined around and across it was solid adamantine vines, not willing to allow any to enter.

A notch in the centre, like that of a keyhole, flattened to an intrinsic symbol had me pausing. It must be the key, but I had not witnessed such a key before. Running my fingers over the flat surface, I felt the indents and grooves of the symbol, somewhat representing a star in its harsh lines and grooves. The ancient power was growling in anger as it was unable to unlock its embrace like it did on the door upstairs.

The sense of Theo nearing as he drew closer to the estate had me whipping my gaze back to the staircase that ascended to the manor above.

Cursing under my breath, I hurried up and around the stairs, my feet almost slipping on the smooth stone twice.

Arriving at the top, the door to the manor hallway stood before me. I used my senses, listening, and found no one around, thanking the gods that I would manage to exit and have the sensitive hearing to do so.

Opening the door slowly, just a crack, I peered out. My gold mask touched the door frame as I searched the hallway. Not seeing anyone nearby, I quickly slipped through, shutting it behind me. The sound of Theo's Mustang filled the garage before being shut off and the door slamming.

The garage entrance was a few feet down the hall, the door slightly open.

I watched, my hands behind my back as my heart pounded against my chest. My features remained cool, but I felt the opposite. Theo exited the garage, his jaw tight as he carried a brown folder in his tattooed hand.

He spotted me almost immediately and halted. He eyed me, a brow beginning to raise as we stood eyeing each other. All the while I willed the power to lock the door, for if it was discovered unlocked, I would be found out. "What are you up to, little rose?" he asked, now fully facing me, crossing his arms as he waited on my reply.

"Taking a stroll, it becomes quite boring around here," I forced out, feigning displeasure.

Finally, the door clicked as it locked, which I covered with a clearing of my throat, however, Theo's eyes narrowed on the door behind me having heard the click. I forced myself to remain calm, not to show any form of unease. This was Theo, for God's sake… he was a reaper. Chaos Handler. To try to get anything past him was near to impossible.

Finally, his gaze returned to mine, his body tense as he watched me. Cocking his head, he eyed me up and down in a slow calculating manner, seeming to have a change in his thoughts as his body relaxed.

"Pants," he chuckled to himself, causing me to frown in confusion as I looked down at myself, the jeans I wore appearing fine…

"What?" I asked incredulously as he chuckled softly, his thumb now running across his bottom lip before he looked back at me.

"I just remembered how you hated dresses, and I haven't seen you in pants over the years. Now I'm seeing you in pants all the time since arriving here…" He chuckled with a slight shake of his head. He remembered, *that*…?

"What was that?" Kason asked as he entered the hallway from the kitchen, not having heard the conversation but knowing he interrupted what seemed like a casual talk.

"Nothing, Braelyn was just telling me how boring our home is." Theo smirked at me before facing his brother and not mentioning the topic of how he knew more about me than he should.

"What?!" Kason exclaimed, his blue eyes going wide as he clutched at his chest dramatically before smiling mischievously and crossing his arms as he faced me.

"I'd be bored as hell too if I was stuck with this oversized prick." Laughing, he dodged Theo as Theo's hand was aimed for the back of his head, no doubt to wallop his brother.

"Shut up, don't you have somewhere to be? What happened to hacking the security for our next hunt?" Theo gritted out, annoyed with his younger brother.

"All done. I don't know how they think their systems are even safe with the number of walls they have set in place. It was child's play," Kason answered.

I found myself learning more about him from the exchange.

"You hack?" I asked stepping closer and having both siblings face me at the sound of my voice.

"Yeah, anything to do with tech is my specialty. We all have one. I'll show you sometime if you would like?" Kason smiled sweetly at me. His black hair was wavy at the top.

Theo frowned at his brother, his jaw tensing before he eyed me, his eyes dark. Because of what I did not know. He had been fine not even a moment ago.

"I would like that, thank you," I answered Kason with a small smile.

"All right, let's go," Theo grumbled, his deep voice rumbling in irritation as he passed me, grabbing my arm gently as he led me down the hall.

"Good luck, princess!" Kason called after us laughing.

Theo led us to a large sitting room, the French doors opened as they led to the garden outside, followed by the border of the whispering Woods.

"What was that about?" he seethed, his eyes darkened in anger, before going wide and then scrunching in confusion as he stepped back, running a hand through his dark hair.

The amber in his eyes flashed and he dropped his arms, the stoic expression returning as I eyed him confused as to what the hell that had been about.

"What were you up to, I mean," he said, his expression seeming bored.

"I told you," I said, eyeing him with narrowed eyes before it clicked. The ancient power was purring within me.

"Ah, I see now," I murmured.

His eyes blazed and he looked to the woods before he eyed me yet again.

"There is nothing to see. Don't go imagining things, little rose."

Smiling mischievously, I stepped closer, the heat of him and the smell of his scent filling me. He tensed but did not move as I pressed my body against his, tilting my head back to look at him. "Are you sure?" I whispered seductively, running a hand over his chest.

Theo clenched his jaw before looking at the woods and then back to me and stepping back. "Let's go," he said tensely before walking toward the border, the folder still in hand.

Looking back at the manor, I saw that no one was around and jogged after him as he slipped between the trees. Reaching him, I followed at his side, the woods whispering around me as an old friend.

"What specialties do you all have?" I asked, my curiosity piqued after the short exchange with Kason.

"Why do you want to know?" he asked stepping around a large root of a tree.

"Just curious." It would perhaps help in my plan too…

Theo eyed me momentarily before finally answering my question. "Kason is tech, he can hack anything. Layna is a sniper as I'm sure you already figured out. The woman never misses a shot, but don't be fooled, in hand-to-hand, she's as deadly as any of us. Trey is strategy and leadership. Kind of like the commander of the militia, although if you ask me, he acts like he has a stick up his ass half the time carrying on about rules…" He frowned then chuckled softly as we headed deeper into the woods.

It made sense and what he said matched what I could imagine each of them was like so far…

"And what about you?"

Theo stopped in his tracks. He turned, looking at me over his shoulder and his face blank.

"Chaos and Death, little rose," he spoke, the rumble in his voice causing me to freeze before he turned and started forward again.

I watched him go, the danger of him clear for anyone to see. I stood frozen as I eyed him. He disappeared behind a tree before I found myself following.

"Well, that's disappointing," I spoke casually, passing him as I sensed his confusion, smiling internally with smugness.

"Why is that?"

"Because if you are chaos and death, then there is no escaping you, is there?" I sighed dramatically.

Theo chuckled, surprising me but easing my chest a bit.

"No, I guess, there isn't. I wasn't planning on letting you go no matter what anyway," he spoke, murmuring the last part to himself under his breath, my sensitive hearing picking up on it immediately.

Stopping, I turned to face him.

"Why not?" I gritted out, standing my ground. He stopped before me; his eyes startled and confused that I had heard him. Not giving him a chance to question me, I pushed on through. "You hate me, I hate you. So, why not just let me go?" I snapped my agitation directed at myself. If he let me go, I would return to the torturous life on my family's estate, no doubt punished for my failure, but if I stayed, I did not know how I would do what was expected… the power hissed at my thoughts, enraged by the thought of harming Theo. I was angry at myself for my mind battling with what I wanted, what I needed, and what was right.

"I. Do. Not. Know." He seethed stepping closer.

"That makes no sense," I snapped at him, crossing my arms defiantly as I raised my chin. Hecate expected me to seduce him. How in nine hells was I to do that when we could not stand each other? I would start with my plans of seduction, only to always have it backfire on me…

"*You* do not make sense!" he hissed at me, his jaw clenching and fist crumpling the folder he held slightly.

"What the bloody hell does that even mean, Katopodis?!" I seethed, yanking the mask from my face, the coolness of the woods washing over my heated face.

"You make no fucking sense! What are you?! Why was there a hunt order placed against you?!" he yelled, throwing the folder at my feet, its contents spilling across the dirt.

Looking at the papers, I eyed him with narrowed eyes and knelt, picking up pages with what appeared to be details on my family, me… very little about me…

"What is this?" I gritted out, reading the contents. There were pages of my mother, father, and Dorian ranging from photographs, birth certificates, school records, and everything else one could imagine. Even medical histories, including blood types.

"You fucking tell me. Your birth certificate is no longer in existence, there are no records of you whatsoever. Even in our world, that is not fucking normal! The only records of your existence are of mandatory events," he snapped, crossing his arms as he watched me rummaging through the papers.

I paled, realising just how dangerous this had become with Theo digging around. He would get me killed, alongside Dorian and the entire family of both Sarris and Katopodis… himself. I shook the thought of it as they were already targets and pushed against the power that threatened to take over in a fit of rage.

"You went digging into my family?" I gritted out as I stood, my hold on the power thrashing like a manic feral animal against my hold.

"Yes, I did," he answered, his tone stoic as he stood before me, like an arrogant god himself.

"Why?" I pushed out against clenched teeth as I shook my head distractedly, the power threatening to expel itself as my chest rose and fell in short pants. My panic had me sweating, my eyes squeezing shut as I struggled to hold on to the feral ancient power. I had always needed to release its leash intermittently over the years, but for some reason, and a factor I had not taken into account at all when being sent here with Hecate's plan, I had near to no control over it when it came to Theo Katopodis. It would be my downfall. I was sure of it.

"I need to know what happened twelve years ago and whom I am protecting. Why I am protecting you," he finally answered, his voice low.

I felt my hold slipping on the power, but at the sound of his words, I felt it recede, but still simmered beneath the surface as the threat he had posed against Dorian and myself if Hecate found out was too great.

"I need you to go," I whispered in a strained voice, the air buffeting around me in pulses as the power steadily readied to be released.

"No," he said, sounding determined.

It was at that moment that I understood I may not be able to carry out Hecate's instructions of killing him. Something in me snapped and I fell to the ground, all the power receding in a slow slither to the darkest parts of my being. It was then that I almost recoiled at the realisation that the power had not been in a rage against Theo, it had been protecting him, *from me…*

Moments passed by in a tense silence… my laboured breaths rattling between us.

"What happened?" Theo asked, kneeling beside me, his voice tense.

Such a loaded question… a thousand ways to answer…

Looking up at him, I simply shook my head, breathing deeply through my nose as I calmed myself. The papers lay across the ground before us, and he continued watching me. I would have expected him to go running after witnessing me moments ago, or rather apprehend me. He had remained, a look of determination on his face before he sat down beside me on the ground, dusting his tattooed hands across his bent knees. "I know you are different. I'm not a fucking idiot, Braelyn. It takes more than just pretty green eyes and shuddering air to be in this situation… whatever the fuck it is," he spoke, his irritation clear but not directed at me.

Looking at him, I sighed, knowing I wouldn't be able to tell him even if I wanted to. Hecate had been sure to cover her tracks thoroughly. I only had myself to count on… It was physically impossible for me to say or even write down Hecate's name regarding any of this, nor the plans, my training by her.

Nothing.

The sting at the base of my skull from earlier was just a taste of what it would be like if I tried to. My only redeeming feature over the years had been Dorian. I could speak with him on the matter as he had the same wards placed on him regarding speaking of the plans, his familiar involvement allowing us to converse together on the matter. Sighing, my mouth felt dry as I answered him.

"I don't know how to answer you. As for what happened just now, I do not even know what I am." It was the truth.

I had lived my whole life in the dark. Theo placed a hand under my chin, making me look at him.

His eyes scanned mine for what seemed like an eternity before he looked away in thought, then back at me.

"I will find out what I can, even if I must fucking knock some heads in to get the answers. I'll get answers for you, and for me…" he trailed off, dropping his hand and looking to the woods again.

I watched, something twisting in my gut at his determination.

"Why is this so important to you?" I asked, my voice croaking slightly.

He began tossing a dagger in the air, a form of distraction. Up and down, the blade gleamed as the filtered sunlight hit it from above.

"You weren't the only one punished," he mumbled in anger before standing in a rush, dusting the fallen leaves from his pants.

"What?" I asked, confusion covering my features.

"Come on," he mumbled, ignoring me, and outstretching a hand. Looking him over, I finally took it, having him pull me to my feet. "Let's get out of here."

Theo

I had been fucking pissed after traveling to The Agora.

My contact was not the witch that I had seen days ago to sever the Servile bond, but instead Proteus, subject of Poseidon who could grant the wish of knowledge to his captor.

I had managed to capture him years ago, not using my wish for knowledge relating to the past, present, or future.

Instead, I had allowed him to hide in the dark twisted environment of the hidden market, not having to return to the sea.

I had managed to capture him during his afternoon nap in the mountains on a hunt four years ago and had no use of him – until now that was.

I had been more focused on just getting the jobs thrown my way done. However, I had not anticipated being royally fucked over by cashing in my wish for knowledge when he came up empty, using his gifts, or a paper trail.

How the fuck was that even possible? It was like she did not exist…

I returned home when I found her in the hallway. It was obvious she had been sneaking around, the discernible click of the door leading to the armoury confirming my suspicions. How in nine hells she had managed to get in was a mystery, but I found myself impressed.

There would be no way she would be able to make it through the vault door, so I had remained silent, wondering if it was morbid curiosity that led her there, or something else. She was a complete mystery, but I found myself intrigued.

When I had taken her to the woods, it had at first been because something primal in me had almost snapped completely at the thought of her with Kason. It was ridiculous; however, I had no control over it.

When I had allowed her to see the reports, a simple pathetic gesture of all that Proteus was able to provide me with, I had seen something in her snap.

My eyes had blazed amber in recognition of danger before I willed it away without her having noticed. The air had been vibrating in static pulses, buffeting in visible waves, pushing falling leaves in a soft tumble away from her as she had been staring wide-eyed at the papers.

The smell of fear coming from her had my mind clearing as I watched her struggle for control of whatever *it* was, *she* was.

When she had told me to go in desperation, I knew at once that I would never be fucking going anywhere.

And nine hells did it shock and agitate me…

I had also almost admitted to what had happened to me all those years ago. It was then I decided we both needed to clear our heads and ushered her back to the manor, swiftly depositing the paperwork in my bedroom, changing into my casual attire of dark jeans, a black shirt, and my collectible sneakers, and escorting her to the garage.

"Where are we going?" she asked, standing rigid in the garage, that stifling princess aura of hers exuding confidence once more.

"Holy Roller. Now get in, little rose," I said, unlocking the Mustang.

I had originally wanted to take the Ducati but found myself stopping short at the reminder of her mask which would not allow her to wear a helmet. She eyed the open passenger door and then got in, closing the door with a sigh. "What is 'Holy Roller'?" she asked, her seatbelt being fastened as I started the car.

"It's a bar. We usually go there to play pool. The others will no doubt make an appearance," I answered, the garage door opening swiftly as I pulled out and travelled down the driveway, the adamantine gates open and shutting swiftly behind us as we drove down the long twisting road.

Tall trees lined it on either side, the shadow from the surrounding hills now casting sections in darkness as the sun hung low in the afternoon sky.

"You play pool?" she mused sounding as if she did not believe it at all.

"Yeah, you?" I asked, raising a brow at her as she turned to look out at the surrounding area whizzing past us.

I did not receive an answer, only a nonchalant shrug as she bit her bottom lip. The image stirred something in me, and I forced myself to stare ahead at the road as we neared the highway. Cars of all shapes and sizes filled the lanes as we whizzed past. Braelyn was like a child, excitement in her eyes as she took everything in, even opening the window all the way so that the wind blew across her face and neck.

A small smile played across her mouth, and I found myself smiling too.

Realising what I was doing, I cursed myself and refrained from looking at her again.

Pulling to the curb after entering the city, skyscrapers surrounded us.

"Here, put this on," I reached into my pocket, retrieved the bracelet, and handed it to her.

"What is this?"

Perplexed she took it, rolling it between her slender fingers.

"It stops any mortal from seeing who you truly are. They won't see the mask, only what they want to see," I watched her intensely as she eyed it and then me.

The understanding was clear across her features as to how she may appear to someone not of our world. Finally, she wrapped the golden serpent around her wrist. She startled as the golden snake coiled of its own accord, slithering, and wrapping tightly along her wrist and forearm before returning inanimate.

It was a trinket from our family trove passed down for generations.

"A few rules," I started as I turned in my seat. Braelyn turned to me; it was clear she was frowning behind her mask.

"I thought I had left all of that behind," she snapped in anger. I almost cringed as she referred to her life being locked away.

"You did, but while we are here, you need to stay close to me, don't go venturing off with anyone, and for fuck's sake, don't fucking spike my drink again," I growled the last part in the agitation.

I had yet to mention what she had done to me on her father's estate, and it still had me simmering. The anger slipped from her face and was replaced by a mischievous smirk.

"I have no idea what you mean, Katopodis." She then unbuckled herself and exited the car, leaving me scrambling out my side and glaring at her over the roof of the car.

"The fuck you don't. I don't know how you did it yet, but I will."

"There seems to be a lot you don't know." She chuckled at me, making my blood pressure rise before I shut my eyes, forcing myself to calm down.

This woman will be the fucking death of me if I don't kill her first...

Opening my eyes, I looked around and she was gone.

Yep, I will be killing her first.

"Fuuuck," I groaned lowly, slamming my door shut and locking it as I hurried into the Holy Roller, its red neon sign glowing against the city pavement outside.

Entering the doors, the grunge aesthetic met me along with the smell of booze and smoke.

Metalcore played through the surrounding speakers, and it was still fairly empty inside. Only a few people were near the bar and a few more were seated at high tables to the right. I spotted her nearing the pool tables at the back left and began heading over.

The fucking bartender whom I had an itch for ages now to pummel, made the stupid move of heading straight toward her as she examined the pool cues hanging from the wall.

Making swift movement, I reached the back of him and yanked on his leather jacket. He stumbled backward to a halt, my hand still gripping him tightly.

"T… Theo," he stammered.

His lip piercing glowed under the lighting and his brown hair was in desperate need of a wash. *Fuck's sake.* I internally cringed.

"Beat it," I hissed, shoving him off, causing him to stumble, staring at me wide-eyed, only earning a scowl from me.

He eyed me then Braelyn, understanding shining in his eyes. *Good.*

"Just get me the usual. Two of them," I sneered at him before shoving past and heading to the thorn in my ass who was racking up the balls.

"What was that about?" she chuckled, not looking at me as she now lined up her cue.

"Nothing," I muttered, crossing my arms.

"So possessive," she murmured, eyeing me from her lowered head as she bent and lined up her shot. I did not respond as the sight of her bending over the table had my mouth going dry. With a solid hit, the crack of the balls filled the air, pulling me from the thoughts of what I would do to her.

"That is three times in one day. First at breakfast, then in the hallway, and now again. If I did not know better, I would say you like me, Theo Katopodis." She smiled at me sinisterly, leaning a hip against the pool table.

"Do not flatter yourself, little rose. I just do not like sharing what is mine. It has nothing to do with liking you," I said purposefully making myself seem as bored as could be with this situation.

Grabbing a pool cue of my own, I stalked past her, ignoring the stiff way she had stood as I spoke, but quickly recovered herself.

Taking a shot, I sunk the ball and immediately took another shot. I missed, which I never do as the asshole was here with the drinks and smiling at Braelyn.

She smiled back at him, flicking her hair over a shoulder before he departed. I glowered at her and him then back again, still hunched over the table. Braelyn sauntered over placing my whiskey beside me on the pool table's edge.

She leaned over, her mouth brushing against my ear as I tried focusing on the prick across the room, her and controlling myself.

"I wonder if your lies taste as sweet as they smell, Katopodis," she whispered before standing and walking away.

My mouth opened in disbelief at her words. I watched her back in tormented fascination.

Using my own words against me… the shiver that worked its way from the base of my spine had me fighting for control. I quickly covered my expression before she turned, cue now in hand.

"You could always find out," I said standing and smacking her ass harshly as I stepped back from the table and around her.

A small yelp escaped her, and she eyed me for a moment, the memory of this morning and the shower surely running through her mind as it was with mine.

I remained watching her, but I chuckled internally as the bartender had seen me touching her and his face fell. Returning all attention to her, she appeared bored as fuck – an expression I was the master of.

"Huh," she finally shrugged as if the thought bored her, not enticing whatsoever.

What? What?!

I could not stop myself as I pinned her to the wall, her small frame pressing against me in the most torturous manner.

"I told you we were not finished, did I not, little rose?" I asked her, my mouth hovering over hers.

It was the first time I realised that I *hated* the fucking mask she wore. I wanted to see her eyes, see everything.

My eyes flashed amber briefly as the door to the bar opened. Pushing away from her swiftly, I drank from my whiskey as Trey, Layna, and Kason headed our way.

She quickly recovered herself, showing no sign of what had been occurring before my siblings had entered.

"Who's winning?" Layna asked, arriving near us first, followed by Trey and then Kason.

"Who do you think?" I answered behind a sip as I hid the smirk.

"For now," Braelyn answered as she stepped forward, not looking at me. Our word's true meanings were only known between the two of us.

"This should be interesting," Trey spoke up and he grabbed a stool near the corner.

"Twenty on Braelyn," Kason said to Trey, slamming the bill on the high table.

"What the fuck is this?" I snapped frowning at them.

"Sorry T, but my money is on the princess." The traitorous bastard smirked at me.

"Your loss then," I mumbled.

I watched agitatedly as Trey was the only one who bet on me, Layna making herself a traitor too. Taking a sip of whiskey, I did not care. It would be great to see the idiots lose their money.

Braelyn took a shot, sinking a ball with the precision of a pro, each of us stilled as she stood, rounding the table, and lining up her next free shot. I brushed it off as beginner's luck and realised just how wrong I had been.

My siblings were watching with wide eyes and open mouths as shot after shot she sunk her balls. She had not even let me have a chance to defend before she sunk the black ball, officially ending the game in a matter of a minute.

I watched in fascination, my mind calculating how she would be able to do it and what other talents I was unaware of. The others paid up, Kason and Layna erupting into laughter and taunts as Trey eyed me, noting the calculation in my seemingly bored expression.

He was no doubt trying to figure her out, as a blind girl, talented or hyper-aware or not, should not have been capable of playing in the manner she had.

"Care to teach me anything else?" Braelyn said mischievously as she stood before me, cue still in hand.

"You are full of surprises, aren't you?" I spoke in hushed tones as the others began racking up the balls for a new game of their own.

"It would appear so," she shrugged and went over to her whiskey, downing the contents in one go.

I could not keep my eyes off her and noticed her stiffen as the front door of the bar opened, and Ezio stepped inside.

I frowned at his appearance, wanting to beat his face in. Braelyn spun around from her spot across the pool table and her gaze met mine. I noticed the rapid beating of her pulse in her throat, the moisture that gathered near her brow and finally her thumb spinning away at her golden signet ring that sat on her forefinger.

Ezio headed over, having spotted us immediately and the bruises I had left upon his throat from the other night were turning yellow already, having healed slower than what was normal for our family, yet faster than a mortal human.

Why hadn't he healed already?

"Cousins!" he exclaimed excitedly as he entered our corner of the bar, the pool table separating me from him. Taking a sip of my drink, I met eyes with him, the threat in mine, clear.

"Braelyn, how lovely it is to see you again." He turned to her, ignoring what I had instilled whilst pinning him down.

My eyes flashed amber, Trey beside me noticing as I set my whiskey down harshly.

"Don't," was all he said with a shake of his head. Trey knew I could not stand the prick, but he did not know of our altercation on Braelyn's estate or that he had done something to Braelyn in the past.

The thought of me not knowing *what* had me grinding my teeth as I watched him.

"Then I suppose it is only lovely for one of us," she responded, standing her ground.

She very much exuded that fierce princess, and even though she was shorter than him, she appeared larger as she held her ground.

"Now if you will excuse me, I don't intend to hang around the filth in this place," she finished, my siblings sucking in a breath at her words and me grinning like a Cheshire cat.

She was fucking brilliant as she headed toward me. I noticed her still spinning her ring and grabbed her hand as she stopped beside me.

Stroking a thumb over her hand, I handed her my drink, blocking her from everyone's view. "You are okay," I whispered before turning back to the rest of them, Ezio seeming to have his balls kicked in.

"With me," I deadpanned as I stalked past Ezio toward the back exit, my eyes letting the prick know that it wasn't up for debate.

Trey got up to follow, but I quickly shook my head at him.

"You all stay here with Braelyn. I just need to have a little chat," I growled out.

"T, don't do something fucking stupid," Trey spoke quietly as he eyed me then Ezio. Always the fucking diplomat…

"It's just a chat. Relax." I laughed menacingly then glared at Ezio who stood before me. "Outside. Now," I gritted out.

The asshole smirked at me before turning and exiting through the back door, the cool air outside like a balm after the warmth of inside, yet it did nothing to cool the rage within me.

The metal door slammed shut behind me and I ventured further into the alleyway, Ezio remaining where he stood near the door. I paused, my hands in my pockets before I turned and faced him.

"You know, Ezio, I always knew you were a fucking piece of shit, but stupid is a new one…" I gritted out, watching him with a cocked head, my brows furrowed in anger.

"Perhaps I wasn't clear enough the other night," I indicated with a tip of my chin to the bruises on his neck.

Ezio smirked before chuckling and then stepping closer.

"For someone who hates her guts, you are being selfish, cousin. We could share."

The prick didn't even get a chance to finish his sentence as I snapped. My eyes blazing amber, I got to him and felt my fist connecting with his jaw in less than a second.

Bending over, I yanked his shirt up, his head dangling back against the pavement.

"You will not speak about her, go near her…" Hissing I shoved him back, his head slamming to the ground and I kicked down at his shin, the bone snapping audibly.

Ezio groaned, his eyes wide in pain as he watched me turn and walk toward the door. He would heal…. *Unfortunately.*

The fucking prick can count himself lucky I didn't kill him right here. His only saving grace was that Braelyn was inside and I wasn't in the mood for Trey's shit tonight.

"Has she made that soft little moan for you yet?" I froze at the sound of Ezio's pain-filled slightly slurred words.

"What the fuck did you just say?" I turned slowly, my eyes glowing and my muscles trembling as I clenched my fists.

He smirked at me, sitting up on the cold ground. "She does make the most exquisite sounds." He laughed sinisterly, spitting blood to the side.

I started forward, ready to annihilate him when the door to the bar opened, and Kason called out to me.

"Yoh, T." An inhale of breath, then a low whistle. "I don't even want to know what the fuck is going on here, but we need to go. We've got a hunt order."

Breathing deeply, I eyed Ezio who still lay on the ground, blood dribbling down his chin.

"I'll be there in a moment," I sneered back. The sound of keys being pulled from a pocket and thrown to me had me reaching up and grabbing it with my right hand, no need for me to take my glowing eyes from the fucking scum on the ground.

"Now. It's Code Red. We have five minutes tops to get there. Now let's go," Kason called back to me, his voice going serious for once.

I frowned in confusion and looked back at him.

"Code Red?"

"Did I fucking stutter?" Kason frowned at me then left back to the confines of the bar. Looking back, I swore loudly as Ezio was gone, having disappeared into The Shiver.

Swinging my Mustang keys on a finger, I turned and entered the bar, the heat swarming around me and my eyes immediately found Braelyn standing near the front door beside my siblings, waiting for me.

"You will have to come with us," I seethed as I passed them and exited the bar to the busy street.

The others each climbed atop their bikes, the engines roaring to life one after the other as they climbed atop and fastened their helmets.

"Get in, and buckle up," I called out to Braelyn before climbing in the driver's side.

My blood was still an inferno within my veins at the words that spilled from Ezio's mouth. She did as she was instructed, the golden serpent reflecting from the neon light above the bar.

"What is Code Red?" she spoke up as I pulled out of the parking, trailing closely behind my siblings.

We were speeding through the city and finally exited on the highway, heading east at incredible speeds.

"Code Red is ordered to take out one of our own that went against orders. Extermination by any means necessary," I mumbled, a tick working its way into my jaw as I gripped the steering wheel tightly.

"You will need to stay in the car. No fucking exceptions. Do you understand?" I shifted gears and turned to her.

"Okay."

"Good, you shouldn't even be with us, but we don't have the option of taking you home first," I gritted out, changing lanes swiftly and passing cars that seemed to be standing still.

Just then, Trey called through and his voice filled the car.

"We are heading to the shipping yards. The target is Ajax."

"What the fuck do you mean the target is Ajax?!" I could not fucking believe it.

Ajax was Calista's brother and one of the best warriors. His ability for speed made him almost unstoppable.

"We have our orders. You know better than to question them. A Code Red is not taken lightly."

"What the fuck did he do, Trey?"

"You have your orders," Trey's voice carried over the speakers before he ended the call.

"Fuck!" I slammed my fist to the steering wheel and ground my teeth.

"Is he speaking about Ajax Thalassa?" Braelyn spoke up from beside me, now fully facing me.

"Yeah," I sneered, shifting gears, and passing my siblings.

Time seemed to slow down as we passed Trey who led out in front. Our gazes met and I could not hide the scowl on my face before I raced on ahead, the Mustang roaring as I pushed it as hard as it could go. I chanced a glance at Braelyn and was surprised that she seemed comfortable at such speeds and immediately felt my mood darken as the shipping yards came into view.

"This isn't fucking right. Ajax wouldn't go against orders," I mumbled to myself as we neared.

The massive fog lights lit up the area that was covered in darkness, and mist rolled in from the shore.

Shipping containers were lined up and stacked. Some new, some rusted and crimson from age and battling the raging waters and salt-filled air for far too long. Cranes lined the docks, passing cargo to and from ships.

"I've never seen the sea. Well not here anyway… and I've never been close enough to appreciate it," Braelyn whispered before looking down at her hands in her lap.

Her demeanour had been different after Ezio's arrival, and I could pick up on her dark mood at the current situation.

"It's nothing but a bunch of salt-infested water and fucking sand that gets everywhere," I grumbled, unable to help my mood even though some part of me was astounded at how little of the world she had seen.

Coming to a stop a few yards from the entrance, I killed the motor and took in every detail of the shipping yard. I had been here numerous times in the past as this was the same yard that shipments for the gods ventured through.

Weapons, drugs, souls….

All a means to an end for them.

"Remember what I said about staying in the car. Lock the doors and for god's sake, do not do anything fucking stupid to gain anyone's attention. Lay low." I turned to her as the others pulled up silently behind me, their lights and engines already cut off to not gain anyone's attention.

"I know," she spoke, turning to face me and brushing a hand over her arm absentmindedly. Over the Servile brand.

A shiver of pleasure ran through me, almost making me moan. I grabbed her hand, stilling her actions. "Don't. Touch. It." I gritted out as the wave subsided and I could concentrate again.

"What? What do you mean?" she asked confused, looking back and forth between her arm, my hand holding her, and my eyes.

"Just… don't fucking touch it. I don't want to be shot again," I grumbled, unbuckling myself and opening the door. The smell of salt in the air was like a smack in the face, the fine mist of the ocean sticking to my skin.

"You *what?!*" she exclaimed, before quickly covering her mouth with a hand and I was glaring at her.

"I told you to lay low, don't raise your voice smartass. I do not want to be shot again, so just don't fucking touch the mark. It's… distracting." Her hand fell away and her mouth fell open as I closed the door and headed to the trunk, opening it to reveal my weapons and a spare suite of armour.

"What was that about being shot?" Layna spoke up beside me as she reached in for her rifle.

"Nothing, mind your business," I quipped back at her, fastening the woven adamantine jacket across my chest.

"Touché," she mumbled, checking her scope and barrel.

"This doesn't feel right," I spoke to her after grabbing my guns and ammo as I fastened them to my body.

"Yeah, but orders are, orders T. You know that." She sighed, slinging the rifle across a shoulder, and grabbing ammo for herself. "Try not to think of it as our friend. He is a target. If we don't do this, we will be the ones with a Code Red issued. Try to remember that," she spoke softly for just me to hear as Kason and Trey were heading over from scoping the area a bit further up.

"There are two at twelve, four at three, and no sight of Ajax but he is here. It's just a matter of finding him," Trey spoke to us all as he reached into the trunk gabbing his weapons.

I placed my mask over my face, my hood being pulled up as I was shouldering past my brother and stepping onto the road, looking up ahead to the docks when my Chaos Handler gene took over. Erupting into a swarm of ravens, multiple points of view flew through my mind. Every guard, every worker, every god-forsaken puddle was accounted for as my ravens flew like death across the wind, the spray of the ocean covering me. I came to a stop in the yard behind a container and eyed the dock workers and the guards.

They would never know what was about to hit them and it made me sick for the very first time. Something deep in my gut did not agree with this hunt order…

I turned my head as I leaned a shoulder against the container, crossing my arms as I waited. I spotted Trey and Kason entering the yard, each splitting in opposite directions. They went completely unnoticed by the workers and guards. Kason of course had his headphones on. I had asked him once why he did it, but I never received an answer.

I guess we all have our secrets then…

Standing up straight, I rolled my neck as we all got into position. We would wait to hear from Layna, who no doubt would be heading for the top of the uninhabited crane. It would be the best spot.

"Comms check," Trey's voice spilled through my mask.

"Check," came Kason's voice, followed by Layna.

"Theo?" Trey spoke through the comms again, checking if I heard him.

"Fuck off," I grumbled, not in the mood for any of this.

"Guess that means he can hear you," Kason chuckled, his voice crackling through the comms.

A few moments of silence followed where the only sound in the shipping yard was that of the churning sea, gulls flying overhead, workers calling out to each other, and the cranes being operated as they moved cargo to and from the anchored ships.

"I'm in position, ladies. North crane. It appears there is only skeleton staff aboard the vessel and twenty men in total near the bridge. I don't see Ajax anywhere. Give me a moment to scout the area before you have clearance," Layna's voice called over the comms before silence fell again. *"Uh, we may have a problem... Calista is here with Ajax."* Well, this evening just kept getting better. *Fuck!*

"Anyone else?" Trey called over the comms.

"No. No one else I recognise. They are heading to your position. Try to keep this clean. We don't need the entire shipping yard in a blood bath if we can help it. They will be coming in to view in three, two, one.... I have officially lost the visual. Good luck. I'll keep an eye on this side." She finished as we held our position, the carrying voices of Ajax and Calista grew louder as they headed our way.

Shit, Calista and I had been fuck buddies, and we had worked well together and I knew she would fight us to the death for this...

She had already been blowing up my phone incessantly since the weekend after I had bonded with Braelyn and quite effectively avoided her. *"Theo, you take down the target, and we will subdue Calista,"* Trey spoke, having me whip my head in his direction.

"I must take down the target. Why the fuck can't you? Don't have the stomach to take down one of our friends, brother?" I sneered down the comms, my voice rumbling in rage.

I did not receive an answer, only a heavy sigh filled my ears. I looked back at them as they approached where I stood waiting and listened to their conversation.

"None of it makes any sense. I know what I saw, Calli," Ajax spoke to his sister, shoving his mousy-coloured hair back from his forehead, the curls bouncing back up due to the sea spray in the yard.

"You cannot get involved. You know what will happen," Calista whispered back, her head turning back to the cargo being loaded onto the deck of the ship.

"Theo, you need to get to work." Trey sounded agitated over the comms from across the yard.

"And you need to fuck off," I growled back pushing away from the container and stepping out from my spot, directly in their path.

"Theo?" Callista called out as they froze in their tracks.

Ajax had gone a shade pale at the realisation of why I was here.

"What….? No…" Callista struggled with her words as she eyed me and then looked at her brother and then back at me.

"Code Red?" Ajax finally spoke, his nerve regained as he stood to attention, his body tense. I couldn't answer them, thankful for my mask for once in my fucking life. A nod was all I gave him, and his jaw grew tight.

"You cannot be serious!" Callista shouted, stepping forward, and immediately her throwing knife dropped from her wrist to her open palm, the threat clear.

Trey and Kason rounded her from the back which she and Ajax noted with a turn of their heads before they eyed me.

The real threat.

"All of this because of what he saw and…" Callista started but was grabbed by Ajax on the arm as he faced her in earnest.

"Not another word or another Code Red will be issued against you," he spoke with a clenched jaw.

A silent conversation passed between them as they eyed each other, their eyes never leaving the other. Ajax lifted his gaze, finding Trey and Kason behind Callista, and nodded at them before stepping back.

"Ajax!" she screamed, her eyes wide and struggling against their firm hold as they grabbed her.

"Get the fuck off me!" she growled at Trey and Kason before her gaze found mine. "Don't you fucking do this Theo!"

Ajax stepped toward me, his sister still firmly in my brother's grip.

"Take her away where she won't see," he called out, no fear in his voice.

I nodded to Trey and Kason who began hauling her away to a container, her screams beginning to gain the attention of the guards.

"Guys, we have a problem," Layna called over the comms.

Braelyn

I had been sitting in this car for well over twenty minutes and the ancient power within me grew agitated with each passing second.

My mind had been going over the evening's events, getting stuck on the appearance of Ezio and his disgusting words thrown at Theo.

I had been eavesdropping by use of my sensitive hearing and had almost dropped my drink as soon as the words left his mouth.

I would have gladly left Theo to finish the pig off, but the situation changed when Trey received a call from Dante. He had gone stiff, slightly pale before he finished the call and quickly recovered his composure.

His gaze had met mine and I recognised the look.

It was a look of torture, yet having no choice in the matter, simply following orders for fear of the consequences. Kason and Layna were still busy in their pool game, bickering with one another when Trey walked over to them and gained their attention.

I was not paying attention to what was being spoken as I was concentrating on the matter outside of the bar when the two words of Trey's conversation caught my attention.

Code Red.

I now found myself sitting in Theo's Mustang on an empty road with a view of the ocean and shipping yard up ahead.

Something felt off, a sensation I had never quite experienced before. Sitting up straighter in my seat, I peered through the darkness toward the yard and the power within me hissed as it prowled against my bones yet again.

I couldn't see anything that would indicate something was wrong. Absentmindedly, I began spinning my ring, the cold metal smooth against my skin.

The air within the car suddenly began buffeting against the windows, the shockwaves of it audible against the glass.

I shuffled in my seat once more, growing uncomfortable in my skin as the ancient power began prowling and hissing with more hostility.

As soon as I looked back toward the shipping yard, a massive explosion filled the area.

Plumes of smoke and a great wall of fire rose high into the sky, illuminating the docks and the surrounding clouds glowed ominously. I couldn't stop myself as I exited the car, the smell of salt, smoke, and brine filling my lungs.

I didn't think twice as I began running down the road. Beach sand was blowing across its surface from either side. The ancient power within me was roaring in fury as I pushed myself further and harder than ever before, each step thundering in time with my heart; the air buffeting away from my feet sending waves of sand scattering.

I was almost there when I saw a beam of white light shoot up toward the sky before a waxy dome began descending around the yard, becoming invisible after its wake.

I knew once it was down and kissed the ground there would be no getting in.

As I ran, I shadow stalked from one shadow to the next, gaining ground faster than before, and managed to enter the yard just as the shield came down. Pockets of air still puffed out and vibrated around me, the power slithering around my legs and torso as it hissed angrily.

Looking around, I did not spot anyone, only the falling ashes and debris met my sight between the shipping containers.

The source of the explosion from what I could gather was near the dock, the bright glow of flames flickering and reflecting against the metal containers that surrounded the area.

Shouts up ahead of me caught my attention and I entered the shadows, shadow-stalking in bursts of great speed to the source of the sounds. I remained in the shadows, coming up with the sight of a ship that had begun slipping beneath the water, a large part of its hull blown to smithereens.

Burning debris littered the area and what appeared to be workers and guards were scrambling for what to do. I had yet to see any of the Katopodis siblings and the power growled ominously at the thought of not finding Theo.

Deciding that they were not in this vicinity, I shadow stalked around the yard, finally coming across Kason and Trey who were in the middle of a fight with Callista Thalassa.

She fought them vigorously, her skills shining through. It was no secret that she worked alongside the Katopodis Household, her family a step down from them and equally enforcers for the Reapers.

A blur of speed ran past where I had been hiding and was swiftly followed by a swarm of ravens.

Theo.

A lone raven circled back and flew sporadically around where I stood hidden in the shadows before its beady eye turned amber and its gaze met mine. I knew Theo had realised where I was at that moment and was about to say something, that I did not know, but it flew away, disappearing in the direction the others had gone.

The ancient power within me urged my body to follow and before I knew it, I was disappearing in bursts around the yard, trying to get to where Theo was.

Ajax Thalassa was a blur of speed as he raced around the yard, Theo chasing him with his ravens and appearing intermittently to fight him before chasing him down yet again, a massive dark cloud of feathers and eyes following closely behind.

A sound caught my attention near the large yellow crane up ahead of where I stood. Looking up, I spotted a flash of red hair as Layna appeared to be in hand-to-hand combat with a white-robed assailant.

It was impossible to see who the person was. Layna fought her enemies with precision, the fight turning more precarious as they balanced along the yellow bars of the extension arm. A grunt nearby had me whipping my head in the direction of Theo and Ajax.

Theo stood over him, his knife bloody and breathing heavily behind his mask. His gaze met mine and Ajax who now lay across the ground found me too, his eyes somewhat hazy through the pain before he looked back at Theo who still held me to the spot with his amber eyes.

"Don't trust anyone," Ajax sputtered, coughing up blood as he forced himself to sit up.

"I never do," Theo grumbled turning back to Ajax, his voice muffled and even scarier behind his mask.

Ajax was breathing sporadically, the definitive rattle and gurgle of blood filling his lungs and chest sounded off as he pushed himself back against a container, his head slumping to the side and eyes growing heavy.

A large crash of metal sounded off in the distance and had Theo and I both whipping our gazes toward Layna who balanced along the crane's extension arm approximately one hundred and twenty feet in the air.

The robed figure dodged her move and countered with one of their own. Theo and I were a blur of speed as she was thrown from the crane, her slim figure falling, arms and legs flailing as a mass of red hair reflected off the flames of the blown-up hull below.

Ravens erupted and flew toward her, and I shadow-stalked at incredible speeds to reach her.

She was falling faster and faster, not even a scream escaping her. Theo got to her first, his ravens disappearing and converging to a whole as he appeared beneath her, grabbing her to him and holding her close and they both fell, the ground rushing up beneath them.

It was then I realised that he was unable to save her as his ravens could not carry another.

The ancient power in me roared as I rushed to them, its hissing and rumbling deafening in my head.

"No!" I screamed, my throat ripping raw as the strangled cry escaped me.

Time seemed to slow as I entered a shadow and found myself in a place I had yet to ever be.

Darkness surrounded, hissing and roaring filling the space of the great void. Flashes and shivers of shadows in bursts of starlight and cloaked masses race before my eyes.

My hair floated lazily around me, the ancient power roaring louder than ever before the void began rushing around me.

Up ahead, I caught sight of Theo and Layna as they fell, clutching at each other.

I spotted them through a smoky film, their features distorted.

Rushing ahead, I reached for them, slipping forward through the void, and grabbing hold. The salt-tinged wind assaulted me in a great flurry as time once again raced.

Theo's eyes found mine as I grabbed them, my mask having been lost in the dark space I had found myself.

The power latched on to them and in a great burst of power, the air shot out and away from us as we were sucked into the dark space yet again, before landing harshly on the ground beside the Mustang.

We landed in a painful heap beside the road, sand erupted around us before raining down. We breathed heavily, Theo beneath Layna as they clutched to each other, and I rolled away. Shivering uncontrollably in a sharp burst of power.

The beach sand rolled and puffed out before sucking in toward me and then out again. I began counting to ten, trying to regain some control but the ancient power seemed stronger than before and it refused to submit, growling at me as it prowled across my ribs.

I did not notice when Theo and Layna sat up and stared at me wide-eyed, Theo's mask already being removed and thrown down in the sand. I could not stop shivering; my teeth chattered against each other and forced me to bite down.

"Braelyn," Theo whispered, nearing me as Layna was pale and staring at me like I was a ghost.

Oh, I was so much worse…

"Little rose," he said softly, coming into view and grabbing my face softly.

I finally managed to look at him. His eyes glowed amber as he held my gaze, his face showing an emotion I could not decipher. "Theo, what…" Layna started but cut off quickly as he cast her a threatening look.

"Check on Trey and Kason and don't you fucking breathe a word of this," he ordered her. She sat in the sand staring at me in fear before she finally shook her thoughts and grabbed for his mask, placing it over her head, and began calling the others to check-in.

"Little rose." He turned back to me, his thumb swiping in soothing motions across my cheek as he whispered, "You are okay." He spoke tenderly, never letting me go.

I could not tear my gaze from his and felt the power calming.

"Are y… you, okay?" I found myself stammering as the shivers remained but were easing up slightly.

"I am okay, thanks to you," he whispered and pulled me close against his chest and just held me as the shivers continued and the burst of power still stirred the sand around us.

"Theo," I heard Layna call to him.

I pushed away from him as we both turned to face her.

"They are okay, they are cleaning up and heading back here. They don't seem to have seen what happened with… well… shit I don't know what to say," she spoke, scratching her head as she eyed us and settled her blue gaze on me for a moment then back to Theo.

"Get her out of here. They cannot see her eyes."

Panic like never before drowned me as I realised the full impact of what I had done.

Layna now knew my secret and I saved them instead of following through with Hecate's mission.

Oh, gods.

Theo nodded then stood, pulling me up with him as he led me to the passenger side of the Mustang. Opening the door, he helped me in as I struggled with my panic.

Our gazes met yet again, and he squeezed my hand before shutting the door and heading to his sister, who now stood and was dusting sand from her pants.

"You cannot tell them or anyone about her," he started before she turned to him.

"There is a hunt order against her. For years there have been, Theo. You know this and yet you have been keeping her a secret," she snapped at him.

I could see the way he stiffened, his jaw going tight and fists clenching at his side. "However, before you get your panties in a twist… I will keep quiet about everything. But as soon as we are done with this mess here, you have some explaining to do, brother. I will not have you going through what you did twelve years ago. Now go before they get here," she spoke sternly and began heading down the road.

Theo watched her go for a few silent moments before turning back to the car and eyeing me through the windscreen.

"Fuck," he moaned, pinching the bridge of his nose, and exhaling loudly. He dropped his hand and clicked his neck then headed to the driver's side of the car.

"Let's go home, little rose." He sighed as he started the car, its engine roaring to life before he turned and headed back toward the estate.

It was a silent ride and I found myself staring at the shipping yard through the rear-view mirror as it grew smaller in the distance and the waxy dome began to dismantle itself, removing any trace of our being there.

Braelyn

Theo and I sat in silence in the parked Mustang.

We had arrived in the garage of the Katopodis estate about five minutes ago still reeling from what had occurred.

"You will need to shadow-stalk back to my bedroom. Chances are high that my parents are up and about, they may see you if you don't…" he finally spoke, turning his amber-rimmed aqua gaze to mine.

A nod was all I gave him, some of my nerve having returned to me.

I would not appear weak before any of them ever again. My panic earlier had been a mistake. Giving it no further thought nor delay, I vanished into the shadows, heading through the manor and up the stairs.

Theo had been correct. I spotted Dante and Alaia deep in discussion in the kitchen as I passed.

Entering Theo's room, I exited the shadows and removed the wig. Beach sand fell like rain upon the floor as it moved within my grip.

I could feel my skin chaffing as the sand remained stuck in my clothes. Theo had been correct in saying it got everywhere…

The sound of the door opening, and closing had me turning to find Theo entering. His clothes and hair remained covered in sand; a particular clump sat spread across his left cheekbone.

Walking past me, he headed to the bathroom, all the while shaking a hand through his black locks sending sand spraying across the room. The sound of the shower turning on caught my attention.

I headed over to the bathroom and found Theo hunched over the vanity with his head hung low.

He had removed his jacket and shirt, which now lay sprawled across the floor. His tattooed hand gripped tightly at the marble counter; his rings were still covered in what appeared to be blood. Ajax's, I assumed.

His friend he had been ordered to assassinate. "You can shower first," he spoke, his voice deep and rumbling before he lifted his head and his gaze met mine in the mirror.

I had never seen him appear so vulnerable. The toll of the evening, Ezio, Ajax, and his worry for me and his family shone in his eyes.

Without a second thought, I walked over to him, never breaking our gaze. He watched me in silence as I approached him from behind.

I could convince myself that this was me following Hecate's plans of seducing him, but I would be lying to myself.

Reaching him, I held his gaze in the mirror as I wrapped my arms around him and pressed my cheek against his bare back. I could feel the way he stiffened at my touch and was unsure of my embrace.

"I am sorry," I whispered against his skin as I shut my eyes and felt the heat of his back against my chilled cheek.

"What for?" he asked, a tremor working its way through his muscles and his voice sounding deeper than usual.

"For everything." Theo stilled and finally exhaled, allowing himself to relax somewhat in my hold.

He released the vanity with one hand, placing it over the contours of my own as I held his torso. He ran his fingers along mine before weaving them together.

"You have nothing to be sorry for, little rose," he whispered before straightening and turning in my grip so that he leaned against the vanity, my front pressing against his as I continued to hold him in my embrace.

"You have nothing to be sorry for. I should be thanking you for saving my sister. For saving me," he murmured as he lifted my face to his. We stood in silence yet again. The steam of the shower still running began to fill the space. Theo ran a hand softly down the side of my neck, across my collarbone, and then my shoulder and arm before returning to his starting point. A shiver worked its way through me which he noticed, yet this time, he did not smirk or tease me about it, only stared into my eyes intensely, the amber rims of his irises spinning like liquid gold.

Very slowly, he slipped his fingers beneath my shirt, pulling it away from my shoulder before repeating the action on the opposite side. My shoulders lay bare to him, and I bit my lip as he bent forward and kissed across their planes affectionately.

Standing again, he began loosening the buttons that ran down the front. One torturous button at a time, he undid them all before removing my entire shirt. Bending forward again, he kissed across my face softly, hesitating at my temple before dropping his mouth to the base of my throat, a hot sensuous lick causing goosebumps to erupt across my body.

In one swift move, Theo had my bra undone, his fingers trailing down my arms as he pulled the straps down and removed them, letting them fall to the ground. I noticed a flash of pleasure as he trailed his fingers across the Servile brand, his words from earlier making sense.

His own eyes closed momentarily at the sensation of it.

My mind was lost to me, only he and I existed. I ran my fingers across his tattooed skin, the hard planes of his muscles flexing under my touch.

Grabbing a hold of his pants, I began undoing the belt, then his button and zipper, his erection already straining beneath the woven adamantine fabric.

"Stop, you don't have to," he voiced out, sounding strained as he grabbed my hands, halting my progress.

"I want to," I spoke up, peering into his eyes.

I noticed his pupils dilate and he closed them briefly before seemingly reluctantly letting go of my hands.

I watched him as I dropped to my knees, pulling his pants and underwear down in one slow movement, all the way to his ankles. I had yet to look at what had remained hidden, and instead trailed my nails slowly back up his legs, over his calves and his thighs before grabbing a hold of his ass from behind and squeezing it firmly.

Theo sucked in a breath, goosebumps of his own erupted across his bronzed and inked skin.

Finally, I allowed myself to look at what lay before me, and I sucked in a nervous breath at the sight of him.

He was larger than I imagined, the thought both daunting and exciting as he stood to attention.

"You don't..." he began to say but sucked in a haggard breath as I bent forward, licking my way from his base, along the underside to his tip which was already dripping with need. "Fuuuuck," he hissed out, his hands now gripping the marble vanity behind him.

The sight of his reaction spurred me on. Repeating the action, I slipped him entirely into my mouth, the tip of him hitting the back of my throat. Theo tensed and moaned loudly, throwing his head back as he shut his eyes, his knuckles turning white as he gripped the marble.

"Oh gods," he moaned as I began sucking and licking him faster, my hand gripping his ass tightly as I knelt before him.

The tangy saltiness of him filled my mouth, only getting me more aroused. Every moan and tensed muscle of him was a glorious sight.

Swirling my tongue along his shaft as I pulled back, only to suck hard on the tip of him, Theo grabbed my head, forcing me back down, his head still thrown back and eyes shut tightly. I let him fuck my mouth repeatedly. Pushing himself deeper down my throat than I thought possible. His moans grow louder…

Suddenly he stopped, pulling himself slowly from my mouth as he finally looked down at me. His eyes were glowing amber as he then looked from mine to the sight of his cock sliding out of my wet mouth. His grip on my hair tightened as he drew himself out to the tip, my saliva coating him as he then slowly and torturously watched on as he slid it back in, the tip passing my throat and his balls nearing my swollen lips.

He met my gaze again before removing himself completely from my mouth, his mouth hanging open in pleasure before he bit the inside of his bottom lip.

Pulling me to my feet, he kissed me slow and sensually, his mouth and tongue devouring me. Wrapping my arms around his shoulders, and sliding my fingers through his raven hair, I pulled him lower, deepening the kiss. The feel of his wet erection sliding across my bare stomach had me moaning into his mouth. Theo began undoing my pants, dropping swiftly to the ground, and removing them entirely before he stood, his mouth finding mine once more.

The entire bathroom was filled with steam at this point, the shower still running behind us. Theo walked us back to the shower, never breaking the kiss as we stepped over the discarded clothing and banged against the shatterproof glass of the shower door.

Theo reached behind me then and opened the door, the spray of water covering us as he grabbed both sides of my face, kissing me fiercely. He led me to the back wall, the coolness of it like an electric shock through me. Pushing back, I nipped at his lip, causing him to moan.

He gripped my buttocks with both large hands and squeezed as he pressed me firmly against him, rolling his erection against me.

I squeaked as he spun me around, pressing my face against the cool shower wall, his hand on the back of my neck, the other gripping my hip that he pulled back to him, the spray hitting the base of my spine and running down between my spread legs.

"If you want me to stop, you need to say so now, little rose," Theo spoke, his voice hoarse and gravelly as it deepened with his arousal.

"Don't stop," I managed out after a few lungsful of air. "Gods, don't stop."

Theo groaned, his fingers flexing that held my neck and my hip. I almost jumped when he slid his large hand down between my thighs, trailing it back up, finally reaching my aching core. A moan escaped me as he slid his hand over my sex, back and forth, the bundle of nerves screaming for more as pleasurable waves ran through me.

Finally, he slid not one, but two fingers into me, fucking me with his hand while his other still had me pinned by the neck.

"Shit," I moaned through a hiss against the wall. A silent moan had my eyes shutting and my mouth opens in pleasure as suddenly Theo replaced his fingers with his cock. One mighty thrust had me coming undone around him. "Fuck," he moaned, his face pressed into my hair as he stilled. "Fuck, little rose," he growled in agonised bliss.

We both were breathing harshly, and I began moaning along with him as he began rolling his hips behind me, his cock sliding in and out. My walls clenched around him, and the smell of our joined arousal filled the space of the bathroom. In and out he thrust, starting slow but when I felt the first shiver of a second orgasm work through me, Theo began fucking me hard. His grip on my hip and neck was brutal as he thrust in and out of me, pushing and stretching me further than I thought possible.

"Oh, gods," I moaned, just before a wave of the most intense orgasm washed over me.

I felt my body stiffen around his cock, my muscles tensing as he pounded into me. My eyes rolled back as he wrapped his hand around my throat and pulled me back against his chest as he pounded into me from behind, never faltering.

His large hand gripped me, his fingers making their way to my lips.

Riding out my orgasm, I sucked on them, having him moan even louder behind me.

"Gods, little rose. Fuck…" he hissed in between panting breaths.

Reaching behind me with my right arm, I ran my hand up his neck and into his hair at the base.

Grabbing hold, I tugged on it and Theo roared as he buried himself in me. His cum filled me up, his cock twitching within my still-clenching walls.

Theo shuddered as he began rolling his hips slower, riding out mine and his pleasure, pulling every drop of ecstasy from our undoing. Time seemed to slow down where there was nothing else but he and me as one. On and on we moved together, greedy for more of the pleasure the other needed and gave. The water of the shower spray coated us, our skin sliding against each other in perfect harmony…

Slowly he slid in and out of me, both of us moaning softly. He released my hip, grabbing my face with both hands, his fingers slipping from my mouth as he turned my face to the side and up, placing his lips against mine as he kissed me sensually.

The heat of his dripping cum and sliding cock had me gasping in his mouth.

At last, we stood unmoving under the spray. No thrusting, no moans, no need except the soft feel of each other. Slowly he slid himself out from me and turned me in his grip, embracing me as he continued to kiss me. Pulling away for air, we eyed each other, his eyes now back to aqua, yet shining brightly.

Neither of us said a word, only watching the other. Stepping forward, he led me further into the spray of the shower, its water still remarkably hot.

Reaching past me, he grabbed the shower gel and loofa, lathering it up before he began running it across my skin in slow sensual movements. It was a side of him I had never seen.

A gentle side…

He leaned forward as he washed me, laying a soft kiss on my forehead, and lingered there before pulling away. I watched him and lay a kiss on his chest, wrapping my arms around his muscled back as he washed down my spine, his large, tattooed hand holding my hair to the side. "Careful, I might start to think you like me," I said in a contented whisper, enjoying the peace while it lasted.

Theo froze in his movements, his chest rising with a deep intake of breath for he too sighed heavily.

"I think you already know the answer to that, little rose. It's been the same answer for over twelve years," he answered before continuing to wash my body.

"I'll keep your secret if you keep mine…" I teased, kissing his chest once more before stepping back and grabbing the loofah from him. He watched me in silence as I trailed a soapy line down his abdomen, his muscles tensing as I went.

Reaching back up to his shoulder, I began washing it when he surprised me with a sudden kiss that left my toes curling and gasping for breath.

He leaned his forehead against mine, eyeing me through lowered wet lashes as our hair dripped from the spray of the water.

"Deal," he murmured, then kissed me again.

Theo

I lay in bed, Braelyn beside me in the darkness of the early morning hours.

Both of us had been exhausted after the evening's events, not just the most gods mind-blowing sex I have ever had.

Turning in the large bed, I lay on my side, looking at her. Her midnight hair fell in long luxurious waves to her waist, her equally dark, long, and magnificent lashes resting against her skin as she slept.

She was beautiful. There was no denying it.

The more I watched her, the more in awe of her I became.

I could kick myself as I thought over all the years, she had been in plain sight but my anger over the loss of her twelve years ago had me shunning any woman away, fuelling my rage and disgust for the Sarris princess – the princess of the house who most likely issued the hunt order against the girl in the woods all those years ago…

Frowning, I sat up in bed, careful not to wake her.

Why would they issue a hunt order against their daughter? It made no sense.

I was missing pieces of the puzzle that was Braelyn.

Rubbing at my face, my phone vibrated beside the bed. Leaning over, I grabbed it and sighed. I knew this was coming… I just did not want to deal with a new shitstorm so soon.

Careful not to wake Braelyn, I grabbed some sweats and pulled them on, looking back at her one last time before I exited the room and followed the stairs down to the floor below.

Turning left, I ventured down the dark hallway, my hands in my pockets and my bare feet cold against the marble floors.

I passed Trey and Kason's rooms, followed by Layna's, and continued.

No one in this household was allowed to enter any of the other's bedrooms.

The original House Katopodis occupants had ensured that one's personal space remained that way and a haven. The house had been warded so long ago, and with such ancient powerful magic that even if one did try to remove the wards, it would be futile.

Finally, I reached the large Ashwood doors and opened them, revealing the dance studio. All the lights were off, however, the reflection through the floor-to-ceiling windows on the wall of mirrors allowed it to be light enough to spot Layna seated on the floor up ahead. Her gaze watched out of the windows across the woods, seemingly lost in thought.

She did not turn to me as I approached and sat down beside her, my arms hanging over my bent knees.

Silence ensued for a few minutes.

"How long have you known? Who she is?"

Layna finally spoke, her voice drained.

"Since the ceremony," I deadpanned. I could not lie to my sister, not after tonight. Silence followed for a heartbeat before the next question.

"Were you planning on hiding her true identity from us forever?" She finally turned her head looking at me while I contemplated my answer. I wanted to protect Braelyn, but I did not want to alienate my family either. I had also made a promise to her that I would not expose her or betray her… I was a man of many faults, but my word once given would not falter.

"In all honesty, yes, I would have kept her identity a secret from everyone forever. That has changed now considering she revealed herself by saving you and me. You know we both would have died had she not intervened, Layna. Don't fucking forget it," I grumbled, reiterating the fact that we both were only having this conversation because of the woman upstairs.

"Hmm," I received an answer from her as she looked out at the woods again.

"Are you going to say anything?" I asked, needing to know so that I could prepare to get Braelyn the hell away from here if need be. "Layna?" I snapped, facing her fully and my temper rising.

"You know…" she started, her eyes lost in some memory, "I was sixteen when they dragged you away for questioning you about some girl with green eyes. I fought them, and we all did. Even Kason tried and he was only eleven at the time."

"We didn't see you in months. Mom and Dad were beside themselves, unable to go against the gods and goddesses for fear of having you assassinated along with the rest of us. When you eventually arrived home, you refused to speak to anyone, bandages covering every inch of your torso and arms. That light you had burning inside you before they dragged you away was gone," she spoke, her voice solemn and I felt the anger in me disappear.

We had never spoken of how it was back then… each of us moving on, avoiding it altogether, and never bringing it up.

I had not realised or stopped to think that my siblings had fought for me, my parents distraught…

"I do not assume to know what you went through. All I know is that you were never the same… and all for protecting some girl none of us knew…"

I looked away, the memories, the nightmares of what had been done to me by Hades himself flashing across my mind had me clenching my jaw and my skin burning.

"Where is she?" Hades sneered as he stood before me. My thirteen-year-old body dangling from adamantine chains in his interrogation room.

I was in the underworld, the screams, and howls of the forsaken filled the air. Hades growled in annoyance as he stepped closer, his hands setting alight and gripping the chain.

I groaned, clenching my jaw shut as they heated around my wrists and torso.

"You will speak eventually, young Theo Katopodis. Now… tell me everything you know of the girl with the green eyes. You were reported to have been spotted with her in the Whispering Woods. What is her name, and where does she come from? How did you meet?"

I felt my skin burning away for what must have been the twentieth time that day. The smell of my burning flesh filled my lungs as I breathed heavily through it. "Look at me, you insolent child!" Hades snapped, his eyes blazing with the hatred and fire of the underworld.

Lifting my painful and tired neck, I glared at him, not saying a word.

Gods damn me but he could do what he wanted; I would not give up any information on the girl. I did not even know her name.

"Very well, I have other methods to try… Your family possesses a unique healing ability passed down from my blood… which means this will be so much fun for me, you little brat!" Hades snapped in anger, turning to his table of torture devices along the obsidian wall.

I managed to lift my head long enough to witness him reaching for an adamantine blade. The metal is so sharp and thin that it would cut through anything like butter.

My head dropped in exhaustion; my breathing laboured as his booted feet came into view.

"Last chance," he spoke cheerily, before roaring in anger when I defied him yet again with my silence. My head was yanked up harshly by his left hand, his face a hair's width away from mine. "Shall we see what happens when the skin of a Katopodis is peeled away, over and over? Shall we see how far we can push that healing gene?" He did not give me a moment to take in his words before the blade began skinning my torso, the blood dripping and my skin dropping like ribbons to the floor beneath me.

I blacked out after the second strip had been removed, still clenching my jaw, refusing to scream for him… Green eyes and a smile greeted me before flashing away to a memory of the rose etching against the willow tree's bark, and then there was nothing. Only being awoken to further skinning and passing out.

To the blissful sight of her and the rose…

Rubbing at the rose tattoo on my neck, I looked away… the memories haunting me even all these years later.

"Is she worth it, Theo?" Layna finally asked, breaking me from my memories.

I turned and found her watching me, eyeing my tattoos that she knew I had gotten to cover any inch of my body that Hades had defiled…

I had gotten them once I was eighteen, finally ridding myself of the armour and gloves used to hide my sorry state…

"Yes, she is," I finally spoke, determination in my voice as we watched each other.

Layna looked away and then at me again.

"Fine."

"Fine?" I asked, needing clarity.

"Fine. I will not say a word. It is your secret and hers to keep... just be careful, Theo. Please..." she softly spoke as she got up from the ground, holding a handout for me as she did.

Grabbing it, I stood, now much taller than her.

"Thank you."

"Don't thank me, little brother... The decision is yours to make. I just hope you make the right one," she answered, stepping around me, and heading to the door.

"Kason and Trey were asking where you disappeared to. I told them you decided it best to get her out of there after you were done so that she didn't see anything that wasn't necessary." I nodded in understanding, receiving one in return before she exited through the doorway, leaving me alone in the dance studio.

A shiver of pleasure worked its way through me from the Servile brand, causing me to look down at it.

It was a tickling pleasure, not sexual as Braelyn's absentminded caresses had been. I raised my arm and cocked my head in thought as I watched the brand twist and change along my skin, black roses sprouting along the thorny vines before it settled, covering a great portion of my tattoos.

Flexing my hand, then my elbow, I eyed it in contemplation, not entirely sure what it meant... Perhaps because we had sex? No, that couldn't be right... other brands from past Servile pairings would have changed over the years. Flashes of images bombarded me, making me flinch.

Braelyn's voice, though younger, called out for help, sobbing before being washed over by gurgled water...

"Braelyn!" I hissed, immediately running for the door.

My heart was beating rapidly in my chest as I rounded up the stairs to my bedroom, finding her tossing and turning in her sleep.

Images of her nightmare, or rather memories bombarded me, causing me to shake my head to stay focused on the present.

Rapid pulses of vibrating air shuddered along the silk sheets as I neared.

"Braelyn!" I hissed, climbing atop her, and pinning her down as she thrashed. "Little rose! Shit..." I called again. It was useless...

I froze and looked around as a rumbling growl sounded in my room, followed by a hiss. My eyes flashed amber and I found no source for it, other than the woman beneath me.

"Braelyn," I whispered, my mind torn between her mind, my own, and whatever the fuck she was.

Out of ideas, I grabbed her face, pushing my lips to hers hoping to the gods it worked.

Slowly, the images faded from my mind completely and she calmed. Pulling away, I watched as she blinked slowly, coming to… "Theo?"

I sighed in relief as she said my name; a small part of me was relieved it was my actual name too… not back to Katopodis or asshole.

"You were having a nightmare," I mumbled, still looking down at her naked form beneath me. "Of the well…" I added after she remained silent.

At the sound of my words, her brow scrunched together in confusion before she met my gaze again.

"How did you know it was of the well?"

"I saw it," I gritted out, my muscles still tense in anger at what I had seen.

"What?" she snapped sounding agitated, sitting up in a rush, causing me to shuffle back. The sheet dropped to her waist, leaving her bare. "What in nine hells do you mean you saw it?" She was frowning at me, waiting for an answer.

"The Servile brand changed, I assume it was because of that," I grumbled, trying my hardest to not stare at her naked form.

It was fucking useless…

Braelyn lifted her arm, inspecting her brand, turning it this way and that, noticing the roses that had appeared.

"Why?" she asked, sounding unsure of herself before she looked to me, catching me sitting across her legs, arms folded, and head cocked as I ogled her.

"Fucking concentrate, Katopodis. It's not like you haven't seen me naked before. Gods," she snapped.

Hissing at me and smacking my arm. Hard. Fuck the woman was strong.

"They are a god-damned sight to behold though…" I replied, my eyes still glued to her perk breasts.

"Prick," she seethed, placing a flattened hand across my forehead and shoving me off her as she stood, the sheet dropping and revealing her completely.

Rolling over on the bed, elbows bent, I placed my fist against my jaw as I watched her go.

"You fucking like my prick, darling!" I called after her and chuckled as I dodged one of my sneakers being thrown my way at lightning speed.

"Don't flatter yourself," she called back from the closet.

"Don't fuck with my shoes!" I called back to her as another shoe narrowly missed the side of my head and bounced off the window behind me. *This fucking woman and my god-damned shoes!*

Another shoe came barrelling from the closet, airborne like a missile.

I watched in horror as one of my most expensive shoes flew past me and disappeared from the view out of the window and fell into the courtyard, landing with a splash of apocalyptic proportions within the fishpond.

"You fucking brat!" I roared, my eyes flashing amber as I stormed into the closet, finding it empty.

"You can't just hide in the shadows forever, little rose!" I sneered, taking in my closet.

"Oh gods," I whispered horrified, finding my sneakers' laces all tied together in the most horrendous knots I had ever seen in my life.

A giggle sounded behind me, causing me to turn, and found the culprit lounging across the bed grinning at me. She was dressed in nothing but her underwear, golden mask in hand.

"Oops," she grinned, her eyes taking in my tatted body. "Although, I will say, my plan on getting you where I wanted to be worked wonderfully. The view is spectacular from over here, Katopodis."

My mind blanked. My fucking mind was left speechless by the audacity of this woman… "Cat got your tongue, Katopodis?" she grinned sinisterly at me, making a show of her eyes brazenly fucking me where I stood.

My blood heated and I found myself reaching her in seconds, pinning her beneath me on the bed.

"That's more like it," she whispered, biting her bottom lip and grinning as my hands gripped her wrists above her head.

"Stop fucking with my shoes," I hissed, my body pressed down on hers making my train of thought hazy.

"And whom the fuck taught you to tie knots?" I frowned at her.

"I was hoping you would," she said, pushing forward and licking up the side of my neck.

My eyes shut at the feel of her, and it was only then that the true meaning of her words sunk in. *Holy fuck!*

My eyes snapped open, and I found her grinning at me yet again.

"Who would have known that the little Sarris princess had a naughty side." I grinned back at her mischievously.

I held back a moan as she wrapped her silky legs around my hips, rolling and grinding slowly into me before sliding her foot down my calf and back up.

Slamming my mouth to hers, I began meeting her rolling hips with mine, the friction of my sweatpants against her getting me hard faster than what should have been possible.

Braelyn gasped, allowing my tongue access to her mouth.

She tasted sweet, and sinful as she met me stroke for stroke. My hands holding her wrists grew tight before I slid my palms over hers, over fingers interlocking and holding on tight.

"I need all of you," I whispered against her swollen lips, both of us panting and the smell of our arousal floated around the room in an intoxicating waltz.

"So, take what you need, for I too need all of you," she whispered back.

Our eyes locked in silence as the implications of both our words sunk in, neither of us had expected it as our eyes watched on in anxious revelry…

Slower this time, I leaned over her, my lips touching hers softly before I kissed her deeply and sensually, the inferno in my blood blazing still.

She kissed me back tenderly, her head tipping back into the bed as it grew in intensity. She squeezed harshly on my hands before releasing her hold on me, only to wrap her arms around me, forcing me down against her chest while she embraced me completely, every part of her intertwined with my body.

She moaned as I bit down on her lip, harsher than I intended and the taste of blood filled our mouths. I was high on her if such a thing was possible.

I was taken off guard as she rolled us over, her strength once again catching me off guard.

Before I knew it, I found myself being the one pinned to the bed.

Gripping her hips, I slid my fingers under the band of her underwear while she sat up. I watched in heated gaze as she reached behind her slowly and unclasped her bra, the lace falling loose around her shoulder and voluptuous breasts. She watched me in return as she slowly slid one arm from her bra, then the other, letting it fall in a delicate heap against my abs.

"What," I started to ask when she reached to the side of us, almost getting off me completely.

I immediately shut my mouth when I saw what she held in her hands. It was her golden blind mask. She bent over me, her naked breasts pressing against my chest as she kissed me deeply, sliding the mask over the top of my head, leaving it covering my forehead, my ink black locks standing in a disarray.

Fuck me…

My aching cock throbbed beneath her as the implications of her actions had my body singing.

Leaning back and breaking our kiss once more, she grabbed my hands from her hips, keeping my fingers locked around the band as she went on bent knees and then stood, forcing me to slide her underwear off completely.

The smell of her arousal hit me full force and I bit my lip at the sight and smell of her. Climbing atop me once more, she proceeded to grip my sweatpants, hauling them down and off, resulting in my erection springing to attention, pre cum already dripping from its head.

"Oh fuck," I moaned, shutting my eyes as she licked its dewy substance away before straddling me yet again.

"Place your hands behind my back," she instructed in a sultry voice, leaving no room for argument…

Doing as instructed, she rolled her dripping sex slowly across my cock as she grabbed the forgotten bra from my abdomen and reached behind her back, wrapping my hands in a tight grip, and knotting it.

She continued to roll her hips, sliding up and down my cock. Both of us moaned in pleasure as I watched her eyes close and her head tip back as she gripped my fastened wrists behind her.

Gods, I needed to bury myself inside her.

She released my wrists, leaving them tied behind her and resting on the curve of her ass as she bent over and kissed me hard. I wanted more as she pulled back but found myself in the dark as she pulled the golden mask down and over my eyes.

"Fuck," I hissed as she rolled her wet sex against my cock, the feeling intensified by my loss of sight.

I moaned loudly as she started kissing, licking, and nipping her way down my throat, paying special attention to my nipples as she went lower.

Groaning, I squeezed my arms around her in a rush, my wrists still bound behind her back, and bucked, effectively lifting her. She squealed startled and immediately replaced it with a loud moan as I dragged her over me, holding her in place above my face as I began devouring her.

Her hands gripped at my hair, the tug of it stinging as she began riding my mouth. She was heavenly as she moaned and dripped over me. I paid special attention to her bundle of nerves before shoving my tongue as deep as I could inside of her.

"Oh shit!" she moaned breathlessly, and I felt her quivering over me, her thighs squeezing the sides of my face.

I knew she was about to come undone, and halted my actions, earning a few curse words. "Fucking beg," I seethed beneath her, the taste and smell of her having me struggle for control.

"Fuck you!" she hissed, trying to move her hips, seeking the pleasure I granted her.

"I said, fucking beg, you spoiled brat who keeps fucking up my shoes!" I reiterated with a gruff voice before biting at the inside of her thigh. I could not see a thing as I remained blinded and bound, but I could only imagine the glare I was receiving.

"Ah, fuck!" I yelled as she yanked harshly on my hair, trying to angle my face to her core. Pulling my head away, I broke free of the bra holding me and flipped her over, myself being on top and resting between her open thighs.

Using my now free hands, I gripped her thigh harshly and used my other to lift the mask. "I said, fucking beg me."

"And I said fuck you! I will not beg you, Katopodis!" she seethed, cheeks flushed and breathing heavily.

"We will see," I smirked, leaning forward and running my tongue up her dripping slit.

She moaned loudly, her back arching as she shut her eyes. Repeating the action a few times, I had her a moaning mess beneath me and when I inserted two fingers within her, I knew she was close.

I halted yet again and removed them, sitting back on my haunches as I grinned at her. She punched down at the mattress and roared in agitation before glaring at me.

Still grinning, I made a show of licking my fingers still coated in her arousal.

"You know what you need to do," I smirked.

Big mistake...

My eyes went wide as she glared at me then slowly began smirking at me in return.

My mouth fell as she lay back down, spreading her legs wider and leaving every inch of her on full display before me. My smirk completely disappeared as she ran her hands sensually across her breasts, pinching the nipples and arching her back in pleasure. Her hand then slipped down her toned stomach and slid between her legs, sliding up and down.

Breathy moans left her lips and had me reaching for my cock.

Fuck… I watched her as she pleasured herself, her fingers playing with her clit and covered in her juices. I couldn't stop myself as I watched on in absolute awe and arousal, stroking my cock in time with her hand.

When she inserted her fingers and arched, moaning loudly, I snapped.

"Don't you fucking dare!" I seethed against her mouth after grabbing her legs and dragging her beneath me.

Her hands were now being held at her sides. I slammed my mouth to hers at the same time I slammed my cock inside her.

Both of us moaned loudly as I began fucking her hard, the bed rocking beneath us. My blood boiled with the need for her, and her wet, silky pussy gripped me hard.

"Shit," she hissed against my mouth as I fucked her into oblivion.

"Only *my* mouth, *my* hands," I growled against her lips, "and only *my* cock," I slammed balls deep into her proving my point as she moaned loudly, "will make you come! *Only me*!" I growled out, pressing down on her firmly, the sound of our bodies filling the space as I continued.

I felt her tensing beneath me, her mouth opened in a silent moan, eyes squeezed shut as she came hard.

Her walls gripped my cock like a vice grip, almost sending me over the edge too.

I gritted my teeth before kissing her, shoving my tongue in her mouth and never slowing down in my thrusts.

She kissed me back hard, each of us starving for the other. Pulling back, I pulled her up with me, before turning her around roughly on the bed, slamming my cock back inside her as she lay face down on the mattress.

"Hold the headboard," I grumbled, my body filled with a fever for her.

She did as she was told, grabbing the bars that lay just within reach. Grabbing the back of her neck and her hip, I began thrusting harder than before.

I closed my eyes in ecstasy as she came a second and third time, her grip on the bars white-knuckled.

Looking down, I watched as her ass bounced and my cock disappeared within her only to pull back out, gleaming with her slick arousal.

"You are mine," I growled out, straining to last just a bit longer until I had proven my point. "Say it," I added, still pounding inside her.

"Fuck you," she growled back, sounding breathless as she finished and I felt her begin to tighten around me yet again.

Slowing, I repeated myself.

"Fucking say it, little rose."

Soft moans of pleasure and need filled the room from her as I denied her so close to the edge.

Slowing my thrusts down, even more, she turned and eyed me, her face flushed and gleaming with a sheen of sweat. I glared right back at her, almost coming to a stop as I waited. My balls and cock protesting me.

"I'm yours," she finally said, her voice shaky.

"You're mine," I added right after, a smirk playing on my lips as I immediately began thrusting hard, going balls deep yet again.

I felt her clench around me before she moaned loudly, her body pulling taut as wave after wave of pleasure washed over her. I felt my balls tighten, the familiar tightening and heat in my abdomen and base of my spine, and moaned loudly as I came inside her, my hot come filling her up.

I thrusted inside her deeply, burying myself to the hilt before I collapsed atop her. Both of us breathed heavily, moaning softly as the aftershocks of our orgasm still pulled at us.

Nuzzling into the back of her neck, I breathed in deeply, the smell of her sweet scent filling my lungs.

Placing a tender kiss against her skin, she sighed in contentment beneath me. Reaching out beside us, I intertwined my tattooed fingers between hers, having her squeeze me back.

We lay like that in silence for a while before I finally pulled out of her and rolled to the side. We watched each other, our hands still locked together as I pulled the sheet up and over us, pulling her close and wrapping an arm around her.

"What?" I asked, my voice hoarse as she smiled at me in amusement, her green eyes shining.

"Never took you as a cuddler is all," she whispered back, smiling wide now.

"Oh, shut up, before I change my mind," I grumbled.

In all honesty, I had never been a cuddler, but here the fuck I was, cuddling.

Fucking pathetic, Katopodis… what next? Some gallant gesture? Fuck's sake…

The things this woman was doing to me. We lay in silence, both of us drifting off to sleep when my eyes snapped open and narrowed on her.

I lay glaring at her, causing her to sense it and open her eyes confused and frowning at me. "What is it?" she asked with a yawn.

"You owe me some new fucking shoes… again."

I seethed in anger.

She eyed me wide-eyed before erupting into a fit of laughter, the sound carrying around the room.

"I am fucking serious. Do you even know how much those cost me?"

"You have fifty more. More than most women." She giggled, kissing my cheek, and then snuggling down to sleep, completely ignoring me.

Sighing in agitation, I glared at her one more time before going to sleep.

Fucking hells…

Braelyn

Hurrying down the steps toward the ground floor, I slipped into the shadows as the voices of Theo and his siblings carried through from the courtyard just outside.

The door opened, with Theo who entered the manor followed closely by his siblings who were laughing at him.

"Fuck's sake, I am going to wring her little neck!" he growled out, shaking water from his shoe that had ended up in the pond outside.

He froze, turning his head, his eyes glowing amber and his sight landed directly on the spot in which I stood…

He shook it away quickly, his eyes returning to normal before his brothers and sister noticed. I grinned at myself, the thought of last night heating my body in the most delicious ways.

After we had fallen asleep, we had awoken for more rounds of pleasure, both of us insatiable, devouring each other's bodies until the sun had risen into the sky.

My body was certainly feeling the effects of it all. My muscles were stiff and aching, bite marks and bruises covering my inner thighs, breasts, neck, and most of my skin. Theo wasn't fairing much better.

I had managed a particularly noticeable mark on his neck. The sound that had erupted from him in ecstasy had me almost orgasming as he pulled me impossibly closer as my mouth latched on to the spot…

We had been overcome by an almost animalistic need for one another, lost in a haze of lust, need, and claiming each other. It had been the oddest thing; the need to *claim*...

I grinned as I noticed the mark on his neck as they continued down the hallway, Theo shaking out his shoe the entire way, pond water dripping across the marble floors.

He was dressed in his armour this morning; the only one it seemed...

Strange...

I had awoken to him gone from the bedroom. His entire shoe collection of valuable sneakers had been removed from the bedroom in their entirety...

And I knew for a fact that it was in their entirety, as I had checked... there was not even a single shoe that remained.

I chuckled at his paranoia as I had gotten dressed. He had left a note on the desk saying he had meetings to get to and would see me after or perhaps in between.

I watched as they rounded a corner, disappearing. Stepping from the shadows, I looked around the hallway, and the courtyard before me.

Sunlight filtered through the leaves of the tree, creating a glittering effect across the surface of the pond.

"Kason!" I heard Theo roaring from the room they were in down the hall.

"Chill dude! I was just asking if she would."

"Don't even fucking think of it!" Theo roared again before Kason came running from the room and straight past me down the hallway in a full sprint.

"Hello princess!" he winked as he passed me. A swarm of ravens burst from the room and raced after Kason, passing me like a black cloud of death. Kason as well as Theo knocked over numerous priceless antiques as they went, chaos erupting everywhere.

I stood in horror as I heard a crash down the hall and Kason swearing.

"They will be okay, it's nothing new," Trey spoke, causing me to turn back around to find him as well as Layna standing outside the study's door down the hall.

"Uh, what are they fighting about?" I asked, chancing a look back at where they had gone as more crashing, and curses sounded out.

"You."

"Excuse me?" I asked perplexed.

"It appears that Kason wanted to show you how he does his tech side of things today, but Theo isn't going to be here, so…" he drifted off, eyeing the end of the hall as Kason slid across the marble floors, within view for a second before disappearing around another corner.

Theo followed him, his anger clear with each calculated step before he too disappeared.

"He appears extremely territorial over you… I wonder why that is?" Trey asked, ever sounding the bored diplomat as he turned his gaze back to mine.

"Trey, quit it. You know Theo has always been… um… extra," Layna piped in, scowling down the hallway as an extremely feminine high pitch squeal sounded out before silence filled the manor at last.

"Pay up," Layna spoke to Trey as she sighed, leaning against the doorframe, her hand outstretched toward Trey.

"Nine hells, how do you always know? You are going to bankrupt me," Trey groaned as he dug in his pocket, handing a wad of cash over to Layna.

"Who do you think taught him the ball twist?" she said casually pocketing her wad of a small fortune.

Ball twist?

Just then realisation dawned on me of what had occurred as Kason came limping around the corner, head hung low as he gripped his groin, Theo following closely behind, no injury in sight. *Oh!*

Ohhhh… so the squeal had been… Kason….

Gods…

"Don't tell me you were an idiot betting against me again?" Theo grumbled as he stopped before me, facing Trey.

Kason was an odd shade of pale as I watched him limp away toward the pond. He stopped beside it, glaring daggers at Theo before unceremoniously falling back into the water, sighing as the water covered his groin.

"Bit dramatic, don't you think?" Theo called to Kason through the open doorway which led outside.

"Fuck off… Let's see how you feel after having your ball sack almost twisted right off. Asshole…" Kason grumbled, rubbing his pants.

"I may enjoy it," Theo smirked at me, causing Layna and Trey to fake gag.

"Right, that's enough testosterone for me. I'll see you guys later," Layna said, pushing away from the doorframe and heading toward the garage.

"I've got shit to do too… I'll see you later," Trey spoke to Theo, only glancing at me where I stood beside his brother before he too ventured down the hallway.

Theo and I stood in silence watching Kason wincing in the pond.

"Did you need to do that? All he wanted to do was show me…"

"Yes, I did," he grumbled, pulling me along with him toward the stairs.

"But why?" I asked, not letting him just shove aside the fact he basically castrated his brother a moment ago.

"As I have said before, little rose, I am very touchy over what's mine."

"Oh, that is utter bullshit Katopodis," I scoffed at him.

I found myself facing his amber eyes that blazed as he whirled around and frowned at me.

"So, we are back to Katopodis now? What is next? Prick? Asshole, God Killer?" he whispered, stepping toward me, causing me to step back.

"I was going to go with dickhead but those would do too." I smirked up at him.

Theo blinked at me a few times before he burst out laughing, his eyes returning to amber-rimmed aqua.

"Gods, that fucking mind of yours…" he whispered against my mouth, grabbing my hips as he stepped between my legs. "So fucking brilliant…" he murmured before kissing me deeply.

A small whine escaped me as he pulled away, smiling at me.

It was a rare sight to see Theo Katopodis smiling and it caused a strange stirring in my gut. The giddiness disappeared and was replaced by a sickening twist as I watched him…

I had allowed myself to become distracted.

Hecate…

I quickly recovered myself, smiling sweetly once more before he noticed. It was too late as he frowned slightly before recovering himself but saying nothing.

"I must go to the underworld. Hayden has some shit I am supposed to collect because of the Servile. I shouldn't be gone long," he spoke, his thumbs caressing just under the hem of my shirt where he gripped my hips.

"Do not get up to shit while I am gone," he said, his voice taking on a serious tone as he eyed me.

"Me? Never…" I winked at him, eyeing his mouth.

"Your name should be shit-stirrer…" he sighed. "I'm serious, Braelyn, don't get up to shit while I am gone."

"I will be perfectly fine. Stop worrying. We hate each other, remember? You would be so lucky for something to happen to me," I spoke teasingly, stepping away from his grip and angling to head down the hall toward the kitchen.

Theo grabbed my hand, halting me in my tracks. He eyed me in silence, his gaze calculating as it usually was.

"Don't fucking trust anyone," he whispered before dropping my hand and turning on his heel.

I stood and watched him go, the threatening aura of the man filling the enormous manor.

I should not trust anyone. Including his family?

I certainly had not planned to, however, he did not feel I should either, and had me re-evaluating a few things mentally.

One last glance as he rounded a corner, and I was on my way to the kitchen. The smell of something delicious had my mouth watering the closer I got. The sound of humming filled the air, followed by the distinct sizzle of something being sautéed.

Entering the kitchen, I found Alaia hovering near the massive eight-burner stove.

It appeared the humming I had heard was from her. It was easy to discern that she indeed was blessed with a beautiful voice.

"Good morning, sweetheart." She smiled at me, her blue eyes shining brightly against the red of her hair.

"Good morning," I answered, being sure to shield myself from her empathetic power.

"Help yourself to anything in the fridge. I'm almost done with an omelette. Would you like one?"

I still found myself confused by the fact she always seemed to be cooking.

"Yes please," I answered, grabbing a seat on the island.

Alaia returned to the stove, frying onions and peppers.

"Where are all your staff?" I asked, immediately cursing at myself for having the thought slip from my mouth.

"We don't keep any, dear. We find the privacy much better… I'll also let you in on a little secret." She smiled mischievously, now turning to me and leaning her elbows on the counter as she eyed me.

"I enjoy cooking far too much to allow someone else to do it for me. As for the rest of the manor… well having four children and a husband comes in handy. No laziness in this house is allowed. They may hate me for it, but I consider it part of a different form of training… discipline and respect. Not all training needs to be centred around combat and strategy." She winked at me and then turned back to the stove. I gaped at her, looking around the great expanse of the manor and finding it difficult to believe they maintained it all themselves.

Where in nine hells did they find the time?

"Dante takes me on a date twice a week which lasts a few hours. He thinks I don't know it, but he gets a gardening and cleaning crew in while we are out." She scoffed as she flipped an omelette.

"He should be here soon to take me out." She chuckled, plating up the most delicious-smelling omelette I had ever smelt in my twenty-five years of life.

I found myself confused as she slid the plate before me and began cleaning up near the stove. Craning my neck, I looked around and did not find her plate of food.

"Are you not going to eat?" I asked perplexed as she had been cooking before I entered.

"No, sweetheart. That is for you. Theo asked me earlier to make you something to eat while he is out. Now eat up." She smiled, squeezing my shoulder as she passed, continuing her path as she cleaned the kitchen around me.

I watched on as she wiped at the counters, storing ingredients away and depositing the cut-offs in a concealed recycling bin near the sink.

I almost groaned loudly as the first bite of food filled my mouth.

Gods the woman knew how to cook.

I had not realised just how hungry I was until I began devouring the omelette. I murmured a thank you behind a hand-covered mouth as Alaia sat a large glass of orange juice beside me just as Theo's siblings entered the kitchen.

Trey was dressed in smart-casual attire, clearly heading off somewhere that dictated a slightly more formal attire, yet not too stuffy. Layna was dressed in a gorgeous green summer dress that complimented her red hair beautifully.

"Where the fuck are you going?" Trey scowled at his sister as he opened the fridge grabbing a bottle of water.

"Trey, your god-damned language!" Alaia hissed.

Trey cocked an eyebrow at her as he took a sip of water.

"You are one to speak, Mom. Great example there…" he scoffed amused.

I found myself grinning as Alaia's wide eyes were covered as she held her forehead in frustration murmuring, "This family…"

"You look beautiful," Alaia finally said to Layna as she dropped her hand and recovered herself.

"Who are you going to see?" Trey asked once more, scowling at her this time.

"None of your fucking business," she hissed right back at him, snatching his bottle of water and downing it in one go.

"I'm going to be late. Call me if you need me!" she called back as she exited and disappeared from the kitchen.

"My water," Trey moaned as he watched her go. He ducked a second later, the empty water bottle hurtling through the air toward where his head had been a moment ago. I could not help my laughter as he flipped her off and it reminded me of throwing shoes at Theo.

I immediately felt a blush covering my cheeks and tried focusing on my food once more.

"Ow, shit!" Trey cursed. Alaia picked up the bottle and whacked the back of his head with it.

"No trash. Now throw it away and leave your sister alone. Gods, you are all in your twenties and still need scolding," Alaia grumbled, smacking the bottle against his chest, and holding it there.

Trey still rubbing his head grabbed it from her and sidestepped to the trash, effectively throwing it away.

"Where is Kason?" Alaia asked, rummaging through the fridge.

"In his room. I think he will be there all day. He needs to hack a site today and Theo almost ripped his balls from his body." Alaia froze at Trey's words, her arm still stretched into the fridge gripping the cheese.

Shaking her head, she sighed. "I don't even want to know what it was this time."

Trey finally acknowledged me seated at the kitchen island and eyed me before turning back to his mother.

"I need to go," he spoke softly as he leaned down and kissed her forehead and left the kitchen too.

I was watching him go and making a mental note to keep my guard around him. The way he watched me was unsettling.

It was a look of suspicion.

"Well, now that you know what a bunch of hooligans you are stuck with, I will say goodbye too. Dante should be getting back soon, and I need to get ready for our date." She smiled sweetly at me before exiting the kitchen.

I sat in silence, my omelette finished and my orange juice before me. It appeared everyone would be busy today, leaving me with the perfect opportunity to do some snooping.

I needed to find a way into the armoury…

I focused my hearing as I closed my eyes behind the mask. The typing of a keyboard and music through headphones upstairs from what I assumed to be Kason.

The sound of a Ducati starting up, heavy-footed feet balancing the bike before kicking up the kickstand and leaving the garage – Trey.

There was no sound indicating Layna, who had already left. The sound of a large vehicle entering the garage before being cut off and the sound of the door opening before once more masculine feet walked across the marble floors, met by smaller footsteps.

"Hello," Alaia's friendly voice spoke to Dante in the garage.

The soft shuffles of clothing as they embraced. "Where are the kids?" Dante's gravelly voice asked.

"Out. Kason is home with Braelyn. She will be okay."

"Hmmm," Dante hummed in response as the sound of him opening the car door sounded yet again, this time, from the other side.

"What is it?" Alaia asked concerned.

Silence followed, my heart beating faster as I waited on his response. Finally, he responded. His words cut me in an unusual way than expected.

"I asked Mathias if he or Kaisley would like to see her, and he refused… I just do not understand how they could be so cold to their daughter. He made a strange comment that Braelyn needed to remain focused," he grumbled, his agitation at my family clear.

"Dante," Alaia sighed before continuing, "You have enough stress with the issue of the hijacked shipments and now the attackers last night that intercepted the kids. All these meetings… Calm your heart for the girl. If they will not be a family to her, then she most certainly has gained one in us."

"It is not proper to abandon your child." Dante hissed.

"My dear I agree, but we cannot start an argument with the house we have had issues with in the past. Leave it. We will make sure she is taken after. I am sure Theo will too…" A scoff from Dante.

"That one of ours is as stubborn as you."

"Exactly why I have faith in him," Alaia said, the smile clear in her voice.

I felt my chest tighten at their words and stopped listening in on their conversation. The ancient power in me that had been unusually dormant this morning slithered awake at the sound of their words, its growling vibrating against my ribs.

Taking a deep breath, I spun my ring in contemplation. I found myself staring at the Servile brand across my hand and forearm. The black roses and vines seemed to hum with the ancient power's prowess.

I tried to wrap my mind around the past day's events. The brand change was a surprise to both Theo and me as we did not know of it happening before. Theo had seen visions of my nightmare as soon as it had transformed, leaving me highly uncomfortable at what else he may discover.

Hecate's plans…

I sucked in a deep breath, shaking my head as I reminded myself of needing to get done with my mission. The longer I took, the greater the consequences. Then there was the greatest mystery of it all…

Last night when I had entered the shadows to reach Theo and Layna, I had entered a place I had never been before.

Time had seemed to slow down, the great void dark and lit with iridescent starlight, growls, and flickering shadows that prowled just out of sight…

Where had I gone? Where had I stepped into? It also should have been impossible to take anyone with me. The realisation had hit me this morning, having me shaking in anxiousness. In my desperation, I had not stopped to think.

No one has ever been able to travel through shadows unless holding the ability themselves; should not have been able to be dragged from one spot to another. The more I thought about it, the further I paled as to the reality that both Theo and Layna should be dead, even if I had reached them.

It hit me like a punch to the gut.

Shaking myself from my thoughts, I regained myself, downing my orange juice and pushing away from the kitchen island. A quick check confirmed that it was indeed just Kason and I at the manor.

Kason remained upstairs in his room, music blaring and typing away furiously at his keyboard.

Checking through the bond, I found the link between myself and Theo a somewhat fragile band being stretched far in all directions; the bond was not capable of reaching as far as it needed to whilst he was in the underworld, a different plane of existence. It reminded me of a cell phone with very little signal, only the barest amount yet still utterly useless at getting through to another line.

Shadow-stalking, I found myself upstairs within the confines of Theo's bedroom. Looking around, I tried to decide where to find the key to the armoury. Surely, he would have a key… each of the siblings should as they would need access to its locked confines often.

Sighing, I allowed the ancient power a bit of room, still holding tightly to its invisible leash as it growled and snapped, stretching in the air around me.

The air was buffeting, sending the sheets rippling and papers across the desk fluttering intermittently.

"Find the key," I spoke to it, spoke to myself.

It was odd, as I had never done so. I had always known it as being me, yet somewhat separate… My eyes widened as the ancient power began slithering around my body, tendrils of its influence reaching out across the room in miniature vibrations as it searched, recoiling as a viper before searching in another direction, its hold on my being pulling tight, my chest heaving forward.

Soft buffeting sounded against the windows as it expanded in its search for the key. My heart jackhammered in my chest that perhaps I had made an incredible mistake by letting it go within the confines of the bedroom… allowing it to roam with so little space with Kason nearby was risky.

Willing it back, I received a hiss in reply as it focused on a spot in the closet near the floor. Using all my strangled willpower; I pulled on its force, whimpering in exhaustion as it pounded and circled on the floor.

I was startled as I was yanked forward by its invisible force, my eyes wide before it growled, returning to me in agitation, growling as it circled me, slithering across my bones once more.

I eye the spot in the closet and caught my breath before shadow stalking directly to the spot the ancient power had been drawn to.

I knelt on the hardwood floor inside the closet, shoving boxes aside.

Picking up a box filled with board games, I rose an eyebrow in disbelief that Theo of all people owned such a thing and shook my head incredulously as I placed it to the side.

Running my hand over the floor, I could not see nor feel anything and groaned in frustration.

As I knelt and examined the floor, the familiar burn at the base of my skull beneath my hair had me wincing.

"Braelyn," Hecate's voice filled my head as I breathed heavily through my nose, ignoring her as I searched.

Pain lashed through my head, causing me to muffle a scream with my hand.

"You will answer me!" Hecate screamed through my mind.

"Yes, Hecate," I hissed right back, struggling to catch my breath. The ancient power roared and growled, its maw snapping at Hecate's intrusion.

"Have you located the Heart of Ouranos?" Steadying my breathing, I focused on my answer.

"I have not. I have located the armoury and am in search of a way inside, which is taking me longer than expected," I replied, my fingers gripping my hair.

The sting of her magic burned across my scalp. I gritted my teeth in fury as a surge of pain scored its way through my mind due to her anger.

"Have you managed to win him over?"

Gritting my teeth in disgust, I looked back to the bedroom, to the bed… "Yes," I murmured.

"Good. Remember child, beauty may be dangerous, but intelligence is lethal… I am growing impatient, complete your task before I send someone to do your job for you," she snapped in anger before vanishing from my mind, the sting leaving and having me sigh as I closed my eyes.

"Bitch," I hissed under my breath kicking at the box of board games.

The contents splayed across the floor, having me grind my teeth in agitation.

Reaching over, I began gathering the mess of tokens, figurines, and fake money. I paused as a deck of cards I recognised lay on the floor before me.

Lifting them, I found them to be the exact deck that Theo and I had been playing with on that final day in the woods.

Shoving them into the box, I lifted a sheet of instructions and froze as something gleamed, sticking out from under another board.

Shoving the box and boards aside, I reached for the item. Holding the metallic object up, I sighed in relief as the key now lay within my grasp.

The adamantine key appeared as a nine-pointed star, a serpent coiled in its centre and a long chain attached.

Slipping the chain over my head, I hid the key beneath my shirt as I gathered up the mess I had created, moving the boxes back into position.

Standing and checking everything again, I backtracked to the bedroom.

Stopping as I reached the edge of the bed, images of last night ran through my mind and steeled my nerve of completing *my* mission as soon as possible.

Listening for Kason, he was still in his room, working away at whatever hack he had been instructed to complete.

Exiting the room, I shadow stalked to the ground floor, the locked door to the armoury before me. Exiting a shadow, I held my hand before the lock, willing the ancient power to aid me as it had the previous occasion, I had found myself standing in this very spot.

I sighed in relief when a small buffet of vibrating air encircled the handle, reaching within the lock, its vibrations causing the slightest rattle.

Finally, the lock clicked as the power receded, its curiosity slithering along my limbs and the item inside calling to me, its power pulling me nearby. Listening for Kason and anyone else, I opened the door, shutting it quietly behind me. Darkness engulfed me, and the stale damp smell of the ancient staircase filled the air.

My eyes adjusted immediately behind my golden mask, allowing me to see once more.

Stepping forward, I made my way down the spiralling steps. The stonework was smooth beneath my feet. Lastly, I reached the circular antechamber.

The ancient murals depict the clash of the titans humming with influence. I dared not to touch the wall again as the memory of the ice-cold bite against my skin and up my arm had me recoiling from the sight of it altogether.

Turning toward the colossal door to the armoury, I reached within my shirt, gathering the star-shaped key that was the size of my palm. I eyed the door, then turned and eyed the antechamber calculatedly. I checked for any triggers or traps that may spring once opened and found none.

Touching the door gingerly, vibrations pulsed through my hand and the door causing me to recoil.

The power within me stilled, seemingly watching on in curious tentativeness.

Toying with the key and eyeing the lock, I placed it in the centre of the door. A snap of power hummed to life from the adamantine door, causing goosebumps to rise across my skin.

Inhaling and holding nervous breath, I stepped forward once more and turned it. I stepped back, the power within me hissing and snarling as it slithered around my limbs. The vine-like bars across the door began to twist and slide away with a groan.

I watched in trepidation as they, at last, slid from view and the door clicked open. Looking back to the stairs one last time, I turned and entered the armoury.

The cavern-like structure loomed before me. Artefacts from the age of the gods' first roaming the earth filled the space, weapons of every manner, and artworks lined the walls and tables within. Columns rose high to the rock ceiling, seemingly carved right from the hillside itself.

Stepping forward, slowly placing one foot before the other, I looked on in awe at the sight before me.

Gods'...

My family had nothing in comparison to House Katopodis. How they worked as enforcers for the other houses, namely House Sarris was beyond me.

Removing my mask as I eyed the artefacts, the cooled air from being beneath the earth relaxed me. The ancient power slithered around me, seemingly calming too.

"Oh gods, how…" I started under my breath as I looked around, having no idea how I was to find what it was I needed.

Eyeing the items stored around the great room, I noticed that they seemed somewhat organised. Weapons filled a large majority of the space to the left, tables down the centre holding ancient artefacts. The back wall was stacked with original ancient artworks and the to the right, trunks lined the stone wall.

I could cross off the left side of the room then. Stepping forward, mask in hand, I walked down the centre alongside the tables of artefacts.

Jewels, vases, and a hodgepodge of trinkets covered the space.

I halted as I eyed the golden serpent Theo had given me yesterday when we had gone to Holy Roller. Guilt kicked me in the gut, and I forced myself on. Nearing the rear, I had still not found what I was looking for.

Heading back up an aisle, the armoury door up ahead, I began opening trunks, frowning as tomes and books were all that I discovered within.

Shutting the lid of a trunk, I cursed under my breath, spinning on the spot. It had to be here somewhere.

No other house had been recorded as having it. It was why I had been reading over the books from my family's library at home regarding artefacts…

Rubbing at my eyes in frustration, I then opened the lid to another trunk finding yet more books. Slamming the lid closed, my finger caught on a splinter, the sting causing me to rear back. "Shit," I hissed, examining my finger.

The small piece of wood stuck in the tip. Grabbing a hold of it, I gingerly pulled it out, relief filling me as the sting dissipated.

Blood pooled on the tip as I eyed the piece of damned wood and dripped to the ground before I inserted it in my mouth. Chucking the splinter aside, the ancient power in me snarled, its attention on the floor at my feet.

Looking down, I watched with a frown as the drop of blood began sliding along the floor, almost marble in shape.

I followed in confusion and trepidation as it disappeared beneath the tables of artefacts and trinkets. Bending down, I watched it continue rolling, exiting the aisle on the other side.

Dropping to the floor, I rolled under the table, coming up on the other side, just in time to see the ball of blood enter a stack of weapons and ammo. Frowning, I ignored the grumbling of the ancient power within me as I drew near.

The pulsing energy of that ancient force's call slammed into me as it had when I first arrived on the estate.

My eyes widened in the realisation that what I sought was here, its draw calling to me yet again.

Shoving ammo and weapons aside, I noticed an adamantine box near the rear, purposefully hidden from sight.

Smiling in relief, I reached for the box, the surface cool and smooth against my fingertips. Reaching further to grip it better, my cheek pressed against the hilt of a sword, its metal biting against my skin.

My outstretched fingers, at last, gripped the box. Holding tight, I reared back, my cheek imprinted with the hilt of the sword as I eyed the box.

A trail of blood ran along the side, still wet. Wiping it with a thumb, it smeared across the surface. It appeared my drop of blood had vanished within the box, slithering through the hinged gap, so small that it would be impossible for anything else to get in.

Stepping to the table behind me, I set it down, shoving aside a vase from the early seventh-century BC.

The time of Homer…

Kneeling to be at eye level with the box, no larger than an ordinary shoebox, I held it with both hands, my fingers flowing over the intricate designs that embellished its smooth reflective surface. Frowning in frustration, I cursed under my breath as I stood, flipping the box this way and that.

I could not seem to open it.

Gods'…

Setting it down, I took a step away, my hands on my hips as I contemplated how to open it.

I could not be sure if it was indeed what I needed and would need to hurry up so that I would not be caught… growling in frustration, the ancient power within me had gone incredibly still, its attention on the box and the force within that called out as a siren's call.

I knew in my gut that what I sought lay within, however, I needed to be sure, god-dammit! "Open it," I whispered to the ancient power within me, hoping that it would respond as it had twice this morning… Nothing.

Grabbing the box, I spun on my heel eyeing the rows and rows of weapons. Throwing knives, daggers, swords… even maces and whips lined the space.

Each was as deadly as the last. Eyeing a slender dagger, I placed the box on a rack of ammo and reached for it. The ancient power within me suddenly roared, catching me off guard as a swift wind appeared behind me, and pain scorched across the back of my head, having me fall against the stored weapons.

Pushing myself aside, dazed and confused, I looked up at my attacker.

"Ezio," I reared back, eyeing the box on the shelf and my mask beneath the table behind him.

"Hello love," he sneered at me, lunging forward. Eyes wide, I vanished into the shadows, reappearing behind him, near the table.

Roaring and growling pounded in my head as I grabbed the closest thing to me and smashed it against his head.

The ancient vase shattered to pieces. Ezio spun around, breathing heavily as we scowled at one another.

Oh, gods, I did not have my mask on, and my eyes were on full display. I felt the warm ripple of blood from where he had hit me at the back of my head as it dripped down my neck.

"I see you still like it rough," he sneered, causing my anger to spike and the air began vibrating around me in pulses visible to the naked eye.

"That's a new trick," he smiled sinisterly at me before vanishing within The Shiver.

The ancient power within me was hyper-focused as it sent its senses out all around me.

Tendrils of its influence arced around me. Ezio appeared, only to reappear in different areas around the armoury.

Taunting me.

Eyeing the sword that was just within reach to my right, I snapped my attention back to him as he appeared a few feet before me.

"I must say, the green eyes are a lovely surprise too. So much prettier to see up close, instead of imaging behind whispered words and secret distances." My stomach dropped.

Someone had been speaking to him, revealing my secret.

Not waiting a minute longer, I kicked him in the gut, sending him backward with a heavy groan. Grabbing the sword to my right, then the box, I shadow stalked to the door.

Facing Ezio, he roared in anger as he vanished within The Shiver once more.

Shit, shit, shit…

Removing the key from the door, I watched in a panted breath as the doors began to shut, Ezio still nowhere to be seen.

A stirring of air to my left had me spinning around, the heavy sword sweeping out. Ezio's figure appeared for a moment before disappearing once more.

Blood droplets against the stone floor were the sole evidence of where he had stood a moment ago.

Running, I jumped through the shadows up the staircase, my heart beating against my chest. Slamming against the door to the manor, I tumbled forward before righting myself, the box tucked tightly against my side, the sword firmly grasped within my right hand.

Warm blood still dripped down my neck, and my head pounding in pain.

"What the…" Kason began, standing frozen down the hallway, a sandwich hovering before his mouth as he looked at me wide-eyed.

I watched as his shocked eyes took in my bleeding head, the box, and sword, and finally my eyes…

The sandwich dropped to the floor as a barely audible word escaped his mouth. "You?"

I did not have time to respond as the air to my right shifted, the ancient power within me sensing the opening of The Shiver. Dropping low, I spun, sweeping my legs out, effectively knocking Ezio's legs out from under him as he appeared. I, unfortunately, dropped the armoury key, leaving it lying across the marble floor.

Looking back at Kason, I vanished in the shadows, sprinting and jumping in a great burst from one shadow to the next as I headed toward the Whispering Woods.

I had no idea where I should go, but anywhere away from the manor seemed appropriate.

I had just burst through the French doors and made it across the expansive lawn where Theo had led me before our walk to the woods and was knocked over by an incredible force.

Rolling across the grass, the box slipped from my hand, tumbling down the slightly sloped embankment toward the tree line.

Ezio rolled, pulling himself to a stop as we eyed each other yet again.

Pulling myself up into a crouch, sword in hand, and at the ready, I chanced a look to the side, wanting to see where the box had gone and Ezio lunged.

Dropping, I rolled down the embankment, him following closely behind.

Digging my fingers into the soft ground, I pulled myself to a stop, swinging the sword in a wide arc and Ezio narrowly missed its blade.

Just then Kason appeared through the doors, his face still in shock as he looked between me and Ezio.

"What the fuck is going on?!" Kason roared at us, his attention now focusing on his cousin.

I did notice however the glances I was receiving as if I were a fabled creature.

"Apologies, little cousin, but I need her," Ezio snapped, lunging for me yet again.

I tried to get away, however, I was too slow. Ezio grabbed my ankle, yanking me back and beneath him, and visions of the past almost paralyzed me in fear.

The ancient power within me hissed, the air vibrating around me, the leaves across the lawn rustling as pulse after pulse, its anger grew.

Ezio pressed down on me, Kason running toward us, words being shouted at his cousin as we struggled in bruising grip with one another. Time seemed to slow down as I struggled, bucking in panic, images of a living nightmare drowning me.

Hands groped harder.
Hands covered my screaming mouth as I screamed for it to stop.
The betrayal. The disgust.

I managed to rip my arms free, punching him in the face, followed by an elbow to the throat.

Ezio fell back, his hands gripping his face and coughing on strangled breath.

I scrambled to get away, managing to get to my feet, my blond wig falling to the ground just as Kason reached us.

Our eyes met.

Kason slid across the grass, his arms grabbing a hold of me just a moment too late…

Ezio roared in fury, lunging for me, and winds swept around us before darkness and shadows swallowed us whole.

The Shiver embraced us.

Theo

Arriving on the banks of the joining of the Acheron and Styx, I scowled at the barren landscape.

My ravens allowed me to travel to the underworld, unlike other demigods or mortals.

Only the gods and goddesses could enter the underworld at will, however, all of us needed an invitation or the arrival would be impossible.

The smell of the underworld assaulted my senses, causing my agitation to grow.

It was astonishing how smells could bring you right back to a memory.

However, my memories of the underworld would much rather be fucking forgotten.

Scowling, I looked around.

Charon was supposed to have been ferrying me across the great river as my ravens would take me no further, the rules of the underworld forbidding it.

Crossing my arms and clenching my jaw, I looked around. Hayden appeared to have been doing a good job of tidying up the place. It was beginning to appear as it should have been all along.

There in the distance stood the palace across the great lava lake and volcanic fields.

Just beyond it, the area for the souls of the redeemed.

I still doubted there was such a thing as anyone good, but even so, they were housed for eternity in the glades.

To my right, darkness swept over the land, the pits of Tartarus housing the Titans in the furthest, deepest, and darkest part of the realm. Evildoers were housed nearby, yet far enough that they would never reach another cell.

Each mortal, demi-god, and elf had a selected area within the underworld, appropriate to the standings of their soul.

"Fuck's sake," I growled as I looked around, wanting to get this over with as I had been having a nagging feeling all morning that something was amiss.

Looking up at the sky, I was greeted by an endless view of stars.

Sighing, I turned my attention back to the river, Charon coming into view.

Dropping my arms, I waited as he brought his boat alongside the shore, his hooded figure remaining silent.

"Took you long enough," I snapped at him, climbing aboard, and having the boat rock with my added weight.

The water of the river rippled, and my only reply was a gruff huff as he pushed away from the banks.

"Here," I spoke, digging a chocolate bar from my pocket and handing it over.

Charon snatched it, his lithe fingers, pale and almost translucent peeking from his robed figure before the bar vanished into a pocket.

I discovered years ago that he had a particular taste for chocolate, and it had been our form of currency ever since. We continued in silence, both of us preferring it that way.

After a few minutes of floating along the river, Charon led us under a bridge leading to the palace, the boat drifting silently to the hidden chamber beneath. Pulling alongside the obsidian wall, I nodded at him and climbed out, the boat rocking as I went.

Steps led ahead, sconces covering the walls, lighting them in a soft glow. Following them up two at a time, I reached the guarded entrance to the palace.

The higher demons eyed me coldly as I stood before them. I grinned at them, knowing they hated my fucking guts.

"He is expecting me." I smiled cockily, my eyes widening to indicate they moved the fuck out of my way.

They ignored me, having me sigh.

"All right then. I see we are still not over the whole *I killed your brother* bullshit…" They eyed each other before staring dead ahead, still ignoring me.

Frowning as I did had not the time for this, I shoved them out of the way roughly. I ducked as the one swung his mace near my head, grabbing the pole firmly in my grip.

I shoved it back, knocking the wind from him before spinning and knocking them both out with the blunt end of the pole.

"Pathetic," I grumbled, chucking the mace away and stepping over them. Shoving the doors aside, I halted as Hayden stood a few feet away, arms folded and eyeing me with a raised brow. "You need better security," I waved him off, approaching him.

"Exactly why I had those two there. They have been giving me issues. I knew you would take care of them for me," he smirked wickedly.

"I'm not here to sort out your staff, *my lord*," I frowned at him, emphasising my sarcasm.

"Oh, I know," Hayden spoke, his words edged with double meaning. "Follow me," he mumbled, turning, and walking ahead.

I watched him go, blowing out an irked breath as I shoved my hands into my pockets and followed at a casual pace behind him. We walked along the great halls.

The obsidian walls rose to cathedral heights, sculptures of the history of the gods and goddesses, creatures of long ago peering down at any passer-by. Starlight appeared to hover within the palace, illuminating the ceiling in specks of silver and frosted orbs.

"It's just in here," Hayden called back, him eyeing me over his shoulder.

I followed him inside the room. It was a lavish space, the ceilings equally as high as the hallways. A fireplace lined the wall, large enough to house an elephant, and a long dining table, with enough seats to host all the gods and goddesses at any single time.

Chandeliers hung from the ceiling, gold and flaming as they added lighting to the items strewn across the surface of the table.

"How the fuck am I supposed to get all of this back?" I asked in an irked huff, raising an eyebrow at the number of items.

"Watch your tone," Hayden snapped, his eyes flashing crimson before dying back down with a quick shake of his head.

Eyeing him calculatedly, I finally asked what was at the tip of my tongue, not giving two shits if he took offense.

"How's the head doing?" I indicated with two fingers at my forehead before pocketing my hand once more. "Apollo mentioned that it's been taking you some adjustments since your… return."

More like fucking resurrection…

He was silent for a moment, a distant look in his gaze. No doubt of the life he left behind… his twin and mate. Being stuck in limbo for just over two years would surely have done the job of loosening a few fucking screws.

"Apollo speaks too much for his good sometimes," Hayden mumbled, crossing his arms as he eyed the table, lost in thought. "But he does speak the truth and is fair… so I guess he was right. It's been an adjustment," he finished looking at me then at my arm, and frowning.

Looking at my arm, I frowned at him, "What?" I sneered; the Servile brand was still locked in by his multi-toned gaze.

"When did you get that?" he asked dropping his arms and standing straight.

"At the Servile a few days ago."

"But the black roses…" he trailed off.

"Only appeared last night. What the fuck is the issue?" I snapped, my gaze noticing every detail of his anxiousness and foreboding.

"I've read about it before," he said, starting for the door in a hurry.

Scowling, I charged after him, our footsteps thunderous down the great halls. He was a blur of speed as he rounded corner after corner, me following behind with a furious gait. I knew the brand was unusual, however, his reaction had me in a foul mood.

Entering a library, Hayden went over to a large desk, papers and books were strewn haphazardly across the space. Ancient maps lay open across the floor.

"Been a bit busy I see…" I scowled at the mess, sidestepping a rather large map.

Looking down near my feet, it appeared to be a section of the underworld I was not accustomed to.

Hayden shuffled papers and books.

"Where the fuck did I put it?" he mumbled, shoving aside a rather heavy tome. "Old habit," he grumbled as I raised an eye at his choice of words…

Perhaps we would have gotten on better before he become the king of the damned… although I doubted it.

I couldn't fucking stand most people.

"Here," he pulled out an ancient piece of parchment, reading it over silently before spinning it to face me across the desk.

Eyeing him suspiciously, I placed a finger on it, dragging it nearer, and then peered down at it.

The words were written in ancient Greek, yet perfectly decipherable…

As soon as wolves roar and ravens flee
A betrayal brings to life a new life
There comes a day when what is green turns to moonlight
A creeper of shadows
Manipulator
A man clad in crimson, born of emerald sight
Shall bring forth the overthrowing of royalty
As soon as the blind man sees once more,
Siblings bring forth the clash of Titans
It shall be on the day that the true one reveals herself,
The two-faced one brings forth an almighty darkness
Upon the day the water rises to the sky, the guilty shall reap
Once stars fall from the sky, a surrender awakens the downfall of an empire
When the moment comes that the wolves howl together,
The young one shall cause the rise of what was forgotten
The black rose and thorn shall conquer.

I read over the words numerous times, my heart beating faster as some of the words made sense. I was sure to conceal any thoughts I had on the matter, my casual aloofness never faltering.

"An old piece of parchment with the mention of a black rose is what has your panties in a twist? I think you need to get out more," I grumbled, eyeing the paper, forcing it to memory, and shoving it back toward him.

"There has never been a changing Servile brand. I know because I've been stuck in here for weeks going over every single fucking part of the way things run. You know it too," he snapped at me, heading over to a large bookshelf that rose high along the ceiling.

"There was a hunt order attached to it. A hunt order that your family has been assigned to and has yet to complete," he grabbed a large book, opened it to the correct page, and slammed it before me.

"Your point?" I asked, feigning boredom and not daring to look at the hunt order before me.

"That was twelve years ago... the same time there are records of you being here for months. Why were you here, Theo?" he growled the words, his eyes flashing crimson before dying back down.

"You need to get out more." I chuckled sinisterly, turning to leave.

"Don't fucking take me as a fool just because I haven't been here all my life! I know and have seen more than you would care to even know! So, get back here, you aren't going anywhere!" Hayden snapped, the doors to the library slamming shut in my face.

Clenching my jaw, and closing my eyes, I sighed. My anger flared and I smiled sinisterly and turned to face him, my eyes glowing amber. "You must have the wish to die a second time." I sneered, neither of us breaking eye contact.

"Oh, fuck off," he scoffed, returning to his gathered documents and back to his old habit of cursing...

"Open the door, Hayden," I grumbled, my jaw clenched.

"No," he ignored me, not even looking in my direction.

"Open the fucking door!" I roared, my feet moving toward him with purpose now, eyes blazing amber.

"It's her, isn't it?" he asked casually, not bothered in the slightest by my threatening demeanour.

I froze, unable to believe the situation I found myself in.

"It is her, isn't it? Braelyn, right? She is the one they were after?" He now sat and eyed me with a raised brow.

Fuck...

I'm going to have to kill another god...

"Sit down and stop glaring at me. As you said... I have died before, remember?" He scoffed. "Sit," he added more firmly as I remained standing.

Grinding my teeth, I stepped forward, grabbing a chair across from him and dragging it with a loud groan across the obsidian floor before falling heavily upon it, my legs open wide, and arms crossed.

"What do you want?" I hissed, my eyes still glowing.

Hayden watched me, his gaze was far too all-knowing. He leaned back in his chair, scratching at his jaw as he eyed the papers and then my arm.

"I've had my fair share of prophecies as you well know." He started then looked away, crossing his arms.

"Your point?" I asked, not knowing where this would be going.

"I lost everything. My mate, my twin brother, my life as I knew it... all because of the will of the gods and goddesses," The way he spoke was almost blasphemous and dripping with venom. Considering he was now one of them astounded me.

"So what I want is for you to have the pieces you need, figure it out, and fucking do with your life as you dictate," he spoke firmly, his eyes flashing crimson flames and holding my own where I sat.

I could not fucking believe it.

"Why?" I asked in an agitated grumble, my scowl still in place. For all I knew, this could be a trap...

"Because fuck The Fates... that is why. I do not need to give you any further reasoning. Do with the information what you wish. I have enough going on with fixing the mess Hades left behind and trying to locate Persephone. I do not know what it all means, the words far too cryptic and my patience too thin, but I am sure a Chaos Handler like yourself can figure it out." He smirked at me.

I eyed him suspiciously and he sighed.

Standing from the desk, the doors opened by his will alone, allowing me to leave.

"I am not one of them," he murmured, stepping past me toward the door. "I will have the cache delivered to your manor. I am sure your hands will be full enough with what's truly important," he called out as he exited and left me alone in the library.

"Fuck," I hissed out, rubbing my eyes in frustration.

Lifting my head, I looked across the desk.

The prophecy as well as the hunt order lay before me. Running my hand through my black hair, I reached for the prophecy, reading it over one more time before pocketing it. Next, I pulled the large tome toward me, reading over every detail of the hunt order.

It appeared there was an anonymous tip of me being sighted with the girl with green eyes in the woods twelve years ago. Mathias had issued the hunt order to my family, and immediate apprehension or assassination if necessary was listed.

Why the fuck would he do that? Order such a thing against his daughter? And who had been the witness?

I was back to square one about the order, however, I now held in my possession the prophecy that started it all.

Shoving the tome back after ripping the page away and pocketing it too, I stood and headed for the door. I headed down the twisting colossal hallways, Hayden nowhere to be seen, and exited to the antechamber.

Charon was waiting in his boat, the water lapping against the obsidian enclosure. The guards remained unconscious. I had done more damage than necessary and shrugged indifference as I stepped over them and down the steps.

Hopping over the wall to the boat below, I stood, finding my balance easily as it rocked back and forth. The sound of the side knocking the wall and water splashing as it lapped against its surface filled the enclosed space.

Charon paid no mind to my rough entrance, barely showing any movement as he remained standing, his ore still firmly in hand. Sitting down across the ancient wooden seat as before, Charon started forward, the glow of the underworld greeting us as we exited from under the bridge.

Staring ahead, I found myself grinding my teeth in frustration over all that I had learned.

Hayden's willingness to hand over the prophecy and hunt order had my mind reeling. I had never stopped to think that perhaps he would hold some grudge against what was done to him…

I rested my elbows across my knees as we continued down the river and checked the bond. I could not locate Braelyn and it had my mood darkening. I had guessed it would happen as I was in the underworld, however, the nagging feeling of something being wrong had me flipping my dagger back and forth as we continued our way.

Charon reached the shoreline where I was to exit the boat and I paid him no mind as I got up and leaped to the sand-encrusted bank. He continued his way, not hesitating for a second.

Sheathing my dagger, my eyes blazed amber just before I erupted into a swarm of ravens, their wings flapping in a cacophony of chaos before spiralling high into the sky. The starlight greeted me as I pushed on forward, higher, and higher. Faster.

A swirling vortex of shadows opened before me. Not slowing down I erupted through it, the setting sun greeting me above the Whispering Woods. I had been longer than expected… the time moving differently within the underworld. What should have been an hour, maybe two over here had now been multiple hours due to my delay in the library with Hayden.

Flying on ahead, my ravens swooped low and twirled as they entered through my bedroom window.

Swarming into a tight mass before I found myself standing beside my bed. Looking around. Braelyn wasn't in here.

"Theo," Kason's voice had me looking up toward the door.

His expression had my gut feeling hollow as I watched him stand from his perch on the steps just outside. He could not enter.

"What is it," I demanded, walking toward him with purpose.

"He took her," he spoke.

I froze, my heart beating rapidly.

Charging at him, I had him pressed against the wall of the stairwell.

"What the fuck do you mean? What happened?!" I seethed in his face.

"Braelyn is gone," he snapped, shoving me off him.

My world came to a halt as I watched him, finding the truth in his eyes.

"You better tell me everything right now before I fucking kill someone and you are the first on my list." I sneered, shoving my black hair back from my face. I checked the bond, finding no sign of her, my face going pale.

"Now!" I roared shoving at him.

"She came out of the armoury," he snapped, heading past me and down the stairs.

He was swift in his movements, and I followed him, the manor still seemingly empty of all other family members.

"What the fuck do you mean?" I asked, pushing past him, and coming to a stop as we reached the ground floor.

Drops and smears of blood lay across the marble floors, leading from the armoury door, down the hallway and disappearing through the French doors to outside.

"Tell me everything!" I roared, slamming a fist into the door that led down to the armoury, splinters flying in every direction.

"I was busy in my room all morning with that hack. I came downstairs and got a sandwich and was headed back to my room when she came barrelling through the god-damned door with a box, and blood dripping down her neck," he began explaining, his expression becoming angered as he crossed his arms.

"It's fucking her. All the time it's been her. I saw her eyes. Her mask was off," he snapped, reaching into his back pocket and shoving the golden mask at me.

I didn't have time for this, so I snatched it from him.

"What happened next?" I gritted my teeth, my hand clenching at my sides.

"Ezio came after her. She was wielding Ares's sword. It should have killed her the moment she fucking touched it. She wielded it like it weighed nothing and it seemed she got a few slices in on him. He was a fucking madman as he went after her." He blew out a heavy breath and then began down the hall in a hurry.

I followed closely behind, the chaos outside greeting me and my decision to kill the motherfucker sealed. I should have ended him long ago.

Gods, if he had her, who knew…

"He followed her outside. There was a tussle. She fought like one of us, never letting go of that fucking box. I tried to get to her. She seemed to freeze up when he tackled her. I managed to grip her just as they disappeared into The Shiver," he finished in a rush.

Stepping forward, I walked on ahead.

Drops of blood scattered around the lawn. A bit of lawn ripped up as someone had dug their fingers into it along the embankment. Looking around the yard, I noticed the fallen leaves scattered across the lawn, pushed together in circles around where I stood. Like ripples in a pond…

Pulses of vibrating air.

"Did he say anything?" I seethed, standing, and looking at Kason.

"Just that he needed her," he mumbled, looking around the yard now too, his eyes settling on the Sword of Ares that lay across the lawn to my left, blood still coating its blade.

Picking it up, I scowled as I eyed it. She should be dead by holding it. I was the only one in my family that could without its power killing me.

Its curse…

"What is she, T?" Kason asked, eyeing the sword.

"I don't know," I mumbled.

"She cut him with it?" I asked, eyeing him and then the blade. A nod was his only response.

Running past, him, I entered the manor, barrelling down the blood-smeared hallways and gripping the splintered door to the armoury.

Shoving it aside, I entered the stairwell, hearing the door bang harshly against the wall.

Kason's footsteps followed closely behind me as I descended the stairs, finding the vault door still open, the hinges frozen in hoarfrost, causing it to have jammed.

What in nine hells were you doing down here, little rose?

It was clear there had been an altercation within the armoury, items strewn across the floors, and shards of an ancient vase littered the floor near the back. Looking around, I headed over to the left, weapons lining the wall, and shoved them aside as I searched, Ares's sword still firmly in my right hand.

"Have you told anyone about this?" I snapped at him in my search for the item.

"No. I thought you would have had a good reason for hiding her."

"Good," I responded not delving any deeper into his statement.

Lifting a heavy-lidded chest and dumping it at my feet before opening it. Throwing the items aside, I found what I needed.

A small vial of swirling shadows greeted me. Pulling the cork with my teeth and spitting it aside, I held it over the blade.

"Come on, fuck's sake," I growled, not wanting to waste any more time.

My breath held as the shadows slithered their way down from the glass vial, reaching out like a predator ready to strike the blood-covered blade. They circled, rearing back like an asp, and engulfed the blood. Crackles and flashes of subdued lightning formed within its grasp before it pulled away, retreating to the vial.

Dropping the sword with a loud bang against the stone floors, I reached for the cork on the ground and sealed the vial.

"The Shadows of Mirrors won't help you find him if he is still in The Shiver," Kason said in earnest as he stepped toward me.

"He won't be in The Shiver forever, he needs her for something and will have to leave eventually," I grumbled, shoving the vial inside my jacket pocket.

"What box did she have," I asked, trying to figure out what the hells she had been up to and forcing myself to think with a clear head, not the blood rage I found myself in. "I don't know, I have never seen it before and it is missing." He cursed under his breath.

"How the fuck did she even get in here?" Kason snapped in anger, kicking over a stand filled with daggers of all sorts.

"She is certainly full of surprises," I grumbled bending to gather up the sword and looking at the vast collection of weapons.

Gathering what I needed, I strapped numerous weapons and ammo to my person, including the sword sheathed now to my back, its deadly power a hum along my spine.

"Where are you going," Kason called after me as I rushed from the armoury, taking the steps two at a time, up and around to the ground floor of the manor.

"Theo!" he called out loudly as he still made his way up the stone steps.

"I need you to hack everything on Ezio. I want to know fucking everything," I growled as I stopped short of the trail of blood down the hallways marble floors.

"Okay T, but what are you going to do?" he asked exasperated.

"I am going to get her back and fucking kill our bastard of a cousin."

"That's all good and well but you don't even fucking know where to start looking for her. She was dragged into The Shiver. She could be anywhere in the world if she is even still alive…"

"She is fucking alive!" I roared, kicking at the table that lined the hallways with artefacts on display.

"What about the rest? What do I even fucking say to them? Mom, Dad? Trey, Layna? What about the hunt order against her?" Kason spoke quieter, my anger slipping through the cracks as I stood before him.

"You tell them," I spoke sinisterly as I walked closer to him, stopping beside him and turning to look at him over my shoulder. "That I am going after my fucking wife, and if any of them stop me or somewhat get in my way, they will meet the same fate as Ezio," I growled out, my eyes glowing amber in my rage.

Kason eyed me, his eyes wide and I started forward swiftly, my heavy booted feet echoing down the hallway.

Entering the garage, I hopped atop my Ducati, revving it loudly as I shoved my helmet over my head.

Clicking the button just below the bottom rim of the helmet near my chin, a shield much like the dome covered my person, the weapons and large sword disappearing. Kicking the kickstand, I started forward just as the doors opened wide enough, racing like a bat out of hell as the enormous adamantine gates opened before me, shutting quickly as I passed through. Opening the throttle, I raced down the winding road, trees reaching toward the heavens, fading sunlight filtering through, casting a glittering glow upon the earth.

Leaves flew up as I raced past, the sound of the motor roaring through the hills.

"Fuck!" I screamed within my helmet, finally allowing myself to release some form of tension over the current situation.

I geared down, pushing the bike faster as I went, cursing myself for not listening to my gut this morning.

My instincts had told me something was wrong, and I fucking ignored it! Idiot!

What had she been doing down in the armoury and what box had she taken? How in nine hells had she not dropped dead as she wielded Ares' sword?

Swerving around cars as I neared the onramp, I opened the throttle fully as I joined the six-lane highway.

Cars were specks in my vision as I raced toward the city, my destination growing closer as I got further down the seemingly endless lanes.

What the fuck did Ezio want with her?

Kason had said Ezio mentioned he needed her for something. What was that? And how the fuck did he know about her?

My blood turned to ice as a realisation hit me. He must have been the anonymous tip-off twelve years ago. He had been living with us at the time, a fucking snake I couldn't wait to kill back then either…

Profanities flew from my mouth; my anger was barely being leashed.

Exiting the highway, I raced through the streets, finally having The Agora come into view.

Parking my bike, the seemingly normal market stretched out before me.

Stalls of produce, artwork, and anything you could imagine filled the space. Awnings covered each stall along the streets as the market inhabited four city blocks. Civilians meandered through the stalls, children laughing and parents handing out wads of cash to vendors as their kids squealed in delight.

Not bothering to remove my helmet, I flicked a second switch as a large group passed me and disappeared entirely.

A little boy stopped, having noticed me disappear before his wide eyes, and pulled his oblivious mother to a stop as he stared at the spot I had been.

I ignored them, making my way through the crowded street, the mother still trying to figure out what had spooked her son…

I wasn't here for the mortal market.

No.

I was here for The Agora, the underground dark market of our world.

Shoving aside a curtain to a stall a block down that appeared inconsequential, shadows swarmed around me, caressing me in recognition as no mere mortal.

Stepping through their embrace, I found myself in the Agora, a different kind of market where witches and monsters traded in secrecy.

I passed on along the streets, many calling out to gain my attention, bidding sounding off in the hall down the darkened street.

The bidding hall was a horrific place to be. Artefacts, monsters, and sometimes even creatures of the light were traded off for whatever reason their captors desired, usually to never be seen again. The smell of rot and blood filled my lungs, having me grind my teeth in an effort not to hurl my guts up.

There…

Hauling myself through a makeshift door made of forgotten or stolen road signs, I crashed into the small, confined space, grabbing the creature, half a man, as he scrambled back in fright.

He kicked at me with scaled legs, only angering me further.

In one swift move, I had managed to subdue him, his face pressed against the tiny table that sat in the room.

"You are going to tell me fucking everything, or Poseidon will be the last of your worries, Proteus." My anger was slipping through, and I noted the reflection of my glowing eyes against the tinted visor from within my helmet.

"You are going to tell me every single fucking thing about the prophecy of the green-eyed girl and the black roses." I sneered, shoving myself away from his quivering form and removing my helmet.

"Now."

Braelyn

Gods, my head was pounding in pain, my mouth feeling like it had been stuffed with cotton…

I tried stretching in bed, but my arms and feet refused to move.

I frowned, opening my eyes only to shut them tightly as lights surrounded me, blinding in their brightness.

Yanking my arms, the distinctive snare and sting of being bound had me panicking.

Forcing my eyes open through the glare of the lights, I was assaulted with the memory of Ezio. Being attacked, only to be yanked within the darkness.

Shadows swam around us, each of us fighting for control as we floated in the empty void.

Snarls and roars filled the space, shadows, and starlight flickering around us.

It had been then I knew what the space I had previously entered had been… I had ventured within The Shiver, only this time, I was not alone.

My mind had gone blank after a particularly hard blow to my already injured head, only to have me waking up gods knew where.

The ancient power within me seemed to be stuck in a deep slumber, the cotton feeling of my mouth the onslaught of dehydration.

Looking around the room, my eyes fought against the glare of the lights. The entire ceiling and walls were covered in large bulbs, their light leaving not a single shadow to be seen as they surrounded me.

As I looked down, it appeared that I was chained to an adamantine chair, both my legs and arms tightly bound.

My heart raced as I yanked, only to have the chains bite painfully into my wrists and forearms. Red welts already forming along the surface of my skin.

"Ezio!" I yelled my anger building and was met with only silence.

The ancient power within me stirring, yet still deep in slumber. What in nine hells had he done to me?

"Ezio, you bastard!" I roared again, yanking my limbs harshly, the chains ripping open the welts, leaving me bleeding.

Breathing heavily through my nose, I looked around yet again.

"Shit," I mumbled not finding any shadows at all.

The prick had been smart, ensuring I had no means of shadow-stalking. Gazing at my surroundings, I discovered that the room that held me was not of any modern construction. Stones lined the floor and walls, worn smooth through the ages. A door before me had a heavy adamantine surface, like that of a cell door with a slot to slide open for viewing.

Wake up…

I mentally urged the power within me. Nothing.

Groaning internally, I whipped my head up at the sound of someone unlocking the door. I scowled at Ezio as he swung it open, his clothing changed, and freshly showered.

He moved with ease; however, I had not missed the stiff movement as he twisted around to close the door.

The injury from the sword had yet to heal. His head, nevertheless, was as good as new.

It was the first time I cursed the Katopodis bloodline for its healing abilities.

"Hello sweetheart," he smirked at me, standing near the door.

I remained silent, my chest heaving in anger as I gritted down my teeth. I chanced a quick look to the floor and behind him but found no shadow. The bulbs lit him up from every possible angle.

"I will admit, I was surprised you managed to survive The Shiver. It was a risky move on my part… Desperate times and all that…"

I remained silent as he spoke, wishing that I could rip his throat out.

"This morning had been messier than I intended." He frowned, crossing his arms, and cocking his head.

The blue of his eyes had the same cool tone as his cousins. He eyed me then, his face scrunching in disgust as he took me in.

"Gods', you reek of him," I looked away, biting the inside of my cheek as I inhaled deeply. "Was Theo better than me?" he snapped, causing me to look back at him.

I made a show of looking him up and down in boredom, my fingers gripping the chair tightly. "He is better than you in every sense of the word," I finally responded, looking away yet again.

Memories of Ezio and I together raced across my mind. He had always been kind to me, showing me attention at the House gatherings as we grew up.

No one else ever did.

Everyone else stayed away, too intimidated by the blind princess of House Sarris, or simply because I was a joke to some.

But never Ezio.

We had started as friends, which soon became more.

I had given him my body at nineteen, my foolish naïve heart finally feeling accepted by someone. It had turned dark after that, his demeanour changing over time in our stolen moments. His possessiveness turned to fury.

His caresses to bruising grasps.

On our final encounter, he had held me down, refusing to take no as an answer when I had asked him to stop, his grip on me painful and his words scaring me…

I had avoided him as much as possible after that, only Dorian picking up on my sudden change of heart toward the man before me.

He never knew what had happened. No one did.

Shaking the thoughts, I looked back to him, counting to ten to calm my nerves and rid my mind of the nightmare that still scarred my heart and mind to this day.

It was the reason I had failed and gotten myself captured.

My panic over him pinning me down had frozen my mind and body in fear, resulting in me being here now.

I would not make the same mistake again…

"I highly doubt that." He snapped, his anger showing through yet again. The true Ezio.

I scoffed, deliberately triggering his temper to snap. He flung himself forward, gripping my shoulders painfully as he scowled in my face, his chest heaving, and jaw clenched.

He was about to open his mouth to spew his venomous retort.

Not waiting for a second to pass, I threw my head forward, our skulls connecting in a painful crash.

Ezio stumbled back, both of our heads now dripping with blood. I was dazed, shaking it away fast, the pounding headache that had awoken me now roaring through my skull. He wiped at his brow, the crimson liquid smearing away. His eyes widened before they landed on me and narrowed.

"You will pay for that." He sneered, turning on his heel swiftly and exiting the room, the heavy door slamming closed with a loud bang behind him before the sound of it being locked filled my ringing ears.

"Prick," I seethed under my breath, eyeing the chains once more.

The Servile brand covered my arm, the chains gripping it tightly. I tried locating Theo through the bond, not sure of what else to do, and could not locate him at all. How in nine hells was I going to get out of here? What did Ezio need me for and… *shit!*

The box from the armoury, I had lost it during our fight outside. Slamming my back against the chair in anger, I tilted my head back and closed my eyes, my heart beating rapidly as anger and fear coursed through me.

Kason had seen me. Seen me with the box, who I truly am…

God-dammit, I needed that box now more than ever.

Hecate… Oh my gods, Hecate…

Surely by now, the news of my discovery would have found her. She would not allow this to go unpunished. Allow me to go unpunished… Surely, she would not leave me here either?

Yes.

Yes, she would if it meant her part in any of this was wiped from the plane of existence…

"Shit," I mumbled, frowning at the door, trying to figure out what to do.

Don't touch the mark. Its…. Distracting…

Theo's words ran through my mind. Looking back at the mark, I began twisting and yanking my arm in any manner I could.

The chain's friction rubs across its surface. I continued until I could not anymore, my skin peeled raw from the chains.

I had lost track of time, my eyes growing heavy as I looked to the door, the glare of the lights making my eyes hurt.

I tried in vain to fight off the sleep that called to me, my eyes closing of their own accord, only for me to pull awake with a start.

I continued fighting off sleep for what felt like hours, eventually succumbing to its embrace.

My head fell forward, hair dangling across my face as I remained chained to the chair.

It was a restless sleep.

Memories of Ezio, the horrors of my upbringing, and finally Theo…

I found peace in the thought of him and jerked awake as the door sounded before me yet again. Ezio appeared, his brow already healed, and he stalked toward me, not saying a word.

I watched him in silence.

He rounded the chair, disappearing from view, and gripped my shoulders, his fingers digging in painfully. I held my breath, not allowing myself to freeze under his touch as I did before.

My jaw ached as I bit down, staring at the open door, and the equally brightly lit hallway beyond it.

"Where is the box containing the heart of Ouranos?" he spoke in my ear, his breath blowing against my cheek.

I remained silent and his fingers dug into my flesh.

"Where is it? You had it," he snapped, gripping my hair painfully and pulling my hair back so that I was now looking up at him.

"Your quiet tongue will not keep you safe forever, Braelyn. I will still get what I need, with or without the box. It would simply be a bonus…" he sneered, his blue eyes searching mine for a moment as I glared at him, resolute in my silence.

Ah, so he was not after the box.

It had simply been me…

What were his plans for me?

Noticing that I had no intention of speaking, he shoved my head forward harshly and released my hair before stepping around where I sat.

Lifting my head, I tilted my head, this way and that trying to ease some of the stiffness in my muscles. I looked at him, the hatred clear in my gaze.

"No one is coming for you," he spoke, a smirk on his lips.

"Then why keep me locked up?" I finally asked, my voice croaking from hours of silence.

"Ah so that pretty little mouth of yours does still work," he smirked, crossing his arms.

I glared at him, disgusted that I had ever allowed him to touch me, and me, him …

"I need to run a few tests. The tranquiliser seems to not be working the way it should, and I cannot have that with what I have planned. So, tell me, what in nine hells are you?" he spoke, eyeing me from the tips of my toes to the top of my head.

I ignored him yet again, the threat in my eyes clear.

Little did he know that I had no idea what I was. We were both in the dark where that was concerned and if he thought I simply refused to tell him, then all the better.

He cursed under his breath before reaching into his pocket and extracting two syringes.

One empty, one with a silver liquid that swirled around and around as if it contained essence. "Fine, we will do it my way then," he scowled stepping forward.

I jerked against the chains as he neared, the efforts futile. Ezio shoved my shoulder back against the chair, keeping me still as he placed the empty syringe against my arm, stabbing its needle in deeply before extracting my blood.

I tried to pull away, shake, anything to stop him but found myself feeling dazed as he stepped away. The second filled syringe was now being pulled from my arm; its contents emptied within my veins.

The room began spinning, Ezio's blurry figure swaying before me.

"I will… kill… you," I managed to mumble, trying to fight against whatever sedative now dragged me under.

He remained silent, heading to the door. I squinted my eyes as I tried holding on to consciousness, the sight of the door slamming shut after him sounding out in my muffled ears. My tongue had gone dry.

Drier than it had already been and stuck to the roof of my mouth. I felt myself tipping over, my body jerking in a response to the sense of falling and darkness surrounding me once more.

It was in the moment that I finally succumbed that I imagined that most faint sensation of a caress down my arm, across the Servile brand.

I woke with a jolt of what felt like electricity running through my veins.

The vibrating burn of it was reverberating across my bones, my teeth grinding as I heaved against my restraints.

Falling back as the sensation passed, I exhaled heavily.

I opened my weary eyes further to find myself tied down with yet more adamantine chains to what appeared a gurney.

Tossing my head to the side, I squinted through the bright lights to see that I remained in the cell as before, however the chair had been replaced by the cold surface of the gurney, wires attached across my body. Stretching my neck to the right, I spotted a monitor.

The electrodes attached across my body sent my vitals to the illuminated screen. The jagged lines across the display in time with my rapidly beating heart.

My clothes had been removed, leaving me bare in the cold confines of the room, except for my underwear.

I froze, the thought of Ezio undressing me while I had been drugged had the panic building within my chest.

"You are a strange specimen," Ezio's voice sounded from the left.

Whirling my head in that direction, I almost winced aloud at the stiff and painful movement of my neck. I found him standing across the room, his eyes focused on a tablet as he swiped across the screen, frowning at whatever it was that he saw.

Yanking my arms and legs, to free myself from the gurney, I hissed as the chains dug painfully into my skin.

"Don't bother. Those are made by Hephaestus himself. The same ones that were used on Prometheus. Having access to my family's armoury does have its perks," he called out casually as he continued to read the screen of the tablet.

He did not bother to look in my direction. I watched him in silence, imagining all the slow torturous ways I would kill him once I was free. His frown deepened and he looked up to the monitor and then the screen between his hands.

Ezio stepped forward, heading to the monitor. I craned my neck, watching him as he passed. He stepped before the monitor, tapping the screen as he brought up different charts that I had no way of knowing what they meant. "Interesting…" he mumbled to himself, swiping across the different charts.

I felt myself frowning.

What was it that he was looking for? And more importantly, what is it that he found?

I yanked against the painful constraint of the chains as he turned to me, the tablet having been set down on the trolley that housed the monitor.

My chest heaved in the rapid concession as I yanked and pulled futilely. Ezio reached for the electrodes on my chest, removing them and attaching them to the tabs that had been stuck across my forehead.

I writhed in pain, tossing my head back and forth to stop him from attaching them to my head.

"Enough!" he seethed as he gripped my jaw in his one hand, his fingers digging in painfully. My chest continued to heave as I glared at him. The venom gaze reflected in his own.

I yanked on my chains as he held my face in his iron grip and used his free hand to attach the electrodes to my forehead. He stepped away, ignoring me.

I watched him furiously as he stepped toward the monitor yet again but bent down and reached for beneath the trolley.

I could not crane my neck far enough to see what it was he was doing but felt a surge of electricity blast its way through my head as he stood.

A remote in hand.

I heaved, my eyes straining, and my breath caught as amps of electricity, enough to be painful, yet not enough to kill me surged through my head and down my body.

He released his hold on the button pressed beneath his thumb and I sagged back against the table. My muscles twitched and ached as Ezio continued for another five minutes. Intervals of torturous electrocution had me wishing it all would end.

He finally set the remote down, inspecting the electrodes across my forehead, and returned his attention to the monitor.

My eyesight had become hazy. Each breath felt like a boulder was atop my chest. My fingers twitched uncontrollably as little spasms worked their way through each muscle and tendon.

"How?" he muttered to himself as I stared through blurry eyes at the brightly lit ceiling, my ears ringing loudly.

"How is it, that there's the faintest trace of a second heartbeat and brain waves…Pregnancy has been eliminated…" he thought aloud now staring at me as if I was the world's greatest mystery.

I could not reply even if I wanted to. What should have been startling news to me at the sound of his voice, was only a minuscule annoyance as I struggled for breath.

"What are you?" He gripped my chin again, forcing me to look at him.

He remained only a feint outline before me, washes of colours and shadows swimming in my vision as I struggled to focus.

"What are you hiding behind those pretty green eyes?" He growled.

I felt the pain only slightly through my tingling and slightly numb skin as his grip tightened in his anger.

I knew my jaw would be bruised.

No doubt a kaleidoscope of blue and purple would appear across my chilled skin.

"What. Are. You." He sneered, bending so that he was so close, his breath fanned my face.

"I," I croaked, struggling to find my voice. My body begging for an end.

"I," I struggled again.

Ezio loosened his grip only slightly as he eyed me, still hovering over my face.

"You are what?" he asked, the sick excitement clear in his voice.

I inhaled a shaky breath. Not from fear. But my muscles still dancing with the after-effects of the electricity that had flowed through my body only moments ago.

"I am going to kill you," I managed a whisper, smiling sinisterly at him as I closed my eyes against the glare of the lights.

Ezio froze for a moment, only to grip my jaw harder and shove himself away from me in fury. I kept my eyes closed as the sound of something being thrown across the room reverberated through my ringing ears.

I could hear through the ringing how his breathing was laboured as he struggled with his anger.

"Theo will find you. I do not doubt it. But I will be the one to kill you," my voice croaked against the dryness in my mouth and my aching throat muscles.

My tongue itself still tingled and the taste of metal covered it.

I opened my eyes as a needle pricked my skin, shoving deeply within my neck.

"I don't think so," he growled, stepping away with an empty syringe in hand.

I felt the liquid enter my veins. The cold yet burning sensation travelled through my body. My head began to buzz. Burning and shivering as if a swarm of bees was trapped inside of it. I turned my gaze to Ezio.

His figure was still blurry, but I knew I had my eyes locked on him as my vision darkened on the sides.

The effect of the drug pulling me under.

"The gods themselves won't save you from me."

I smiled.

A death promise on my lips.

Ezio stood watching me as my vision turned dark yet again. I let the darkness call to me, embracing it with a smile on my face.

There was no sense of time within the darkness.

No beginning and no end.

In the darkness, growls stirred. Echoes.

The sound of wings beating, and the whispers of shadows danced around me.

I was not afraid.

My consciousness calmed as the growls and snarls grew louder as they neared, and wisps of obscurity embraced me. I waited in the darkness. Waited for the powerful wings to draw closer.

There was something familiar about the sound. Something homely.

Flashes of silver.

Flashes of ice and frost and death. It surrounded me, cocooning me.

A familiar slithering of power and rage flitted against me as the flashes of hoarfrost grew brighter. Each flash beating like a war drum in time with my heart.

A great maw appeared before me.

Fangs dripping silver and slithering shadows in the darkness and hisses of a frost filled the void. The maw closed as obsidian scales reflected in the darkness before me.

Shining like the night sky. Like death itself.

Two large green eyes, lined with silver and demise.

The slits of its pupils an endless chasm of shadows held my gaze in greeting.

In rage.

In a promise of revenge.

"There you are," I whispered.

Braelyn

I lost track of time as Ezio continued his experiments in the brightly lit cell.

Only to have him drug me over and over, sending me to the endless depths of the dark void I now cherished.

I did not know if I had been in captivity for hours, days or weeks.

All sense of time had been lost to me. I remained steadfast in my silence.

Not answering any of Ezio's questions. My promise of his death by my hands were the only words to leave my lips.

My body, the little that I could see of it in the brief moments of consciousness, was peppered with bruises.

Bruises from the experiments, the endless stabbing of needles, and finally Ezio's damned hands.

I had decided in my silence that his hands would be the first to go. I would remove them from his body, a painful and bloody mess silently promised to him.

In a few moments, I had been awake. I watched him curse endlessly as he pondered over every detail. My charts, my body.

Everything about me.

But what he had not realised is that in those moments he was studying me, I was returning the favour.

I now found my previous fear of the man utterly ridiculous.

His too-fast temper, his lack of patience. His superiority complexes. It was all a joke to me. I had even noticed how the wound from the sword I had wielded on the day of my capture was still not healed.

His Katopodis bloodline should have easily healed it by now.

He would wince ever so slightly with every movement.

In his moments of anger, he would split the wound open yet again, leaving his clothes covered in blood.

I would remain silent in my observations but found myself smiling every time he would bleed.

Which only infuriated him further.

I had also noticed how his fingers held a certain tremble every time he was near me.

Every time he reached for the god-damned drugs to put me to sleep. It was so faint that had I not been looking for it, I would never have noticed.

I would never have seen the tremble as he placed the needle in my skin.

"You need to bathe," he muttered, inserting a different liquid into the syringe.

I watched him silently as he pulled the plunger down. A crimson liquid filled the syringe before he chucked the vial aside carelessly.

My eyes narrowed on the substance as he flicked a finger against the syringe, ensuring no air lay within it.

I had not seen this substance before. The drug that he had been using on me had been of a silver hue.

He noticed my eyes suspiciously and stepped forward, that subtle tremor and wince clear for me to see.

"You are of no use to me dead," he grumbled and inserted the needle in my neck which no doubt was pockmarked with puncture wounds by now.

I narrowed my eyes further at him as the usual buzzing in my head did not sound out. My eyes remained clear, and my breathing was even.

Just what had he given me?

He began unlocking the chains around me, the ones that wrapped around the gurney and my legs slid off and fell with a heavy clang.

I wasted no time and kicked at him furiously. I narrowly missed his jaw and he whirled on me. His temper snapped as it always did.

"You will lay still. Not one movement," he hissed, and I widened my eyes in horror as my legs of their own accord lowered to the chilled gurney.

I lay frozen within myself as he began untying the rest of the chains. The chilled air against my cracked skin was biting.

I felt panic rise within me but shoved it down, reminding myself that I had training, I was smarter than this, and felt the panic recede as I tried contemplating what he had given me.

"Sit up," he grumbled, stepping back as the last of the chains that held me down fell to the floor. My stiff body responded to his command, and I felt my muscles and tendons protest the movement as I tautly sat up on the gurney and eyed him.

"You will follow me. You will not attempt an escape. You will not attempt to harm me. You will follow me without causing a scene and not do anything else." He sneered, his aqua eyes holding mine.

I knew I could still speak of my own accord, but I refused to give him the satisfaction.

I only scowled at him, my eyes remaining narrowed on his. He did not say another word and stepped back, heading for the door. I screamed internally as my body climbed from the gurney, my feet hitting the freezing stone floor of the cell.

Ezio opened the large, heavy adamantine door, its hinges creaking as he swung it wide. The stone corridor lay before me, and I found no shadows as he began leading me down its great expanse.

Bulbs hummed in the silence as they lit up every possible surface from every direction.

There were no other doors for nearly three minutes of walking until finally we reached the end of the hallway.

My muscles burned as they stretched out after so long. Another heavy adamantine door stood before us. Ezio turned to me with a tick in his jaw.

"Do not bother trying to shadow-stalk." I eyed him with fury as he opened the door and stepped through the threshold.

I began following and found myself in what appeared to be one of the pleasure houses of the gods. The sun shone brightly through the massive stone arched windows, the ocean a turquoise gem in the distance, and white cliffs lining the shore.

Ezio led us down the centre of a great room, curtains of gossamer billowing in the breeze, and salt-scented air filled my lungs. I spotted endless shadows and willed myself to shadow-stalk.

I immediately regretted it as I found myself flickering on the spot, pain slicing through me, my very blood burning me.

I sucked in a breath as my body flickered painfully in and out of focus and Ezio turned to me, a cruel grin on his face.

"I warned you. The blood of The Gorgons will not allow you to escape."

Gods, he gave me the blood of The Gorgons. It explained my frozen state. Any who peered into the gaze of a Gorgon would be frozen… It must have been altered by one of the Houses as a weapon… No doubt the scheming drug masters of House Farmako.

It would also explain the pleasure house I found myself in. Drugs were on the menu, as well as the pleasures of the flesh…

"Now, follow me," he grumbled, turning, and leading the way once again.

Seagulls sounded in the distance above the sound of crashing waves and my aching body began following.

We passed large alcoves. Cushions and lavish adornments of a multitude of jewel tones covered the space.

The smell of something sweet mixed in the air with the salt of the ocean far down below the glittering white cliff where the limestone and marble structure found itself upon.

I did not spot anyone and found it odd that not even one of the sex workers was to be seen. I kept my thought to myself as Ezio halted beside a large fountain waiting for me to catch up, the ceiling domed above us, and columns reached high to the ceiling.

Ivy and jasmine twined around the columns… the source of the sweet smell was finally identified.

The water running down the fountain bubbled and splashed serenely, and a myriad of colourful fish swam about. The entire setting seemed at odds with Ezio himself as well as what I knew the pleasure houses to be.

Ezio turned on his heel, heading to the left of the fountain and the arched window to the right allowed me to glimpse further down the coastline below.

I followed him, my feet leading the way no matter how harshly I fought against my own body.

He finally came to a halt before a wooden door, the brass knocker on it shining brilliantly against the flame of the sconces that hung from the wall beside it.

He dug in his pocket, retrieving a set of keys. I eyed it and remained frozen as he unlocked the heavy door and pocketed the set again.

With a harsh push, the door swung open revealing a bathing pool. Mosaics covered the floors in an array of colours and scenes of the gods.

Aphrodite's visage was clear in many of the scenes. I gritted my teeth as I unwillingly followed Ezio inside.

Far too aware of my lack of clothing.

"You will bathe yourself and wait for me here. There is clothing in the armoire across the room for you to get dressed. You will not attempt to escape at any time. You will remain silent until my return. You will also not attempt to open the door for anyone." He ordered, eyeing me suspiciously.

I found myself scowling at him from where I stood.

My dirty hair clung to my neck and down my back.

I indeed was in desperate need of a bath. However, I would much rather rip the smug look off his face.

"Good," he sneered with a wicked smile in my silence.

I watched him go, the poison in my blood not allowing me to launch myself at him. He exited with the sound of the door being locked behind him and I felt the hold on my body lift ever so slightly to allow me to move around the confines of the bathing room.

I noticed the large arched window and walked over to it, placing a hand on its carved surface as I leaned out and peered below. A sheer drop met my gaze.

White cliffs led down to jagged rocks in the crashing surf below. There would be no escaping from here then.

Stepping back, I looked around. Ferns and jasmine grew within the large chamber.

A chaise the size of a bed was nestled comfortably in the corner on a raised platform. Gossamer curtains swayed in the breeze as they surrounded the bathing pool and chaise.

On the other side of the room, a large armoire stood, its wooden surface carved with scenes of pleasure and writhing bodies.

Suitable for a place such as this.

The deep bathing pool sat in the centre of the room, colourful mosaics surrounding it and beneath its surface.

I should just refuse to bathe, forcing Ezio to be near my filthy and reeking body… But the instructions were clear, and I gritted my teeth as I furiously against my will removed my underwear and stepped toward the pool.

I took a step down, almost moaning as the water was warm around my aching feet, up to my ankle.

The water had been enchanted by the gods, no doubt Aphrodite herself, to remain at the perfect temperature.

My aching muscles seemed to relax immediately, and I stepped further down into the water's depths.

I froze mid-step as it reached my thighs.

Gods! I could not go any further. The water, the depths...

The feel of it covering my skin... I backtracked up a step, the water now just covering my knees. I ground my teeth in frustration and tears welled in my eyes as the fear took root.

My body wanted to force me forward, as I attempted another step back. I fought against myself.

My body trembling and silent tears running down my dirt-covered cheeks.

I was near hyperventilating when I managed to force myself to sit on the steps, the water barely covering me. I almost sagged in relief when the force on my body seemed to fade, seemingly accepting my position in the water.

With shaking hands, I began unwillingly running water across my body, tears still streaming down my face as I gritted my teeth. My jaw began to cramp up and my eyes blurred with unshed tears.

My chest ached as I willed the fear and sobs down deep within myself.

I spotted jars of oils beside me and reached for them with shaking hands.

Opening the jars, I found it to be bathing products and continued my tortured pursuit of cleanliness.

When it came to my hair, an audible sob escaped me, and I dipped it beneath the surface of the water between my legs as I bent forward.

Once it was wet, I reared back in haste, hating the water being so close to my face.

Water ran down my face, causing me to squeeze my eyes shut to stop screaming.

I had never been capable of bathing since the well-house...

I could only tolerate showers and there would be no great body of water threatening to drag me underneath...

Showers – the water ran off me as fast as it appeared.

Lathering the substance from the jar, I washed my long black hair... the sweet-smelling aroma filled my nose as tears dripped from its tip and over quivering lips.

I eyed the water before me as I lowered my hands from my hair.

I would need to rinse it.

Leaving my head in the water longer than before...

I smacked the jars aside in frustration, their contents spilling over the mosaiced floor. Oils and soaps formed pools of reflecting liquid across the floor and dripped over the edge of the pool.

I eyed the water, trying to ignore the flashbacks of the well-house.

Inhaling a shaky breath, I slowly bent over, lowering my head between my legs and the tips of my long hair entered the water, suds, and oils floating across the surface in incandescent ripples.

Panting uncontrollably, I forced myself lower, the edge of the water now sloshing against my scalp.

Groaning as I fought back my sobs and with shaking hands, I hastily rinsed my hair.

I was not even sure if I had removed all residue of the soapy suds and oils as I recoiled as fast as a viper.

My chest heaved and water splashed around me. My nails scraped against the edge of the pool as my grip threatened to snap off pieces of tile.

Closing my eyes, I counted to ten and repeated it numerous times as I willed my heart to slow.

When I finally opened my eyes, I noted how the evidence of the suds in the pool had vanished, along with the spilled jars to my side. New jars stood perfectly aligned and filled beside the edge.

Enchanted indeed...

Scowling at the water before me, I truly hated myself at that moment.

The fear having so much sway over me.

I had been enduring torture in an experiment, yet a simple bathing pool had brought me to near hysterics...

Not bothering to rinse my hair thoroughly I exited the pool, water sloshing behind me and the sound causing a shiver to run down my spine.

Closing my eyes briefly and exhaling through my clenched jaw, I started toward the armoire. I yanked on the wooden handles, opening both doors wide. Water ran down my body and the distinctive drip sounded at my feet.

Thankfully, I was not cold in here as it had been in the cell Ezio had been keeping me in. I scowled as I eyed the garments hanging inside.

Growling my displeasure, I grabbed one of the atrocious garments and slammed the doors closed as I stepped toward the large chaise. I looked back for my underwear where I had left it and found them missing.

Of course, they would be missing!

My anger grew as I slipped the silk fabric across my body. I should have never complained about the dresses my mother had me wear at the Servile ceremonies.

I yanked on the fabric across my skin and kicked the chaise in frustration as it was futile. The fine ruby-red silk chiffon was so thin and delicate that my breasts were on full display. A scrap of material barely covered my nipples and a thin line hung down between my breasts and legs and fell to the floor. The same could be said for the back as it barely covered anything.

It was approximately six inches across… and that was me being hopeful.

The material was twisted like that of a rope as it created a form of a halter neck and long traces fell around my neck like a god-damned collar. My blood boiled at having to endure the humiliation of Ezio witnessing my naked body further.

I caught my reflection in a mirror beside the chaise and stepped forward, still tugging at the material.

I frowned as I saw my body.

Bruises covered my arms, jaw, and neck, the areas that had been chained down were chaffed raw and numerous welts covered my skin. I had surprisingly not lost any weight and struggled to think back to how long ago I had eaten. Surely it couldn't have been so long ago if I had not lost weight… I had unfortunately lost track of time after being drugged so many times, it was impossible to figure out how long Ezio had kept me here.

Wherever here was…

The ocean and cliffs beyond the chamber and holding up the pleasure house were not familiar to me.

However, my knowledge of travel was extremely limited.

I only knew what I did from reading and the occasional movie with Dorian…

What was Dorian doing now? Had he noticed my absence? Was he okay back home by himself with our mother and Hecate?

My blood simmered at the thought of someone harming my brother.

I turned away from the mirror and with my hands on my bare hips, I looked around the chamber.

I had been instructed to bathe and stay within the room. Not attempt to escape and not answer the door for anyone…

I chewed my bruised lip as I scanned the room. There had to be something I could do or find or…

The faintest trickle of a sensation ran along my arm like that of walking through a spiderweb, causing me to scratch at my skin. The sensation flared to life yet again, more persistent yet still dull.

My eyes grew wide as I realised it was the Servile mark.

Theo!

I frantically rubbed at the mark, hoping to the gods that it was him and not just my body reacting to all that it had endured. I waited in the silent chamber.

The only sound surrounding me was that of the ocean outside and my heavy breathing. I huffed in frustration as I felt nothing.

I attempted to rub at the mark vigorously a few more times but only ended up with more angry welts.

I still could not locate him through the bond, and it appeared that the sensation I had felt was seemingly just my imagination.

Screaming in defeat, I fell back against the chaise, scowling dead ahead to the world outside, trying my best to ignore the large body of water within the room.

I had yet to figure out what it was that Ezio wanted from me and why it was so important he figure out what I am.

I had remained silent during his experiments, only reminding him often of my promise to kill him.

And I would.

Eventually…

If he thought locking me up would break me and cause me to spill all the secrets he yearned for so desperately, he had another thing coming. I had endured far too much over my twenty-five years of life and I would endure this too.

Hecate's venomous voice echoed in my head over and over…

You are a weapon, and weapons do not weep, they do not break…

I was dragged from my thoughts as voices sounded near the door of the chambers.

Launching to my feet, I crept closer. Silent as a phantom breeze.

I noticed shadows beneath the bottom of the door, two of them. I crept closer, being sure to not allow my own shadow to fall on the floor near the door, and focused on my sensitive hearing.

"I need more time," Ezio's voice spoke quietly. "You have two days," a haunting voice spoke, the scratching of it sending chills down my spine.

"The auction is tomorrow. If I am unable to make the trade, the next one is only a week after that."

"Two days. No longer," the rattling, hissing breath spoke, and they drifted away as terror filled me.

An auction? My blood ran cold as the thought of Ezio possibly selling me on auction was like a punch to the gut.

Terror was soon replaced by rage, not of my own but the ancient power within me as it stirred.

Most likely awoken from whatever deep slumber it had been forced into by my panicked emotions. I let its rage consume me as it uncoiled itself, slithering and hissing around my bones protectively.

I shut my eyes briefly, relieved that it had returned. Its anger flared as it remained confined to the innermost workings of my being.

Slamming adamantly against the hold.

I did not know why it had been slumbering or what held it in place, caged like a roaring beast… but I knew that once it was free yet again…

Once I was free… Ezio Katopodis would suffer by my hands.

I willed it to recede, to show no evidence of its awareness as the door sounded.

The sound of jingling keys filled the air and Ezio stood on the threshold as he pushed the wooden door aside.

He appeared pale… no doubt from his festering wound and the encounter with whatever horrid stranger was on the other side of the door only minutes ago.

I held my chin high and glared at him as his perverted eyes took me in.

Every inch of my skin was caressed by his beady eyes. I felt sick to my stomach.

The red silk barely covered anything at all.

It served no purpose besides wrapping me like a gift in a red bow.

"Very good," he mumbled with a grin and my eyes narrowed on him.

Theo

My mind was reeling as I mounted my Ducati in the streets of the Agora.

It had taken much persuasion to get Proteus to talk.

His fear of the subject was clear.

The hunt order and prophecy still tucked securely within my breast pocket felt like a hot iron against my chest.

Gripping my helmet between my tattooed hands, I watched the civilians of the city absentmindedly as they strolled through the streets and vendors called out.

Shit.

For once in my life, I was torn as to what to do… Retrieving Braelyn was my priority and non-negotiable but after that?

Proteus had made clear the seriousness of the situation and that should my family not stick to their duty, there would be blood spilled…

Checking through the bond, I still could not locate Braelyn. I had my theories about this too and needed to think fast about what my next plan of action would be.

Why did Ezio need her?

The slimy bastard always had an agenda and his words when he took her made it clear that she was needed for something.

She was alive. I knew it.

Gritting my teeth in frustration, I pulled my helmet over my head and clicked the buttons to cloak myself. Luckily it was so late, the streets were not as busy as earlier and no one even noticed as I and the motorcycle disappeared from their view.

The cloaking held steadfast as I started up the bike, revving it loudly. No sounds would be heard by the mortals as the cloaking shield contained every minuscule detail.

Pulling away from the curb, my phone started ringing through the helmet's speakers. I ignored it as I got onto the highway.

Ezio's home was my next stop. I doubted even he would be stupid enough to be there, but I needed to work out some more details "What?" I snapped finally answering the call as it began ringing in my ears for the sixth time in a row.

"Where are you?" It was Trey.

"Hunting," I gritted out, swerving lanes.

"Cut the shit. Don't make me get Kason to track you. Now, where are you?" Trey snapped.

My older brother was serious as usual. I knew that by now Kason had surely filled everyone in on what happened and Trey, ever the sucker for the rules, would only want to get this over and done with.

I had my faults. Plenty of them.

But Trey's biggest fault was his sense of duty over everything else. I couldn't have him getting in the way of finding Braelyn and ensuring her safety.

"You are already tracking me. Don't be so coy," I grumbled and ended the call.

Increasing my speed, I began racing down the highway, the sun already threatening to rise over the horizon for a new day.

Spotting a rather dangerous bend in the road, I increased my speed.

The guardrail looms closer and closer. Standing upon the bike, I balanced as I stuck the throttle to maintain speed. My eyes glowed amber as the barrier neared, the passing cars on the highway oblivious to what was occurring around them.

Removing my helmet, I threw it aside, the wind racing past making it disappear within a blink of an eye somewhere alongside the highway…

The roaring wind around me whipped like a lashing as the bike raced down the highway. I was now crouching atop, balancing as my black hair was blown back from my face and my eyes narrowed.

The speed the bike was going would seem a blur to any passing vehicles now that my helmet had been discarded. The shield and tracking installed in it were destroyed by its destruction a mile back as it crashed to the ground.

The remaining means of tracks were about to be destroyed.

I evened my breathing, my eyes glowing brighter as the bend grew closer.

Waiting for the last possible second, to ensure the bike did not veer off into any innocent vehicle, I pushed off the bike with a massive leap, erupting into a swarm of ravens.

I watched as the bike met the barrier, exploding into a million pieces as it was torn apart, and the majority flipped over the edge.

By destroying the bike instead of just abandoning it, I had destroyed all evidence of my visit to the Agora. Kason would not be able to retrieve any data.

I was certain that they had only just begun tracking me when Trey had called and would find nothing but scraps of metal once they arrived.

Cars came to a screeching halt at the sight of the impact. Tires squealed against the asphalt and the smell of burning rubber and fumes filled the air.

Casting a look to the horizon, I narrowed my attention on the estate in the distance.

Wasting no time, my swarm of ravens swirled and flew at incredible speeds across the highway and over residences and woodlands.

I circled the estate Ezio lived on, finding it eerily quiet. Just as I had predicted.

Swooping low, I encircled the manor, peering in every window. It was dark, with no sign of movement. My ravens rotated and circled the front courtyard, vanishing and leaving me standing as I glared up at the front of the house.

Clenching my fists, I looked around the perimeter, each step crunched beneath my boots. The gravel driveway seemed to tremble with every step.

Taking the six steps up to the front door, I eyed the door, ready for any attack. I caught a glimpse of my reflection in the glass panes of the surrounding windows and my eyes burned brightly.

Amber gold, a promise of violence…

I released two ravens to scout the perimeter as I kicked the door open.

Splinters rained down over the threshold and the door banged against the interior wall.

Clicking my neck, I slowly, purposefully stepped inside and halted.

Ezio was many things, but a bastard was at the top of the list. He no doubt had his home rigged for intruders. Especially if he was insane enough to go against me so directly.

I craned my neck as I took in his foyer.

The hallway led straight ahead with a large staircase beyond, flanked by hallways on either side. To my left and right were a study and a formal sitting room. His home was nothing like that of the Great Houses but was still considered a manor by its grandness.

I grinned sinisterly as my Chaos Handler gene took over, noticing every minuscule detail. The traps he had set were clear as day for someone like me.

Idiot.

Rolling my shoulders, that deep dark part of me that thrived in chaos was eager to get this over with. Amused and excited in a sick way of eradicating the traps Ezio had set.

My eyes narrowed in anticipation as I slowly took a step forward, the first trap being triggered by the pressure plate beneath the hallway runner.

A click sounded up ahead and I immediately leaned back as adamantine wire, as fine as hair was released from the hall.

I watched as it passed over me and embedded itself in the doorframe behind me. Had I been someone else, it would have decapitated me in a second.

Whipping myself up, I immediately rolled to the side across the cold floor as another faint click sounded and arrows were released from my right, thudding loudly as they dug into the heavy wooden door of the study.

Pushing up in a rush, I ran down the hallway, zigzagging as adamantine spikes pushed through barely noticeable slots in the wall. Their edges were as sharp as a razor blade.

Launching myself, I landed with a roll upon the staircase landing, the hallway I had been in a moment ago was now a deathly collection of spikes and blades that reflected in the light of the encroaching dawn.

"Fucking idiot," I mumbled to myself as I stood and eyed the adjacent hallways. Ezio's traps seemed a bit overkill and a bit barbaric, even for someone from our world. I frowned as I watched each spike slide back into place within the walls. All evidence of their presence vanished.

Why did he even need this shit?

He helped run pleasure houses. The Katopodis estate did not even have such preposterous traps…

Ensuring there weren't any medieval torture devices ready to spring on me, I stepped off the staircase landing, my boots echoing against the vacant space.

I began down the hallway yet again, the spikes remaining in the walls after being triggered already. I turned right and stood before the study door.

Grabbing a hold of one of the three arrows embedded in the wood, I yanked harshly and eyed it.

Adamantine forged arrows… I frowned as I eyed it.

"What are you up to?" I grumbled and tossed it aside before yanking the door open.

Ezio's study lay within. A large mahogany desk stood in the centre, a large window behind it looking out to the gardens outside.

A black leather couch took up the left of the room and a great bookcase to the right. Eyeing the room, I spotted no traps and stepped inside. I headed to the desk, immediately gripping the drawers, and yanking them open. Rifling through the contents, I found nothing of consequence…

Stepping back, I eyed the computer on the desk and immediately sat down, powering it up. I easily got past his firewalls and passcodes.

Kason had taught me a thing or two…

I was going through his files when my arm tingled, and I shook it away as I read over ledgers and more crap to do with the pleasure houses.

My arm tingled again, and I froze, looking down at it as my fingers hovered over the keyboard.

My heart began racing as I realised it was the Servile brand.

Braelyn.

Yanking my jacket off, I rubbed at it, trying to get the sensation to return, and cursed loudly, throwing a stapler across the room when I felt nothing and could not locate her through the bond.

Running my hand through my hair and clenching my jaw, I returned to going through the files on the computer. There was nothing of importance.

"Fuck!" I shouted, pushing back from the desk chair that banged against the wall behind me and caused the window to rattle.

I inhaled deeply as I clenched and unclenched my fists and stared ahead trying to think of what else to do.

I was staring at the bookcase when I noticed a certain book that had been placed between the others, but not shoved all the way in.

I cocked my head as I eyed it across the room and stepped around the desk. I headed toward it and halted when I noticed what book it was... Reaching out, I yanked it from the shelf. The adjacent books fell over, now leaning awkwardly against each other.

Hesiod's Theogony.

The original copy dates to seven hundred B.C. What was he doing with this? As far as I knew, it was meant to be in the armoury at home.

Flipping it over and paging through its delicate pages of age-worn parchment, it was indeed the one from home.

The stain of barbeque crisps left by tiny fingers still covered the back cover...

My mother had given me the hiding of my life when she discovered me in the armoury at eleven years old, crisps being shoved in my mouth as I browsed casually through the artefacts of our world, bored out of my mind as the rest of the family dealt with my aunt and uncle's funeral.

Ezio's parents...

Frowning, I turned the book over once more, not finding any clues as to what he would be doing with the book containing the origin stories and lineage of the gods.

Flipping through the pages, a piece of parchment fluttered out and landed atop my boot.

Reaching down, my finger still book-marking where I had the book open. I picked up the parchment, scowling as the texture felt off.

Almost like leather.

Holding it up to the window, where the sun had begun to rise, I cursed as I recognised the strange texture.

It was human skin, used by the dark witches of the Agora – The daughters of Circe.

They used it for their spells and invitations, any form of writing done in code as the ink would stain the leather-like substance.

"What the fuck are you up to, you little shit?" I spoke to the silent room, my temper flaring at Ezio's involvement with the daughters of Circe. Whatever he was involved in and needed Braelyn for had turned even darker than even *I* could imagine.

I set the book down on the desk, open on the page where the coded skin had fallen from, and placed both hands flat beside it as I peered down at its contents.

The book was open with a chapter that read about the origins of the titans and my blood turned to ice.

Siblings bring forth the clash of Titans.

A verse from the prophecy...

Was Ezio after her because of the prophecy? But even if he was, what could he possibly do with the information and Braelyn?

Closing my eyes briefly, I sighed heavily through my nose and opened them, staring out of the window.

"Stop trying to hide like a fucking novice," I gritted out.

I turned, leaning against the desk, and folded my arms across my chest.

"Sorry," Layna spoke quietly as she and Kason stepped into the study.

"Where is Trey?" I asked, annoyed that they were here.

"He is helping Dad try to smooth things over with the gods, Apollo included," Kason said as he stepped further into the room.

"And why are you two here?" I asked, keeping my voice deathly monotone.

Kason looked to Layna who eyed me intensely. Her blue gaze never left mine. It appeared she was searching my face for something, and I was about to leave when she finally spoke.

"We are here to help you."

"Help me or follow the hunt order?" I growled, turning back to the desk, slamming the book closed, and gathering the coded skin up in a swift, angry movement.

"Here to help you. To get her back," I stopped what I was doing and turned back to them, my brow furrowed as I looked at them each.

"Why?" I finally grumbled, not sure why they would be doing this as it went against orders. Against everything we were trained for and led to believe growing up.

Hell, they didn't even know Braelyn that well except for a few passing words the past few days.

"Family first. That is why," she snapped at me, Kason nodding in agreement as he too crossed his arms.

"She might be new to the family, but that doesn't make her any less family than you are, and you should know we would never abandon you, T," Kason finally added, determination in his voice, not his usual goofy cockiness.

I eyed them in silence.

The seconds ticked by.

The large clock on the wall the only sound in the room besides are shared breaths.

Nodding finally in agreement to them helping, I was still reeling over the fact that Ezio was a step ahead of us. I would deal with the consequences of the gods and whatever shit storm Trey and my father were dealing with later.

"Any idea what the hell this is?" I tossed the skin to Layna who caught it with ease.

She scowled in disgust as she held it and lifted her gaze to mine momentarily as she peered at it again, tracing a gloved hand over the inked code.

"Daughters of Circe?" she frowned and passed it to Kason who grabbed it gingerly and inspected it.

"Oh, grow up," Layna hissed at Kason as he turned pale and began gagging at the human skin between his fingers.

He shoved it back at her and bent over, hands on knees. His gags sounded aloud in the study. "That is revolting!" he moaned loudly and stood, his cheeks blown up as he exhaled heavily through his nose.

"How the fuck can you call yourself a reaper and gag at a piece of dehydrated skin?" I asked him, my brow raised.

"Oh, gods," he moaned and hurried behind the desk, hurling in the trash can.

Layna and I cursed loudly, both scowling at him as he popped back into view.

"Better?" I grumbled, scowling at my idiot brother who appeared a shade of green.

"Yeah, I think so," he began, sounding cheerier, and instantly shoved a hand over his mouth as a gag threatened once more.

His eyes went wide.

"Kason!" I growled out. "I swear to god if you fucking throw up one more time, I am going to throw you off of Ezio's balcony – what… what are you doing?" I asked incredulously as he moved to the window, opened it, and hung out as he peered up to the balcony above us.

"Checking if it's worth it," he called back, grinning.

"God's fucking help me," I grumbled as I wiped my hands down my face. "At least the window is open, so we don't have to smell that shit," I glared daggers at him.

"I think it's something about a sale… no, that's not right either," Layna spoke up behind me, frowning at the coded skin between her hands.

She was educated in most languages and texts. It would be difficult for her to come across a dialect she couldn't understand.

"Oh gods," she mumbled, her eyes snapping to mine.

"What is it?" I lurched forward, Kason stepping forward too.

"It's an auction."

"You mean…?" I asked, not even wanting to finish the words myself.

"It's an invitation and clearance for the auction house in the Agora," she finished.

My world stopped. No one got in there without clearance. Even reapers like us. It was a vile place where the most atrocious acts of savagery took place…

Kason and Layna spoke, but I heard nothing besides the rapid beating of my heart as it grew louder and louder.

Each beat was like the beating wings of death. My chest pulled tight.

Gods'…

What was happening?

I struggled for breath, my chest pulling tighter. I bent over, my hands on my knees and eyes wide in panic.

Layna and Kason knelt before me, eyes widened and fearful as they called out to me.

I couldn't hear, I couldn't breathe…

What the fuck?!

Kason had his hands on my shoulders, yelling at me as I stared ahead seeing nothing and hearing only my heart.

A sharp pain erupted across my jaw and the world began coming back into focus as I found myself sprawled across the floor of the study. The beating of my heart slowed, the sound returning gradually, and my chest tightened, allowing me to breathe.

Sucking in a lungful of air as I stared at the ceiling, I loosened my jaw, the pain flaring.

I looked over at Kason and my eyes narrowed, snapping amber.

"Oh, shit," he called out, eyes wide and his hand still being held in a fist.

I sat up, never taking my eyes from him and he took a step back placing his hands in the air, palms up trying to placate me.

"Dude…" he said, looking to Layna for help then back to me.

"Run," I sneered in a deadly silent tone.

Kason did as I said and managed to make it to the door before, I was up and slamming my body into his, resulting in both of us slamming into the bookshelf as I yanked him back.

Books tumbled across the room, the shelf broke, and I had him by the collar of his shirt as I heaved him up against the still-standing part of the shelf.

"Help?" Kason called meekly to Layna who remained by the desk with her arms crossed and eyes narrowed on us in irritation.

"Let him, go you idiot," she hissed at me from behind.

"You ever fucking punch me again…" I seethed in Kason's face and then chuckling sinisterly, I allowed him to imagine what it was I would do to him.

"Oh, shut up, T. You were having a panic attack. Kason just got the shot in before I could…"

I scowled at Kason who remained in my grip with his eyes still wide in fear.

Shoving off him I whirled on my sister. "Panic attack?"

What shit is this?

"Yes, a panic attack." She rolled her eyes at me and turned her attention to the desk where the book and skin layers were.

"Now if you guys are done, can we finish figuring out what we need to do?" she called out.

I had a panic attack. A fucking panic attack?! I never…

"You think Ezio is going to the auction house to sell or trade Braelyn?" Kason spoke to Layna, stepping around me and weaving between the scattered books and pieces of shelving.

Scowling at them and the thought of me having a god-damned panic attack, I forced myself to calm down and push aside the ridiculous notion. I had never in my life had a panic attack.

Shit, I had seen and done enough in my life, including killing Hades himself and sleeping like a baby…

"He isn't going to sell. It will be a trade," I spoke up from where I stood.

They both turned to me, waiting for me to elaborate.

"He has no reason to sell. Ezio is beyond wealthy. He said he needs her. So, he needs her for something in return."

"Okay but what?" Layna asked, her frown deepening.

"Does it even matter what he needs? The issue is getting in somehow and getting Braelyn back," Kason spoke up, looking between us and crossing his arms.

"Yes, it matters what he needs. Because if he is willing to go to such lengths then it can't be anything good. The daughters of Circe never dabble in anything good…" I answered and rubbed at my painful jaw as I glared at him.

Little shit…

Kason noticed my icy look and suddenly found a rather peculiar piece of fluff fascinating on his sleeve and then the ceiling…

"What is Ezio doing with this?" Layna frowned, holding up the ancient book.

"That's what I was wondering about," I grumbled stepping forward and taking it from her as I flipped through the pages.

"You need to tell us everything that you know. No more secrets, T," Layna called out to me as she eyed me, her arms crossed, and hip cocked. "You know more than we do. It's obvious."

I lowered the book. Searching her face and then Kason's who stood just behind her.

"Theo?" Kason urged me, his voice solemn and he took a step forward.

"We have always stuck together. Family first. That is our motto and I know I fuck around like everything is a joke most of the time, but it doesn't change that family comes first. We aren't known as the Bloodhound Brothers for nothing. Let us help you. Let us help her…"

I watched him, knowing he spoke the truth and Layna waited patiently for me to speak.

I needed to be honest with myself that I needed them.

"This is what I know," I sighed, gritting my teeth and retrieving the prophecy and hunt order from my jacket pocket, placing it on the table for them to see, and stepping back.

They both looked at the pieces of parchment and then at me before stepping to the desk and reading them.

"Where did you get these?" It was Layna who spoke in bewilderment as she picked them up, inspecting both.

"It doesn't matter," I wasn't about to screw over Hayden for giving them to me.

That was for sure…

"What matters is that the hunt order still stands. This means that now everyone knows it's Braelyn, we still must complete the order or all of us will be executed. Code Red…"

"Shit," Kason muttered, rubbing at his jaw as he stared at the order in our sister's hands.

"The prophecy is why there is a hunt order," I continued, feeling my muscles tense with trepidation, and anger….

A flurry of contradicting emotions.

Layna passed the hunt order to Kason as she began reading the prophecy out aloud.

"*As soon as wolves roar and ravens flee. A betrayal brings to life a new life. There comes a day when what is green turns to moonlight. A creeper of shadows. Manipulator.*" Layna whipped her head to me still holding the parchment before her.

"She is a shadow-stalker," she said barely above a whisper.

I nodded and Kason scrunched his face in confusion.

"Braelyn can shadow-stalk?"

"Yes," I answered, my jaw clenched, and Kason's eyebrows rose in shock.

"*A man clad in crimson, born of emerald sight. Shall bring forth the overthrowing of royalty. As soon as the blind man sees once more, siblings bring forth the clash of Titans.*" Layna continued reading aloud. "The emerald sight I assume is her eyes, but the rest doesn't make sense." She frowned as she read it over again.

"Siblings… Do you think it means… us?" Kason asked looking between us in silent contemplation.

"It could be, but I don't know," I answered running a hand through my black hair.

"*It shall be on the day that the true one reveals herself, the two-faced one brings forth almighty darkness. Upon the day the water rises to the sky, the guilty shall reap. Once stars fall from the sky, a surrender awakens the downfall of an empire.*"

"Okay, now that makes absolutely no fucking sense…" Kason said as Layna finished reading the verse.

"Empire means the gods…" I muttered in irritation.

"What? How do you know?" Layna asked, her eyes wide.

"Why do you think they issued the hunt order? She is a threat to them. A threat to their empire." I growled out.

It's the only thing that made sense and Proteus eluded as much…

Why she was a threat was still a mystery.

"*When the moment comes that the wolves howl together, the young one shall cause the rise of what was forgotten. The black rose and thorn shall conquer.*" Layna and Kason's eyes snapped to my exposed arm, covered in the Servile brand.

Expanded across my tattoos, it covered my hand, wrapped around my thumb and all along my forearm, ending at my elbow.

Kason raised his gaze to meet mine first and I looked back, giving nothing away.

"Well… No need to explain the final line… but the rest? Wolves?" Layna frowned again and chewed her lip as she pondered over it.

"She has sway over the sacred wolves of Whispering Woods," I muttered remembering how the wolves had aided her the Friday before the Servile.

When I had encountered her, not knowing who she was then…

Stepping around them I picked up the hunt order Kason placed on the desk and snatched the prophecy back from my sister's grasp. I pocketed both quickly.

"She does?" Kason asked bewildered. His eyes were wide, and Layna watched on silently, equally perplexed.

"Yes," I snapped.

I did not feel comfortable exposing her this way but knew I needed their help.

"Shit…" Kason mumbled after a whistle. "I knew I liked her, but now I fucking love her. She's so hardcore!" He grinned at me wagging his eyebrows.

My eyes flashed amber and I stepped forward. "Enough," Layna snapped at us both and I shook my head trying to rid myself of the need to maim my brother.

Why was I territorial?

I always had been, but this was almost feral… raw instinct…

It didn't matter to me in that instant that he was my brother.

If it meant keeping Braelyn, I would have killed him and it had me turning away as I squeezed my eyes shut, forcing the instinct down deep.

"Theo?" Layna called to me, and I turned around, exhaling as my eyes returned to normal.

Her hard gaze searched mine and she spoke to Kason. Her ice-blue eyes never left mine as she said, "Kason, go and search the rest of the house for anything that may be useful."

"But."

"Just do it," she spoke sternly when he began to protest.

"Alrighty then, I know when I'm not wanted," he muttered, rolling his eyes and leaving the study with a quick worried glance in my direction.

Layna and I stood in silence until we were sure he had ventured upstairs.

"What was that about?" she asked, keeping her voice low.

"Nothing."

"Cut the shit. It's not the first time it has happened. You are usually near borderline psychotic, but this is not the first time you have wanted to kill someone for saying something about her… You would never willingly hurt one of us, I know that, but when it comes to her, you look like you would without a second thought… Don't think I haven't noticed."

"Borderline psychotic?" I asked, as I crossed my arms and smirked.

"Don't deflect. I taught you that shit, little brother," she growled at me.

"Fine. I don't know why or what it is but the thought of someone laying any sort of claim on her gets my blood boiling." I snapped and clenched my jaw in anger.

Layna was silent as she eyed me, face stern, and her eyes then travelled down the length of my body.

"Do you think maybe that she is…"

"No," I snapped not allowing her to finish the fucking ridiculous notion.

"Mmm…" she murmured and stepped away from me and headed to the door of the study. "You are so quick to dismiss it, but you know the truth," she said and then exited.

I watched her go and clenched my jaw which had already healed entirely from Kason's blow. I could not let the possibility of Layna's train of thought get in the way.

I had already considered it, but if I accepted that it may be true… I may as well be the one to annihilate my entire family…

I just hoped it did not come down to choosing, which is why I needed to figure this all out and get Braelyn back safely as soon as possible.

Theo

Layna, I, and Kason did a thorough sweep of the house.

There had been nothing to find except the indication that our cousin was indeed highly paranoid or had amassed for himself dangerous enemies.

Traps were set throughout the house.

Ezio worked in the running of the pleasure houses. What kind of business did he get himself involved with that he felt the need to protect himself so?

It was beyond fucking ridiculous.

The sun had now risen beyond the horizon and cast its stagnant heat over the manor. Exiting the front door, we halted upon the gravel driveway. "Okay, so what do we know?" Layna asked, braiding her red hair back while she spoke.

"Braelyn is some badass queen?" Kason mumbled and I exhaled loudly as I attempted to control myself.

"Really? Focus… Gods," she scowled at him after a glance at me, before listing off the details, raising a finger for each point.

"The prophecy is about her, but we don't know all the details. The gods issued the hunt order because of said prophecy…" I nodded, standing with arms crossed and still eyeing my brother in irritation.

"Ezio, our wonderfully idiotic cousin, has taken her because he needs something from the daughters of Circe. It is safe to assume he is the anonymous tip-off that alerted the gods of her presence twelve years ago."

The prick better be savouring his time because once I found him…

We had discussed it at length during our search and it made sense. He had been living with us and he knew about her to kidnap her… what he needed in return now was a mystery. "We need to get into the auction house tomorrow. The codex on the skin listed tomorrow's date. So how do we get in?" she asked, chewing her bottom lip again as she looked at me.

"You know how I plan on getting in," I scoffed and kicked at the gravel bored with this conversation and my temper barely in check.

The Shadows of Mirrors in my pocket had not indicated Ezio's location yet, and I had the suspicion that it wouldn't work at all.

The asshole had found a way to truly cover his tracks.

There was no way he could be in The Shiver for so long…

It was a miracle that I hadn't gone on a rampage, destroying everything in sight already. But I knew I had to be smart about this and not let whatever fucking feelings I had to distract me from a safe extraction…

"Your plan of going in there and slaughtering everyone and everything won't work, you fool. There are wards that we cannot even get past. And they will notice us from a mile away. Ezio will be long gone before we even get close to him." She shook her head at me and scratched her head as she looked off into the distance, deep in thought.

"We sell something of our own," Kason spoke up, looking between us.

"That could work, but they won't let reapers in…" Layna sighed.

"Then we need someone who isn't a reaper to get in," Kason rubbed at his neck frowning.

I snapped my eyes to Layna as a thought hit me.

"Dorian."

"Are you out of your damn mind?" Layna hissed back almost instantly.

"He isn't a reaper and I'm pretty sure that he will want to help when he hears the news if he hasn't already…" I wouldn't back down.

It was a smart idea, and my sister knew it.

I eyed her knowing her reasons for hesitating, but her tactile mind finally relinquished. "Fine," she grumbled irritated but agreeing.

Just then Kason's phone began ringing and he fished in his pocket for it and stared at the screen.

"It's Trey." Answering the call, he stepped away to speak to our brother whom no doubt was dealing with the biggest shitstorm our family had yet to come across.

"I'll call Dorian to meet up," Layna called to me before walking over to the tree line that encased the driveway.

I eyed both siblings.

Kason was tense. His eyes drifted to me intermittently as he spoke. Layna spoke in hushed tones as she spoke to Dorian. I sighed heavily as I tilted my head back. My body was tensed like a live wire.

Or more accurately a bomb ready to detonate.

I absentmindedly rubbed my hand over the Servile brand and gritted my teeth in anticipation of any form of signal from Braelyn. There was nothing.

"Fuck," I mumbled and was pinching the bridge of my nose when Layna called to me.

"Dorian has been kept away from all meetings. He didn't know what was happening. Mathias has banned him from interfering in any way."

"Will he help?" I asked, crossing my arms.

"As much as I hate it, yes, he will. With no hesitation. He's going to meet us in the Whispering Woods. He says there is a willow tree that Braelyn always used to go to. He sent me the coordinates."

I almost laughed at the fucking irony.

"Don't bother. I know exactly where it is," I spoke, giving nothing away to the hurricane of emotions.

As far as anyone would see, I appeared calm, collected, and deadly. I tried ignoring my sister's inquiring stare and cracked my neck, releasing some of the built-up tension.

We looked to Kason who was still on the call with Trey and held the phone away from his ear as Trey began yelling something.

"Yeah, okay dude," Kason finally spoke and ended the call with a sigh and roll of his eyes. "He is especially prickly today," he mumbled as he walked over to where we stood.

"What did he say?" I asked trying to remain in control of myself. I was teetering on the precipice of losing.

"Well, the gods are questioning if we have been knowingly harbouring someone that has been under a hunt order for twelve years. Mathias is being questioned separately. Apollo is with him." He scratched at his jaw again before he continued.

"The hunt order still stands regardless."

"We knew they wouldn't change their minds though. What else?" Layna spoke, noticing Kason fidget where he stood.

"Kason?" I snapped, irritable.

"The box that she had when Ezio took her? It's the Heart of Ouranos…"

Shit.

"Nine hells," Layna whispered, wide-eyed.

This just became more complex.

"We need to find it and get it back, otherwise a Code Red will be issued to House Thalassa against every single one of us," he added, his voice deep and solemn.

"I'm sure Calista will enjoy that. Retribution for her brother…" I grumbled.

A tic worked its way into my jaw.

"What was she even doing with it?" Layna snapped at me, and I felt my eyes blaze amber at her tone.

"I don't fucking know," I gritted out.

But I planned on finding out.

My little rose wouldn't have been in that armoury and with the box unless it was something important.

"Don't even give me that look. Put those god-damned eyes away. I am not your enemy, baby brother," she hissed at me taking a step forward.

"Then drop the fucking tone, Layna." I snapped back, dropping my arms at my side.

"Guys…" Kason called out as we faced off at one another.

His voice was ignored.

"Why was she in the armoury? Why did she take the Heart of Ouranos, Theo?!" she snapped yet again, and my temper snapped as we glared at each other.

Kason noticed and was between us in a second, arms out against each of us. He gripped my shirt as well as Layna's tightly. My breathing was heavy, and my sneer turned into a sinister smirk as we continued glaring.

"That's fucking enough! How did I become the mature one here?" Kason snapped and shoved us both back. "It doesn't fucking matter! She was there, she had it and we can try to figure it out with a million possibilities, but what we need to figure out is how to get her back, as well as the box." Kason was simmering with that rare wrath that hardly ever showed itself and Layna finally turned her eyes away from mine.

"So, what's the plan? Because we cannot stand around here all day," he asked running a hand through his wavy black hair and blue eyes looking between us each.

"We are going to meet with Dorian and figure it out from there," Layna spoke with her irritation still showing through.

I watched them in silence, with my arms crossed.

Whatever shit Braelyn had herself involved in…

Gods.

She better have a good reason.

I already was thinking over a million possibilities of getting her out of this mess but…

"Use the coordinates. I'll meet you there." I growled out and my eyes snapped amber just before I erupted into a swarm of ravens.

I left the estate, heading in the direction of the Whispering Woods. The start of a plan began forming in my mind.

I just hoped it would work.

If not, blood would be shed, and no one left standing.

I was getting Braelyn back no matter what.

Braelyn

I had lost track of time yet again as Ezio drugged me, causing me to drift in and out of consciousness intermittently.

I could recall glimpses of being carried through the pleasure house, then darkness.

I awoke again in the cell. The glare of the lights blinded the cold and damp room.

I could only assume that more tests were being run on me and awoke to the sound of chains rattling. I tried pulling away from the gurney, only to realise that the chains were wrapped around my throat like a collar tied to a leash.

My anger flared as I found my focus on the cell door as I lay in my drugged stupor.

The ancient force that resided within me had curled itself so deep within as it slumbered that it was a struggle to find it still safe there.

A faint speck of power in the darkness out of reach…

Forcing myself up by my elbows, I noticed the chains that Ezio had previously used to tie me down across my legs and chest were nowhere to be seen.

Sitting up, I grabbed at the fine, dainty chains now wrapped around my neck, finding no way to remove them.

I managed to chip my nails as I pried and pulled uselessly against the cold metal, finding it misleadingly strong.

Grabbing the long reflecting piece that dangled from the back, I began gathering it and felt it pull taut.

Swivelling where I sat, I then noticed it locked to an eye-hook in the stone floor.

Growling in frustration, I stood from the gurney and immediately regretted my decision.

Grabbing a hold of the side, I waited for my balance to return and the humming in my head to cease.

Once the world had stopped spinning, I began my slow walk around the bed, finding myself kneeling gingerly before the hook. I yanked at the chain.

Nothing happened.

Trying once again, using all my force, even leaning back as I pulled, the ridiculously delicate chain held.

Breathing heavily, I glared at it, seemingly willing it to combust under my gaze.

"Ah. You are up. Good." Ezio's smug voice sounded from near the door. "Just in time as predicted. Seems I got the dosage pinned down exactly right." He grinned at me as I turned my head in his direction and narrowed my gaze on him.

I remained crouched before the hook. The dainty chain still clenched between my hand's tight grip.

"Don't bother," he mumbled, stepping further into the room.

I watched him in silence as he came around the gurney, stopping beside me and crouching down to my level.

"Another little masterpiece of Hephaestus," he picked up a piece of the chain and rubbed it between his fingers as if in contemplation.

Not wasting a second, I launched myself at him, wrapping the chain around his neck and pulling it tight.

Ezio scrambled, trying fruitlessly to remove the chain as I pulled tighter.

His face began turning red as I deprived him of oxygen and wrapped the chain around my hands, pulling the length impossibly tighter.

I dodged his kicking legs and growled in anger wishing he would drop dead any second.

A rustling of pale robes entered the cell and rushed to where I held Ezio's life in my hands.

I did not dare to remove my eyes from Ezio's enlarged, bloodshot blue ones.

So much fear…

I could hear the slowing of his beating heart and pulled tighter.

A sudden sting in my arm had me whipping my head around.

I found a syringe now being emptied into my bloodstream by a robed figure. My head began to buzz, and I shook it hastily to remain focused. Just a little longer and he would be dead… just a little longer…

"Not yet, Tsalmaveth," the robed figure spoke in hushed tones for only me to hear.

I struggled for focus, and he removed the syringe from my arm as my grip on the chains loosened.

Shaking my head dazed yet again, I yanked on the chains, only to have my grip leave me. They fell to the stone floor of the cell with an audible clang that echoed around us.

Ezio immediately scrambled away. His breathing was laboured as he eyed me and then the figure with wide eyes.

He continued to rub at his neck. Red welts were visible.

My body began to feel heavy.

The weight of the entire world crashing down on me. I managed to turn back to the robed figure. I could not make out much.

My vision had begun to swim. I caught glimpses of a pale, tanned robe. Brown leather boots. A hood concealing the majority of the induvial from view.

I did a double take.

As useless as it was as I was pulled under by the drug.

Green eyes…

Not the same shade as myself… but *green*… I frowned, slumping against the stone wall, bulbs digging into my back as I did so.

"Who…" I managed to mumble but my mouth seemed stuffed with cotton as the buzzing in my head grew louder.

The robed figure eyed me in silence. Only his gaze showed through his concealment.

A scar ran over his right eye…

Ezio began cursing loudly and the individual turned his attention away… his eyes narrowing on Ezio.

"Get up," the man snapped from behind his face wrap and stood, leaving me slumped against the cool stones.

To try to turn my head in their direction as Ezio managed to stand, leading them out, was hopeless.

I stared ahead as my focus waned.

The final image I had managed to hold on to was of the cell door closing behind them as my vision turned dark.

I awoke.

The gods only knew how much longer after I had been drugged.

I shifted against the soft leather seats and looked around. The world passed by us in a blur through the windows of the car.

Looking down at myself, I remained dressed in the horrendous attire from the pleasure house. The dainty shining chain remained around my neck; the end fastened to somewhere behind the seat.

I turned and froze as Ezio was seated beside me; his neck was covered in angry welts as he glared at me.

I smirked at the sight sinisterly.

"Thank the gods I can rid myself of you soon enough," he grumbled and ran his finger over his downturned lip lost in thought as he looked me up and down.

"You almost killed me, you little bitch," he seethed.

The venom was clear in his tone.

"Pity I failed. Next time you will not be so lucky," I deadpanned and looked out of the window.

Ezio remained silent at my death promise. No doubt unsure whether he should believe me or not.

However, I knew in my bones that he would be wiped from the plane of existence by my hands. He was on borrowed time, and I intended to collect.

As I watched through the window, I noticed that the Whispering Woods were in the distance. Their silent call to me was clear even from this distance.

I frowned, unsure of where we were headed. Looking forward, past the unnamed driver, I saw the city in the distance as we headed towards it. How long had I been in Ezio's captivity?

Was Theo even looking for me or was he relieved to be rid of his ties to me?

The latter thought had an ache erupt through my chest which I quickly shoved away.

He hated me. He had made it clear numerous times… and I hated him. Perhaps this was my way to free myself of the ridiculousness of the Servile bond…

Even though I thought it, I knew I would never believe it.

My mind and dare I admit it, heart, knew better…

If no one else knew it, I would be okay…

I wanted to know where we were headed and where his mysterious companion had disappeared to but instead held my tongue. My silence would frustrate Ezio as it had been since my capture.

I knew it.

He would eventually be foolish enough to try and gloat, revealing more than he should.

Sighing, I adjusted myself in the seat and watched as the world outside flew past.

Searching internally, I was relieved to find the ancient power still there… coiled tightly in slumber within the depths.

I sensed its presence yet was blocked from it. A wall was cast down between us.

In the moments I had no connection to it when I first arrived in captivity, I had felt lost…

Alone.

I had always been somewhat afraid of power. Afraid of myself… yet in that dreamlike state where I had seen it for the very first time when it had looked me in the eyes, I had felt at peace.

It was a separate entity, yet so deeply woven into the fabric of my being, that we were the same.

"You are not even a little bit curious about where we are going?" Ezio finally spoke.

I ignored him completely, hearing him shuffle in his seat beside me.

Typical, and just as predicted…

"Very well. Enjoy your final moments of freedom. It won't last long," he attempted taunting me into enquiring about our looming destination.

I could fathom a guess it was the exchange that I had overheard them speaking about. I would know more once arrived and decide how I would get myself free of him.

Turning my head slowly, I eyed him with narrowed emerald eyes.

"I would suggest that you do the same, Ezio. Each breath you take is the countdown to when I shall remove the life from your appalling body." I then smirked and readjusted myself to gaze out the window.

My chin held high and the chains reflected off the setting sun. "I shall very much enjoy it." I sighed wistfully.

"Bitch," he sneered, causing me to snicker lowly.

"Oh, yes, I am. You have no idea. Absolutely none. You do not understand what you have just done to yourself." I chuckled sinisterly, not bothering to look at him.

My power had been subdued, lost in a deep slumber. I had assumed it was caused by the chains created by the gods' blacksmith.

I could have easily killed him now, yet I wanted to know what it was he needed me for as well as the fact I remained constrained to the vehicle by the shining chains.

So, I continued to be shackled in the seat beside him, listening to his rapidly beating heart.

So much fear… why was that?

Ezio remained silent for the rest of our journey, not even looking in my direction. The city surrounded us in darkness and flashing lights.

The sun had set a few minutes ago. We drove through the streets, skyscrapers looming overhead. I wondered how many secrets they had been witness to. I watched in silent awe as civilians walked down the streets, chatting and completely oblivious to the control the gods had over their everyday life.

I noticed as we passed, a person exchanging cash for drugs down a darkened alley.

Fools.

Even the drugs they lusted after were controlled by the gods…

Cars passed in a blur, and we finally came to a stop near the back end of a market. I watched silently as the market filled with shoppers of all ages.

Vendors calling out for the most attention. It was quieter where we had parked and the driver opened his door, exiting and leaving us alone in the vehicle.

I was watching him when Ezio suddenly lunged, inserting one of his god-damned syringes into my exposed thigh, immediately pushing the plunger down as the crimson liquid filled my veins.

Nine hells!

My temper snapped. Yanking the syringe out, I lunged at him.

"Stop!" he yelled, and my body halted, frozen by his command.

I gritted my teeth as I loomed over him shaking with my forced restraint. The syringe was held tightly in my grip with the needle hovering over his widened, fear-filled eye.

Just one slight movement forward and the needle would be embedded in it.

"Sit down," he snapped. I clenched my jaw as I did as he said.

The drug made it impossible to fight his every command.

"Give it to me," he sighed and immediately screamed as I stabbed the needle through his outstretched and waiting palm.

"You did not say how to give it," I sneered back as I watched him with a raised brow.

Ezio cursed loudly as he pulled the needle from his hand, blood began pooling in his palm before his fist swung at me, connecting with my jaw.

My head whipped to the right and pain erupted through my face.

I controlled my breathing as I felt my rage boil through my blood. My black hair was a curtain covering me before I slowly sat straight up, my eyes locking on his.

I tasted blood in my mouth as it coated my tongue and spat it at him before throwing my fist against his jaw.

I watched as his head whipped back and I wiped at my mouth, seeing my fingers coming away crimson.

Ezio glared at me, his face covered in my blood and spit.

"Consider yourself fucking lucky, I cannot do more damage as I need this trade to go through," he growled as he wiped at his face angrily.

I smiled widely. Sinisterly.

Blood coated my teeth, and I was sure I looked maniacal. Ezio's heart increased in speed, indicating his fear of me.

Good.

He should be scared.

"You will speak to no one. Always remain silent. You will do as I say. No violence whatsoever. You will not shadow-stalk. The chains and drugs prohibit it, so don't even fucking try." He snapped irritably before opening the car door and exiting the car.

The door slammed shut just as the driver opened my side, saying nothing and refusing to look at me. He reached behind me, unlocking the chain from behind and handing the god-damned leash to Ezio.

I wanted to scream and curse at him, cause a scene yet I couldn't as his command was law over my body while the drug remained swimming through my veins.

"Clean her face," he snapped at the driver and held tightly to the end of the chain.

I watched Ezio silently as the driver wiped at my face and handed me a bottle of water to rinse my mouth. Ezio wiped at his face and then his bleeding palm against his black suit pants, all the while never taking his grip from the chain. Once he was satisfied I was clean enough, he yanked on the chain, pulling me from the car. The driver bowed to him before retreating to the car and driving off.

I scoffed at the fact that Ezio was being bowed to.

He may be a Katopodis but did not reserve the right to be bowed to. He was a nobody in our world.

Ezio glared at me and pulled me forward, close enough that his ridiculous leash was concealed between us, and walked along the quiet part of the street, heading to a vacant vending stand.

Walking through the back, the feeling of tendrils caressing across my skin had me sucking in a breath before its hold was released and we entered a market of chaos and creatures of our world.

"Welcome to the Agora," he mumbled, keeping me close as he led us forward.

Looking around, my skin crawled.

This place was wrong.

So much darkness and ancient cruel power dripped down its surfaces.

A few people that I recognised as witches, daughters of Circe, watched us go as Ezio pulled me along toward a building up ahead. Creatures and witches lined the street, waiting to gain entrance.

Loud calls and cheers erupted from inside and had me careening my neck to see better. It sounded much like bidding. I stopped dead in my tracks, my eyes snapping to Ezio who bemoaned irately and yanked on the chain as he headed to the back of the building.

I tried by all my might to stop myself, to yank back but a simple word from Ezio had me walking diligently beside him. I screamed within myself, wanting to run in the opposite direction. "Ezio Katopodis," he muttered to someone at the door before they disappeared.

I willed myself to calm down, counting to ten in my head as I spun my ring. Around and around. Ezio appeared nervous himself, which only had me re-evaluating my circumstances further.

He brought me here for a trade, but for what and with whom. If he was scared, then my chances were slim as the object to be traded…

"This way," a woman spoke, her face concealed by a mask of wood, only slits for breathing cut into it and a bloody handprint covered its cracking surface. Ezio nodded and began forward, the leash pulling taut before I was forced forward.

The sounds of the bidding in another part of the building carried down the dirty halls. We followed the masked woman, her dress covered in what appeared to be dried blood and charcoal-covered fingertips.

As we passed a set of stairs, screams erupted and had me halting. Ezio yanked on the chain, and I found myself staring into its dark depths before he pulled me too far away. The woman opened a heavy wooden door, indicating for us to enter.

"The goods appear damaged?" she spoke muffled behind the wooden mask.

She stepped forward, towering over my short stature and grasping my jaw. The site of Ezio's punch flared with pain under her bruising grip. "Apologies. We had an issue while in transport," the asshole replied, nodding his head to her in a form of an apologetic bow.

"It appears she can give as well as she is given." The woman cocked her head as she eyed Ezio's purple jaw and cheek, before cocking it the other way, somehow inspecting his bleeding hand.

A chill ran down my spine as the sound of her inhaling deeply scenting Ezio's blood within the room.

Ezio shuffled on the spot. His heart rate increased as she eyed him, smelling him. "You will wait here until you are called," she spoke as she soundlessly drifted toward the door.

"Do not damage the goods any further. The master will not have damaged goods tainting his establishment. You will take her place if I return to any further… issues, young Katopodis…" With that being said, she shut the door as she exited, but not before sniffing at him yet again.

A clucking noise escaped from behind her mask. Ezio had gone pale, his eyes never leaving the door. Now that it had been shut, I noticed the gouges across its surface.

Taking a step closer, I saw them for what they were.

Scratch marks, left behind by fingers, eagerly wanting to escape.

I turned my gaze to Ezio, seeing that he saw them too.

Sighing dramatically, he turned his attention to me.

I was still forced to remain silent, but I could have some fun by getting under his skin.

I raised my chin smirking at him before walking over to the barrel that sat against the wall.

Taking a seat, I crossed my legs serenely and wove my fingers together over my knee as I waited.

The chain connecting to his grip slid across the filthy brick floor and clanked loudly. In the distance, the cheers and roars of the bidding sounded out.

We had waited for what felt like hours.

Ezio had remained standing, shooting glances at me throughout the wait.

Some were fearful, others hateful. I ignored him the entire time, sitting as if I was not doomed, which seemed to confuse him if the looks were anything to go by…

The door opened with a loud creak and the woman from earlier stood in the doorway, her head cocked at me and then at Ezio.

"Come," she hissed and began silently down the hallway. The sounds of the bidding become fainter the further we followed.

"Where are we going?" Ezio called out to her, having noticed the same.

"Instructions from the master," was her only response as she rounded a corner and stood before yet another heavy wooden door.

"You will wait here," she spoke to Ezio and held out a blackened hand for the chain.

"Where she goes, I go," he snapped defiantly.

"You will wait here," she repeated, the clucking noises sounding between each word.

Ezio looked to me then back to her, knowing he held no sway in this place, and gingerly handed over my leash to her outstretched hand.

I ignored him as he watched me much like a piece of meat he was ready to fight over.

The woman proceeded to open the door. A bathhouse lay within. More masked women stood waiting in line.

Five of them to be exact.

Ezio began to protest as she led me through, and he was cut off as the door was shut in his face. I watched them with trepidation as I was led forward.

The masks not giving any hint of what lay beneath the blood-soaked wooden surface. I was stopped before them, and they started forward, immediately grabbing for the red pleasure house attire.

I struggled against their ice-cold grasp only to have the chain yanked and a clucking noise escaping the woman that held me in her grasp. "The master wishes you be presentable for the bidding." She snapped.

I froze in my struggles and looked at her and down her grey blood-covered dress…

I wanted to ask why but found the words stuck in my mouth as Ezio's command still held.

I relinquished my struggles and allowed them to disrobe me. I stood bare before them staring dead ahead and my chin held high. I would not appear weak. I would not appear afraid.

I was Braelyn Sarris, princess of the highest house of the gods.

And I was a weapon.

I remained steadfast as their hands washed me, leaving no spot untouched. I gritted my teeth in anger at the feel of them.

The only thing adorning my body was the reflecting dainty chain that wound around my neck multiple times and left only the leash dangling down the back which remained firmly in the grasp of the unidentified woman.

I remained stoic as they then began rubbing scented oils across my skin, leaving my skin shimmering with a golden sheen.

They then led me forward as the one brought forward a black dress.

I ignored them as they placed my arms through the sleeves of wrapped and twisted organza before they fastened the back. The black material shimmered and reflected, laying across my shoulders, and falling to a plunging neckline. They then fastened a golden, metal corset across my waist, fastening it tightly in place.

The gold was woven in intricate swirls, delicate silver stars, and crescent moons moulded between each swirl.

I could barely breathe as they fastened it further, my waist being pulled impossibly small. They then led me forward, the organza flowing behind me as it swept across the floor, a slit allowing my right leg to step through as it ended near my hip. I was forced into a chair as they began clucking at each other, tugging at the tendrils of my long black hair.

I found myself staring at my reflection as they brushed and pinned my hair. I barely recognised myself.

Not due to the attire, but the person sitting staring back at me.

My emerald eyes shone back. My face was yanked to the side as chilled fingers began smearing makeup across my face.

Coal lined my eyes, smudged across my eyelids, and light rouge added to my cheeks. My lips were covered in further golden tinted oils, shining brightly against the lights. Another woman shoved my face forward and placed a golden tiara on my head.

I hissed against the sting as the heaviness of it bit into my scalp.

I glared at them in the mirror as it was fastened, and strands of my hair clipped around them.

They managed to cover the tiara's combs and left the rest of my midnight hair hanging down to my waist.

A headache already threatened by its weight.

Looking at myself in the mirror with narrowed eyes, I wondered why they needed me done up so… The tiara was of solid gold, and rays reaching for the heavens created a halo around my head. The part directly atop my head was a mix of moons and stars and reflecting emerald and navy gems.

A pull on the chain had me looking to my right, finding the woman cocking her head at me as if inspecting if I was fit enough for whomever this master was…

"Come," she hissed and pulled the chain as she started forward.

I barely managed to stand in time as the chain pulled tight and I stumbled after her. My bare feet were cold against the floor.

I managed to right myself as I scowled at her back.

Gods. This corset was tight…

She opened the door, finding a brooding Ezio leaning against the filthy wall. He opened his mouth to say something to her but shut it as his eyes met the sight of me.

I raised my chin, clasping my hands before me, and narrowed my eyes at him before stepping past them and stopping.

I still could not speak but raised my brow in a silent query. *Well? shall we get this over with?*

Ezio watched me in silence and asked for the chain back, which he was handed immediately. He wrapped it around his hand, clenching it tightly.

"This is taking longer than expected. Should I expect further delays?" Ezio spoke to the woman.

She cocked her head eerily at him and walked ahead, not answering him. I followed, not bothering to wait for Ezio who scrambled after me, shortening the leash as he wrapped it further around his fist.

"I will admit, you seem eager, which… disturbs me…how someone could be eager for their imminent demise," he muttered, his eyes running the length of me.

I ignored him, staring ahead as we continued down the hallway.

I was not eager.

If anything, far from it…

Yet I would be damned if I let this fool of a man think he could break me.

The ancient power within me stirred and my steps faltered briefly, which Ezio smiled at, assuming he had gotten under my skin. I dared a look at him and narrowed my coal-lined eyes as he smiled smugly as we walked.

Fool.

A god-damned fool is what he was.

As predicted, the drug was wearing off… I had noted that the drugs had begun wearing off sooner the more he gave them to me. It would only be a matter of time. My biggest challenge would be the chain. The power stirred again, its maw opening wide in a huff as it coiled around my bones in a silent, weakened greeting.

The woman halted behind a worn heavy curtain.

Grime lay upon its woven tapestry and the roars and bidding cheers sounded from the other side. Ezio paled.

"I was told that my involvement would be anonymous. My identity is hidden."

"No anonymity. You shall stand beside your object, your goods, during the trading." She snapped back, shoving aside the curtain.

I would have objected to being referred to as an object but found myself frozen as a sea of creatures, big, small, humanoid, and nightmarish filled the roaring crowd.

Daughters of Circe could be spotted bidding and mingling with the crowd. Their presence was strong in the bidding hall. The ancient power within coiled itself tighter around me and I cleared my throat as I regained my composure.

Shoving my shoulders back, I waited for Ezio to lead the way. I had to hide my gleeful smirk at the sound of his plot already not going according to plan.

Ezio was arguing with the woman when she shoved him out of the enclosure and the hall went silent.

I watched as the chain led to where he stood with every eye in the room upon him.

Ezio righted himself and began pulling on the chain to get me closer.

Breathing deeply, I grabbed the end of the chain, halting his pulls.

A tic worked its way into his jaw, and he began toward me.

Each step was thunderous.

Raising my chin, I looked at the woman one last time and walked out before the crowd and right past Ezio who froze confused as I walked ahead. I stopped in the middle of the raised platform and adjusted my dress skirts and stared at my Servile brand for a moment, at every rose and thorn that covered my skin.

At last, I exhaled, shoved my shoulders back, and stared ahead, every bit the princess I was.

The leash still led to Ezio who stood frozen much like the crowd.

At the sight of my eyes, the hall erupted into a frenzy.

Theo

The auction house bidding hall was pandemonium.

I shoved my way through, my eyes on the lookout for any suspicion, especially from the daughters of Circe who littered the space.

Layna and Kason were in their designated spots, Dorian with them, hopefully sticking to the plan. The smell of sweat, rot, and decaying blood filled the space.

Thank the gods for the face covering that lay across my mouth and nose.

The golden serpent coiled around my forearm, under my shirt, and covered from view. It was risky… the serpent only covered its wearer's appearance from mortals, but most of these creatures were stitched together by human parts they had won in bids.

Hopefully, it would mean the serpent would do its job. I had managed to sneak in under the pretence of bidding with a large crowd that had arrived together. Taking the risky front entrance to keep Dorian within sight.

Dorian gained entry easily as he was not a reaper, and no one had recognised him.

Kason and Layna had used the rooftop entrance. Dorian had left my side shortly after entering, I just hoped the fool would not lose his nerve in this place…

The crowd roared as the bids continued. Many creatures bumped into me, causing my temper to flare.

I scanned the crowd, noting a daughter of Circe heading my way.

Her body was clothed in dark wrappings, not an inch of flesh to be seen, save for her black eyes. Trinkets sewn over the wrapping – souvenirs from conquered foes glittered under the soft yellow lighting of the hall.

Disappearing through the crowd, I headed in the opposite direction effectively losing her.

As I rounded a particularly gruesome creature, pieces of human body parts stitched together, the crowd had gone deathly silent.

I looked ahead and my eyes blazed amber as I spotted Ezio standing awkwardly on the stage. A thin shining chain gripped tightly in his grasp and attached to something behind the curtained entrance.

He scowled and stepped forward, gathering the chain in his grip when the other end was yanked back and halted.

Ezio's jaw ticked as he moved forward thunderously, and my world stopped. Braelyn stepped forward from behind the curtain.

She was a goddess of the night as she swept past him in her black shimmering gown, leaving him dumbfounded where he stood.

I watched in awe as she stopped, adjusting her midnight skirts, the golden tiara reflected the lights of the hall.

She seemed to pause, her dark hair a curtain around her as she appeared to be looking at her arm.

At her Servile brand.

I reached for my own as I watched her, still frozen where I stood.

The crowd was stunned to silence, her beauty captivating everyone. She then pulled her shoulders back defiantly and lifted her chin, staring dead ahead like a fucking queen and the crowd went utterly mad.

Those eyes… those god-damned gleaming emerald eyes!

I shoved my way forward, everyone in the crowd doing the same.

I managed to trip up a few in my way, them dropping to the ground, lost amongst the host of bodies.

Someone grabbed me, and I managed to snap their arm as I surged forward. I reached the front, stopping as I caught sight of a line of daughters of Circe blockading the stage.

She was so fucking close.

I caught sight of Dorian and my siblings across the hall, all wide-eyed, and the master of the auction house stepped forward.

Looking back at her, she appeared stoic, staring ahead as she held herself regally.

"Silence!" the auction master called out and the hall turned silent once more.

Vulcan stood tall beside Braelyn, and it was then I noticed the fucking chain wrapped around her neck like a dog's collar.

Her leash was being held by Ezio.

I breathed heavily through my nose and clenched my fists wanting to tear him from limb to limb.

"The goods shall be a trade. No monetary transfers." Vulcan searched the crowd, and I lowered my head slightly as he gazed in my direction before turning to Ezio and speaking in hushed tones.

The crowd moaned loudly in displeasure, and many vacated the space, bitter at not having any eligible item to trade. Luckily, I had anticipated Ezio was not after money and came prepared.

The daughters of Circe lining the stage inspected prospective items.

Those they deemed somewhat worthy were sent to the left of the hall, waiting for the exchange to commence.

Dorian stepped forward; his item concealed in a velvet pouch. The daughter of Circe inspected it and nodded to the left. Dorian gave nothing away of his relief as he went and stood beside the others.

He had come dressed in a hooded jacket, a pair of dark pants, and boots. Nothing of his usual attire. I casually made my way closer to where he stood but kept a respectful distance from the group of bidders.

I never took my eyes off Braelyn and noted how her skin shone like liquid gold.

My admiration was cut short as I noted the puncture marks littered across her body, as well as the bruise shining through her makeup along her jaw.

My eyes snapped to Ezio with wrath and a small part of me found amusement in the evidence she no doubt got her shot back at him as his jaw and cheek were turning purple.

Good girl…

Thankfully, she had not noticed her brother as he walked right past her. She remained to stare dead ahead, silent and filled with deathly rage. I would notice that wrath anywhere.

My body hummed with rage as I held myself back.

If this were not the Agora and certainly not the hive of the daughters of Circe, I would have grabbed her and been out of here… Unfortunately, even as deadly as myself and my family were, there were moments we knew that the chances were stacked against us – such as now.

The crowd remained large, causing us to remain undetected. Dorian caught my gaze and I nodded to him subtly he then looked over to his sister, most of his face covered by the hood.

Vulcan and Ezio headed over to where the group of bidders stood, taking the four steps down from the stage.

The chain attached to Braelyn clanged against the floor, slithering after Ezio like the snake he was.

They inspected many items, leaving a man and then Dorian.

Dorian kept his head low as they stood before the man and inspected his item. My breath caught as I witnessed what he held for their inspection.

It was a shimmering scale. About the size of the man's arm.

It reflected as he turned it over, the darkness of the room seeming to be drawn to it.

Swallowed up.

It was a scale of Typhon. Father of monsters… Rumours had swirled for millennia that three scales were scattered around the world. I had never believed it until this moment.

My eyes blazed amber as they narrowed on the ancient piece of pure evil.

Ezio grinned sinisterly before hiding it.

Shit.

They inspected Dorian's item not paying much attention to him and his offered trade.

Dorian had offered one of the many treasures from our armoury. The snake head of one of Medusa's many snakes.

It would not turn anyone to stone, yet its power of freezing anyone for a few mere seconds the wielder willed was still a dangerous aspect of it. They returned it to the velvet pouch and stepped away.

Dorian's gaze met mine and it was clear he was thinking the same as me.

There was no way he would win the bid. It was apparent that the mysterious man who held a scale of Typhon would be chosen.

If not for the scale, I would have been certain he would have won the bid as the others held what I would consider trinkets.

Jewels, a sword, even a pendant that belonged to Helen of Troy…

I searched across the hall for my siblings and found them in position. We were unable to use coms as we usually would as the Agora interfered with any form of technology making it impossible.

"Very well," Vulcan spoke as his tall form loomed over everyone.

The man, half creature, and machine himself were near over eight-feet-tall. His golden arm pointed to the man beside Dorian and beckoned him over.

I sucked in a breath anticipating how this would go through.

The man stepped forward, the large dark scale tucked beneath his arm and wrapped in silk.

"It appears your bid was a successful one. Please complete the trade." Ezio yanked on the chain, causing Braelyn to stumble before her eyes snapped to his.

Hatred and a death promise were clear in those green eyes.

She yanked back the chain and sneered at Ezio as she walked over to him, the chain still in her grasp as she whipped it casually up and down. Each time it connected with the bricked floors; the sound echoed across the hall.

I managed to catch sight of Dorian as he rushed forward, but it was too late.

"Fuck!" I shoved past the crowd, trying to get to him in time.

Pandemonium erupted in slow motion before my glowing eyes as my Chaos Handler took over, noting every detail.

Dorian rushed forward, his hand gripping the snake's head and aiming it no doubt for Ezio. A pale-robed figure dropped from the ceiling, snatching the scale from the man before he could be noticed, and rushed through the back of the stage.

The daughters of Circe turn their attention to Dorian and rushed forward.

I surged forward managing to get to Dorian and disappearing into the screaming crowd with him. My hand gripped the back of his hood as I shoved him along.

"Are you fucking stupid or just have a death wish for all of us?!" I hissed at him, getting him near the exit as screams erupted through the crowd and many rushed towards the doors.

Layna and Kason arrived just as we turned and noticed Braelyn using the chain in her grip as a whip as she snapped it back and forth, her eyes narrowed on Ezio and Vulcan.

Ezio's cheek was bleeding and he yanked harshly on the chain, pulling her forward. "Get him the fuck out of here!" I shoved him at Kason and shoved my way back to the stage.

"You better get her!" Dorian shouted after me as he struggled against Kason's firm grip and Layna tried covering his mouth with wide eyes.

"Remember, we need the box!" she called after me.

If not for the fact that Dorian was with us, my siblings would have remained. But we had decided that should this happen, the responsibility of getting Braelyn would be mine alone until Dorian was secured.

We sure as hell didn't need to explain why the prince of House Sarris had been killed after their princess had been kidnapped from our care.

Gritting my teeth, I pushed my way past everyone, finding myself surrounded by the daughters of Circe.

I chanced a look to the stage noticing Vulcan disappearing through a hidden door, leaving Ezio and Braelyn struggling for control of the chain.

"All right ladies, I just came to collect what's mine," I called out, dropping my face covering and raising my hands placatingly.

"Reaper!"

"God killer," they hissed after each other, closing in around me.

The snap of the chain as Braelyn whipped it back and forth at Ezio sounded out like thunder in the now vacant hall.

"Okay, now you are just wasting my time," I growled, dropping my arms and my eyes blazed.

I had taken note of every detail in this place. Chaos was me and in one swift movement, I set about a chain reaction of events that would seem like pandemonium, yet every detail was calculated.

Throwing my hidden dagger, I embedded it in the lever for the stage lights.

Sparks flew and one by one the lights went out. Throwing another, I managed to topple over a large stack of broken furniture that was on the side of the hall as the dagger pushed the top piece slightly off balance but enough to cause the desired effect.

Furniture crashed over half of the witches. Their screams filled the hall and the snapping of the chain continued.

I knew Braelyn would be able to see in the darkness, just as well as I, and I launched myself at the remaining daughters of Circe.

They moved with unnatural speed. Their agility was like that of a viper.

Flashes of their dark-coiled magic flew at me. Their magic was instant death.

Dodging them, I managed to slit the throat of one before spinning and stabbing the back of the other. I just managed to eliminate the final one when the doors to the hall burst open and more of them entered.

"Took you long enough," I sneered with a wicked grin, and they rushed forward. Erupting into a swarm of ravens, my chaos ensued.

The screams of the remaining witches filled the air as they were torn apart and ripped open by beaks and talons.

They had come running just as expected leaving a chance for Layna, Kason, and Dorian to leave undetected, it also meant that Braelyn and I would be able to sneak away without interference once I was done with them.

I returned, my ravens now gone as I took the steps onto the stage and my gaze met with Braelyn for a moment.

My thigh was bleeding as one of the witches had managed to slice apart one of my ravens. Blood dripped upon the dirty floor from beneath my armour.

It didn't happen often, but in the rare moments one of my ravens was killed, the effects would show on my body even as my armour remained intact.

I stepped up to the final step after ensuring all the witches were dead. Braelyn's eyes widened at the sight of me, but it was a mistake as Ezio lunged at her, wrapping the chain tightly around her, holding her arms close to her side as he held on tight from behind her.

"Let her go," I growled and started forward but stopped when he tightened the chain, causing her breath to stall.

I stopped where I stood, my eyes narrowed at him. She had managed to get him a few times with the chain. Slices covered his face and angry-looking welts littered his skin where the clothing had been torn.

Ezio's head snapped back as Braelyn slammed her head back at him.

His hold on the chain dropped and she spun herself, the leash loosening, and black organza skirts flared.

She looked at me in worry and heaving breaths, then behind me as I sensed a blast of dark magic launched at me.

I never felt the impact as her eyes flashed silver and her pupils slit like that of a cat for a second before returning green.

A shield of vibrating air buffeted around me as I was surrounded, shielded entirely.

I was crouched to avoid the impact and turned to watch as the daughter of Circe behind me was choking on shadows, the life being drained from her before she dropped to the ground, a bundle of bones and taut skin. Every piece of woven dark fabric that had covered her sagged around her dead form. Any trace of living essence was ripped from her.

Darkness coiled and slithered around the corpse before dispersing to the shadows once more.

My eyes widened and I turned back to Braelyn as the vibrating air around me flickered and then fell.

Ezio was dragging her through the back door, a syringe still stuck in her neck as she lay lifeless in his arms.

Running across the stage, I yanked the door open and ran faster and harder than I ever had in my existence.

Blood continued to run down my leg in warm drips as I pushed on.

I followed the sound of Ezio's hurried footsteps down the filthy, enclosed hallway. I tried using my ravens, but pain sliced through me as I flickered in and out of form.

The wards for the holding cells... Fuck!

Pushing through the door of the auction house that Ezio had just exited, I found myself back in the Agora. The streets were in chaos. I spotted him further up ahead, heading towards the exit to the mortal world. Shoving past creatures and humanoids alike, I pushed through the wards and found myself on the street of the mortal market.

Tires screeched and Ezio sped away with Braelyn in the passenger seat beside him. She has slumped over awkwardly, the fucking syringe still in her neck.

Erupting into a swarm of ravens as the wards held no sway here, civilians' screams were a chorus through the market.

I followed the car as he sped up through the city streets.

My ravens banged and surrounded his car, causing him to swerve and almost hit an oncoming car. Tires screeched as cars swerved out of the way and he exited the city, speeding toward the highway.

I needed to be smart about this because if he crashed, then Braelyn would no doubt be injured.

So, I instead followed overhead, no longer banging at his windows. I trailed him down the coast, a swarm of darkness and feathers and beating wings promising retribution.

It was impossible to know where he was headed and the longer I waited, the riskier it became of getting Braelyn back safely.

White cliffs rose ahead of the road and the waves of the ocean crashed violently against them down below.

I knew where we were headed now. The pleasure house of White Peak.

It had been abandoned in the past year for renovations.

Renovations Ezio oversaw…

I could fucking hit myself for not thinking of it. My anger flared and I swooped low, forming as I landed with a heavy thump upon the roof of the car. Ezio swerved and I crouched low, finding my balance. The wind rushed past me. The smell and taste of salt coating my mouth.

Ezio swerved violently attempting to throw me from the roof as he sped up.

Removing my knives from my boots, I slammed them through the car roof, anchoring myself.

My breathing remained steady as I readied myself. As predicted, Ezio slammed on the brakes. Tires screeched and smoked as the car came to a violent stop and I was flung forward. Using the momentum and my grip on the knives, I slid forward, flipping and slamming my booted heels through the driver's side of the windshield.

Glass sprayed, and I turned my face away as I kicked Ezio in the chest with both feet.

Releasing the knives, I launched myself at him as he reached for his gun.

I pounded on his face. One, then two times and snatched his wrist, forcing it to the side as he fired out his side window.

Glass rained around us. Snapping his wrist, he howled in pain. I grabbed the gun and shoved it against his temple.

Ezio froze, his face covered in blood and the inside of the car littered with shattered glass. I looked over to Braelyn and gripped the syringe, removing it from her neck.

Glaring back at Ezio in wrath, I punched him and placed the barrel of the gun under his chin, forcing his face up to look at me.

"Why?!" I screamed at him.

Ezio chuckled choking on blood and I reloaded the gun, pressing it harshly against his forehead, my eyes blazing amber and my tattooed hand gripping his neck.

"You hurt her. I will fucking kill you!"

"Oh, Theo… You have no idea what you have got yourself in the middle of," he chuckled again and spat blood to the side.

"Where is the box containing the Heart of Ouranos?" I seethed, wishing I could just splatter his brains over the car interior and be done with him.

"I don't know," he muttered.

"Liar!" I squeezed his throat tighter and pressed the gun closer.

"I have no idea where that fucking box is. It would have been a bonus for the trade, but I don't have it. Maybe you should be asking your little whore why she had it." He seethed.

I monitored his pupils, and his breathing for any sign of a lie and found none.

I snapped hitting him again.

His head slammed back, and I readied to empty the gun in his head. There was no use keeping him alive if he did not have the box.

I tightened my hand on the trigger when another car rammed into the side of us, tossing the car over into a barrel roll. Glass and sand flew through the interior of the vehicle as we rolled.

Over and over, it went.

Metal groaned and buckled. We came to a stop near the cliffside, my head swimming and coughing up dust from the road.

I had managed to land up in the passenger seat of the overturned vehicle where Braelyn had been seated.

Shaking away the fog that clouded my mind, I looked over to Ezio, finding him gone too.

Craning my neck, I spotted the pale-robed figure that had stolen the scale of Typhon standing up ahead, Braelyn lying unconscious on the dirt road beside him, and Ezio dusting off his clothes.

Looking around I noticed no other car.

"What the… fuck," I groaned as I tried shuffling out of the car but found myself stuck as my leg was pinned beneath a twisted piece of metal.

Dirt crunching beneath booted feet sounded to the side and I looked over.

Brown boots met my gaze through the broken window. The robed figure crouched; his head still concealed by the robe. I narrowed my eyes at him and yanked uselessly at my pinned leg. I froze as he lifted his head and green eyes met mine, the rest of his face covered. A jagged scar ran over his brow and eye.

But his eyes… they were green.

A pale shade compared to Braelyn's yet green, nonetheless.

He watched me in silence and his eyes slit as Braelyn's had when she had saved me. The metal of the car began buckling around me.

It was then I realised that it had been him that caused the car to roll.

How he had managed to get Braelyn and Ezio out was beyond me.

A sinister smirk shone in the stranger's eyes before he stepped away, standing up yet again and walking away as the car began pushing in around me.

"Fuck you!" I called after him.

He did not stop until he was beside Ezio, seemingly in an argument.

Braelyn stirred where she lay, and my heart stopped.

She was okay…

I just hoped my siblings found her.

Turning my gaze from them, I pushed back at the buckling metal as the air seemed to compress it in around me.

Glass rained over my head as a larger piece of still intact window shattered, sounding like a gunshot going off.

My eyes blazed amber in the night as I yanked and pushed at the buckling metal.

I attempted erupting into ravens, finding myself unable to as my leg remained pinned.

Banging my fists against the metal, I roared in anger as I bled and struggled.

Braelyn

Growls and snarls sounded in my head. The smell of salt filled my lungs and I struggled to open my eyes.

Finally, I managed to and found my vision blurred as the sight of what seemed to be a wrecked car in the distance greeted me.

The snarling of the power within me grew louder and ever more insistent.

The sound of roaring from the vehicle made me stir.

Why did it sound familiar?

My breaths left my gaping mouth, causing little puffs of soft white sand to billow around my face.

I blinked rapidly, trying to regain my sight. The familiar buzzing in my head continued and banging against metal from the car had the power roaring.

My vision returned and the buzzing stopped, almost as if the ancient power had burned all traces of the drug from my system.

"You will give me what I want! That was the deal!"

"I will do no such thing. You have failed in your end of the bargain. You have caused a scene. He will be much displeased by your actions," Ezio argued with someone.

A male.

The male's voice remained stoic.

"Kill him and the rest of them!" Ezio roared back at the stranger.

"You will remember your place," he answered in a deathly tone.

Ezio remained silent and the car in the distance groaned as the metal buckled further.

The power within me had me jolting as its anger and desperation were targeted by the car and the men who stood beside me still unaware of my awakening.

Standing in a rush, I ran for the car. Sand pushed aside from my bare feet as I ran as fast as I could.

Strong arms gripped my biceps halting me in place.

Slamming my foot down upon the male's boots, He moaned before I hooked my heel around his other foot, sweeping his foot out from under him at the same time I slammed my aching head back.

I connected with his chin and his grip loosened. I then slammed my elbow in his ribs and whirled around as he staggered.

My eyes slit as I eyed him for a second then ran to the car.

He was there in a second, gripping my elbow as he yanked back.

The ancient power in me snapped in fury and air boomed around me, forcing him back. He placed up an arm to cover his face from the whirling sand.

Theo's roar caught my attention before I felt the ancient power lock its sights on the stranger before me.

"Release him!" I yelled at him, his pale green eyes meeting mine.

Ezio stumbled to where we were and was breathing heavily as he looked between us. "How is the chain not working?!" Ezio yelled at the stranger who still eyed me in silence then at the vehicle where Theo struggled against the crushing metal.

The ancient power within me recognised the stranger as the one responsible for the power surrounding the car.

"Now," I growled at him, the ancient power within me sounding through my voice.

I would have been startled were it not for the pure fury I felt racing through my veins at the thought of this man harming what was mine. The robed man tilted his head as he eyed me further then nodded subtly and the groaning of metal stopped, the sound of a particularly large piece bending away, and Theo's heavy breathing sounded out.

"What are you doing?!" Ezio yelled and started for the stranger who stood and never took his eyes off me.

Ezio roared and shoved at the stranger's shoulder. His green eyes slit as he turned to Ezio.

"The chains don't work for she has laid claim on him. Any harm toward him will cause her to break through." He snapped and air swept Ezio's feet out from under him, leaving him lying flat on his back in the sand and coughing heavily as buffets of vibrating air held him down in its crushing grip.

"We will meet again, Tsalmaveth," he gritted out, almost in anger toward me, before turning and walking away.

Wasting no time, I turned and ran to the wrecked car, finding Theo climbing from the broken window.

Cuts littering his body were healing before my eyes and I launched myself at him, throwing my arms around him and holding him tightly. "Little rose." He croaked and slammed his mouth to mine as he sat in the sand beside the car.

The ancient power within me purred at having him safe and Theo wrapped his hands around my neck as he deepened the kiss.

The clanking of chains sounded and then a heavy thud as they fell upon the sand. Theo still held most of its links in his hand.

Our peace was short-lived as two gunshots sounded out and my ears rang. Theo immediately covered my body with his own, shoving me beneath him into the sand as the sound of crunching footsteps grew closer. We were both breathing heavily and when I looked down under Theo's sheltering body atop mine, I noticed two bullet holes in his legs. Crimson poured from the wounds, covering my legs as the dress was a crumpled mess around me.

One in each leg.

Adamantine bullets… nothing should have been able to get through his armour, but adamantine bullets from close range would…

Theo clenched his jaw and was yanked away from me as Ezio gripped his shoulders and glared at me.

Before I could stop him, Ezio entered The Shiver. Shadows crept around him and a pale Theo before they disappeared before my eyes.

Shaking, I stood hastily and the power within me roared.

My eyes turned to slits as the power took over. Its determination was now my own and the two pools of blood soaking into the white sand were the last thing I saw as I entered The Shiver.

Sand blowing out from the spot I had stood. A deathly rage took over me and using the Servile bond, I followed Ezio.

Followed Theo into the void between worlds of darkness and shadows. Whispers and roars.

Flashes of silver greeted me, and a phantom breeze licked its way around me in the dark void.

I appeared at intervals, searching, and watching. Shadows formed around me, and roars sounded and echoed in the distance.

The ancient power within me was unrelenting in its sway over space.

It was then I understood. Understood what this place was to it. To me.

Some natural force, some ancient intelligence whispered the truth through my mind as I searched as if a great barrier that had been in place for eons was finally crumbling down…

In a blast of power and sway, it roared as a wave of its authority ran through the void.

There.

It had found Ezio.

It roared around me, shadows twirled, and flashes of silver mist readied themselves as my eyes narrowed.

Sweeping forward like a ghost in the night, I found them.

Theo lost consciousness in the void due to his blood loss. Ezio's eyes widened at the sight of me.

My hair floated enchanting, hauntingly around me.

"How?!" he yelled in fear before vanishing again further into the void.

I sneered and found him an instant later. It continued like that until finally, he exited The Shiver, me close behind him as he dropped Theo's unconscious form on the pebbled shore of the lake in the Whispering Woods.

"How?" his voice trembled, and his eyes remained wide in fear and awe.

"How can you enter The Shiver? Theo should have died the instant I dragged him in there. How did you find me?!" he started meekly and ended up yelling at me.

His chest heaved in anger. The ancient power roared loudly, this time for him to hear and he began quivering as he stood before me, having stepped over Theo's crumpled form. The forest quieted around us. Even the waters of the lake had ceased their lapping of the shore.

"You took what was mine," I spoke in a deadly tone, the ancient power's voice conjoined with my own as it reverberated out around us. "You dared use

The Shiver, *my domain* as a means of destroying what is *mine*," I continued, and the wolves of the Whispering Woods howled in the distance in recognition.

Ezio took a step back from me as I stepped forward.

He paled as buffets of vibrating air rippled out from me, stirring the pebbles at our feet and the water of the lake.

"What… what are you?" he whispered as he began trembling and took another step back, ending just beside Theo.

I snickered sinisterly. "I am your worst nightmare," I whispered and smirked at him.

Theo surprised us both as he stood in a rush, pale as the moon, and wrapped the chain he still held in his grip around Ezio's neck and pulled tight.

Ezio struggled against him, his face turning red from lack of air and pebbles were kicked out of the way.

"Run," Theo croaked, his eyes struggling to remain open.

"Run back home." He struggled further and yanked back again before continuing. "Run to our room. You'll be… safe," he finished in a whisper, his eyes drooping further.

Ezio pushed back and stumbled backward, crashing to the pebbled shore with a loud crunch. They struggled and fought for control.

Pebbles clattered around them as they were shoved out of the way.

I roared and started forward when another gunshot sounded out and they disappeared within The Shiver yet again.

I roared in anguish and fury and shadows gathered around me before I entered the void.

I halted as the power cast its attention to the centre of the lake, the moonlight reflecting off its surface.

Shadows formed ten feet above its surface before both Ezio and an unconscious Theo plummeted. They broke through the surface of the water with a great splash, sending waves out to the shore.

I started forward, freezing as the water touched my bare feet. The ancient power within me roared and growled, urging me forward as the fear took over.

I gritted my teeth as I trembled looking out across the lake, wishing I would see Theo resurface any second.

Ezio appeared on the shore, drenched and water dripping from him.

"You better go get what's yours," he spat venomously at me with a heaving chest before disappearing through The Shiver yet again.

"Theo!" I cried out as I trembled in fear beside the lake and my eyes searched for him. Groaning loudly when he wasn't resurfacing, I yanked the heavy tiara from my head, the pins snagging painfully on my hair. With trembling hands, I removed the metal corset and dress in a hurry.

All the while, the power roared and screeched in urgency as it paced back and forth across my bones.

Trembling from fear, I closed my eyes briefly and steeled my nerve.

I forced my locked limbs forward, swallowing my tears as I pushed through the water. The feel of it covering my bare limbs and splashing across my face felt like knives digging their way through me.

I wailed as I began swimming across the lake, tears streaming down my face as I pushed on to get to the centre where Theo had gone under.

Treading water once I reached it, I closed my eyes and gritted my teeth.

Looking up at the moon, I swallowed a lungful of air through silent tears and dove under.

Darkness greeted me, and I almost screamed as the water surrounded me.

Its iciness sliced and held me as I swam deeper. My eyes adjusted to the darkness, and I could see as my lungs began to burn and I struggled further to keep from screaming in terror.

Down below, Theo lay unconscious upon the lakebed, with rocks, and weeds swaying in the water around him.

The power within me roared at the sight of him and I swam faster and harder than before, fighting against the fear of the water.

The fear of drowning.

Reaching him, I gripped him under his shoulders, placing his back against my chest. I kicked furiously, struggling with his lifeless weight even in the water.

My lungs burned and I kicked toward the surface. The moon's rays glittered across its surface.

Flashbacks of the well-house slammed into me, and I froze, almost losing my grip on him.

The power roared and the memories left me. I kicked harder, swimming for the surface.

Trails of red floated through the water as Theo's legs bled out, and his shoulder from the newest gunshot wound.

The power roared at the sight of it and tendrils of its power reached out, staunching the blood flow.

I was nearly drowning when we finally broke the surface.

I sucked in copious amounts of air and turned my attention to Theo as his black hair covered him and stuck across his forehead.

Swiping at it, I cried out loud as his head rolled to the side of my shoulder and there was no colour to his face, his lips were blue, and a grey tone covered his skin.

"Hold on. Please… please don't leave me," I wailed as I pushed towards the shore.

I attempted shadow-stalking to the shore but found I could not as the power concentrated on stopping Theo's blood flow from his wounds. Swimming with my back to the shore, I tried ignoring the water lapping at me.

I wanted to scream and eventually did as we neared the shore.

I was trembling and struggling with my grip on Theo's heavy and water-slick body.

I didn't stop for an instant of relief as I felt pebbles beneath my feet.

Dragging Theo further up the shore, I collapsed with him just beyond the brake of the lapping water.

My chest heaved as I allowed myself a second to catch my breath before beginning CPR on Theo. His heart was beating, but barely and the power roared at me as I continued pressing at his chest and expressing my breath within his mouth.

His lips were like ice, and I could not stop myself from crying as I trembled and begged him to wake up.

My hair stuck to my bare back and across my neck as he began coughing up water and I cried out in relief. Theo rolled to the side, continuing to cough and I patted his back.

"Oh, thank gods," I whispered, still crying softly.

Theo rolled on his back and looked at me in silence.

Weakly, he reached out his hand, wiping a tear away with his thumb before twirling a piece of my wet hair.

He rolled his head to the side and looked out to the lake and then back to me, his eyes scrunched in confusion. "You went in after me?" he croaked.

"Yes," I whispered and couldn't stop the tears that fell as the feeling of the water overtook me then and the overwhelming relief of Theo being safe crashed into me.

Theo coughed up more water and some colour returned to his face as he closed his eyes in exhaustion.

"Gods, you make me sick," Ezio's voice sounded from the tree line and my gaze zeroed in on him. Theo began to protest but I was before Ezio in an instant and dragging him within The Shiver.

We struggled for control, the power roaring and wanting a taste of his blood for retribution.

"Why?" I yelled at him, wanting to know why. After all the years of his tortured love, his kidnapping… attempting to destroy what was mine, I needed to know.

"Because Theo had everything, and I had nothing! It's my birth right and I deserve it all as much as him!" he yelled as we struggled within the void, and I froze him in place at the sound of his words. The power and my sway of The Shiver bending to my command. Ezio struggled against the invisible bonds holding him in place and he then looked at me wide-eyed.

"You want to eliminate the Katopodis and place yourself as head of the House?" I gritted out.

Ezio spat at me, and I growled in warning. His face paled at the sound of it.

"You have no idea what you are involved in, do you?" he thought aloud. "What the fuck are you?!" he yelled then, asking yet again.

The same question everyone wanted the answer to.

"Let me show you," I whispered sinisterly as my eyes flashed silver and slit. Ezio struggled against the bonds, his smell of fear filling the void. Growls and snarls sounded just behind me as the power revealed itself to him and Ezio stilled, tilting his head back as the power rose. "Drakon…Wraith," he murmured in fear. "D… Death," he finally stuttered.

"Darkness, shadows… yes," I answered, continuing with his list and my voice was joined by the power behind me as it coiled its immense body around us in the darkness.

The void flashed with silver and roars sounded in the distance.

Calls…

"Do you recall my promise to you?" I asked softly as my eyes narrowed and I lowered my head as I watched him, and my voice echoed across The Shiver. He dragged his gaze back to mine and the power behind me snapped at him in a warning.

My hand reached out, caressing his injured cheek in a taunt as he began struggling. "You bitch," he hissed at me.

"I am so much worse than that," I spoke softly, hauntingly, and dropped my hand.

The Drakon behind me roared and Ezio whimpered as he struggled in fear. Silver tendrils of power reached around him, caressing him as he screamed, and I watched on in silence.

"You are no longer welcome in The Shiver. You are no longer welcome in *my* realm," the words left my lips with finality and the tendrils of power snapped around Ezio like a viper. His screams and struggles began to quieten as life was drained from him. His eyes bulged and his skin turned ashen and began pulling taught and recessed across his bones.

Gripping his hands, with tendrils of power, I twisted until they snapped clean of his arms. His mouth widened in a silent scream.

"You will not be hurting anyone else again," I watched silently as the life left his eyes. A milky cloud covered his once-blue eyes.

The power roared and hissed and Ezio's form began turning to mist before me… disappearing further into the void.

The creatures of The Shiver boomed.

Wraiths swooped past in a frenzy as they devoured what was left of his crumbling corpse.

I watched in silence, my hair churning around me as the Drakon coiled itself around me purring in satisfaction at Ezio's demise.

The wraiths growled at each other, fighting over the remaining dust and mist of Ezio.

The power hissed in a warning, and they ventured off.

Flashes of silver and moonlight filled the gaps between the shadows and booms sounded out, echoing around the darkened space.

Theo

"Braelyn!" I yelled out, as I watched her shadow stalk in an instant to where Ezio stood. They were there one second and gone the next as she grabbed a hold of him, and shadows swirled around them.

"Fuck!" I shouted, before falling back against the pebbled shore.

I coughed up more water and my chest heaved, burning. My legs warmed as blood began pooling beneath my armour from the wounds I had endured.

Had Braelyn staunched the blood flow somehow? I gritted my teeth as I forced myself to sit and looked out to the lake.

She had braved the water to save me. I knew it was her greatest fear and I did not know what to make of it.

Pushing my hands to the slick stones, I rotated and pushed up on them to my knees. My thighs and shoulder protested in agony.

My eyes blazed amber as I breathed through the pain and shook my head as a wave of dizziness threatened.

I needed to get to Braelyn.

Gods… how the fuck was I going to do that?

"Theo!" Kason's voice sounded out as he came running from the woods, Dorian and Layna followed closely behind. We had caused more of a commotion than I realised…

"Shit," he murmured as he slung my good arm around his shoulder and helped me up.

I gritted my teeth as the pain surged and Kason steadied me.

"Where is she?" Dorian rushed over, breathing heavily.

"The Shiver," I groaned out and Layna eyed my wounds.

"Ezio did this?" she grumbled with her brows scrunched together. I nodded in confirmation, and she immediately dropped her backpack, digging through its contents.

"Why is she in The Shiver? How?" Dorian snapped.

His concern for her was clear in his demeanour and tone.

"Ah, fuck!" I yelled, clenching my ass cheeks, and pulling forward as Layna stepped away in a rush.

She had pulled my pants down slightly from behind and injected me with a healing serum before I had noticed what was happening.

My ass burned but I sighed in relief as the pain subsided considerably and the blood flow ceased. My healing gifts could now hurry up the process.

"A little warning next time." I snapped and dropped my arm from Kason's shoulder so I could stand again without aid.

"I don't know how the fuck, but she can enter The Shiver. She dragged Ezio in with her just before you got here," I spoke to Dorian and gritted my teeth as I cracked my neck.

I needed to get to her. I began pacing the shoreline, deep in thought of how to get to her as quickly as possible.

"Fuck!" I screamed, kicking stones.

"You were supposed to keep her safe!" Dorian snapped at me, and my attention zeroed in on him instantly, my eyes glowing amber.

"Care to fucking repeat that?" I was already moving toward him to make sure he could never utter another single word when Layna stepped before me.

"Move," I growled, side-stepping her instantly and too fast for her to intercept.

Dorian glared at me.

I launched myself at him and he dodged. I swung again connecting with his cheek and then two shots to the ribs. Dorian held his ground, spinning and knocking my feet from under me and getting his shot in. He moved like a reaper, and I found myself shocked for once in my life. *That seemed to be happening far too often with the Sarris siblings as of late...*

My anger flared and I tackled him to the ground, landing punch after punch before he rolled, pinning me, and doing the same thing. Two gunshots rang out around us and we both turned to look at Layna.

"Enough," she hissed.

Dorian's hood had fallen back to reveal his blond hair as he turned back to me, his lip bleeding as he scowled.

"You were supposed to protect her," he hissed and then shoved off me.

"Fuck you. So were you," I snapped back and got up glaring at him.

He knew it was true. He had done a shit job of protecting her all her life.

Dorian sneered and walked back to Layna and kept walking until he sat down on a rock staring across the water.

"You know nothing." He finally snapped and wiped the blood from his lip.

"Then fucking tell me," I snapped back.

"T," Kason started, frowning at me.

I glared at him, shutting him up instantly.

"Tell me!" I roared.

"I can't!" Dorian yelled standing again, his chest heaving, and my eyes scanned him.

He wasn't lying. He could not tell me.

My eyes narrowed on him as I scowled. Shadows began forming on the shore and Braelyn appeared. Her hair was still slick from the water of the lake, her body was bare except for her underwear.

Ezio was nowhere to be seen. Her eyes met mine and she rushed to me, flinging her arms around me tightly.

She was as cold as ice, the feel of her almost stinging.

Her skin vibrated at a nearly imperceptible frequency.

"You are okay?" I asked as relief washed over me, pulling her away and searching her green eyes.

She nodded, and I noted the swirling silver that appeared almost ghostly in the greens of her eyes.

"Ezio?" I whispered, inspecting her for injuries and finding none. Her wounds were completely healed. No trace of the bruises could be found.

"Dead," she deadpanned, with no hint of remorse for only me to hear.

The sounds of guns being cocked around us had me lifting my gaze.

My father and Trey exited the woods, along with the hounds of Hephaestus. They growled as they neared slowly.

Nine of them circled and I gritted my teeth as I looked at my brother and father.

"What are you doing?" I was tensed, ready for anything.

"The hunt order stands. We cannot allow the entire family to be issued a Code Red. I am sorry Theo," my father spoke, guilt and shame riddled his features and he looked at Braelyn as if in pain.

"I am truly sorry," he spoke softly to her, and she tensed.

Trey remained silent and for once he didn't seem to agree to his orders as he looked down, his face scrunched in a frown.

Dorian shifted and the hounds turned their attention to him. Braelyn growled and everyone froze.

"You will not touch him," she said and the hairs on my arms stood on end at the tone and pure undiluted power that exuded from her.

The hounds whimpered back before turning their attention to her and snarling.

Growls sounded out around Braelyn, the same ghostly sinister snarls, and growls that I had heard in our room when she had been having a nightmare and I tensed.

Looking down at her, her eyes were swimming in quicksilver, like mercury dancing within their orbs. Howls sounded in the woods, and everyone looked around in trepidation.

It was her sway over them... the sacred wolves of the Whispering Woods.

I was sure of it.

"I can't let you do this," I snapped at my father and Trey who stepped closer.

"Don't make me choose," I gritted out in a threat as they neared, and the hounds circled closer.

Their metallic fangs snapped, and their pointed black ears tilted back.

"I am warning you," Braelyn whispered menacingly.

She was trembling along with the pebbles at our feet, and I knew whatever ungodly power she held was teetering on the edge of a precarious blade.

Dorian side-stepped closer to us, and the hounds lunged.

Chaos erupted as they snapped and snarled, their venomous saliva dripping and splaying across the area.

"Stop!" Kason yelled and lunged for Trey as he aimed at Braelyn, effectively knocking his rifle up as the shot rang out.

Dorian reached us and Braelyn roared in rage as a wave of pure wrathful power erupted from her sending the hounds rolling and wincing.

My family dropped to their knees, gripping their ears.

Pebbles rose and shot out in every direction leaving the sand bare around her feet. I watched in awe as the wave of power extended to the Whispering Woods, leaving the tall ancient trees bending and swaying under her might.

I looked back to Braelyn and saw her eyes slit, all trace of their green gone as she surveyed my family as prey readied to be slaughtered… and then grinned like death itself.

Braelyn

The power in me snapped at the threat posed toward Dorian.

It recognised him as someone dear to us, someone worth protecting. It too never took its attention from Theo at our side, ready to destroy any threat posed toward him in an instant.

I had been trying to hold it back, not wanting to harm any of Theo's family, and failed as it took control when the gunshot had gone off.

Its rage became mine, all sensible thought gone, and I roared in wrath.

Its power, my might, shook the earth beneath our feet as a surge of power ventured forth, bringing everyone to their knees and the Whispering Woods bowing in recognition of my influence.

Its silent whispers filled the air and wolves howled in the distance answering my call.

"You will not harm what is mine. You. Will. Not." I growled out, grinning at them promising pain and death should they try me…

"Little Rose," Theo called in trepidation from my side, still crouched from my surge of power, his own eyes glowing a brilliant amber.

Growls filled the air once more as the wolves arrived, their massive forms prowling from the tree line and fur hackled.

The hounds rose once more, noticing the threat, and stood off in a show of dominance against the wolves twice their size.

I looked over to Dorian who watched on, his face gone pale as he slowly looked at me. "Brae?" he asked, unsure of my new show of power.

One of the hounds lunged and the wolves attacked.

Snarls and whimpers sounded out as they were torn apart one by one until nothing was left except for metallic mechanical parts and bloody gore.

I began to walk away, trusting this was over and the power relinquished some control back to me and I staggered.

There was silence from the rest of Theo's family as they breathed heavily, the wolves holding them in place. Should one of them dare make a move against me, they would soon regret it.

"We cannot let you go," Trey called out and the sound of his gun being reloaded had me stopping where I stood.

The wolves snarled and the Drakon growled loudly around me, remaining unseen, the air beginning to vibrate once more.

My back was to them, Dorian and Theo standing close to me.

"You really should," I managed out against the Drakon's sway as its rage increased and the wolves snarled, their maws snapping loudly as they circled.

"We cannot," he said.

My head lowered and I squeezed my eyes shut, fighting for control, the Drakon's rage, my own was overcoming all common sense again.

My eyes snapped open, swirling silver and slitted pupils as I gave in, relinquishing my hold on it yet again and the rage of everything took over.

"Very well," I whispered and twirled back around, my black hair swaying as I did and my eyes meeting Theo's cool ones.

I could not read him; his expression was of stone.

I looked back to Trey, who had his rifle aimed at me, the red laser shining between my breasts, directly over my heart.

"I dare you," I smirked, and Theo frowned stepping before me, the dot now between his lower ribs.

"Get the fuck out of the way, Theo."

"You will need to kill me to kill her," Theo sneered, his eyes blazing.

The sound of his words and the rifle aimed at him set my rage flaring.

With a twirl of my wrist, a shudder of air rippled out and the wolves attacked.

Shouts, grunts, and shots rang out as the Katopodis household fought off the wolves.

Dorian grabbed my arm and hurried as he dragged me away, but I pulled back, lost in the blood lust.

Trey was wounded and Dante and Layna screamed as a wolf managed to snap down on her leg before she shot it between the eyes. "Stop it, Brae! Let's go!" Dorian pleaded with me.

Theo was immediately in the mix, fending off the wolves from his family.

None of them dared attack him and he was swift as he moved between them, fighting each off and killing them one by one.

Blood covered him and he erupted into a swarm of ravens. A dark cloud of death as he swooped between the carnage.

I would not leave without him.

"Braelyn!" Dorian yelled bewildered by my behaviour and spun me around to look at him.

A shot rang out, only this time, blood splattered across my face, awakening me from the haze as Dorian stumbled.

His grip on my arm loosened and he fell to the ground, wincing in pain, and blood pooled from his neck.

"No!" I shrieked so loudly that everyone dropped to their knees and the trees swayed. The lake quivered as ripples spread.

"No! No!" I repeated as I dropped to the pebbled ground beside my brother, ignoring the sting of the stones against my skin, and pressed against Dorian's neck.

Crimson liquid spilled between my fingers, its copper smell filling the air.

A second shot rang out in the chaos and my body jerked as it passed through my shoulder.

I gasped as pain flared and my eyes returned to normal.

A second and third shot rang out, each knocking my breath away as they passed through me.

Dorian's eyes struggled to remain open, and I whimpered as I pressed further and harder against his neck, urging the blood flow to cease. Using what power I could grab onto, I urged it forward to heal Dorian, or the very least staunch his blood flow.

A roar of anguish sounded, followed by rage as Theo appeared beside me, gripping me tightly.

I tasted blood in my mouth as I struggled to look at him.

I coughed and watched through hooded eyes as blood sprayed over him and Dorian.

My skin began to tingle, and I lost sensation over my extremities.

It was a wave of numbness that licked its way over me.

Caressing.

Glorious relief swept over me as the pain receded.

My fingers slipped from Dorian's neck, and I scrambled uselessly to reapply the pressure.

"Little rose," Theo called to me, sounding far away.

I swayed in his hold and removed one bloody hand from Dorian's neck to place against his cheek. Crimson smeared across his golden skin, and I sagged, my forehead pressing against his. "No, no, no, don't you fucking dare leave me," Theo mumbled in a panic as he gripped me tighter, pushing the hair from my face.

His lips pressed to my bloody ones as he begged.

"Please, please, please, stay with me."

"I'm s… sorry," I managed, only to cough up more blood.

"I tried to… fight it," I whispered just before my vision darkened around the edges and I sagged against him.

Theo roared in anguish as he rocked holding me to him, his one hand holding mine firmly against my brother's neck, in a final effort of helping me to save him.

"Stay with me. Stay with me," he murmured repeatedly as darkness swallowed me deeper and I felt yanked within the familiar void and hold of The Shiver.

Growls surrounded me as the Drakon encircled me in the darkness and I stood before it in the form of wisps and shadows.

A Wraith.

Its scales were smooth as silk as it brushed against me in a comforting caress.

Breath as cold as hoarfrost blew over me as it now faced me.

Green-slitted orbs swirling with silver looked back at me, its maw open and fangs dripping shadows.

I was not afraid. It was a part of me, and me it… "Save him. Save them both," I managed to instruct it as the thudding of my slowing heart pounded through the void.

Its reptilian eyes narrowed on me, a huff of ice and shadows and it opened its colossal maw as a roar shook The Shiver around us.

Shadows and flashes of silver encased me as it slithered around once more, and my heart drummed its final beat as an explosion of obscurity.

Theo

"Braelyn?" I whispered, my chest feeling as if it were splitting in two for the first time in my life as I held her to me.

My one hand was bloody and pressing hers to Dorian's neck.

His blood flow had ceased at the wound, but he remained alive, albeit pale as death and unconscious.

"Little rose," my voice cracked as I whispered to her.

She had turned as cold as ice in my embrace.

No, no, no.

I dreaded pulling away from her to witness for myself the sight I knew would greet me, but I needed to.

I needed to see it to believe it.

She couldn't just be… gone…

Gritting my teeth, I pulled her and my hand away from Dorian's injured neck and placed hers against my chest. She was completely limp against me.

Brushing her matted dark hair away from her face, I pushed her forward, cradling her neck with one hand as the other held her waist. Her head rolled lifelessly to the side and my breath caught painfully.

Braelyn was gone.

Her skin was as cold as hoarfrost and her lips were blue.

Blood stood in stark contrast to her now snow-white skin, coating her almost everywhere.

Three bullet wounds punctured her body.

One through the shoulder and two through her abdomen.

I shook as I fought against the pain and my eyes swam with unshed tears.

It would be the first time in my life I had cried. Not even Hades' torture came close to this… I squeezed my eyes tightly as I pulled her back against my chest, her head nestled in the crook of my neck.

Swallowing back the pain that wreaked havoc inside me, I breathed in her scent deeply and gritted my teeth as I fought for control of my shaking hands and body.

"Theo," Trey's traitorous voice sounded from behind me, near the tree line.

My eyes snapped open and blazed amber as fury and wrath scorched my veins.

"Theo…" he called again, guilt and shame sounding through each word.

I ignored him, barely containing my anger.

"I needed to. It needed to be done. We couldn't allow the entire family to be killed because of her," he pleaded his case uselessly.

My gaze searched out across the lake, its surface still and reflecting brilliantly under the moonlight.

Braelyn had faced her biggest fear to save me. She had saved me, and my family killed her. Peering down at her still form in my arms, I placed a tender kiss upon her head.

My family remained silent behind me as I laid her down gently beside Dorian's unconscious form. Her head rolled to the side, and I stood slowly.

Her entire body was covered in blood… blood that now coated my hands, my body, and my face.

"Theo?" my sister called out, her voice breaking from unshed tears.

I cocked my head to the side, clenching my fists and wrath flared and scorched through me. "Theo, I…" Trey started, and I whirled around, my eyes blazing in the night as they locked on him.

The bastard still held the rifle loosely in his grip. I narrowed my eyes further, menacingly as I seized him in my sight.

"Theo, he didn't have a choice. We all didn't. I'm so sorry," my father spoke and took a step forward around a fallen wolf with his bloody palms raised.

My sight never left Trey as the world around me seemed to disappear from focus.

All I could see was him shooting Braelyn, *over and over again* and my control snapped.

"You took her from me," I seethed in a deathly whisper, and my family held their breaths. My chest heaved as my breaths came in rapid concession, my blood boiling in fury.

"You took her from me!" I roared and launched myself at Trey.

I was a blur of speed across the pebbled shore and my fist connected with his face and ribs before he dodged the third hit. Bones crunched beneath my blows and my skin split open. Mine as well as Trey's.

"Stop!" my father called out.

Hands grabbed at me as I continued my assault and Trey barely managed to protect himself. The image of Braelyn's lifeless form kept assaulting my mind and my wrath was her retribution.

Trey gave up protecting himself and allowed me to pummel him.

My family grabbed for me, trying to pull me off but it was of no use.

Layna was screaming at me to stop, Kason was grunting as I elbowed his jaw, and my father pulled at my waist.

"You're killing him!" one of them screamed but it was an echoed whisper over the roaring in my head.

They wouldn't be able to stop me. No, not until I was done, and Trey's blood spilled as hers had.

Growls and snarls filled the air around us, somewhat breaking through my blind rage.

I slowed my assault as the stones beneath our feet began vibrating, pulsing out from behind us, like ripples in a pond. Trey lay upon the ground beneath me, coughing and moaning as I turned my head as my family had and my sight rose higher and higher.

A coldness that bit at the skin and mind seeped and slithered across the earth from where Braelyn lay, leaving frost in its wake.

Shoving away from Trey, I stood in awe as swirls of shadows and mist formed and twirled in the air with the moonlight reflecting and bouncing across its form.

"What... what the fuck is that?" Kason muttered barely above a whisper, reaching for his weapons slowly as the rest of my family had the same mind to do.

"Put the shield up," my father hissed to Layna who reached for her weapons belt, detaching the round metallic device slowly and holding it within her grasp.

It wasn't the large shield, but large enough to hopefully cover whatever the fuck this was. Hisses surrounded us.

Each was an echoing whisper of threats swimming around each of us. With a quick flick of her wrist, Layna flung the shield across the shore, and as it hit the ground. A flash of light illuminated the area as the shield erected itself. It was at that moment all of us flinched as the flash illuminated the beast within the swirling mist and shadows.

It should be impossible, yet here it was. A Drakon.

They were supposedly extinct for millennia, children of Typhon.

Its scaled tail was seemingly connected by shadow to Braelyn's lifeless form as it held her in its protective embrace, Dorian too.

The growls, the snarls, and hisses that I had heard around her had been… a Drakon. But not normal as our world's history had depicted them… no.

It was a wraith.

No corporeal form, shadows, and mists made up its scaled reflective form.

A bringer and harbinger of death itself…

The earth shook beneath our feet, like a war drum as the shadows dispersed, leaving the Drakon exposed in its mist and wisp form.

Green-slitted eyes, swimming with quicksilver, the same as Braelyn's had been narrowed on us, its huff of breath sending chilled pulses in our direction.

My sight locked with its own and the world stopped around me.

There was a familiarity to it.

A familiar fierceness as well as rawness, covered by the will to protect what was its to keep and untainted chaos.

A silent understanding seemed to flow between us, and I felt as if I had been awoken somehow. It opened its maw wide, fangs dripping with shadows reflecting the moonlight and it roared.

My family dropped, shielding their faces as the air blasted by us with its raw power and I felt my bones rattle within my flesh.

Shit… no wonder the gods feared her…

My eyes snapped to Braelyn, who still lay lifeless beside the wraith's form.

It lunged at my family then, snarling and snapping at them as they dodged out of the way just in time. It had gone right past me, seeming not interested in harming me.

Gunshots sounded out and my father and Layna took aim, Kason wielding his daggers.

Nothing worked as it snapped at them, slithering through the bodies of the wolves as it continued to lunge.

My eyes blazed and I launched myself into the air, my ravens taking flight and attacking as well as distracting the beast.

None of the weapons worked against it, simply passing through its wispy form.

"Nothing's working!" Kason yelled as he rolled out of the way of its snapping fangs.

Layna was dragging Trey's beaten and bloody form away when its sights landed on them. Her eyes widened in fear as she noticed its attention on them as she held Trey beneath his shoulders. Not thinking twice, I formed before it, putting myself in its path toward them.

It growled at me, its fangs dripping shadows mere inches from my face.

My hair was being blown by its ice-cold breath as I stared it down. I noticed my amber eyes and blood-covered face reflected in its haunting gaze. My skin prickled against the cold and frost collected on my eyelashes and the tips of my ears. Its eyes narrowed on me for a second as it whirled and refocused on my father and Kason. My foot snagged on clinking metal as I started forward.

I ignored it and took a further hastened step only to be dragging whatever it was with me. Looking down in rapidity and irritation, my eyes snapped back to Braelyn's body as the words of Ezio and the stranger from near the wrecked car filled my mind.

Why isn't the chain working?

Snatching up the chain, I eyed the wraith Drakon as it slammed my father into one of the many trees and rushed forward once more.

Braelyn

The sounds of a battle surrounded me in the darkness.

I no longer found myself in The Shiver.

No, it was somewhere… else.

Ticks and gurgling sounded out as the sensation of knitting organs, bone and flesh slithered through me.

Roaring sounded loud as pain sliced through my skull forcing my eyes open.

The starlit sky met me, and the world came into focus slowly as wisps of mist caught the corner of my eyes, followed by flashes of silver.

Pain sliced through me again and I inhaled my first lungful of air, like breaking through the surface of the lake…

It all came back to me then… House Katopodis, the rage, the pain… Dorian!

Forcing myself up, stones slid beneath me, and I whirled, finding him beside me, unconscious yet alive.

Pain carved through me again as the roaring grew louder. Looking toward the noise, I found the sight of House Katopodis fending off my wraith Drakon.

Theo attacked swiftly, the chain that had once been collared around me sliced through its misty form, and pain assaulted me yet again. I swallowed back my scream as I noticed the blood that covered my bare body. My bra strap hung from one shoulder, and I reached for where the bullet hole should be and found nothing except for a large amount of caking blood.

Quickly surveying my abdomen, I watched in awe as the wounds stitched themselves together like… Theo.

My gaze snapped up as the Drakon roared in pain from the chain slicing through its phantom form and it snarled at Theo.

It did not attack him, yet the displeasure was clear in its heated eyes.

"St… stop," I managed a croaked whisper as they continued to attack it.

"Ah," I moaned, squeezing my eyes shut tightly as pain tore me apart again.

"Stop!" I screamed, my chest heaving, and a blast of vibrating air crashed like a tidal wave over them from my spot along the shore.

Theo and his family whirled around, their shocked faces landing on me as if seeing a ghost or something more shocking than my wraith Drakon as I struggled against the pain.

"St… stop," I whispered between laboured breaths, and red welts appeared on my skin, burning as if the chain had been whipped against my flesh.

The Drakon snarled, creeping, and slithering as it readied to pounce yet again. "Enough," I ground out, my eyes flashing silver as I looked at it.

It huffed, sending ripples of power out across the area in anger.

"I said enough," I forced more harshly on choked breaths.

It snarled and reluctantly made its way toward me, snapping its fangs threateningly toward Theo's family.

Mist and shadows swirled around it and me as it growled and disappeared, leaving my own eyes flashing green and quicksilver as it returned within me and The Shiver.

Theo rushed toward me, sliding across the pebbles as he grabbed for my face, searching my eyes as I looked at him.

Tears swam in his eyes, lining them silver before he slammed his mouth to mine in a chaste kiss and held me impossibly close to him.

He was trembling before he snapped his head up and went deathly still, his eyes glowing amber.

"I will fucking break your sword in two and jam both ends so deep inside you if you take one more fucking step closer," he growled out threatening Dante as he stepped in our direction, sword in hand.

"Theo," he pleaded with his son, torn between duty, protecting his family, and allowing me to live.

"One more fucking step…" Theo sneered not looking in their direction.

Dorian stirred beside us, and I removed myself from Theo's embrace, hovering over him. The bleeding had stopped, but he was still in dire need of aid.

"Help him," I pleaded, looking to Theo's family, finding them watching with torn expressions. My gaze landed on Layna who had heartache written in her eyes.

"Please," I pleaded with her.

She looked to Theo who hesitantly nodded in reply, and she rushed forward without hesitation.

Layna crouched beside him, inspecting the wound, and then met my eyes.

"I am so sorry," she whispered, looking back down at Dorian.

"Just help him, please," I begged.

"I'll try my best, I promise." She spoke in hushed tones, looking to Theo one last time and reaching beneath Dorian's arms to haul him up and drag him away.

Once she was far enough away, Kason grabbed for them, helping to carry Dorian away. I watched as Dante picked up a circular device from the ground and pressed a bloody and grime-covered finger on the button.

A shield covering the area collapsed in on itself and he pocketed it.

Kason and Layna continued through the trees, carrying Dorian to safety.

"Go," Theo snapped at Trey and his father who had remained silent.

My eyes widened at the battered face and body of Trey as his swollen eyes found mine.

He looked gruesome. It was a miracle he could hold himself up.

"We need to talk at the very least," Dante spoke carefully as he watched Theo beside me.

The guilt and pain in his eyes as he watched his son then felt foreign as I had never been blessed with such love from a parent. I did not trust him now, especially not Trey whom I didn't doubt was the one who had shot me, but I reached for Theo's bloody hand, nevertheless.

His gaze met mine, his jaw set tight.

"Go speak to him," I whispered and pulled away, wincing in pain.

Theo was silent as he searched my face with his glowing eyes.

He nodded finally after a silent contemplative and calculating moment and stood, watching me as if being certain I would not disappear the second he turned his back.

I had contemplated it, but the draw I felt for him made it impossible for me to flee, even for my self-preservation.

My injuries did not help much either…

He had protected me. For longer than I had ever known, and I found solace in that. The power writhed inside me and across my bones, hissing as Theo neared his father and brother.

Their heads snapped back to me in fear, and I watched them in silence, forcing the power aside and bidding it to aid in healing the pain scattered across my body.

It had been weakened by the whipping of the chain but did as it was asked, growling, and huffing inside my mind as it did so.

I paid no attention to the Katopodis as they conversed in heated, yet hushed tones. Theo slammed a piece of parchment at his father's chest and stormed away.

He headed toward me.

Each step was thunderous in his rage.

"I suggest the two of you fuck off," he sneered over his shoulder as he reached me.

I looked past him, seeing Dante folding up the water-clogged parchment and grabbing Trey by the collar as he steered him away.

He limped beside his father arguing if his hand gestures were anything to go by. I tried listening in with my heightened senses, yet all I heard was a buzzing in my head as I remained sprawled across the pebbles beside the lake. "They are just going to let me live?" I asked Theo as he crouched before me, brushing my hair away from my face.

He didn't answer which concerned me, but it vanished as he placed a tender kiss upon my lips, then cheeks, and finally my forehead.

"Come on," he whispered, his voice thick with emotion as he scooped me up with his arms and stood.

My legs dangled over his tattooed arm and my arms went around his neck.

"What is going on?" I asked softly, not sure of what to expect.

"I'm taking you somewhere," he said and began walking along the shore in silence.

My body ached as he carried me, and my wounds knitted together. I felt myself drifting off into slumber as he carried me.

I awoke as he halted outside a small cabin beside the lake and took the steps one at a time.

Theo reached out, shuffling his grip on me as he turned the wooden doorknob and entered. The smell of dust filled the space as he sat me down gently.

I stood and took in the space before me. White sheets covered the furniture. A small basic kitchen sat to the right and a bedroom and bathroom toward the back.

No walls divided the space.

"We used to come here as kids. Fishing and getting up to shit," Theo grumbled as he switched on the golden lights and began pulling the dusty sheets off from the simple furniture.

It was nothing like the luxuries of the manor, but homey. I remained silent as I watched him. He seemed tense. His jaw was set tightly and his fingers trembling.

"Theo," I called out to him, standing bare near the front door.

"Theo," I repeated, and he stilled, closing his eyes.

"I'll start the shower for you," he muttered and disappeared toward the back and the spray of water sounded.

My bones ached and protested as I turned, shutting the door behind me, and limped toward the shower. Theo tested the water with his hand and looked at me, his expression guarded.

"Let me help you," he said and started toward me slowly. His eyes met mine, now back to his normal brilliant aqua and amber-rimmed irises.

I shivered as he rounded me, his fingers trailing over my shoulder that had been shot and was now healed.

"What's wrong?" I whispered and sucked in a breath as his hot lips feathered across my shoulder.

He did not respond, and his fingers unfastened my bra.

I slipped my arms through the straps and watched as they fell to the wooden floor.

Theo knelt behind me, his fingers trailing softly down my spine before hooking into the band of my underwear along my hips. I sucked in an unsteady breath yet again as he placed a kiss on the base of my spine and slid the underwear down slowly, all the way to my feet.

I stepped out from it and turned as he stood towering over me.

"Go shower," he instructed, his voice shaky even in his alluring deep baritone.

He turned in silence and began removing the sheets covering the bed and side tables. I cast one last look at him in worry and longing as I turned and entered the shower.

Streams of red ran over my body as the blood was washed away.

I closed my eyes to the evidence of so much brutality and began trembling as I washed and scrubbed at my body.

I needed it off, all of it.

Hecate had called me a weapon and weapons do not weep but I could not hold it in any longer as I scrubbed my skin until it stung and turned red, threatening to turn raw.

I sucked back a sob threatening to escape as I squeezed my eyes shut tightly.

Two strong arms wrapped around me and held me close.

Theo held me as I sobbed against his chest, the blood still swirling through the drain as both of us stood beneath its spray.

Theo reached for my hand, grabbed hold of the loofah gently, and wiped at my skin as if it were the most delicate thing in existence.

More precious than any gold or jewels…

My bloodshot eyes met his briefly and his gaze softened as he washed me.

I did the same, only for him to halt my movements and shake his head slowly.

"Let me do this for you, little rose. Let me take care of you," he whispered and placed a tender kiss on my forehead.

Tears welled once again in my eyes and I leaned into him, allowing him to wash every inch of me and my midnight hair before he washed. I had never witnessed or imagined such a tender side to Theo Katopodis, and I was certain that I was the only one to ever see it.

Theo kissed my cheeks before exiting the shower and wrapping a towel around himself and placing one near the shower for me. He disappeared and came back into view with a set of clothes, setting them on the vanity.

"You can stay in there as long as you want to," he spoke softly, his eyes searching mine tenderly before he retreated from view.

I watched him go and tilted my head back under the steady stream of water, willing my thundering heart and racing mind to ease.

Wiping my hair back from my face a final time, I shut off the water and dried myself before grabbing the clothes Theo had left for me.

They smelt faintly of him, and I held them close before dressing.

Theo's clothes were far too large for me.

His boxers slid right down my legs and his shirt fitting like a dress.

I forego the boxers and exited the bathroom towards the front of the cabin. I found Theo dressed casually with his head in his hands as he sat on the couch.

"Theo?" I asked and stepped closer.

His head whipped up and concern was written all over his face.

"How are you feeling?" he asked quietly.

"I should be asking you that?" I replied and went to sit in his lap, running my fingers across his face with a featherlight caress.

I watched as some of the tension left him, and he closed his eyes.

Leaning forward, I placed soft kisses across his face before finally on his lips. As he had done to me.

His eyes opened slowly, and we watched each other in silence for a moment before he placed his lips on mine and kissed me deeply, his arms wrapping around me and holding me close as if afraid of letting me go.

"I thought I had lost you," he whispered as he broke our kiss and placed his forehead against mine, his eyes remaining shut.

"What do you mean?" I asked, frowning, and pulling back to get a better look at him.

He looked up at me and pain swam in his gaze as something in him shattered.

"You were… dead, Braelyn," he spoke, struggling to get the words out.

"What…" I whispered disbelievingly. "How," I started and lifted the shirt I wore, the bullet holes completely healed, and scars left in their place.

"I'm not like you," I whispered referring to his family's healing genetics.

"I know," he groaned and ran his hand down his weary face.

I watched him with narrowed eyes.

"You know what?" I asked slowly.

His gaze met mine and he appeared torn.

"It may be from sharing blood… if the circumstances are right…" he trailed off and I scrunched my face in confusion.

"What? We haven't."

"We have. When you bit me and when I bit you… Also, during the Servile ceremony. We kissed instead of just touching lips after wiping our thumbs across each other…" he answered looking away from my mouth and his face was still lined with tension and something else. "Either way, I… lost you…" he trailed off and shut his eyes.

My heart broke at such pain marring him and I turned his face to mine.

"I'm here," I whispered and kissed him softly, already pushing aside the thought of blood exchanges and everything else.

"I'm here, Theo," I whispered against his lips as I wrapped my arms around his neck and ran my fingers through the soft damp black hair at the back of his head.

Theo's hands tightened their grip on me at the sound of my words, as if needing reassurance. He deepened the kiss and ran his hands over my hips and under the large shirt.

"Gods," he groaned against my mouth as he found me completely naked beneath his shirt.

Theo stood, wrapping my legs around his waist as he made his way to the back of the cabin.

All the way his eyes held mine with so much emotion that I hid my face in the crook of his neck after being overwhelmed by the intensity I found in his gaze.

Theo halted and lay me down gently across the mattress, his large form slowly climbing atop me as he bent over and kissed my neck in gentle promises.

His large, tattooed hands slid through my hair at the sides of my head as he landed his hot lips across mine.

He kissed me slowly; he kissed me deeply…

I found myself lost in him. Theo leaned back, his thighs caging me in as he removed his shirt and threw it across the room.

My hooded eyes took in his physique. Tattoos covered his golden skin, faint scars visible beneath their artwork.

I ran my hand slowly down his chest, his chiselled abs pulling taught as I trailed my hand lower, simply admiring him.

My green eyes met his, and I found him watching me as if in awe.

He then slid his hands slowly over me, his touch a haunting whisper across my skin as he lifted the shirt, pulled it over my head, and bent down to kiss me yet again.

Something was different tonight.

Each touch, each kiss gentle and filled with a myriad of emotions.

I pulled him closer, his bare chest scorching mine as we delved deeper into whatever this new territory was for us.

Theo removed his pants and found himself pressed over me yet again, entwining his fingers through mine as he kissed my neck and across my collarbone, his mouth hovering over the newly formed scar.

He halted, his face showing the pain he felt. "I'm okay. I'm here," I whispered gaining his attention and dragging him from his dark thoughts.

Trying to reassure him, I took our joint hands and placed them over my beating heart.

"Do you feel that?" Theo closed his eyes briefly as he felt my steady heartbeat.

"I won't let them hurt you ever again," he promised, his eyes now holding mine.

I knew he could not possibly be able to protect me from everyone and everything, but the promise found its way into my heart.

Pulling his face to mine, I kissed him deeply, trying to convey how I felt.

I felt safe.

I felt… I would dare not say it.

Admit it… yet the feeling boomed in my chest as if in finality.

I would find no way from the hold of Theo Katopodis.

And I did not want to.

Theo deepened the kiss, his hips pressing further into mine as I wrapped my legs around his, my body moving with his in a steady, slow, and passionate rhythm and already waiting, ready for him.

"Look at me," he whispered as he pulled away from my lips and his one hand was placed on my heated cheek.

I did as he asked and felt as he slowly, as if savouring the feel, glided inside me.

His eyes began to glow amber, and I found my swirling silver in their reflection.

My breath caught and my chest heaved as the sensation of him filled me.

My body felt on fire as he began moving against me, slow in his movements and his eyes never left mine.

I could not help but close my eyes and my mouth fell open in a silent moan as he urged me toward the edge of bliss.

Heat pooled within me as it built, and he moaned breathlessly as my body gripped him tightly.

A wave of ecstasy crashed over me and I gripped him closer, rocking with him.

Theo crashed his mouth to mine, swallowing my moans, his tongue caressing mine. My hands slid down his taut back and I gripped his behind tightly, the flesh firm beneath my palms.

I rode the high out, our rhythm delicate as my heart raced.

Flipping him over, my hands slid through his dark locks, and I continued to kiss him as his fingers ghosted down my back and then up again, sliding through my hair.

I rocked my hips, the feel of him filling me impossibly full.

Theo groaned, closing his eyes tightly as I rode him. His mouth found my neck again and my own hooded eyes slid closed as he licked and nipped ever so gently against my skin.

My pleasure built yet again, and I found myself breathless.

Theo and mine eyes locked and it sent me over the edge immediately, his release following almost instantly.

Theo gripped me tighter as we moved as one. My blushed face found its way to the crook of his neck and his open mouth sent hot breath across my temple.

Heat filled my core and I moaned and bit down gently against his neck, causing him to moan loudly.

Both of us lay still, lost in the pleasure of what we had just done and my body trembled with the aftermath.

Theo's soft lips found my temple and lingered there.

His fingers squeezed my flesh intermittently as he trailed his hands over my body.

We lay in silence, our hearts beating in sync with each other.

Rolling my head to the side, I peered up at him as he lay with his eyes closed.

I ran my fingers down the silhouette of his face and his hand gripped mine, placing it over his lips for a chaste kiss before he turned his head to mine.

I watched in awed silence as his eyes dimmed to their natural hue of aqua and he watched me with a tenderness I had yet to see from him, even in his ministrations earlier around the cabin…

"What will happen now? They want me dead…" I whispered, hating to ruin the mood but it had been bugging me.

Theo's eyes dimmed and he looked to the ceiling before turning over, slipping from within me. His arms wrapped around me, pulling me against him again as we faced each other.

"Can we talk about it in the morning? I just want to enjoy this with you before everything goes to shit." He sighed as if the world lay on his shoulders.

"I promise I will not let them harm you," he whispered against my forehead and placed his lips there lingering.

"Okay," I whispered closing my eyes at the feeling of being safe with him.

We lay in silence, the light over the shower illuminating the bed.

"Did you know what you are?" he asked suddenly and hesitantly.

My eyes opened and I sighed, tracing circles over his bare back.

"I didn't. I just knew there was a form of ancient power that lingered within me. Separate, yet the same… I'm not making any sense…"

"You are making sense," he added quickly and kissed my nose before laying his head further into the cushion.

"We can speak about it all tomorrow. Try to get some sleep," he added, pulling me closer and watching me with hooded eyes.

I watched him, the words at the tip of my tongue and I forced it away, only to place my lips against his, pouring all the words I would not say into one kiss.

Theo tensed and then responded in kind before we broke apart, our eyes meeting.

"Thank you," I whispered and closed my eyes. My thanks for so much more than just tonight… Theo tensed, and I opened my eyes again, finding him watching me, emotion swimming in his gaze.

"I promise I am not going anywhere," I whispered and closed my eyes to sleep.

I began drifting off rather quickly, sleep pulling me under as I lay in Theo's warm embrace.

I dreamt of words leaving Theo's lips in whispered tones that caused my heart to soar before it was swallowed up and forgotten as sleep dragged me further…

"I know," I thought I heard from Theo clearer through the haze of sleep, his voice pained, and slumber embraced me.

No dreams plagued me that night. No nightmares…

I was safe at last.

Braelyn

Sunlight lit the back of my eyelids, and I stretched in the bed smiling as I recalled last night.

Something had changed between Theo and me.

The intensity… the passion.

Gods.

Opening my eyes, the sight of the cabin greeted me, and I looked to my side finding the bed empty.

I shook it off as nothing as I rolled over, only to have something snag around my throat.

Frowning, I flipped my long hair over my shoulder, and something felt off.

I felt… empty.

Sitting up straight in the bed, my hand went to my throat, only to have the cool smooth feel of the chain wrapped there.

"I'm so sorry," Theo's hushed voice sounded from the living room as he stood there, his face bleak and pain in his eyes.

"What, what did you do?" I stammered, clawing at the chains and my eyes going wider as the reality of the situation hit me like a punch to the gut.

"Get it off!" I screeched and stood from the bed, my fingers snagging on the chain and almost tripping over the sheets by my feet.

"Get it off right now!" I begged him, my eyes locking with his.

He remained stoic where he stood, and my heart shattered.

Tears welled in my eyes as pain crashed through me.

"Please," I begged and stumbled to stand before him, still naked from last night, except for the chain around my neck.

Theo closed his eyes as if in pain, ignoring me and turning his face away.

"Look at me, you prick!" I screamed, smacking at his chest as hard as I could, and he clenched his jaw before turning his gaze back to mine.

"Take it off, please," I managed between rage and pain-filled sobs.

Tears streamed down my cheeks as I waited for him to remove the chain.

"I can't," he croaked out and gripped at his dark hair, closing his eyes yet again.

My shock and anguish hit me like a train then and I stumbled back a step, watching him in silence and my fingers dropping from the chain.

"You promised I would be safe… All last night was a lie," I managed out in disbelief and horror. "It was all a lie," I whispered to myself and turned back to the bed, my hands gripping my head as I searched around the room, for what I didn't know…

My heart? My sanity? My dignity?

"It was never a lie, don't say that," Theo spoke, pain filling his voice.

"This was the only way to keep you alive and keep my family safe, little rose. Just let me explain," he pleaded for me to understand.

My head rose and I whirled on him.

My eyes narrowed on him as I wiped angrily at my cheeks, removing any evidence of the pain he had just inflicted on me.

"So, keeping me chained up like some feral animal is better?" I seethed and he visibly flinched.

"The same as Ezio had done to me? I see the family ties are closer than you led me to believe," I snapped and turned again, looking for the god-damned shirt I had from last night.

"Little rose," he started, and I grabbed the nearest object, a rather heavy book from the shelf and threw it at his head.

Theo ducked as it crashed through the window of the cabin behind him, his eyes wide.

"Don't, you fucking call me that ever again or I will rip that lying tongue from your deceitful mouth myself." I seethed, my finger pointed at him and hatred clear in my eyes.

I turned fighting back the tears that threatened to fall and breathed heavily through my nose.

Spotting the shirt as it lay beside the bed, I stomped my way over and shoved it on, flinging my hair out behind me before I whirled on Theo who had remained silent.

"Was this the plan all along? Get me to f… feel things for you, only for some cruel joke? Is that what I am? A fucking joke to you?" I stumbled over my words, choking back the painful lump in my throat.

"No, never. I thought you knew that," he spoke softly, his eyes scrunched in torture, or just more deceit I didn't know….

Nor did I care. I couldn't care.

A chasm had been ripped open in my chest and I struggled for my breath.

Placing my hands on my hips, I bent over, shutting my eyes, only to stand straight again and pull manically at the chain around my throat.

I couldn't breathe.

Gods, I couldn't breathe.

"I just," he started forward to me and I held my hand out halting him.

"Oh, just shut up. Shut the hell up, Katopodis! You always thought of me as the stupid little Sarris princess. You made it clear enough. You hate me. You said so yourself." My eyes narrowed further on him before I spewed the biggest lie myself.

"I fucking *hate* you. So at least we can agree on one thing," I spat at him, seeing him flinch yet again as if I'd physically assaulted him.

Good.

"You don't fucking mean that," he seethed, his jaw clenched tight.

"Oh, I think I do," I snapped back and clawed at the chain again, before slumping to the edge of the bed, my movements jerky as I struggled to get it off and pain slammed through my chest like a battering ram yet again.

I halted as my face scrunched together, unable to stop the tears from falling.

My vision turned blurry, and I struggled for air as sobs escaped me and I snapped a nail as I ripped at the chain.

Red welts formed across my neck as the friction from my fingers and linked metal chaffed away at it.

"Braelyn," Theo whispered, grabbing my forearms, and lowering them from my neck as I continued to cry.

I struggled futilely to pull my arms from his grip and finally gave up as a wail left me, and I broke down before him.

"I hate you," I cried, not sounding like I meant it at all.

All power behind my voice was vanquished by my agony. "I hate you," I cried again, and Theo lowered his head, his own eyes turning bloodshot.

"I know," he whispered with strangled words. "I know you do."

I forced my face away from his as I hiccupped, trying to swallow back my tears again.

I counted to ten over and over as I faced the wooden wall behind the bed with Theo still crouched beside me, his hands holding my arms. *You are a weapon and weapons do not weep.*

Hecate's mantra for me echoed through my roaring head and ice-cold wrath took over as I pushed my feelings deep and deeper to the endless depths of my soul.

Yanking my arms from Theo's grasp, he released me as my breathing calmed and I closed my eyes still facing away from him.

I gritted my teeth as I forced myself to calm down further.

Theo used my silent moment to explain himself.

"I promised to keep you safe, and this is the only way I can see to do that for now. I will find another way, but the hunt order stands. You know what a Code Red is. You saw for yourself... I found your original hunt order and there is a loophole. We can capture and detain or assassinate..." he spoke, and I could feel his eyes on me as I kept mine closed, breathing heavily through my nose.

He took my silence as an indication to continue as he stood from the ground, never moving away.

"I cannot let you, or my family, be led to the slaughter. You must understand that, Brae. This is the only way...." He forced out and I shook my head in denial even though his words made sense logically, my heart could not accept them.

"Shut up," I whispered scrunching my eyes tighter as I lowered my head.

"The gods cannot interfere with the hunt order if you wear the chain, but they have issued further orders. The box you stole, the Heart of Ouranos, we need it back or they will issue a Code Red for all of us."

"I don't have it," I muttered, refusing to look at him as I opened my burning eyes, staring at the wall ahead yet again.

"Then who does? Why did you even steal it?" he spoke and reached for my arm but halted as I glared at his hand hovering over my skin.

He clenched his hand into a fist before dropping it.

Gods... those hands...

I had allowed him to touch me in so many intimate ways with those hands…

"I cannot tell you," I snapped.

"You can't or won't?" Theo snapped right back at me.

Turning my head, my eyes narrowed on his as I chose my words wisely, to further get under his deceitful skin.

"Both."

"What the fuck does that even mean?" he growled, and his jaw clenched yet again. *Good, let him get wound up.*

"You are going to get us all killed if you don't tell me something that I can use to get the fucking box back."

"Then I shall dance in the afterlife knowing that you got what you fucking deserved," I snapped and stood glaring at him.

My heart broke further at my own words.

I didn't mean any of it, but I sure as hell wasn't going to let him know that.

Theo's eyes shut as he looked away. His words were soft as he spoke, no malice tainting them, and it froze me to the spot.

Haunting me.

"Yes, I will have got what I deserved, but it wouldn't be what you deserved. I'd rather see you dancing in this life." He walked toward the cabin's front door and exited, slamming the door shut, but not before calling out to me over his shoulder.

"We need to get back to the manor, I will wait for you outside. Dorian is awake."

I stood frozen to the spot as I watched him walk past the now shattered window outside.

Inhaling deeply, I squared my shoulders and raised my chin.

I had no idea where the box was.

I had assumed Ezio had it, yet he had been asking me too.

So, where the hell was it…

Hecate would no doubt be checking in soon wanting it and I pushed the terror aside at the thought of *that* obstacle.

She still expected me to deliver the box as well as assassinate the Katopodis family.

Would I? I didn't know…

I also needed the box to exercise the plan that I had for myself.

To be free of Hecate's hold.

A million possibilities and a million obstacles lay before me, and I did not know what to do.

For the first time in a very long time, I did not know which direction to take.

Looking down at the Servile brand that lay like a tattoo over my arm and wrapped around my thumb, I noticed the tremor in my fingers.

Fear.

Gritting my teeth so hard my jaw hurt, I clenched my hands into fists and exhaled slowly. Stepping around the bed, images of last night flashed like a blade through my mind and I forced it aside.

Opening the cabin door, Theo lifted his gaze to mine as I came down the wooden steps with my head raised high.

Layna and Kason were standing to the side looking particularly awkward, Trey, battered yet appearing somewhat healed stood alone further up the path.

I rose an eyebrow at them all, then looked to Theo.

"Reapers escort?" I gritted out and he crossed his arms over his chest.

"Something like that," he muttered and looked away.

Fine then.

Let them fear me, as they should.

I caught Kason ogling my bare legs as I stepped forward dressed only in Theo's large shirt. "Apologies. If I knew I was to be captured, I would have dressed for the occasion."

My eyes narrowed on Theo as he shouldered past Kason and started down the path.

Kason cleared his throat and held an arm out indicating I follow Theo and Trey up ahead.

I took my time during the walk back with Kason and Layna covering the rear of the path. The Whispering Woods surrounded us, and its phantom caress carried by the breeze passed over me, curiously.

No one spoke the entire way.

Trey and Theo ignored each other, and the tension was clear in Theo's tight shoulders and his clenching fists.

When we reached the manor, stepping through the tree line, I looked up, finding Dante as he stood atop the marble steps leading to the massive doors.

Alaia stood beside him looking rather gloomy. Her usual sparkle that was found in her eyes had dimmed when her blue eyes met mine. A form of silent apology passed between us before she looked dead ahead.

It was the first time I would be using the main doors to enter the manor, and it did not pass my attention that this would be the foremost time I entered as who I truly was, whether I was chained or not...

Dante nodded to Theo before placing a strong hand over Alaia's lower back, leading her inside.

Theo walked over to me, his intention to lead me inside too.

One glare from me halted him where he stood. I stared down all of them, my eyes narrowed particularly long over Trey's form and he looked away, his face unreadable.

Uncomfortable, yes...

I grinned sinisterly at each of them, causing Kason to scratch at his head awkwardly as he looked to Theo for guidance.

"You are all going to regret this," I smiled a crooked, evil smirk at them.

I stepped forward, leaving them behind as I took the steps one at a time.

Standing atop them, I looked back at them before whispering, "You are all going to regret this immensely." With that being said, I turned, continued through the doors, and called out loudly for Theo as I went. The princess I was...

"Take me to my brother."

There was muttering behind me before Theo appeared beside me, eyeing me calculatedly.

He didn't say a word and I did not either, instead staring ahead with my chin raised high as I passed down the hall.

I had not been down this hall before. I noted the massive paintings and priceless artefacts adorning the hall and a massive family portrait that hung from the wall, a table with more family photos just beneath it.

I froze on the spot, staring up at the colossal painting and then at the photos below...

Theo stopped beside me, watching me intently. Picking up a crystal frame, it was a photo of Theo, maybe from about five years ago and he was smiling that extremely rare smile of his that I had only witnessed once.

It was like drinking acid.

My heart squeezed painfully, and my eyes narrowed on him before returning to the rest of the photos.

"You are going to regret this," I sneered and dropped the frame on the floor, causing it to shatter.

"Every single one of you."

I picked up another, shattering it as the first. "One," another shattered and Theo stood watching me with narrowed eyes, "By fucking one." I smashed every single photo frame, the pictures and crushed crystal covering the marble floors.

I eyed him, my face giving nothing away.

I shouldered past Theo, my bare feet stepping around the hazard on the floor.

He ran a hand through his onyx hair, and I continued.

My shoulders pushed back, and my head held high.

He thought of me as a haughty princess before, I would show him one now.

I was Braelyn Sarris.

Princess of House Sarris, the highest of Houses. Wraith.

Shadow-Stalker.

Drakon and dominion of The Shiver.

Death.

I grinned to myself as he followed behind me. They had just let a wolf loose in their own home and she was rapacious…

Acknowledgements

Wow! I don't know where to start! Firstly, thank you to, YOU, the reader! I would like to thank all my friends and family. My husband Tyrone and my two children. Kaylin and Tyler – You guys inspire me every day and more than you will ever realize. Thank you for being the whip-smart, funny, gobsmacking intelligent little humans that you are! My mom and dad, Vanessa, and John, as well as my brother Adrian – thank you for always having encouraged me and even your sobering words of wisdom that you laid out for me. I love you all more than words will ever express and without every single one of you, this would not have been possible. My best friend and equal book-fiend, Liz – You are simply awesome, and your support as well as honest opinions are truly appreciated every step of the way. Finally, I would like to thank Austin Macauley Publishing. You have made my dreams come true! Thank you!

Books by Julene Wood

Immortal Fire series:
    Immortal Fire, Scattered Ashes, Wicked Embers.

House of Wings and Shadow series:
    Chained, Twisted – *upcoming*